Three Rivers of Tears

Three Rivers of Tears

A novel by
Lopa

Published by:
LiFi Publications Pvt. Ltd.
211, 2nd Floor, Gagandeep
12, Rajendra Place, New Delhi - 110 008, India
Phones : (011) 2574 1000
E-mail : info@lifipublications.com
Web : www.lifipublications.com

ISBN 13: 978-93-82536-00-0   ISBN 10: 93-82536-00-0

© Lopa 2012

Lopa asserts the moral right to be identified as the author of this work

First published in 2012

Cataloging in Publication Data — DK
[Courtesy: D.K. Agencies (P) Ltd. <docinfo@dkagencies.com>]

Lopa, 1973-
    Three rivers of tears / Lopa.
    p. cm.
    Novel
    ISBN 13: 9789382536000

    1. Indic fiction (English). 2. Political leadership – India – History – Fiction. 3. Political leadership – Pakistan – History – Fiction. 4. Political leadership – Bangladesh – History – Fiction. 5. India – Ethnic relations – Fiction. 6. Pakistan – Ethnic relations – Fiction. 7. Bangladesh – Ethnic relations – Fiction. I. Title.

DDC 823.92   23

All rights reserved. This book is sold subject to the condition that it shall not, by way of trade or otherwise, be lent, resold, hired out, or otherwise circulated without the publisher's prior written consent, in any form of binding or cover or medium other than that in which it is published. No part of this book may be reproduced, stored in a retrieval system, or transmitted in any form or by any means, electronic or mechanical, recording, photocopying or otherwise, without the prior written permission from the copyright holder and the publisher.

This is a work of fiction. Names, characters, places and incidents are either author's own imagination or are used fictitiously. Any resemblance to real persons, living or dead, or actual events or locales, or organizations is purely coincidental.

Printed in India by Salasar Imaging Systems, New Delhi

Preface

I did not imagine this story. I chronicled the pangs of a nation. I wept with my grandmother's generation, questioned my mother's, and hoped with my own. I wanted to address the events of the Partition and the hatred that has erupted ever since, so many times. Should one expose the stories of an abandoned home, those precious memories passed down as family heirlooms? If this book reminds anyone of the scars they were hiding behind smiles, I ask to be pardoned. I know certain wounds should not be touched; certain doors should not be opened. But precisely because we have suffered, we know how deeply it hurts, and therefore have also the secret to heal it. If this book enables us to come forward with remedies, I would feel comforted. If some light is shone on the already existing commonalities that make us one people, I would feel satisfied. But if this story unites us in heart and mind, it will have achieved its purpose, since external unity is a detail that works itself out once the inner foundation is laid.

Finally I get a chance to thank my well-wisher who happily and enthusiastically rendered service as copyeditor. I shall respect his wish to remain unnamed. I want to thank Karen Ecke for reading the first draft of the novel and helping me with important technicalities. Most of all I want to acknowledge my gratitude towards Dr Debashish Banerji for passing the text through the magnifying glass of his vast scholarship, for his expert comments on art, history, culture, philosophy, and for walking with me through the whole process.

This story enables me to applaud the work of Mukhtar Ma'i of Pakistan and Sunitha Krishnan of India, who save and assist rape victims, having themselves suffered the terrible trauma of rape. I also want to pay tribute to activists like Ruchira Gupta who brush aside threats to their lives to better the lot of sex workers, and Vandana Shiva who fights for peasants' rights and speaks for Earth democracy. I have been inspired by socially responsible directors like Hrishikesh Mukherjee and Shyam Benegal, and have been moved by actors such as Guru Dutt and Naseeruddin Shah.

But the innumerable people of our subcontinent, who have adapted to everything time tossed at them, have been my greatest inspiration. I think of Shahnaz and her family diving under a bunker in Azad Kashmir interrupting a wedding to let the bombs blow over. I ask Ashok, a Kashmiri Pandit, who escaped Srinagar, if he wants to return to his childhood garden. Parmeet's house burnt down during the anti-Sikh riots while his family hid in a Hindu friend's place. I want to share his story of how they returned to the very same place and are still wearing their turbans. From Dhaka I crossed the Padma with Manisha's family, walked by the paddy fields at night and slipped under the barbed wire into India. But I also remained in Chittagong with Vivekananda, casting my lot with the typhoons and the triumphs of Bangladesh. I want my Pakistani friend, Zara's, dream to come true – to see the Taj Mahal, and not be denied entry into India because her husband served in the Pakistani Navy. Praveen, once from Karachi, blushes when I mention Jhulelal, as though I stepped into his sanctum with sandals on. I want him to feel proud of his difference, and not have to wear a camouflage. I want to remind us all we are a people who can hold our rich diversity in one heart, because we have the unique privilege of being blessed with so much history, so much culture, so many religions, so many languages. Above all I want us all to realize home is not a place; it is a state of being.

Contents

Preface		v
Prologue		ix

Part One

1.	Binapani	2
2.	Tushar	14
3.	Nazrul	25
4.	Gypsy	32
5.	Aparna	42

Part Two

6.	Anand	54
7.	Sulaiman	72
8.	Debjani	88
9.	Madhumati	106
10.	Aleya	121

Part Three

11.	Raja	138
12.	Mohan	155
13.	Savita	172
14.	Nirmal	186
15.	Atul	204

Part Four

16.	Jalal	224
17.	Sukhvir	242
18.	Tariq	258
19.	Swami	268
20.	Chitrangada	283

Part Five

21.	Shreyas	306
22.	Roshan	322
23.	Tulsi	345
24.	Yuyutsu	364
25.	Vasant	382

Part Six

26.	Rustum	400
27.	Prahlad	419
28.	Chandidas	439
29.	Rahim	455
30.	Panchali	472
	Glossary	493

Prologue

After the great shuffle that was World War II, the hand of destiny dealt out cards with a shade of generosity. Colonies became sovereign nations reversing time back to another era of their history. The peninsula on the Indian Ocean guarded by the Himalayas also demanded her due. But the land for whom her children had sacrificed their lives in millions was awarded a one-eyed justice. India had her right arm and left hand shorn off to form Pakistan. In August 1947, two different flags were hoisted, two different anthems were sung, and brother turned against brother.

"This is the ancient story of India," said the sceptics, "The whole war in the epic Mahabharata is all about brother conniving against brother, brother slaughtering brother. Such is the irony of our culture that it is not called 'epic' in Indian languages, but 'itihas', history. And everyone knows history has a bad habit of repeating itself."

Greater critics of human civilization pointed out with the last laugh, "Why India alone, look at the other histories – Cain kills his brother Abel, Isaac and Ishmael cannot live together in peace. To this day these regions are torn by filial wars."

About the partition of India, historians would argue, lawyers would compare, leaders would justify, and yet the common man remained unconvinced. The question he asked was not how or why the Partition, but "Was it really necessary?" For if this was a natural division, would the lesion bleed so profusely – in the time of Partition, following the time of Partition and ever since, to this day?

Part One

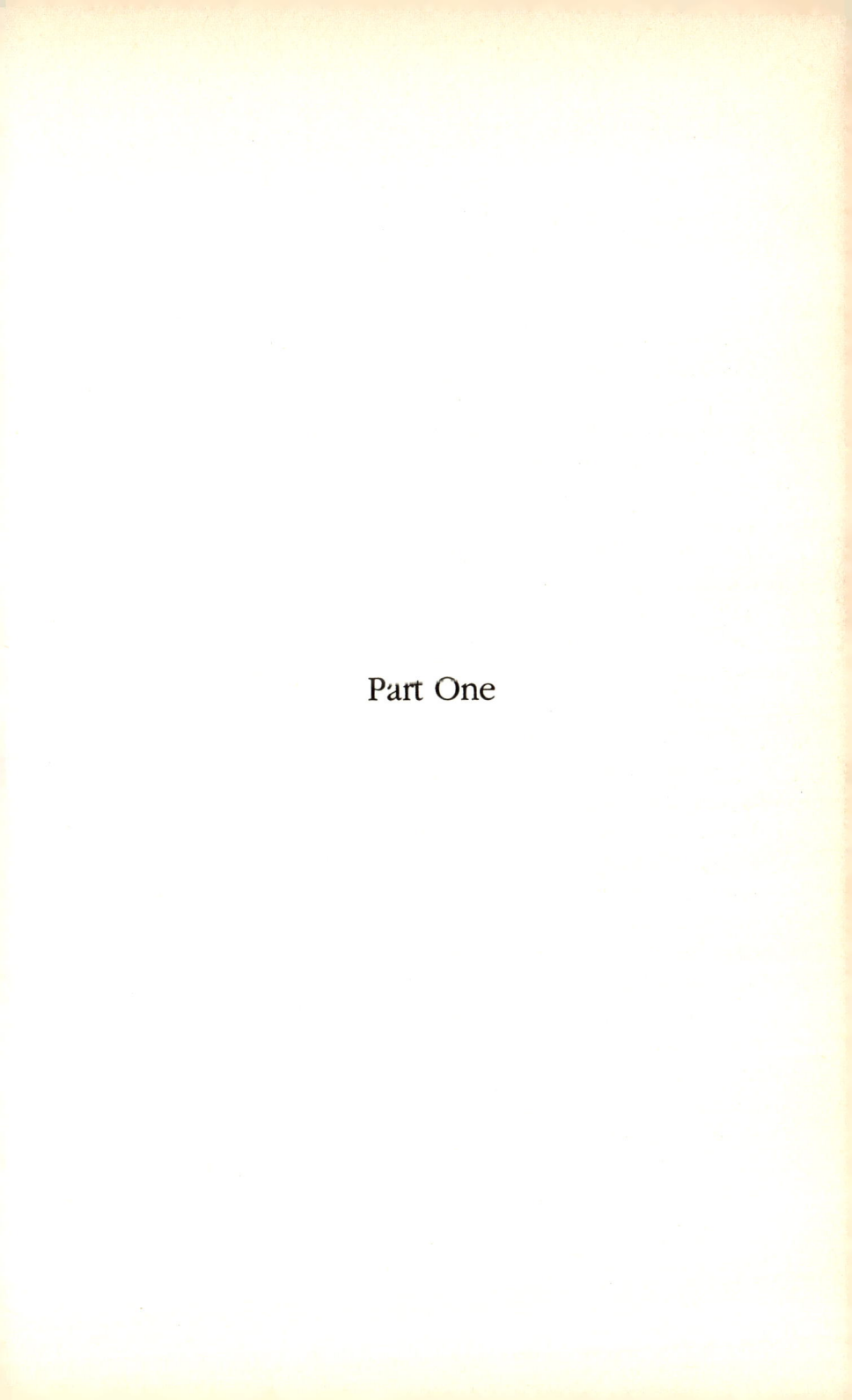

Chapter One

Binapani

Binapani stood at an intersection in Calcutta, twenty-two years after Independence, herself as young as free India. Her country was at the forefront of international diplomacy, and an industrial nation forging ahead into the space age. One of the world's first women prime ministers led the vast populace of this infant democracy. Binapani and her country were proud, progressive, emancipated. The metropolis that hummed around her had been a handful of villages three hundred years earlier. Then, for a hundred years, it had served as the pivot of the British East India Company. While the subcontinent was slowly passing under British control, Calcutta had remained the country's most important city. Then the capital had moved to Delhi, which had been the seat of power for many dynasties, spanning several centuries.

Bengal, with Calcutta as capital, was blessed with pioneers in all cultural spheres. Here, Sri Ramakrishna, worshipped the Mother Goddess by the waters of the Ganga. Here he initiated Swami Vivekananda, who spread the message of Hinduism around the world. Here was born the Bengal Renaissance which would sweep away social and religious prejudices. Here dwelt poets and novelists inspired by humanism. Here was composed the mantra for the freedom struggle of India, Vande Mataram, "Victory to the Mother". Here also lived landowners with hundreds of acres to their title, and impoverished peasants with not a paisa they could call their own. This was a land of sharp contrasts with luxury cars and man-drawn push-push rickshaws, marble temples and deities in sooty tree stump niches, villas and slums, the orthodox and the liberated. It had magnificent superlatives and cringing abysses, like the rest of India.

The age of the youth had dawned. In the Western world they were rediscovering themselves – through rock bands, hallucinogens, feminism, long hair and hitchhikes. They tuned in to subconscious psychology, and tuned out of Sunday school. They protested in the streets against war, and hugged trees to hear the sap flow inside their veins. Inhibitions were tossed out – inhibitions of clothing, smoking, drinking, of sex, of tradition. In India, too, the youth stirred. Binapani, like her Western counterpart, experimented with life within her own latitude. She wore a sleeveless blouse and a silk sari printed with large dahlias was draped voluptuously around her waist. Her hair was worn in a puff at the back of the head, in the style of the heroines of Hindi cinema. A hint of lipstick played with the faint smile on her lips. Her sandals added an inch to her stature. From her nail-polished fingers, she swung an orange short-handled bag, rightly called a "vanity" bag. "Charming!" the world complimented her, and she responded with an affected frown, "Oh, don't mention it."

Binapani stepped past the entrance of College Street as if it were the portals of a temple. Her eyes patted the many bookstalls lined next to each other. The smell of books filled the air – new from the press, freshly bound with the fragrance of glue, old from ancient shelves, musty from locked trunks, naphthalene and neem pressed, bug-eaten but not dead yet. Thin students cigarette in hand, boys with cotton side-bags, bespectacled old men and frothy young girls like herself were all poring over the books, oblivious to the bustle. This was a paradise for lovers of knowledge, a barter house of the pastimes of the intellect. Immortal classics in English and Bengali lay shoulder to shoulder with film magazines and comics. Ideas of great men mingled with the commonplace chatter. Dreams were forgotten, and then revived. Some were languid, some revolutionary.

"Bina-didi, I have something for you today." This was Kanailal calling from his perch up ahead. He addressed his customers as if they were his relatives, as did much of India. Elderly women were mashi – mother's sister. Aged men were kaku – father's brother. Young girls were didi, which literally meant "elder sister", but was a sweet name for little sisters too. And if one wanted to add another measure of sweetness, one said didimoni. Similarly, young boys were dada. And there was ma, literally "mother", the dearest of endearments reserved for daughters and daughters-in-law. Kanailal specialized in Russian books – Binapani's favourite genre. In reality it was Kanailal who cultivated her taste for Russian novels. Often she said, "Kanai-da, you know so much and talk so well. Why don't you take a teacher's job?" to which he replied, "I have it, didimoni. What do you think I do the whole day? I talk with people like you, fresh minds eager to learn. And what's best is that I don't have to correct notebooks and hand out marks. I can spend all that precious time reading these classics."

He handed her a book which smelled of the Indian custom house and the pine trees of Russia.

Binapani read aloud. "And Quiet Flows the Don. Mikhail Sholokhov. Is it about the Bolshevik revolution?"

"Yes, and much more. It is about war and peace, about Cossacks and Hussars, peasants and soldiers, life and death."

"Like Doctor Zhivago? Is there love in the time of war? Excellent. And there are two volumes? Oh, Kanai-da, I am so happy today."

She wanted to start devouring the book right there standing under the makeshift awning of the shop, and looked impatiently at the fingers wrapping her darling volumes with newspaper. Then she heard a familiar voice close by. Two stalls away Aparna was buying a book. Binapani skipped over to her friend's side and pinched her arm.

"Ouch, oh it's you, Bina!" cried Aparna, relaxing in a smile.

"Guess what I got today! A novel of the Russian Revolution. And Quiet Flows the Don. Have you read it?"

Aparna shook her head indulgently. "Bina, how long will you read novels? See this book – New Humanism, by M.N. Roy. Read it. It has the life experiences of a brilliant mind."

"Aparna, you talk like a teacher. I don't like politics. I just like stories."

"But then why don't you read Charles Dickens, James Joyce, Somerset Maugham? Why always the Bolshevik revolution?"

Binapani leapt into her dreamworld. "Because here life is on the verge of something stupendous, the urgent need to test it all, the constant danger of war, the anticipation of a new age, shifting landscapes, noble sacrifices and desperate loves."

Aparna knew there was nothing romantic about war. It was about shortage of food, shortage of work, shortage of medicines, shortage of water. About fear of losing one's loved ones, fear of depleting one's savings, fear of having the roof blown apart, fear of being maimed, fear of death. She had had a sister who died of cholera during the Second World War in Calcutta, when the curfew silenced a weeping child and the sound of throbbing hearts was louder than exploding bombs. Her own father had fought for India's freedom, then went to jail and died there. She was born to a mother in her widow's white, but in a free India. Binapani was a spoilt little girl of a rich family, and she had no right to jolt her awake. So she prompted her sweet dreamer friend, "Drink life to the lees?"

Binapani recognized the quote from their favourite poem and smiled, "Maybe in some past life I was there on the Caspian Sea coast, waving a red handkerchief to a lover on his horse whom I may never see again. That was home, those were the heroic days, a bygone golden age."

Aparna leaned close and whispered in her ears. "And will it shock you if I said those heroic days are back? To India this time? Right above your head a storm is brewing. One event that occurred and has been perhaps forgotten will yet change the future of our country."

Binapani shivered. "Aparna, stop tickling my ear. You give me the goosebumps. Why are you talking in riddles? What so momentous has happened in our country's history?"

"Naxalbari." Aparna had laced her arm around her friend's neck. She was euphoric. She just laughed and dragged Binapani with her out of the honeycomb of bookshops, past the many tea stalls, through the crowd of people returning from office and college.

Binapani tried to curtail their speed. "So tell me about this hero of yours."

"Charu-da?"

"No, the author you mentioned."

"Oh, M.N. Roy. Manabendra Nath Roy as a youth, at the beginning of the century, had his own group of friends with whom to discuss tactics for the freedom struggle. They were making bombs too. Then he went to Mexico, and started the Communist party there, shortly after the October Revolution in Russia. Back in India, he set up the Communist party here. He was involved in the Comintern too."

"Ah, the Communist International organization started by Lenin where the 'Workers of the world, unite!' slogan would be put to action."

"Yes, he also went to meet Mao Tse Tung during the Chinese peasant uprising."

"That's quite an adventurous life!"

"All that done, and once again back in India he took a closer look at Communism and decided there must be a philosophy beyond it, which also transcended capitalism. This is the book he wrote last – New Humanism. It is considered to be as important as Marx's Communist Manifesto."

"Was he alive when India got her freedom?"

"Oh yes, he passed away in 1954."

Binapani would have loved her guru, Rabindranath Tagore, the seer-poet, to have lived till Independence. How glad he would be to hear his song, Jana gana mana, being sung as the national anthem. The two ladies turned the corner of College Street, and went up the stairs of the Coffee House, past the jostling waiters in white liveries calling out orders, "Five coffees, four cutlets, didi, side please." They reached a table which resembled a volcano after an eruption. Four men and a woman could be seen through the curtain of smoke. All greeted Aparna and nodded politely at Binapani. The discussion went on.

"As I was saying, there are two types of people – the exploiters and the exploited."

"Marx studied these two groups within the perimeter of the English industrial system. Lenin devised a political system that he applied on the workers of Russia. Then Mao led the peasants into forming a People's Republic in China."

"The Communist ideal has recognized a deep-seated need in man – the need to love and be loved. He is not given adequate chance in his life to love. Would a man rather share his food with the hungry or watch them die while he grows fat?"

Binapani wanted to interject, "How you all talk – like children! What love? I have seen men beat a gardener who had broken a pot. And what about human greed? It never looks back at what is achieved, but shoots up like a fire cracker to burst in the sky. The boss kicks his clerk. The clerk kicks the peon. The peon kicks the dog on the road. Are you expecting the rich to turn around and start sharing their wealth, because in truth they had always wanted to, but did not know how to? You really have too much faith in human nature." But she remained silent wondering who these dreamers were – art students, poets, or writers maybe.

"All that is needed is a critical mass. A structure, however old or venerated or feared, can then be toppled."

"Look at the French Revolution. Didn't the people, sick and decrepit, property-less and penniless, one day rise up to the cries of Equality, Liberty, Fraternity?"

"Consider the Vietnam War. I predict the Communist north, Ho Chi Minh's soldiers, will win. Ask yourself how it is possible for peasants chewing on roots to survive carpet-bombings from the most sophisticated air force in the world."

"And that too for more than a decade!"

"I'll tell you why. It is their numbers and the power of their conviction."

"Don't forget the guerrilla warfare."

"India is ready for the rule of the intellect – Communism – which is also the rule of the masses, the true democracy. Not this farce of 'voting rights' democracy."

Voices were rising as if they were arguing, but Binapani observed they all agreed with each other. They were just so excited. Then she suddenly felt self-conscious. Her expensive silk sari did not blend with the topic of discussion, or with the speakers. One had an ink smudge on his shirt pocket. Another had no shirt buttons. The woman, Ketaki, wore a wrinkled sari, and Aparna herself was as plainly dressed as the others. Binapani brought her hand to rest in her lap to hide the gold-banded watch.

The man opposite her, the one who spoke calmly, slowly crushed out his cigarette. "So Binapani, what do you do?"

"I am studying English in Calcutta University, for my master's degree."

"Ah, of course, that is how you know Aparna. What do you have in your hand – looks like books, textbooks?"

"No, these are some story books I bought today. Here, have a look." She uncovered the newspaper parcel. The books went round the table and gained a few appreciations.

Ranjan, the small boy with the ink smudge, was a wee bit irritated by the gap in the conversation. "So do you read these as bedtime stories or do you hope to apply them some time in your life?"

Binapani blushed in embarrassment. Ranjan glanced nervously at the other boy, "Tushar, we can't spend time on recruitment now."

Binapani got up, noting her dismissal. "You will have to excuse me. I have to go now, I have not informed them at home I would be late."

Tushar looked pained by his friend's rough behaviour. "Won't you stay for coffee?"

"No, some other time."

She had reached the door down the stairs when she heard a voice calling after her. It was Tushar.

"May I ask pardon for my friend's impatience? He is a firebrand. You will love him once you get to know him. We will meet again on Wednesday. If you liked our desultory thoughts you can join us."

She nodded. If not for the thoughts, she may just drop in to see Tushar's smile again – like the sun breaking through the clouds.

Binapani entered her house, and Gypsy came bounding up to welcome her. He was the house watchman, which meant he was both a watchdog and a Doberman. The gardener stopped watering the plants as she passed by. She greeted him "Bhupenda, is everything going on fine?" But before he could get any word out she rushed by just in time for dinner. She wanted to avoid explaining to her father why she was late. He was the Deputy Commissioner of Police in the north Calcutta zone, and often forgot where his official duty ended and his family duty began. Except for Gypsy, he was master of his destiny and all those around him. At dinner, Binapani asked him,

"Baba, what is Naxalbari?"

"Not 'what is', but 'where is', is the right question. Why do you want to know?" He continued eating, having dismissed the question.

Binapani's mother intervened. "Look up from your plate and answer her. Don't treat her like a child. She is growing and needs to know some things. Knowledge is power. And the right knowledge will give her the right power."

"Oh, don't lecture me, Debjani." spat out her father.

Binapani thought she had asked a simple question, but now it seemed this Naxalbari was not such an easy one. No wonder Aparna was in raptures about it.

Reluctantly, her father answered. "It is a small village in the northern-most district of West Bengal, near Siliguri."

"Is that all? Nothing special about it? Then why did you and ma just have a sour exchange?"

His voice grated in her ears, "Whom have you been talking to?"

Her mother came to the rescue. "About three years back, let me see, it was much before the planting season, yes, beginning of March, in 1967. The court concluded a case which gave a peasant his land. When the poor man came to plough it, the landlord sent his goons and beat him up. So the peasants got together and fought back."

Her father mocked her, a pastime he rather relished, much to Binapani's disgust.

"And fought back! Just like that a bunch of illiterate peasants start revolting? After hundreds of years of torpor? It was not that simple. Some well-read young men, so-called intellectuals, inspired by the Chinese peasant revolution, organized an attack on the landlords."

Binapani was getting interested. "Then what happened? Did people die? Was the police involved?"

"Oh, yes. As soon as the cats appeared the field rats dispersed. In two and half months all was quiet." He clicked his tongue and passed his hand across his neck like a sword cutting it. "These are misguided youth, Naxals as they call themselves after Naxalbari. Now is the time for nation-building. The industrialization of India has miles to go. We need hard workers, we need these boys to refocus their energies."

"So the proletarian revolution was nipped in the bud?"

"Don't use big words you learn in story books. These so-called intellectuals were also like that, mere book readers – theorists. Are they diplomats who know the trouble of governing a country as diverse as ours? Just look at the role model they have chosen – China. The first thing the new Communist government does is attack Tibet. God knows why; because Communism is against religion, or maybe Tibet was an autonomous province and China itched to annex it. The peace-loving yak herders and Buddhist monks are killed mercilessly with such a lack of humanitarian sensibility that the world is shocked. And the Indian Communist rascals choose to idolize Mao Tse Tung. The Dalai Lama had to escape on foot through the treacherous Himalayas. But look at what the democratic government of India does. Not only gives him refuge, but the whole region of Dharamsala to set up his government."

Debjani supplied her wisdom, "Buddhism started in India and returns to India. This is her rightful refuge."

The police officer was now quite incensed, "And the other hero they have is Stalin, that asura, that demon! You know what he does to his political opponents? Puts them all in the same train and blows it up. Politics is all a game of power. Whatever name you give it – this 'cracy' or that 'ism'. It is not 'of the people, by the people, for the people', but 'of power, by power, for power'."

Binapani went to her room, shut the door and jumped on to her bed. This was what she had waited for all that evening. She gathered a pillow close to her heart as if it were her lover, and gently opened the book – And Quiet Flows the Don.

In their bedroom, her parents were arguing.

Mr Banerjee confronted his wife, "Debjani, why is she asking about Naxalbari?'

The lady had acquired a sharp tongue to match her wit. "I thought the field rats were all crushed. Why are you worried if she wants to know some history?"

Precisely because he feared it was not history yet. But aloud he said, "Women who meddle in politics lose their sweetness."

His wife gave an extra punch to the pillow she was arranging on the bed. "Truly spoken like a good Brahmo."

"Look at yourself. If the Lahiris next door knew you talked back to your husband like this, they would not join our Brahmo Samaj."

From the mid-nineteenth century Bengal had seen the birth of extraordinary men in every field. The Brahmo Samaj was started by the social reformer, Raja Rammohan Roy. Suttee, the practice of burning a woman on her dead husband's pyre, was the scorching issue of that age. If that seemed cruel, the alternative was worse. This same woman, if allowed to live, had a harder ordeal to face than death. She was considered a burden to her husband's family, and her father would not have her back either. Often they blamed her for bringing ill-luck for everything that went wrong. Food, shelter, clothing were given her sparingly, and she worked like a domestic servant. But one ill removed would not suffice. The edifice had to be demolished from its rotten base. So widow remarriage was instituted and child marriage was denounced by Vidyasagar, another scholar-reformer of that golden era.

It was the worst time to be born a girl and the best to be born a high caste man. The caste system split society in categories of increasing privileges. A son inherited his father's caste and so the injustice travelled down the generations. Levels of education, economic status and social opportunities were distributed by caste. A low caste family had only one way to upgrade itself – by marrying their daughter to a high caste groom. Often a man of eighty was paid a handsome dowry to marry a child of eight. Such men married several of these hapless girls, and left them widowed. The reformers realized that along with the abolition of child marriage, polygamy and dowry, the caste system would have to be dealt a fatal blow. Women's colleges sprang up and the lower castes were allowed entry in all educational institutions. The best of literature blossomed in that age to restore to woman her honour, to the outcast his pride. Who can forget Bankim Chandra's Devi Chaudhurani, Ayesha, Bhomra? Or, Sharat Chandra's Bordidi, Shodoshi, Kamal? This era has been called the Bengal Renaissance, which spread all over India and supplied the spiritual wine for the freedom struggle.

Debjani continued on her own train of thought. "Removing suttee, dowry, child marriage were all good. But when it came to solving long-term problems of women by educating them, some people had to swallow a bitter pill."

"Men have one role to play and women another. If both do the same things, it causes social disharmony."

"If both do the same things, who will dominate whom? Isn't that the main question?"

Mr Banerjee decided to end this conversation by muttering, "With Indira Gandhi as prime minister every Indian woman has sprouted wings. But wasn't she voted to power because of her father, Jawaharlal Nehru, the true architect of modern India?"

Chapter Two

Tushar

Binapani went to the library and started looking up "Communism". Her fingers leafed through the cards – one, two, three ... ten ... fifteen – until she was beginning to lose hope.

"It must be a terrible feeling not to know where to begin with."

She looked up and found a grinning boy with a goatee and thick spectacles.

"I am comrade Samrat Roy."

Binapani felt a thrill run down her spine. The very word "comrade" had such vibrancy to it, so much tension, as if she was an insider to a fascinating secret!

She answered proudly, "Comrade Binapani Banerjee."

"New to Communism? Let me help you. Shut that drawer and follow me. A good place to begin is Marx's Communist Manifesto. Would you like to read the Bengali translation Nazrul did?"

"Who did you say? Kazi Nazrul Islam, the poet and composer of songs?"

"Yes, the very same man. He was a journalist in the 1920s and even spent some time in jail for his revolutionary ideas."

"Was he a Communist?"

"The Communist party in India was started around that time by M.N. Roy."

Samrat stopped walking and turned around. "Or you know what you should read to get a short cut into the movement? Better read Charu Majumdar's Historic Eight Documents. That will explain it all."

So this was Charu-da, Aparna's hero. She felt embarrassed to ask about the leader they all knew so well and revered so much. But she was itching to know him and Samrat read her inquisitive expression.

"Oh, I forgot you are new to the doctrine. Charu Majumdar, now around fifty years old, was the brain behind the Naxalbari uprising. Oh, you know about Naxalbari? Good. He has formed a militant wing of the Communist Party. Of course, it meant he had to go against some moderate elements within the party, but he has sucked in many of us students. Read the essays and you will know what I mean. And these idealists are not just word-mongers; they are living examples. They don't believe in private property, so they just give it up and live a simple life."

Binapani must have had a surprised look on her face, because Samrat stopped to explain, "It means making do with just one pair of sandals, because that's all you need anyway, the bare minimum of clothes and some food to keep body and mind fuelled, a fountain pen and a few notebooks to write on in a small room." She was reminded of Tolstoy's story where a peasant was promised as much land as he could cover in a day. The poor man runs to his death, and the only land he needs is the six by two feet patch for his burial.

Binapani was glad to have met Samrat and he too was quite pleased to help. He hesitated for a minute before leaving her with the booklet. "If you are not as yet in a group, we would like to have you in ours."

Binapani really liked this honest and simple boy, but she felt herself already initiated. "I have actually joined a group yesterday."

"Whose group is it?"

"I don't know the leader. There was Ketaki-di, Ranjan, my friend from college, Aparna, Tushar..."

"Oh, you are in Tushar's team then. Well, what can I say but that one man's fortune is another's loss. Too bad for us. But you are in very good hands. So long, comrade."

On Wednesday, Binapani chose a plain cotton sari and found an old vanity bag tucked in the storeroom. She could hardly wait for the lecture to end, and made pencil scribbles on her notebook which, by some strange coincidence, resembled Tushar's name. When it was finally over, she hopped over to Aparna's side.

"Tell me about your comrade friends while we walk to the Coffee House."

Aparna smiled at her teasingly, "Looks like sleeping beauty was kissed awake?"

"Aparna, will you stop treating me like a little girl? Please?"

"All right, all right, now wipe that pout from your face. Ranjan is studying chemistry. From childhood he has been tinkering with fireworks, and now he will make some real fire work." She laughed at her own pun.

"Tushar was a brilliant student of political science until last year. His father passed away and he had to take up a job. He does typesetting, and in his spare time reads the pamphlets that pass through the press. That is how he got hold of Charu-da's writings, and all the other ideals of Communism. Ketaki-di is our senior. She is doing her masters in philosophy, but that is to fool her family. Actually she collaborates with the main office of the student's wing. She is very good at writing. We have all read her inspiring works but did not know it was her. You know she writes under a pen name – Pashani."

Binapani exclaimed, "That is quite a cruel name to choose, I mean one who calls herself stone-hearted ..."

"The idols we worship are also made of stone. With our devotion we instil life in them, and one day a stone becomes a divine power with the universal mother's compassion."

"How true!"

"Priyotosh lives in the students' dormitory. He is the best debater I have ever met. No wonder all the students in his hostel have joined our cause."

"Oh, so he is the propaganda minister?"

Aparna was shocked to hear the word. "We don't call it propaganda. That's a dirty word that reminds me of the Nazis. Priyo appeals to a person's reason."

When they reached the Coffee House, two tables were joined together and more boys were pressed elbow to chin. Binapani voiced her father's doubts. "Marx said religion is the opiate of the masses. How can such a doctrine work for Indians? Can you imagine us without religious customs – every milestone in our life is a religious rite. There are more temples than drinking water wells in this country and thousands of men whose very livelihood is religious ministration. And all this is just religion. The foundation below it – spirituality – goes so deep that a mere political doctrine cannot uproot it."

Tushar was impressed by Binapani. "You make a good point. We will take from Communism what we can adapt to the Indian psyche – like buying cloth from the market. One man makes himself a shirt, another a kurta, a third a sherwani. But they all started from the same cloth. That is how an ideology is kept alive. Isn't that what the many philosophies have done with the Brahman? Some keep his infinite qualities, some make him colourless, some give him innumerable forms, and yet some condense him in a book, in a name, a sound. Some call It Him, some call It Her. But essentially we are all talking about the same thing – God, Light, Bliss, Freedom, Immortality."

Binapani still had her doubts about Communism. "It dreams of a classless society. Most of us are sharply divided in the four castes, and have created many more – untouchables, dalits, converts, Anglo-Indians, foreigners. Our inland letter stationery has Gandhi's words on it, 'Untouchability is a crime against God and man.' Yet the lower caste is segregated. And why are the books of wisdom, the Vedas and the Upanishads, prohibited for them? How many reformers have tried in vain to straighten this cur's tail?"

Aparna supported Binapani. "Yes, it is in contradiction to the very foundation of our spirituality – that God is in every person."

On this point everybody agreed – that a corruption of thought had created the caste system.

Tushar elaborated, "It is written in the Purusha Sukta, a part of the Rigveda, that when the Supreme Being wanted to create the Becoming he sacrificed himself for it. Four categories of men sprang forth from his body. The Brahmins from his head, and these are the scholars, priests, teachers. The Kshatriyas came from his arms. They are the diplomats, rulers, warriors. The Vaishyas came from his thighs, and they uphold the structure of society by generating wealth. The Shudras sprang from his feet – the peasants, barbers, washermen, those who burn the dead, and similar other menial labourers. Now the question is, where did the hierarchy come from? Does it say anywhere that the head is higher than the feet, therefore the Brahmin is a better person than the Shudra? This thrusting of an order where there is none, is called the caste system."

"So how did it begin?"

"Simple. The same way as any group overpowers another. A man who is a little ahead in the game chooses some friends and together they make the laws – laws that safeguard their status. Centuries later the source is forgotten and the form is worshipped."

Shubir said, "I would argue that the peasant should be the most respected member of society. Can a man use his mind when he is hungry? Can he fight? Can he do business without being alive first?"

"So what can be done?"

Ranjan cut right to the bottom of the issue. "We have waited long enough for people to change. Now we have to annihilate the class enemy."

Binapani wondered if "annihilate" meant what she feared. Who were these boys, these young students, these university dropouts who believed so madly about a new world, as if it was round the corner? When she looked up after a while, she was surprised to find Tushar studying her. He lifted his eyebrows a little, "Had enough of passive smoking for a day? Comrades, let me escort Binapani to the bus stop, is it? Or do you live close by? Ah, bus stop it is then."

"Binapani, I don't know what you think about us, but swear you will not tell anyone what you learn here. The time is not yet ripe for us to come out."

"I am fascinated by your idealism. All that I admire in fiction is actually very much alive in your hearts. I can almost touch that part of history written in the Russian novels I love so much."

"Yes, isn't it exciting? You and I and all of us will rewrite history our own way."

"I wish I could help more than just being a hungry listener of your thoughts."

"We would love that. I am so glad you offered."

"Really? I am flattered."

"I am not sure I want to tell you, right now at least. You have just joined us, and I am afraid you will make an about-turn and run away."

"Oh, don't you worry about that. Tell me, I am listening."

"Looks like we have to start printing some pamphlets, pay for travel expenses, boarding and lodging ... "

"Is it money?"

Tushar made a grimace and nodded, "Yes."

"Why are you so shy about it? I will try my best."

On the way back home Binapani applied herself diligently on the task. Finally she came up with a pukka plan, a solid strategy. She approached her mother who was stitching a button on a shirt. "Ma, I want to resume my singing class. Do you think baba will allow me?"

Her mother gave her a piercing look, as if she had transferred her needle work to her eyes. "Bina, I am your mother, you can't lie to me."

"No really, I want to start singing again. Those Rabindra Sangeet songs we hear on the radio in the morning are so inspiring."

"You don't want to tell me your secret. That's all right. These days it is better not to know young people's minds. But let me tell you one thing, young lady. We have tried to give you the best education for one reason, just one reason."

"To honour my family traditions?"

"Not at all. That may be something your father drills down

your head at every opportunity, but that is not how I see it. Education is responsibility, it is the power to discriminate, viveka. Use it properly. Choose your friends wisely."

"Thus spake Polonius to his son, in Hamlet."

"Very smart. Now run along and get ready for dinner."

Binapani went to her mother's side, put her arms round her neck and gave a huge hug.

In the corridors of the university campus, Binapani and Aparna met Ketaki, and the three of them started walking towards the Coffee House. When they were near the bookshops Binapani had an idea.

"Let's talk to the bard of College Street." They walked past the many stalls exchanging greetings with the storekeepers.

Binapani stopped in front of Kanailal's perch and instantly earned a flashing smile from the man.

"Kanai-da, what do you think of Communism?"

"It is an excellent dream."

"Dream?"

"Yes, for India. It assumes great responsibility for the common man, the proletariat as they call him – the factory hand, the miner, farmer, tailor, barber, cook, then the banker, teacher, the architect, the mason – in other words, every unit of society that works, with body or mind. It believes he will work voluntarily for the community."

Aparna was surprised, "So you think Indians are selfish? They cannot work for others?"

"No didimoni, the emphasis is not on 'community', but on 'work'. Given a chance we would rather not work, leave alone the back-breaking tasks of peasants and factory workers. We are like camphor. If the stopper is loose, we will evaporate in thin air. We have twelve centuries of *jagat mithyaa* backing us. Why labour for an illusory world? We need to be driven. Some motivated leader has to whip us to action or an ambition has to slap us hard enough to wake us from our sleep."

Aparna was displeased with the argument. "What about the

three-thousand-year-old call from the Upanishads – *uttishthata, jagrata*, arise, awake?"

"Do you hear that bell ring in your ears?"

"I do, just as many others do. Swami Vivekananda rang it yet again for us decades ago."

"Then go forth and build the new world order. I, for one, am ready to discard my pessimism and run barefoot in the street like a five-year-old."

"You have to do it now for it to happen. Only this time it may not be a bell, but the twang of a bowstring."

Ketaki had spoken, and Kanailal looked at her amazed, as if he heard something behind her words he could not believe.

At the table in the Coffee House the topic of discussion was the feudal system. All agreed it was an anachronism that had to be laid to rest. Binapani tried to bring balance to the discussion.

"You must remember that not all landlords are wicked just because they inherited their land. Most are not the real masters. There are hundreds of relatives who share the prosperity if not the perspiration."

"Yes, Rabindranath Tagore was one such man with a heart big enough to engulf the whole world. But one needs to be *that* noble not to succumb to the glamour of wealth and power."

Binapani said, "I know of another such man, who distributed his land among his tenants; as much as he could, and he himself wanted to live the simple life of a poor man."

One of the boys asked, "I suppose his relatives did not allow him that luxury?"

"Yes, he struggled all his life with this dichotomy. But it was an attempt that we shall nevertheless admire."

Ranjan prompted her, "Why don't you tell us, we give up."

"It was Count Tolstoy, the author of War and Peace and so many other masterpieces."

Someone whistled. Binapani continued, "And do you know whom he inspired? Gandhi."

"Is that why the father of our nation wore a single piece of cloth and lived in a hut?"

"Primarily Tolstoy inspired Gandhi with his concepts of universal compassion. Tolstoy had written articles on Christian piety, which found their way to the energetic barrister, Gandhi, in South Africa. They started a correspondence too. That's why when Gandhi set up his community experiment in South Africa he called it Tolstoy Farm."

Ranjan made a bored face. "Non-violence has not achieved much, has it? Look at us, one people in two countries."

Binapani retorted, "That could be because there was not enough non-violence. Gandhi tried hard to make the Muslims feel at home in a Hindu-majority nation."

"That is the problem. Non-violence assumes you are dealing with rationality. It does not consider bigger motivators like ambition and fear."

"Why don't you tell me what more could violence have achieved?"

"Violence does not mean terrorism. It also means being firm. Gandhi had the whole nation's ear. He should not have been so lenient with the Muslim demands."

"I already said he thought the method of appeasement would win their confidence."

Tushar clapped for attention. "Silence, please! Everybody has an opinion on the Partition, and we don't want to get into that discussion now. The task of the hour is the annihilation of the class enemy."

Binapani was flustered after the argument "And what do you mean by annihilation?"

Shubir was laughing at her fear. "We mean 'Jai Hind' style, not 'Hey Ram' style."

"Are you mocking Gandhiji's sacrifice for our nation? How many men can utter the name of the Lord, 'Hey Ram', when he is shot at? That too, ironically, by a man of his own religion?"

Aparna tapped Binapani on the shoulder, "Oh, no, we are

not mocking him. We are contrasting his dove-like methods to that of the hawks of the extremist camp. Our preference is 'Jai Hind', taught by our hero, Netaji Subhas Chandra Bose, because he chose the path of direct action."

Binapani looked at Aparna angrily, "I shudder to think of the consequences he was introducing with his dalliance with the Japanese. They were a much worse task-master than the British."

"Netaji did not think of handing over India to the Japanese. All his efforts were for Poorna Swaraj. Besides, he sought the help of Soviet Russia at first. Only when his request was met with silence, did he turn to Germany. Then the Axis powers promised him weapons and he gathered an army in Singapore."

Shubir continued, "But the pity is that after many twists and turns of history, when independence was granted by a Britain bled white in the Second World War, the transfer of power followed the Gandhian style. And like all negotiations there was a compromise. A line was drawn through the body of Punjab and Bengal, two of the most extremist states during the freedom struggle. And what a ridiculous division! Pakistan has two limbs, one in the Arabian Sea, another in the Bay of Bengal separated by a thousand miles of India."

Ketaki's gentle voice dispelled the heat, "Binapani, what we lament is the exodus of fourteen million people of which half a million were massacred in cold blood. Some people wonder if, within six months of the Partition, Gandhi paid for this national disaster, with his own life."

People became sadly pensive. Tushar sighed, "Blaming is futile. None could foresee the two major events that followed the decision of Partition – one, the bloodbath, and two, the fact that millions of Muslims chose to remain in India."

Suddenly the gentle hum in the Coffee House was disturbed as if the bees had smelled smoke in one corner. Binapani saw Samrat approach Tushar in great haste. He whispered a word and immediately turned and left. Tushar jumped up. "The police are coming. Disperse now, and do not walk together. Ranjan, go inform Hari's table." It was then that Binapani noticed the great evacuation. There was not a table left undisturbed in the huge hall. Was it possible that most of the people in the Coffee House were comrades? Some tables were made to turn over, coffee cups crashed on the floor spraying pieces of bone china all around. Binapani followed the sea of people rushing down the stairs, afraid to look around and betray familiarity. Only when she found herself surrounded by the public in the bookstalls of College Street did she look around for any trace of the men in khaki. There they were, with batons in hand, rushing about, defeated by the dispersed crowd.

Chapter Three

Nazrul

A crowd of onlookers was huddled round a table by a sweet shop. Excited voices cried out encouragements.

"Harder, harder!"

"Don't give up!"

"Use a sudden jerk!"

"Stare him down!"

"Shall I tickle him?" Laughter broke out.

Binapani stood on her toes to snatch a look. Two men were arm-wrestling, panting like bulls, red eyes locked, sweating biceps quivering. This game is called panja which is also used to settle arguments, or ego bouts. An image from a poem flashed across Binapani's mind – *aami mrityur shaathe lorbo paanjaa*, I shall arm-wrestle with death. This was from the poem, Bidrohi, the rebel, by Kazi Nazrul Islam, a poem that sent sparks of fire coursing down the veins. It made every man feel like a hero, a conqueror. She had a brilliant idea. It had to be read in the meeting today. This was the mantra for the rebel. She turned back and sped towards College Street, and went straight to a bookstall. "Sukumar-da, do you have Nazrul's volume of poems?"

"Yes, but you surely have a copy yourself."

"I don't want to buy. Can I borrow it for a few hours?"

"You look possessed, my child. It must be one of Nazrul's poems. Yes, I got it, it must be Bidrohi."

"Yes, it is."

"Here is the book." Sukumar handed her the book and jumped down from his seat. With an agile movement he brought the shutter of his stall crashing down.

"Where are you going so early, Sukumar-da?"

"I am coming with you. I would not let such an opportunity pass."

The abandoned house was humming when they entered. Word went round and wherever they met – in people's homes, in parks, in classrooms, forgotten temples – every day more and more people were seen with bright eyes and shining faces. Within minutes Priyotosh, the orator, had started reading the poem to a spellbound audience.

"*Bolo beer, bolo unnato mamo sheer.*

Tell yourself, O hero,

Say, my head is held high, so high, the mountains bend theirs before mine.

I am a cyclone, I am destruction, I am unfettered.

I tear at my shackles and transgress all law, I mock at fate's pride.

I am the rhythm of a madman's dance.

I embrace my enemy, I arm-wrestle with death.

The cup of my life is again and again filled with wine.

I am the sacrifice, I am the priest, I am the fire.

I am creation, I am cessation, I am the crowded place, I am the graveyard.

I do not bow to anyone but to myself alone.

I am the forest fire devouring the universe.

I am the fury in a storm, I am the crash of the ocean.

I am the thirst of summer, I am the scorching sun.

I laugh the laughter of flowers seated in hell's fire.

I am eternal, immortal, indestructible, bodiless.

I am the unmatched rebel, the brave

I have risen alone above the world with head held high.

I have discovered myself today, all my bonds are broken.

I, the great rebel wearied at war, shall rest only when

The cry of the downtrodden ceases to pierce the air,

And the sword of the aggressor is laid down in the battleground.

On that day, I, the rebel, shall attain my peace."

After the meeting, when everybody was dispersing, Tushar found Binapani.

"Come, Bina, I will walk you to the bus stop." The bus stop came but these two pretended there was no stop and walked to the next stop, and then to the next. A chill wind started blowing as the kites swung upwards. Binapani shivered and covered her back with her sari.

"No, not like that," said Tushar with a naughty smile on his face. He arranged the sari back and put his arm round her shoulder. "Isn't this warmer?"

Binapani whispered, as if the world was eavesdropping on them, "What are you doing? Have you lost your mind?"

"Why? Whom do you know among these passers-by? We will not meet them again in our life. Why should they be masters of our fate?"

"Make a wish Tushar, before the sun disappears round the corner."

He closed his eyes. "Done it."

"What?"

"That we could have fried fish on the Digha beach, together, right now."

Binapani sighed, if only Tushar's wish were a reality. If only he did not have this disease in his brain eating him up. If only they could be like two small children splashing about in the puddle. Why did he have to stake his life for a handful of peasants? She knew the answer only too well, yet indulged herself with these questions.

"Tushar, if I ask you for a boon will you give it to me?"

"Gladly, if it is mine to give."

"Violence does not solve problems. Do not follow its path, I beg of you, please."

"Earth is the heroic spirit's battlefield."

A shiver ran down her back. "Where did you hear that?"

"I will show it to you when we reach the next street light."

"But heroism is not always in extremism."

"Even so said Arjuna in the battlefield of Kurukshetra. But what did his charioteer, the Lord Krishna, say to him? No revolution ever came about through prayer, Bina. Look at the French revolution, didn't heads roll? Look at the Bolshevik Revolution and the Chinese Peasants' War, and the American Civil War, and the freedom struggle of colonies. Which of these was bloodless? Which of them failed?"

"Our scriptures say there is a God in each man. Still will you want to kill?"

"*Na hanyate hanyamaane shareere.* One does not kill the divine spark within. One just kills the body and the prejudices that infect it."

Tushar stopped by the street light and drew out a book from his side-bag. It was the size of the Bhagavad Gita. Binapani was not in a mood for any philosophic discourse. She just wanted him to be safe, for her, for their future together.

"Why are you showing me the Gita, I too have read those words – *na hanyate.*"

"This is not the Gita. It is the gospel of the Satya Yuga, the Age of Truth, written in English for the whole world to read."

Binapani opened the book and read, "Savitri, a legend and a symbol." Below was the signature of the author – Sri Aurobindo. Suddenly she was furious.

"So are you planning to follow the path of Aurobindo and his gang of bomb-makers?"

"Bina, I don't decide these things. The spirit of the age compels."

"Let me remind you where they all went. Many went to the cellular jail in the Andaman Islands. Some of them were hung and some tortured to death. Only a few were released, broken in body and spirit."

"You forget that some were acquitted, including Sri Aurobindo. He was not a bomb-maker, he was the wielder of the pen, and therefore, more dangerous for the government. He was not the sort of orator either to rouse the rabble, but he did appeal to the best in man, and people came flocking to his door."

She had heard about the cruelty of the police. Her father mentioned some horror stories at home, and she knew he had watered them down. And this was just the police. If the situation demanded it, the Indian Army would be brought in. "Tushar, how can you imagine fighting with the country's armed forces? They have tanks and machine guns."

"We too have some. Not tanks, but guns. Besides we will do it the guerrilla style. You know how they are fighting in Vietnam right now, how they won in Cuba and in China."

"But, Tushar, what do you know of using a gun?"

"I personally may not need to do it. We are training the peasants. Eighty per cent of India is the peasant class, and also eighty per cent is starving. Can you guess who these people are, those who are starving?"

"The same peasants?"

"Yes, those who produce food cannot eat it. It is because they don't own the land they cultivate. They get poorly paid for their labour, like it was a job in a factory. The landlord who pays the farmer a pittance, makes a fortune on the crop he sells. That is why we say..."

"Land to the tiller."

"Yes, Bina, you know it. Growing food out of soil, water and sunshine is a miracle. Only God can do it. And some men are specially gifted – to midwife this mother earth. These are the peasants. If you cannot love the earth as a living being, you cannot assist her in production. How can the landlord, who has not even touched her body with his bare feet, leave alone his hand, how can he fathom the relationship between a man and his mother earth?"

They were silent for a long time, moving back into the darkness between the street lights. Tushar continued, "On the battlefield of Kurukshetra, Arjuna faced his enemies and was overcome with love, not weakness – after all, they were his friends and relatives. The true Communist is also a big lover. He does not stop short of loving his relatives, but considers the whole world his own family. Tell me, would you not react if someone beat up your mother, your brother?"

"You make it sound like the bhakti movement of love for the Divine. You know Vaishnavas touch the feet of every person they meet – such is their sense of love. Surely you cannot compare Communism with this deep adoration."

"I am not saying they have the same outward form. But in essence they are the same."

"So one day when the battle is done, you will love like that?"

"When the battle is won, yes!"

"Have you any idea how many people you may have to kill?"

"We don't propose to kill them all. We hope the terror will bring many people around."

"Can you evoke love through fear?"

"Unfortunately, some people don't know what deprivation means, to lose, to be at someone's mercy, to be poor. We have to show it to them. Yes, terrorize them. And after that hope, hope earnestly, that the new age will descend, hope that all this misery will end fast."

Tears ran down Binapani's face. "I am sorry, Tushar. It is just that I am so scared. Scared for you ... for all of you." Slowly they moved away from the street light, and Tushar put his arm around Binapani drawing her closer.

* * * * *

The next time they met at the abandoned mosque, Binapani sensed a tension in the air. Something terrible had happened. Nobody spoke. Everybody was looking at the ground. Tushar looked daggers at her. Could it be the same person who had been so tender with her the other day, the same Tushar she had begun to admire, to love?

He said icily, "Number 55, Bagbazar Street. Do you recognize the address?"

"Yes, that is where I live. What happened? Why are you all so..."

"That is also where the Deputy Commissioner of Police lives."

"Yes, he is my father."

"The man who would rather see us all dead this minute is your father, and you did not tell us?" Tushar was trying hard not to scream. "So did he send you to spy on us?"

Binapani snapped back. "No, that is not true. He does not even know I am here. He thinks I am in a singing class. I swear I will never betray you. I admire your idealism and pray that you succeed." Tushar was as cold as snow, like his name suggested. She looked around and found in every face the same chill ... the same hardness.

"If you don't trust me, I will walk away and forget that I had ever met you." Then she broke down and said through sobs, "I have not chosen my father, have I? But I can choose my friends, can't I?"

Tushar sprang to his feet and wrapped her in his arms. She hid her face in his chest and wept. He was whispering, "I am sorry. I had to prove it to the others."

These others tried to look away, not comfortable with this public display of affection from their chosen leader.

Chapter Four

Gypsy

On the last bend to her house, a car honked in Binapani's ear and made her jump. It was her father's white Ambassador, with their driver Haradhan at the wheel. His eyebrows jumped up, "Madam, from where are you coming?"

It was Binapani's turn to question him, "Why are you parked here?"

Haradhan countered, "First you tell me where you are coming from."

Binapani answered nonchalantly, "From the singing class."

Haradhan tilted his head politely, "Me too."

Now she was on her alert. "Who sent you to pick me up? You know I always come by bus."

"No, I don't know anything anymore. They said you never joined the singing class from last year. Yet you come home late. Are you up to some mischief, some boyfriend maybe or smoking ganja?"

Hashish and marijuana, popularly known in India as charas and ganja, were grown all over South Asia and sold openly in the market. A stream of adventurers from the West – those who questioned, resisted and finally dropped out of society – wandered along the drug routes of Asia in search of a pure idealism, a lasting peace, a beatific grace land. These hippies camped in parks, on the beaches and stayed in run-down hotels, leading lives of collective sharing, altered consciousness and free-wheeling spirituality. Attracted by the novelty of the emerging counterculture, the youth in cities of India also started consuming narcotics and tuned in to rock music.

Binapani pretended to chide her old well-wisher, aware that his complicity was necessary at this point. "How you speak, Haradhan-da. Do I look like such a silly girl?"

"I have seen you shitting in your pants," said the old man, meaning that he had seen her from her babyhood. There were a dozen other expressions one could have used, such as "I have seen you crawling", but that would have been against Haradhan's earthiness. "I will not let you go astray, meet bad boys, or go dancing in those British relics, called clubs. I know all that happens there. My waiter friends have told me. The Bengali society men and women are not that tailless." by which he meant they were like animals in many respects.

"Haradhan-da, it is nothing of that sort."

"All right, I am listening."

"Can't a person have some secrets out here?"

"You want to keep secrets from your old uncle?" he meant himself.

Before he could remind her in which state he had seen her, she had blurted. "No, it is very simple. I will tell you everything, but please do not tell my father. You know how much he hates nursing. But I want to learn it, just as a hobby, you know. So I spend time helping Shoma."

"And who is this Shoma?"

"Don't you remember her? My friend from Yogamaya College." In reality, neither did she, because this Shoma never existed. "She is training to be a nurse."

"All right, all right, now get in," grumbled Haradhan, with no story to take to his adda party with his Nepali watchmen friends. "Your father wanted you to be home an hour earlier. Now you handle the situation yourself."

Adda is the favourite Bengali sport, followed by football and then cricket. It means to converse – exchange recipes, cures and news – spin yarns, debate, critique, joke, strategize – just give your tongue a field day. It means to release a puff of your thought in the air and see it mingle with other puffs. Adda does not discriminate – you don't need legs as in football, or brains like in chess, or luck as in cards. Children do it during tiffin break, mothers do it over terrace boundaries, lovers do it in the

Botanical Gardens, men do it while hanging from the bus, rickshawallas do it with their passengers, temple-side beggars do it and babus on golf courses do it. Some people joke that adda is actually an acronym for "All Day Do Adda", using the word to define itself, thus indicating its unending nature.

The car turned the bend and reached their driveway. Binapani's mother was pacing the balcony upstairs in great agitation. She called to her daughter, "Come up this minute. Quick."

On her bed was spread out a sari of heavy gold embroidery – the Benarasi style – that was used for special occasions like attending weddings and festivals. Beside it lay an open satin-lined jewel case displaying a pair of earrings and a necklace in intricate gold filigree.

Her mother was panting as she tried to wear an old-fashioned earring she had got from the locker that day. "These jewels are so unwieldy. Now get dressed fast and eat something. We don't want to hear your growling stomach. They will be here any minute." She was like a little steam engine on the roll, unaware that she had overshot her station. "Haradhan, take Gypsy to the tool shed, and mind you, lock it well."

Binapani came round to face her mother's upturned face. "Who will be here any minute?"

"An IAS officer and his family."

IAS means the Indian Administrative Service. A position in the IAS is coveted by all aspiring young Indians, who are not strong enough to join the armed forces, or not mathematically oriented to be engineers or doctors. Of the tens of thousands that take the IAS examination every year, a few hundred are selected. Of them some get a real chance to serve the country. The rest lubricate the bureaucratic machinery.

"And so," Binapani knew her mother was trying to hide something, "Why should I have to dress up in a Benarasi sari? And wear all those jewels?"

"His son's name is Debarpan. Now don't begin... Oh my God, is it their car honking?"

Binapani caught her mother's frantic arm. "Ma, listen. I am not going to get married to this boy."

"Bina, it is good for your father's career. Now be a good girl and don't upset him."

Binapani sank on the bed and rested her head on the bed post. She was after all a bronze vase they kept well polished for customers. Or a piece of land watered and ploughed to fetch a proper price. She would be bartered in return for a favour. That was the whole plan, wasn't it, when she was born a girl? Her education, the many books they allowed her, the singing lessons, the expensive saris, the fancy sandals, the fashionable vanity bags, everything, everything was a secret plot to make her more marriageable. Her mother's engine had stopped chugging. She placed a hand on Binapani's shoulder. "I know how bad you feel. All this so suddenly, without even asking you. They are just passing through Calcutta, so it had to be arranged within hours."

Binapani tried hard not to blink as her eyes had filled with tears. "Bina, I know who is in your heart – one of those boys. What, am I right? I say, just play it as a game. We can at least enjoy the sweets and kachoris, while we give our guests a good see-off."

Binapani turned around in surprise "Ma, I don't like this joke at all. No, are you seriously with me?"

"Sholo anna. One hundred per cent," came her mother's smug reply.

Binapani walked into the assembly seated around the table decorated with sweets and salty snacks. The father IAS officer welcomed her using the choicest cliché, "Ah, the perfect image of Goddess Durga."

Binapani's father delivered his oiliest laugh, "Chatterjee, Goddess Saraswati, you mean. Her name is Binapani". Binapani is another name for Saraswati, the Goddess of Knowledge. This Goddess holds the veena, and is thus called Veenapani, the holder of the veena, Binapani in Bengali.

"Oh yes, Banerjee, how right, how right." The two were like old cronies, calling each other by surname.

In this upper caste Bengali society, people's names were read right to left. By the time the right side of the name was assessed, a mass of prejudices had formed. So much so that the left side was often not necessary. A scoundrel with a Chatterjee, Banerjee, Mukherjee, Goswami, Ganguly, Bhattacharya, Chakraborty right side was a better man than a saint with any other "right" side.

After the initial chatter, Mr Chatterjee turned towards the prospective bride, "So, Binapani, your father was saying you have just returned from your singing class. Would you like to entertain us a little?"

Binapani looked demurely at his feet and started,

"*Ei korechho bhalo nithuro he.*

Oh cruel one, what you did was indeed right;

For, if the incense is not burnt, how will it be fragrant?"

"Stop, Bina, dear," said her father, struggling to sound tender. "What if you sang a song for the occasion?"

Binapani thought a little, "Shall I sing 'I have drunk poison losing hope of life'?"

"Sing *bhalobeshe shokhi*," commanded her father without much pretence this time.

Binapani started in a mournful tone.

"Oh love of mine, write my name in the temple of your heart."

Her father walked around the sofa, and positioned himself behind his guests. He faced his daughter and waved his hands to indicate a tabla – the Indian drum – and a sword cutting his throat. It literally meant taal caatchhe – your rhythm is a disaster. He gestured with his hand – faster. Instantaneously she changed her pace, like a set from a Hindi film's dance sequence. Her father grimaced and made the opposite gesture. She was dragging her words again. Mrs Chatterjee extracted a Chinese foldable fan from her vanity bag and started fanning herself. This was no love song, but a dirge. Father played conductor for a few more minutes and then holding his head signalled her to stop before she could complete the last stanza. The other hearers heaved a sigh of relief instead of the customary praise with "Wah wah".

Mr Chatterjee was bright again. "Now you two young people should go in and have a chat. What do you say, Banerjee?" The latter was ready to say yes to dancing on one foot with his hands tied behind his back. So this was an easy favour to grant. He added, "We old folks will talk politics, then cricket, then some more politics. You will get bored."

Debarpan followed Binapani, caressing the frilly end of his dhoti that he was holding so she could notice it was well pleated. The barber is also the men's greenroom specialist. He cuts the hair, shaves the beard, trims the moustache, files the nails, and ends up pressing his fingers deep into the head and applying a mustard oil massage to the body. For an extra baksheesh, he pleats the end of a dhoti.

Binapani put on her most stylish accent, as if she had just passed an audition test for a playback singer. "So Debarpan, what do you do?"

"Call me Deb."

"Is there anything you do other than asking girls to call you Deb?"

The boy dropped his pleats in shock and almost tripped over them, "I am preparing for the IAS exams for this summer. And what do you do, Bina? No? All right then – Binapani?"

"I am doing my masters in literature – English."

There was a long pause. Debarpan feared she would start humming, so he asked, "Is there some special topic from the field of literature that interests you particularly?"

"Yes, I am doing a comparative study of fairy tales. You are smiling. So you think, like most adults, fairy tales are mere fantasy to fool children to eat, or sleep or be quiet?"

"Apart from the fact that the plot is interesting, I don't find anything more in them."

"Fairy tales are the foundation of education. A person who

cannot look back on these fantasies has a vacuum he cannot fill easily."

"Looks like you have given them a serious thought."

"All right then, let me ask you a question. You think the whole of humanity is very diverse, don't you? But you will be surprised to learn the fairy tales hardly differ. Give me an example of a common trait."

Debarpan scratched his memory and found some remnants of stories dropping off like dandruff. The Bengali folk tales are collected under the heading of Thakurmar Jhuli, grandma's sack of tales. It has talking frogs, princes hatching from eggs, demons with spade-like teeth, lands on the moon and bewitched forests. He scratched out Snow White, Cinderella, Rapunzel. Binapani would not let him relax.

"That makes just two of the many cultures. Surely you cannot forget the Arabian Nights?"

"Oh yes, Aladdin and the genie, Ali Baba and the forty thieves."

"And do you remember Baba Yaga of the Russian folklore?"

"Russian folk tales? I don't read anything Russian."

"I am sorry, you have missed a lot of fun."

"I'll have nothing to do with those Communist dogs".

Binapani cut in, "Communist what?"

"Communist dogs. Do you mind?"

"No, not at all," she was her suave self again.

"I was saying they have started their dirty little propaganda tricks right from the bottom up."

"What makes you think fairy tales are political propaganda?"

"Propaganda is like that – very subtle. You don't even realize it. These same children will grow up reading Tolstoy, Pushkin, Chekhov."

"In the same way people read Shakespeare because they heard the Frog Prince?"

Debarpan mused, "Now here's a shrew that needs taming."

He was silent. What was he thinking? Aloud he caught on to the old train of thought, "So what's common among this multitude of tales ... I say it is witches."

"Yes, we are getting somewhere. How are witches different from you and me?"

"They can fly, and curse, and turn children into goats and eat them."

"What you mean is they have magic. But can you tell me what magic really means?"

"We all know it when we see it. One does not have to define it like a school textbook."

"I think one does. Magic is the impossibility of today, but could be a reality of tomorrow."

Debarpan could not believe he was having a serious conversation. "Then we have a problem. Witch-hunts have to be re-established."

"Some hold on to their fantasies and they are the dreamers who make things happen. The others turn into adults."

For Debarpan, it was intense and abstract, and therefore intensely boring. He said, "Where is the toilet?"

"Turn left and at the end of the corridor you will find it."

Binapani was waiting for just such an opportunity. She called out to Haradhan sitting outside. "Haradhan-da, can you open the tool shed, please?"

The driver was massaging a plug of raw tobacco in his left palm with the thumb of his right hand. He looked up at her "Didimoni, this is just tobacco. One does not get drunk on it. You cannot fool me into opening that door. Elder Brother is there."

Gypsy was known as "Elder Brother" by the neighbourhood. In his walks when he announced a good morning to the world within a radius of five kilometres, the cats scaled impossible heights to vanish. He was especially eager to engage his kinsfolk in conversation – the street dogs – that cleared his passage, grumbling away gutturally. Cows started galloping. Chickens became winged birds and flew away. Goats jumped into the waste bins they were chewing from. And the human onlookers laughed at the man straining backwards on the leash.

Binapani bargained, "What if I gave you a plug of that raw tobacco? How about two? Three?"

Haradhan got up, wagging his finger, "Three plugs of tobacco, and not a word about what I did. Is that a pact?"

Binapani swished hastily back to the drawing room. She did not want to miss a second of the spectacle. "Now see what a not-so-Communist dog can do."

Gypsy was bounding indoors. It sounded like an approaching cavalry. He was eager to meet the guests, in other words, the cause of his imprisonment. He went straight up to Mrs Chatterjee, who rolled up like a cornered spider, her legs on the sofa, "O ma go, oh my God, what is this pony doing here?"

Gypsy looked down at her, his eyes moistening like the Buddha of compassion. Then suddenly he put his paws up on Mr Chatterjee's knees, looking straight in his eyes, canine to human. "Hello, old fox. Aha, what do we have here? A sandesh, my favourite sweet! Give us a bite, give us a bite!"

The man swung the half eaten sandesh around trying to avoid the snapping jaws. "Banerjee, do something."

His host was already doing lots of things at that time. He was busy dropping photos from their frames while he looked for a stick behind the furniture. He screamed "Gypsy down, down!"

But Gypsy was an honourable dog, he was faithful to only one person, and that was Binapani's mother. "Silence!" he ordered, showing two rows of sparkling teeth, "My bark is louder than yours."

"Debjani!" yelled the helpless patriarch in his policeman's trumpet call, "Control this beast of yours."

Mother and daughter were peeping from behind a cushion each, rocking in mirth. Through bursts of laughter, Debjani instructed Mr Chatterjee to toss the sweet in the air for Gypsy –

no, he would not mind a half-eaten piece. Gypsy gave a greedy push to the knees and caught the projectile in midair.

Here Binapani could not stop herself from the old habit, "Shabbash, good boy, Gypsy!" Usually this comment was followed by another treat. Gypsy did some complex math and deduced old fox to be the source of the next treat too. For the fox in question had leapt to his feet and, with defiance, had picked up another sweet. This time, he towered over his adversary. Deliberately he popped the sweet in his mouth, two eager doggy eyes following its trajectory. It was a bad idea to incense a creature of such keen sensibility. Gypsy ran for the table, held the edge of the tablecloth in his slobbering mouth, and tugged at it. Sweets, snacks, glasses of sherbet crashed to the floor. Spoons came rushing after to the rescue and clanked on the cutlery. Mother and daughter were gasping for air. Father was approaching the beast slipping on the chutneys splashed on the floor. His hand brushed past an object that felt like a missile. He grabbed it and hurled it at Gypsy. Mrs Chatterjee's dainty vanity bag hit Gypsy's hind quarter.

Gypsy turned to admire the room one last time. "Oh, keep the sweets for me – I don't mind fallen food."

On his way out he felled his last victim – the returning Debarpan – along with his fancy frills.

Chapter Five

Aparna

After the discussion at Tushar's house, when everyone else had left, Binapani looked back at him, "Shall I see you tomorrow then? Where are we meeting?"

Tushar asked her to follow him. "I want to show you something."

They entered his bedroom, which was like a bookstore. Binapani sat on the little place on the bed where a thin man could make a night's stop. In front of her was a framed photograph of Sri Aurobindo. He had many garlands round his neck. Tushar followed her eyes, "That photograph was taken when he addressed the students of the National College he had founded, shortly before he went to jail. The speech is very inspiring – makes you feel like laying your life down for your country then and there."

Binapani turned her head and found Goddess Kali looking at her from a calendar. She was wearing a garland of severed heads which dripped blood and at her feet was a wreath of hibiscus flowers. Turning around, she found a man's sketch mounted on another wall. His hair and beard formed a mane round his face giving him a leonine appearance. His eyes looked at a distant point. Binapani was mesmerized. "Who is that?"

"Go find out for yourself."

Binapani walked to the portrait and read at the bottom, "Above all, always be capable of feeling deeply any injustice committed against anyone, anywhere in the world. This is the most beautiful quality in a revolutionary." The name under it was "Che Guevara".

"Tushar, who is this Che Guevara?"

"He is the proletarian revolution personified."

"He does not sound Russian or Chinese."

"Because he was Argentinean perhaps?" joked Tushar. He came round to face Che.

"Che was a guerrilla warrior. He had played a major role in the Cuban revolution, which brought the Communist government to power. He led by example – worked very hard and lived a simple life. He dreamed of liberating the poor around the world, and organized campaigns in Africa and Latin America."

"Did Che's revolutions succeed?" asked Binapani.

"Cuba was his only success. His ideals were too lofty. He was executed in Bolivia after months of living in the jungles, half dead of disease."

"When?"

"Two years back. He was not even forty. The revolutionary dies, but the revolution lives on. The Che lives." Tushar touched his heart with his fist. After a solemn moment he relaxed. "But I wanted to show you something else. Close your eyes and listen."

They sat on the bed and she complied. He read from a book.

"The earliest preoccupation of man in his awakened thoughts and, as it seems, his inevitable and ultimate preoccupation – for it survives the longest periods of scepticism and returns after every banishment – is also the highest which his thought can envisage. It manifests itself in the divination of Godhead, the impulse towards perfection, the search after pure Truth and unmixed Bliss, the sense of a secret immortality. The ancient dawns of human knowledge have left us their witness to this constant aspiration, today we see a humanity satiated but not satisfied by victorious analysis of the externalities of Nature preparing to return to its primeval longings. The earliest formula of Wisdom promises to be its last – God, Light, Freedom, Immortality."

"Read on, it is the best thing I have heard for a long time!"

"No. Let this sink in."

Binapani repeated as if hypnotized, "God, Light, Freedom, Immortality. Show me the book."

Tushar quickly hid it behind his back. He was smiling

mischievously. She lunged for it, and the hand flew over his head with the book in it. "Not so easy. You have to earn it. Say the magic words."

"God, Light, Freedom, Immortality."

"Louder."

Tushar was now walking towards the door with Binapani following. He ran on into the corridor and up the stairs. Binapani raced after him, still repeating "God, Light, Freedom, Immortality." On the stairs she panted out, louder "God, Light, Freedom, Immortality." They were on the terrace, and Tushar was still running, dragging her after him "Louder, louder." Finally she stopped, inflated her lungs, and flung out the words to the universe, "God, Light, Freedom, Immortality."

His mother's concerned voice funnelled up the stairs, "What has happened, what has happened?"

Some neighbouring terraces started showing signs of curious movement. Giggling like children, Tushar and Binapani crouched at the parapet, out of sight. He handed her the book. It was The Life Divine by Sri Aurobindo. Tushar had read out the first paragraph of this voluminous book.

Binapani had begun to share Tushar's fascination for the sage – Rishi Aurobindo.

"Did he not leave the freedom movement early, I mean really early to settle into the life of a hermit?"

"Yes, he left India's freedom struggle and moved on to humanity's. But he had sown the seeds that would liberate India eventually."

"What an age of giants it was! The Bengal Renaissance had spread fast to become an India-wide reawakening. Why India alone – all the colonies were astir with a new spirit of freedom. If he had not left politics so suddenly India would be free earlier, don't you think so?"

"Perhaps. But he had a greater mission. He wanted to bring about a revolution of another kind, one that would transform man from within. I cannot fathom what all he did, but you are holding a small token of what he left behind."

The day was waning. The clothes on the line billowed like sails. The house seemed to be launching into an ocean of vastness. Binapani was inspired to sing.

"*Shrinvantu vishwe amritasya putrah*
Hear, worldwide, O children of Immortality:
There are realms divine.
I have known a Cosmic Being,
Resplendent like the Sun, above the darkness.
Knowing Him one crosses beyond Death.
There is no other path for this journey."

After a long meditation Tushar spoke. "Bina, the time has come. We will not have any more meetings. We are going to launch our attacks."

Binapani shivered, "How many are you? Do you know the police are increasing their numbers too?"

"We will go underground. Nobody will know where we are, whether in Calcutta or elsewhere. All our manoeuvres will be guerrilla tactics."

"When will I see you, Tushar?"

"We hope the uprising will spread like a wildfire across India – at least the eastern half of India. From Kashmir to Kerala the Communist party has infiltrated every town and village. And they have been training the peasants."

"Tushar, when will I see you next? Answer my question. Don't tell me about your dreams."

"Bina, don't get so agitated. This is our *dharma kshetra*, the battle for our ideals. We do not control the outcome. We are just instruments of a higher force. Now don't cry – especially in front of your father. We want our children to live in a better world, don't we?"

Tushar held her in a tender embrace as she wept bitterly.

"I too want to do something." She whispered clinging to his neck. "I am coming with you."

"Life on the run is not so easy, my dear. And I want you to be safe. You can serve the cause better if you spy on your father. Report to Aparna all that you hear – even if it sounds irrelevant."

"So, can she meet you?"

"I love your jealousy, darling. No, we will always have a different chain of communication. Your contact will be Aparna to start with."

* * * * *

Binapani read the newspapers – English and Bengali – scrutinising every article for news of the revolution. Horrible reports started coming in – a High Court judge killed at his doorstep, the Haldar family mansion burnt to the ground, a landlord in Coochbehar threatened and yielding to his tenants, peasants' huts set on fire, students killed in an encounter, a hideout discovered, a rich man kidnapped, some bodies found minus the limbs, heads discovered rolling in the gutter. This was not the cry of *Vande Mataram*, not the ringing of a worship bell in a temple, but the terrifying laughter of Kali.

When the demon brothers from hell, Shumbha and Nishumbha, had conquered heaven and earth, the dispossessed Gods turned to the Mother for succour. From her body seven Goddesses emanated. But in the battlefield they were challenged by the demon Raktabeeja. From every drop of his blood that fell on the earth, an identical demon arose. Thus he multiplied endlessly and the battle seemed lost. Time and again people try to wipe out evil, but like Raktabeeja it reincarnates. Then the Mother put forth her fiercest form – Kali – the black naked Goddess. She opened her mouth and drank the blood from the quartered demon before a drop could fall to the earth. His heads she strung together in a garland around her neck. Kali was dancing again now in the streets, her bloody tongue lolling, her scythe chopping heads mercilessly.

When Binapani passed a boy in the corridors of her college, she wondered if he was a comrade, whether she would stop seeing him, when a mother would lose her son, how his body would be found. The boys disappeared from those lanes of knowledge and appeared in the streets of the city stripped of life, or in jails to be tortured to death. She still continued with her imaginary singing classes and passed on all the money she could collect to Aparna. Uprisings were reported from Bihar, Orissa, Andhra Pradesh, as Tushar had rightly predicted, from the eastern half of India. Sometimes it seemed the police were winning, sometimes the Naxalites. Often classes were suspended; parts of the city were cordoned off for the "operations". Calcutta was not a safe place to live in any more. Once Binapani was trapped in a crowd of people running away from the police. From her tight spot she could hear guns firing and cries of dying men. Patches of blood were splattered on the wall, on the street, on rickshaw and bus seats, on tree trunks, on railway tracks, everywhere. Explosions filled the air, not the fireworks of a festival, but the real blazing flames turning property to ashes, gunshots silencing lives. Bombs burst in the marketplaces, in crowded buses, in packed cinema halls, in bustling streets.

One evening, Binapani heard her father exclaim on the phone, "Are you sure they will all be there? Ranjan, Priyotosh, Tushar, Shubir?" Binapani stopped breathing and her body froze. Where will they be, and when? Is it too late to inform Aparna? Her mother came into the room and in an instant gauged the situation. It was dark outside and too risky for a girl to walk alone in the streets of Calcutta. But her mother's firm voice woke her up.

"Go now. Take an umbrella. It might rain, or you could use it otherwise."

Binapani walked so fast her sandals slipped off her feet several times. At last she was ringing Aparna's bell.

"Mashima, is Aparna here?"

"No, but you can wait for her. She might have gone to the Coffee House. Are you all right? Here, have some water."

The poor mother of Aparna had no idea of her daughter's activities. The Coffee House meetings were now a pale history. She hesitated, then decided to wait on the road. If she stayed she would surely betray her anxiety to this unsuspecting lady. Every minute of vigil was a torture. Finally she saw the profile of Aparna getting off a bus. They talked and in two minutes Aparna was waving to an autorickshaw. Binapani thanked the rain, for she could hide under the umbrella and cry her fear out.

The next day her father was in a wild mood on the phone. "What? None of them showed up? And of course their hideouts are all empty? If I can find that shuor ka baccha – 'son of a pig' – informer, I will have his throat slit first thing!" Binapani continued combing her hair with a steady hand. At last she had contributed significantly. The next few months she kept contributing – any names he mentioned, even those she did not recognize, any movement of the police he was coordinating, any word even, that may be a password.

In a crowd suddenly she saw Tushar walking ahead and ran to catch up, but it was not him. A passing shoulder deceived her, the slant of a head, and the walking style of another. She wrote his name on the plate while she toyed with her food, all appetite gone. She distributed pamphlets to students in the college corridors, kept heaps of them in bookstores, packaged them within the folds of newspapers. The writings reported about the progress of the Maoist peasant revolution around India. The Telengana Movement of the 1940s in rural Andhra Pradesh had received a new lease of life. The writers urged the public to boycott the elections, to withdraw all court cases, to place no trust in the government machinery. Binapani's father was hardly at home, and when he did return he was angry all the time.

"Why does the government not call these Naxalite leaders to have a talk?" suggested her mother.

"They don't want to talk. They want the government to surrender to them and walk away. Until then they will terrorize the country."

One day five lines in the corner of a Bengali newspaper made Binapani's whole body tremble. Some young men were shot while they were trying to escape. The address was one street from Tushar's house. She ran to Aparna's flat and held out the paper in her shaking hands. The two did not speak, but they knew where they were going.

They entered the morgue and the pungent smell of rotting flesh hit them like a physical blow. There were people raising the cloth from the dead bodies and passing on in dreadful silence. Some stifled cries could be heard. Aparna and Binapani pulled their saris over their faces to hide their identity as much as possible. They started the routine in terror of what they would find. Some faces were hideously distorted. They were all pinched, as if unfed for days.

"Was that Samrat?" asked Binapani after they had just covered a face.

"Yes," whispered Aparna, and held her friend's arm tightly preventing her from taking a second look.

And then they found Priyotosh, and Shubir and Ranjan, and finally Tushar. The men looked terrible, hardly a memory to keep. Aparna stuffed her sari in her mouth to stop vomiting and dragged out Binapani – who had begun to faint. This was the worst time and place for such a scene. There were many more people she knew who were alive and she was not going to be tortured into disclosing their names. Ketaki was tortured and raped in jail. They found her hanging from her own sari.

Out in the street, Aparna dragged Binapani with her, slapping her gently and digging her finger nails in her wrist. "Bina, we may be followed right now. Our life is in danger, wake up, we need to catch a bus and disappear right now."

Binapani was too stunned to remember who she was. She saw her body step onto a bus, then she must have vomited, because her head was hanging out of the window, someone was offering her a water bottle. Aparna was explaining something about acidity. They were walking again and Aparna was pulling her. Then it was night and Tushar was coaxing her to walk till the next street lamp. All would be fine then. He had something important to show her. Then it was Aparna's voice again, and it was daylight. Was she shot at, was she dying, why was she losing hold of her body? Or was someone else dead? They were now in a tunnel, no it was a staircase, somewhere she had been recently. It was Aparna's house. She saw Haradhan-da's face appear at the door, but it was so distorted she could not focus on it, or were her eyes playing tricks? He uttered not a word, slipped a paper in Aparna's hand and vanished.

The chit was surely from Binapani's mother, although it had no signature and was scribbled in utter haste. "You foolish little girls, why did you go to the morgue? Don't you know there are spies over there? Now hide yourselves and do not bring Bina home. Her father knows it and he will kill her."

Aparna's mind burst in rage at herself. She dragged Binapani to the bathroom and commanded her to wash up the vomit from her sari. Binapani felt water splash on her face and saw Aparna's mother wiping her with a towel. "What happened to you two, did you see some murder on the road?" Aparna was throwing together her clothes in a cloth bag. "Is she all right? We need to leave now."

"But where are you going? You have just come in. Bina cannot even stand."

"Ma, she will have to stand. Come Bina, we need to leave."

"Are we going home?" asked Binapani weakly longing for her mother's comfort.

"No."

"Where are you going, Aparna, with all those clothes?" her mother's voice shook.

"Ma, I cannot tell you. It is best you do not know. Best for you and me."

"Aparna, one day your father told me the same thing. And he never returned alive."

"Stop it, ma, I cannot take it now."

"You young people think you know more than us. We have seen the freedom struggle and your father sacrificed himself for it. And now you do secret things without bothering to tell me!"

"Don't start boasting about the freedom struggle – that's what your generation always talks about! What sort of freedom is it, anyway? A broken nation, the pieces constantly at war with each other."

"That is not how the freedom fighters envisioned it. Surely you know better than to talk in that shallow manner?"

Aparna was not listening, "...with a democracy full of corruption."

"All right, do something better and then talk."

"That's the plan, I assure you, ma."

"Do you have to take Bina too with you? She is going to faint any minute."

"Yes, she is my shield." They would not shoot at the Police Commissioner's daughter. Besides Aparna owed her mother an important tip-off.

Suddenly Binapani remembered Tushar and that he was dead. So were the others. She too would find a way to join them. There was nothing beyond the last street lamp – only the eternal night.

They were rushing down the stairs when Aparna asked her to wait – she had forgotten something. She ran back to the threshold where her mother was standing. She stooped and touched her mother's feet. Binapani saw the lady crumple to the ground like a white handkerchief.

Binapani let go of Tushar's hand and walked backwards into the street. He was smiling at her and she too was happy. A vehicle screeched to a halt and angry voices cursed her. Aparna's grip tightened around her waist. She was sleeping on a bed and saw her mother's sister, her mashi, bandaging her forehead with a wet cloth. Mashi pushed a sandesh to her lips, but Binapani shut her mouth close. Then she saw her mother's brother, her mama, looking haggard, unshaven, red-eyed. Did he not live in Bombay? Maybe he was dead too, and she was in a waiting room among the dead where they are sorted. She looked around for Tushar, and there he was, beckoning to her, and she ran into his arms.

When she opened her eyes she saw a little girl sucking on a lollypop. The girl made a gesture to give it to Binapani. Her seat was rocking. She was in a train and her mama was indeed sitting beside her, looking worse than ever. She raised her head weakly. It was drumming madly.

"Where are we?"

"Nagpur."

She rose in a jolt. "But that is in Maharashtra!"

"Yes, we are going to my house in Bombay."

"Why?"

"Young lady, spare me that stupid question. Do you have any idea what we have gone through for you these last few days? Your mashi and me and of course your mother had the worst time of all. Oh yes, that friend of yours too – trying to save you from running under a bus."

"I need to go to the toilet. I can go alone, why don't you rest?"

"And have you jump out of a moving train? I am coming."

"Why does my head ache so badly? I could bang it on the iron railing to stop it."

Her mama heaved a sigh and made her sit. "Shall we eat something?"

"No."

"In Bombay, if you stick to your adamant ways, we will feed you with a glucose drip."

"Feed me some more of those sleeping pills. Wasn't that how you shoved me into this train?"

He shook his head sadly, "You have no idea, no idea ..."

Part Two

Chapter Six

Anand

"That was a superb play. Congratulations!" Anand's father touched his shoulder and walked to the water cooler. Others passed by dropping their compliments in his hat. The Ganapati festival had just concluded in Dadar's Jayanti Colony in Bombay – ten days of worship accompanied by all sorts of cultural programmes – songs, dances, recitation competitions, dramas, quizzes. On the last day was staged the play Anand had directed, the most serious of all items, the "grand finale" as his mother proudly advertised. Anand was tired after the many days of practice and wanted to rest now. Every year he planned to work with adults for plays, but the kids needed to be kept occupied, said the parents. Alas, these were not just docile kids, but hyperactive teenagers eager to extract the last drop of fun from every minute of their life.

Deshpande was talking to him. "I think it is a very good idea to take up a historical event that we all know, and render it in Sanskrit. Otherwise we will not follow the conversation. I like your teaching approach. Keep it up."

Deshpande was gone, and Anand sighed. That had not been his reason for staging Sanskrit plays. By now he was three years into his Sanskrit professorship, and had tried many ways to spread awareness of the language. But it had not been for the sake of the language itself. Every year he and the children of the colony presented a play, and yes they were all from history to pump up the national pride. The first year he had directed Shivaji's encounter with Afzal Khan, where the Maratha king rips open the big Mughal army commander, with the tiger claws hidden in his bare hands. The second year it was Baji Prabhu's battle in the mountain pass with a handful of soldiers against an army of thousands. This year he had chosen Panna's story.

Panna was the governess of the Rajput crown prince, who

was an infant when he was betrayed. The enemy came to slaughter the child and at that moment Panna exchanged her own son, a baby of the same age, with the prince. She saw him being beheaded and the mother in her wept within, but outwardly she concealed her anguish. Thus Panna had saved the future of her kingdom. Her sacrifice is an exemplary act of courage and patriotism rare to find anywhere. Anand, like the characters he chose to depict, lived to accomplish ideals.

Mrs Chauhan came up beaming, "Anand, your play was the best item!" Her daughter had the role of Panna. She had done an admirable job, admirable enough to please the mother. She went on, "I say this is the kind of play we need at every Ganapati mandap. The women of India need to be empowered. If not for Panna's presence of mind, our history would be different. And, of course, which man is capable of such a sacrifice?"

Anand interjected, "That is why I say each woman should have two votes."

She was offended. "You are teasing me. I am not such a staunch feminist as to beat men for the centuries of ill-treatment women have silently borne. I am simply asking for equality and opportunity, like Indira Gandhi got."

Anand inadvertently looked at his watch and then regretted it. She was quick to catch his mood and walked away.

Then Lajpat encroached on his peace. "Splendid job there! Just getting those kids to come and practise is quite a feat". Lajpat's son had acted the role of the sentry with no dialogue. But to make him stand still for five minutes on stage without talking had been a tough job. Anand almost promised himself never to take him on again. But it would be prudent to keep Lajpat in good humour as he was a big contributor of the festival.

"Oh, it was all my pleasure," said Anand attempting to be jovial. "I love these historical events, and what better opportunity than the Ganapati pooja to renew the cultural vigour?"

"Exactly, and revisiting history always gives us a good perspective of the present situation. But now I think you should work on a play on contemporary issues."

"Like lack of cultural awareness?"

Lajpat gave him a sidelong glance, not sure if he was being sarcastic. "Like American hegemony. You know, Vietnam and Panama and Guatemala and Cuba and South Korea and ..."

Anand wiped his forehead. Was he going to name half the countries of the globe? The show could then be a quiz session called "Know your geography". He cut in, "Lajpat bhai, we should then also have a second act showing the Soviet hegemony, North Korea and East Germany and Poland and Romania and Hungary and so on."

Lajpat was softer towards the Soviets, "Anand, the USSR had to retaliate because the Unites States started parcelling out the world for themselves. Consider this – setting the American dollar as the world currency, the nuclear programme, intercontinental ballistic missiles, competition in outer space, exporting democracy – until who knows, maybe the dictatorship of the world! Some superpower had to step in to balance it off! Thank God for the USSR."

"Postcolonial colonialism, or is that politically incorrect? What is it called? Ah yes, imperialism. Nehru and company started the Non-Aligned Movement just for that reason. And within ten years of it we are aligning ourselves with the Cold War parties."

Lajpat clicked his tongue. "But Anand, what can we do? Do you know how much support Pakistan gets from the United States? East Pakistan is all but boiling, and if war breaks out, we Indians, sandwiched in between, will feel the pinch. Pakistan is after all an integral part of our history."

"Not after 1947. We have, once for all, washed our hands of Pakistan."

"How can that be so when we still have disputed territories – Kashmir being the biggest thorn in our relationship?"

"Lajpat bhai, don't let us get carried away with Pakistan. In time all the problems will get resolved."

"I like your optimism, if not political astuteness. Maybe that will win the day for us eventually."

Now Anand wanted to go home and sleep, sleep for two full days. He drained his water and decided to leave the pandemonium behind. The well-intentioned compliments weighed on his spirit. One wanted to spread a political message, another wanted feminism, one more wanted a refresher course on history, and some even thought it was a language lesson. But nobody asked Anand why he did the play, and why he intended to keep doing these plays, in Sanskrit. He was waiting for one person to be so inspired by the power of the language as to want to delve deeper into it, to discover the immense spiritual literature that was available in Sanskrit. That was the foundation of the Indian culture and the rest a magnificent superstructure. He wanted to illumine the timeless in people's minds, to give them a glimpse of the Satyam, Ritam, Brihat – the True, the Right, the Vast. Political messages using Sanskrit indeed! He shook his head hopelessly, that was the last thing in Anand's mind. Adults were simply disgusting. That is why he worked with children even if they were ... well, disgusting too. He was really tired and right now wanted to be leagues away from humanity.

But Professor Anand Deshmukh had no such luck that day. Panna, or the girl who acted as Panna, cornered him. "Sir, where are you going? Aren't you coming with us all to immerse Ganapati in the sea?"

"No, Diya, I was thinking of preparing some lessons. By the way, everybody has praised your acting. Well done!"

Diya beamed and advanced upon him. "You are going to dance with us on the road." She had decided his immediate future with her hands. So there he was, in a crowd of young people like himself, with infinitely more energy than he could muster, dancing to the mad beats of a bellowing drum. One voice in a mike screamed hard "Ganapati bappa," and the chorus finished the phrase, "Morya". He said, "Pudhachiya varshi," and the chorus yelled "Laukar ya" Again and again the alternate cries rose up in the air.

"Ganapati, the victorious,
Return quickly back to us."

Once Goddess Parvati ran her hands over her body during a bath, and with the substance that she collected, she created a boy. She then asked this son of hers to guard the palace while she bathed. He was so faithful to her word that he even barred her husband, Shiva's, way. The Lord was furious and a fight ensued. The boy fought bravely, but at the end Shiva cut off his head. Parvati came out running and found her son dead. She was so distraught that Shiva sent his army immediately to bring the head of the first creature they found. And so, Ganapati got an elephant's head, and since he was such an exemplary protector, he is worshipped as the Remover of Obstacles.

On a chariot sat a big Ganapati bedecked with colourful flower garlands. A host of other smaller Ganapatis were being carried on heads by the devotees. Anand was jostled by the sea of humans to the sea of water. The beach was full of life with similar groups of people beating drums, crying aloud and immersing their holy clay idols. The crowd waded into the shallows of the sea – women in saris, girls, their dupattas wound round their waists, boys in bell-bottom pants, and men in churidars. Diya appeared from nowhere, wild as a gypsy, and pulled Anand by the hand inside the sea. He resisted but a crowd from behind hauled him in. He was fully under water now and gave up fighting the frenzy. The world had won against him. Yes, Ganapati bappa morya. He lay in the shallow water watching the festive fervour all around.

A woman wearing a sari walked past him towards the deep sea. She was not dancing or rejoicing but had instead a determined look on her face. Anand sighed – the only other person defeated by the world. His curiosity was aroused. He watched her advance stubbornly, readjusted his supine position to follow her with his eyes, and when she did not stop even when the water had risen above the level of her shoulders, he got to his feet. Then suddenly he could see her no more. The waves kept advancing towards him, disrupting his concentration. Was that a hallucination of his tired mind? A horrible thought occurred to him – she was drowning! He waded towards the spot he had last seen the back of her head. Finally his knees touched something. It must be her. He ducked his head into the water but it was too frothy. He grabbed whatever he could lay his hands on and lifted it. It was just her sari, but he had located her. He dived in again and yanked up a hand. He kept pulling till the neck showed up and then the head with closed eyes. Maybe she was dead, or had fainted. He fought against the current and lifted the shoulders out of the water. Yes, she had fainted at the very least. Someone had at last spotted them and more people came running to help. Anand could hardly advance when the wave receded, and almost fell over when the wave pushed him towards the shore. Her hands and head dangled lifeless. By the time he touched the sand, a group of revellers had taken a break from their frolic and had gathered around them. Someone immediately set to work to pump out the water the woman had swallowed. The crowd around was thickening and Anand once again felt the nausea of human pressure. He extricated himself and this time he was really going home.

Diya had returned. "Sir, what was that? I saw you carrying a woman back from the water?"

"Yes, someone who did not know swimming I think. She got carried away with the current. Luckily I saw her in time."

Diya rolled her eyes up and began to fall close by, hoping to be supported. Anand watched her crash on the sand, "Good, now you deserve a sea bath."

He marched away wringing his clothes. His sandals were caked with mud, but he admired their tenacity. If they did not have straps, he would have lost them surely, and his footing too.

Anand did not want to think about the incident. Fortunately, nobody spoke about it or even seemed to remember him as the rescuer. Maybe such incidents happen every year; one or two excited novices almost get drowned. Days passed, but the memory still disturbed him, as if something unsolved within clamoured for his attention. The woman had not appeared to be in a frenzy. Suddenly he gasped. She was about to commit suicide! But such a pretty woman in her prime! Why? He could not sit still any more. Who was she? It had to be someone from his colony or nearby because she was part of the same group celebration. Or did she deliberately mingle in the crowd just to perform her final deed, to camouflage herself in the general madness? The woman's face crept up in his mind when he worked on a lesson, in his sleep, when he was correcting notebooks, mid-sentence in a classroom. He had to know the rest of the truth. While people were writing down their New Year resolutions, dreaming up lofty aims and ideals, Anand was entirely focused on one target. It loomed larger in his mind than Sanskrit education and teaching spirituality. She had become his existential crisis. He had to find her.

Anand had taken out his sister, Savita, to the market for buying her Diwali gift. She looked through many stores to choose her salwar kameez, chatted with other buyers and storekeepers, and all the while observed her brother's distant mood and disturbing new habit. Finally she burst out.

"Bhaiya, what is the matter with you? You have been staring at all the girls around and embarrassing me. Can't you hear them sniggering as we pass by? It would have been better if I had come with Aai. Now, will you tell me or not what's wrong with you?"

Anand was shocked. His mind was captivated by that unknown woman, but he had not observed himself staring at girls. Was he looking for her in every female face? He confessed to his sister. The only part he withheld was his suspicion of her intentions. Savita understood, "So she has charmed you with her weakness. That's exactly what I fantasize too. Some handsome prince will some day carry me in his arms just like you did that woman. And there and then he should pledge his entire life to my service."

Anand shook his head. "Correction, I am not a prince, and she was not just acting, she had really fainted, so she does not even know who brought her to the shore."

"Bhaiya, you may not be a prince, but you are handsome

enough, that is, if you remember to shave."

Had he neglected that too, without even noticing it? He had to do something seriously now about this fever. Savita with her large circle of friends came to his rescue. "Pushan is an artist and works part-time for the police investigation department. If you describe this damsel in distress to him, he can draw a likeness of her."

That worked, and Anand had a sketch of the woman before his eyes. Her face was wet and her hair fell in snaky locks around her face. This is how he had seen her pass by. That afternoon Savita rushed into his room straight from college.

"Bhaiya, do you have her?"

Their mother followed her in. "Who is here, can I also see?"

Savita laughed at her mother's innocence, "Aai, no real person is here, just bhaiya's dream girl, on paper."

They were all staring at the face water dripping from her loose hair. Savita had a big frown on her face. She seemed to recall seeing the girl. Then she took up an eraser, and rubbed off the locks of hair that hid the face. When the cheeks and forehead became fully visible, she exclaimed with a sudden revelation. "I think I have seen this woman. She is Raja's cousin from Calcutta!"

"Which Raja? Mohun Bagan Raja?" gasped Anand.

"I know of only one Raja. Yes, the football champion."

Mohun Bagan was the football team from Bengal that won most of the inter-state football tournaments. Every Bengali boy worth his salt wanted to be in the team. And Raja was talented enough to have earned the coveted nickname. The next step in the plan was to meet her. And there too Savita helped. The inter-school football match was scheduled within a month, and surely Raja would be the star player. They could steal the proverbial key to his house during one of these sessions.

So, after his classes, Anand walked to the football arena and scanned the players. There he was, Raja, centre forward, the cynosure of the game, parting with the ball briefly then getting it back to make a showy tackle, and then a pass to himself around the opponent, a skidding kick and the ball flew into the goal – or almost. Anand kept his eye on the kid – indeed Mohun Bagan material. It would not be hard to spend time waiting for the game to end. He backed into the gallery talking to himself, "Smart move Raja, what a pass, good attempt, hard luck, next time." He heard someone clearing the throat behind him. He was so engrossed in the game that he must have backed right into somebody. He swung around "I am so sor...", his words froze in midair. He was looking at her! He had no idea how long he stood staring into her face, but at last he observed her combing her hair with her fingers, nervously. He may have been standing there for an hour. He reminded himself he was a professor in a college, and had a hundred students and was writing plays and ... nothing worked, he had lost his voice.

He just walked away and only then realized he had forgotten even to breathe. His whole system was in a state of shock, paralysis, asphyxia. He stood at the end of the court, looking no more at the game, but floating in ether. Then the game was over and people were walking away. He saw Raja beckon to her, and she got up and joined him. They were gone, the sun had set, a street dog came to inspect him, mosquitoes gathered for the feast, and Anand still stood shell-shocked. He had seen the object of his dreams, the purpose of his life. On that court, with a powerful nobody as witness, Anand vowed to make her happiness his life's primary goal. His second goal was spiritual education for the masses. Otherwise his name was not Anand, which meant "happiness".

That night he and Savita planned a reconnaissance sortie. She would spy into this illustrious Raja's life and learn all about his cousin. Anand waited for Savita to return after college. He had already worn his best shirt and had sprayed himself with perfume. Savita came in, not galloping like the previous day, but dragging her bag.

"Bhaiya, forget about her."

"Why? Is she married?"

"No."

"Then everything else is good news. Tell me, my ears are bursting."

"Her name is Binapani, but everyone calls her bina vani – 'without words'. She does not talk."

"'Does not' is different from 'cannot'."

"'Does not' is equal to 'will not'."

"'Will not now' is different from 'will not ever'."

"'Will not now' is equal to 'not worth trying'."

"Even if your handsome prince brother tries, is he going to fail, you say?"

"Bhaiya, stop playing. She is some sick girl sent here from Calcutta to recover. She will be gone when and if she ever gets better."

"She does not look sick to me. She is the prettiest girl I have seen so far in my life."

"She is sick here," Savita tapped her temple with her finger. In reality, she was already jealous of any other woman claiming even an inch of her brother's affection. And this case was beyond repair. A strange binavani had, without uttering a single word, captured her precious brother's heart.

In a few minutes Anand was at the football gallery. He introduced himself and soliloquized about football and how good Raja's moves were. Then he talked about films and theatres – his personal hobbies. Then he spoke about Sanskrit and related anecdotes of his class. Then he spoke about books. All the while, she watched the game with an indifferent look.

The next day he brought a book and tried to lend it to her. She seemed interested, but saw the title and declined. "I can get you any book you like, in any language, from our library. Is there something you would like?"

She spoke for the first time. "Do you have some book by Dostoyevsky? Crime and Punishment, The Idiot, or The Brothers Karamazov?"

He heard the voice, but had no idea what it said. His mind

went blank with joy. Then he made her repeat the titles, which she did, not concealing her irritation. He would have crossed the Arabian Sea to get the book if it was necessary.

Luckily the library had The Idiot. She grabbed it from him and started wrapping it in some paper she had got.

"Why is that needed?" he asked.

"Keeps the book in better condition," she lied.

Then he could not squeeze a single word into her ear because she had started reading it. The next day she returned it, fully read.

"Get me Solzhenitsyn," and after a pause she added, "If you can, please."

Her command was his duty. He got her a handful of books – all Russian authors. She even betrayed some satisfaction and thanked him.

Anand was coming out of his class, when Raja cornered him.

"Sir, have you been supplying Russian novels to my cousin sister?"

"Yes, she seems to enjoy them."

"They are banned for her. I can't explain. Best you leave her alone."

"Hey Raja, wait, just don't walk away with that little reprimand. I am trying to make her happy. Is that a crime?"

Raja laughed, "Yes sir, you will be punished."

They had struck a bond there, and Anand coaxed Raja to give him the proverbial key to his house. A burning Calcutta, Naxalites, father a police officer, dead lover story came out of Raja. Now Anand saw why the Russian connection had to be snapped.

"By all means," promised Anand. His heart was heavy. She had loved already and would not love again, perhaps. He also understood how deeply she had loved for she was ready to follow her lover to the other world. Maybe she was just plotting another such attempt. Raja and Savita were right. He had walked to the edge of a precipice, and now he could only turn back. Or fall. And, of course, being a level-headed professor of a sublime subject, he chose to ... fall.

The last day before the match, he greeted her, "Kaymon achho?", the two words Raja had taught him, meaning "how are you" in Bengali. She blew out some air that could pass as laughter. "Not kaymon, but camon, like in 'cat'."

"But is it not spelled as kaymon, with an 'é' diacritic?"

"A what?"

"A vowel pronounced after a consonant is represented differently than the vowel if it were standing alone. It does not exist in English, of course. That special symbol is called a diacritic."

"Oh, I see. In Bengali one symbol can have two sounds; those who know the language read it correctly. Besides, the spelling came after the spoken language."

"No," protested Anand, "The spelling came before the spoken language. All the north Indian languages are derived from Sanskrit which does not have a cat-like 'è' sound. Sanskrit and its Brahmi-based script existed before any of its derived languages."

She was curious, "Then we should pronounce it kaymon, like you said."

"No, a language is more than its representation. It is, as you say, in the interpretation of the speaker."

"All right, so where did the 'cat' sound come from?"

"It came from Urdu. Just as the 'fa', 'za', 'wa' sounds. Sanskrit is the ancient language of the Indian subcontinent, the language of the gods as it is called – devabhasha – in which the prolific spiritual literature is written. Urdu is the heady punch of the liqueurs, brought in by the conquerors, added to the indigenous vintage. It is made of Persian, Arabic, Turkic and Sanskrit words. The script is Persian, read from right to left. Other north Indian languages, though more Sanskrit than Urdu, have embraced a lot of sounds and words from these foreign tongues."

"Then why didn't the script also adapt?"

"To a certain extent it did. But that came after a period of pure written language, but mixed spoken language."

Binapani understood what he meant. The early writers in Bengal wrote in a language that was all but Sanskrit, written in Bengali script. But the common man did not speak it. So during the Bengal Renaissance such authors as Bankim Chandra broke the mould and started writing for the people, and that did wonders in helping to educate the masses.

"I don't think the Bengali script changed from the original forty-eight characters that Sanskrit gave us. That is why we have the same symbol for two different 'e' sounds."

Anand had made Binapani talk! He clung on to the thread, "Hindi did adapt though. They have added dots in existing letters, for example to represent 'za'."

"But surely you condemn all languages that are spelled and pronounced differently? They are not logical enough for you."

"And who says logic is essential to a language?"

"Sanskrit lovers."

"Not me."

"Then maybe you are not a pundit." She had a twinkle in her eyes. Anand would take any word – praise or scorn she threw at him – as a compliment. He would kiss the hand that slapped him if it was hers. He would save her again and again from any current that flowed counter to her joy. He gave her the book of his own choice. It was Three Men in a Boat by Jerome K. Jerome. It was a comedy – a world apart from the Russian revolution novels. She lapped it up, and would have returned the next day for some more, had not the football matches ended.

Anand found Raja. "What next?" Raja was supposed to accompany her wherever she went as she was not to be trusted alone. Would he like to share his burden? Yes, he would, gladly. Anand, overjoyed within, agreed with feigned reluctance to comply. But she was not easy to talk to. He had to come up with interesting monologues. She brooded, and sometimes did not hear what was said. He gave her comedy books, fantasies and fairy tales, anything to lighten her mood. But all his distilled waters were wasted on a toughend cactus. He then spoke about subjects closest to his heart, and here she did respond.

"When people speak they actually sing. Each voice has a melody of its own. Over that is laid the family tune, then the regional tune, then the language's own notes, even a national tone. Every spoken sentence is a cultural orchestra."

"Anand, go slow. What do you mean by it?"

"When you pass by a cinema hall, you hear voices from within, but cannot distinguish the words. Yet you can tell if it is a Bengali film or a Hindi film. How? – because of the distinct melody inherent in that language."

Binapani considered the proposition. "If it is a Bengali art film, we will hear a single word, then a long silence, then a monosyllabic reply followed by a spoon stirring tea in a cup. For Hindi, it would be a song with a dialogue in between to create a pretext for the next song."

Anand loved her illustrations. "You are being naughty, I can see. But yes, that is what I mean. Speech has many facets. At the base is the language's unique tune. On top of it are the modulations of emotion, the choice of words, the most common phrases, the emphases, the pauses, the short and the long syllables, the pronunciation, the interjections. All these are variations within a single language. We call them dialects."

"How many dialects are there in India?"

"Thousands. Who can count them? We don't even know about some in remote areas."

"All right, how many languages are there?"

"A language is an approximate grouping of similar dialects. The number is not accurate. In hundreds, I would guess."

"Anand, why do you have to make it all so complicated? I say the answer is fourteen. Every rupee note has them listed."

"That list is the number of official scripts. It does not account for languages which share scripts, or for those which are not written. There is an immense loss of information when a text is written down – as we were discussing the other day. That is why for millennia our spiritual hymns were memorized, passed down from master to disciple."

"But fortunately for posterity, they did get written."

"Yes, but who knows with what compromise. To get back to the original meaning, one has to be a rishi, like the composers."

"So, professor, is that what you teach?"

"No, not yet. The professor came later. I was a Sanskrit lover first. Once you discover the source, you want to follow her tributaries. Then one day you come face to face with a whole civilization – ancient, glorious, mysterious."

They walked in silence up to Binapani's house. Anand half lifted his hands to hold her and give her a shaking.

"Therefore, Binapani, speak. Let the world hear your music. You are Saraswati, Vak, the primordial creative power of sound."

But only silence followed. He lowered his voice, "And now goodbye."

She nodded and turned to leave. This time Anand really held her elbows with his hands, "Not that way."

"Goodbye." she said meekly.

"Thank you."

* * * * *

Binapani overheard her uncle explain to his wife that she, Binapani, would be gone soon, back to Calcutta, when she recovered. And she was better, wasn't she? She was eating at least, if not talking. She had even found a benefactor who supplied her with books. He would keep her afloat through her stormy days. Binapani had resolved never to return home, from where she was thrown out so unceremoniously. But it seemed here too she was unwanted. She had tried to end it all, but someone had saved her life. And now another insane man was trying to steer her broken craft. Maybe he was the only hope she had. But what was she thinking? Why would any person love her? Her heart had died with Tushar. How could she throw herself on another well-meaning man? Thus she pondered about her existence and its futility.

Her mother's letter was a tiny wave in her sea of despair.

"Dear Bina,

There is too much happening in Bengal these days. Along with the Naxalite raids, we have to support the refugees from East Pakistan. Pakistan's two halves have parted ways and a civil war is brewing in the eastern provinces. Students are being killed in Dhaka just like they are in Calcutta, but for very different reasons. Bengalis are demanding freedom, and are being cleansed ethnically. Hindus are targeted first, and they are pouring into India. Luckily for them, the Indian Prime Minister has ordered the borders to be kept open. The frontier states are tight as a drum, though.

Feeding all these people has created quite a shortage of food in our markets. And such prices! One can hardly afford to eat like a year back. I hope you don't feel the pinch in Bombay. Your father is not keeping well – mostly because of the extreme stress at work. His diabetes has increased beyond control. I miss you very much and always pray for your well-being. Gypsy too rushes to the door whenever someone comes, and then returns head down."

There was a postscript – "I am glad to hear you have found some happiness." She had underlined the word "happiness". Binapani's uncle would have relayed the "Anand" inclusion to her life. She noted sadly – she was missed, but not invited back home.

* * * * *

One day, Anand called on Binapani and walked her to the garden as was the custom, as if she was a dog that needed fresh air. But he had a plan. She admired his efforts, though could respond to none. He wanted to take her to see a film, an old favourite that would be shown again. She got permission from her uncle, and Anand got a wink from Raja. It was "Chaudhavi ka Chand", with the enchanting Waheeda Rehman, and the romantic Guru Dutt in the lead roles. The awkward couple in the audience watched the amorous couple on screen poised to sing the famous song. The heroine was lying on her couch, and the hero was approaching. The curtains parted with the wind to reveal a full moon.

Chaudhavi ka chand ho ya aaftaab ho,
Jo bhi ho tum khuda ki kasam laajawaab ho.

Whether you are the full moon or the sun,
Whatever you are I swear by God,
You are the incomparable one."

Binapani felt Anand's little finger touch her little finger. It was strange, but she did not protest, and did not remove her hand from the seat handle.

"Your hair is like dark clouds peering over your shoulders.

Your eyes are two cups full of sparkling wine."

Slowly his finger climbed on her little finger, and then the next finger began its tentative journey.

"You are the draught of joyful love.

You are the beautiful ballad playing on life's lyre.

O charming spring, you are a poet's dream."

Her hand surrendered to the exploration. As the song advanced, and Guru Dutt had reached his beloved, Anand's whole hand was over Binapani's. It covered hers and held it. This moment he would cherish all his life, no matter what happened hence. After the song he dropped his possession, squeezing it gently for a second. He had asked for her hand, and she had consented.

Outside the theatre they did not talk, both shy of what had transpired within. Some boys were loafing around, and found them. They nudged each other and started singing the love song "*Chaudhavi ka chand ho.*" Binapani looked away in embarrassment and so did Anand. The raucous voices accompanied them up the bus. Anand let Binapani sit on the one empty spot and stood guarding her from all other human contact. She felt safe after a long time. If not affection, she at least sensed a languid peace when this young professor was around. They got down from the bus and he was walking her to the house. No words were spoken yet. Then Anand started humming the tune of the same song Guru Dutt had sung, and the eve-teasers had done a playback for him.

Binapani stopped him, "You too, Anand?"

He slapped himself playfully. "Oh, sorry!"

She was smiling at him teasingly.

They had reached the door of her house. Anand stood and she stopped too. He said haltingly, "Aami tomaake bhaalo shaabi", the words Raja had taught him in Bengali for "I love you". This time Binapani laughed out loud. Anand did not know what he did to deserve such a treat, but he would do it again and again, for the next sixty years of his life.

"Not bhaalo *shaabi*, but bhaalo *baashi*," she giggled.

Anand repeated it like a good student, "Aami tomaake bhaalo baashi."

Binapani had now grasped the meaning and not just the words. She blushed and disappeared behind the door, smiling in the dark.

Chapter Seven

Sulaiman

"Osman chacha! Osman chacha!" a piping voice ran into the hut followed by its owner. It was Badal, the gardener's son, from the big house. Sulaiman was tying the cotton towel on his head in preparation for work in the field. "Scream a little louder and Osman chacha will rise from his grave."

"Osman chacha is dead then!"

"You can talk to me. I am his son, Sulaiman."

"Do you still have your cycle rickshaw?"

"No."

"No?" the boy's face crumpled in dismay.

"It is no more a cycle rickshaw, but a cycle van." The boy looked up with wide eyes. "You still have it then?"

"Here, have a look. Isn't she a beauty with her flat board and new tyres? Now I can carry all the sheaves of paddy in one trip."

"Sulaiman mia, can you please help us then? We are in big trouble."

Sulaiman was still admiring his craft. "I will tell you a secret. I got her floating in that field over there during the cyclone. She looks like a wall of some poor fellow's house."

The boy was now tugging at Sulaiman's hand urging him on the cycle van.

"What is the trouble? Tell me first. I have to attend to my field too."

"Boudi is getting her baby right now. Hurry, hurry!"

He mounted his craft and started pedalling, still chatting about her.

"Then some windows came tearing through the air, while I was binding myself to the jackfruit tree. Oh, what a cyclone it was! I can swear nobody in their entire lifetime has seen anything like it. So I watch these windows, with shutters and all, breathing like fish, their gills opening in and out, in and out. And I pray the water recedes soon so that I can catch these wooden fish. And Allah hears my prayers, for even eight hours later, when I free myself from the tree, there they are, stuck in the mud!"

"And what have you done with those windows?"

"I knew you would not guess it. You are leaning on one of them right now."

Badal turned around and admired the railing on the van.

"The shutters still work. Open one and feel the breeze on your skin."

They reached the big house which was once the landlord's mansion. It still belonged to the Chakraborty family, but they were landlords no more. The feudal system in Pakistan was abolished in 1950 and the peasants were given much of the land for a nominal price. But the house with its grand iron gate and the spacious garden inside were not touched. In fact, it seemed the house had not been touched for a century. A pipal tree grew out of the cracked compound wall, gripping the debris with its gnarled fingers. The moss-covered façade of the house looked like green saris hung out to dry from the balcony upstairs. Badal jumped down and rushed to open the iron gate. Sulaiman rode in and saw a lady squirming in pain on the porch – the boudi. He turned to the boy, "Badal, is this your real brother's wife?"

The bare-bodied boy in his shorts did not look like a member of the zamindar's family. He made an irritated click of his tongue. "Not my real boudi. I used to call the young babu, her husband, my elder brother. We all do that, don't you know?"

The mother-in-law came down the steps, tried to help the pregnant woman into the van and gave up the struggle very soon. Badal and Sulaiman hauled her bodily on it where she collapsed, moaning all the time. The old lady tossed in a few towels, a bundle of clothes, and a bottle of water, and gestured to them to move on. She had thoughtfully tied some cash into the loose end of the young woman's sari.

"Badal, go with boudi."

Sulaiman looked at the perspiring boy.

"Mashima, the van is not sturdy enough to carry two persons, and the hospital is too far off for Badal to walk to."

"Then what shall we do?" The old lady's face was creased to the point of tears.

"If you think it is all right, I will drive her to the hospital with care, and bring her back."

The mother muttered, "Whatever you arrange, hey Gopal." She looked up at the heavens with palms joined in resignation.

The lady groaned and twisted around all the way, and sometimes she cried out for water. Sulaiman stopped to wet her lips, and jumped back on his seat. The road was uneven and he started praying too. "Did I face the wrong direction to recite the namaz today? Why did you choose me for this task, Allah?"

But Allah and Gopal were both gracious that day, and they reached the hospital before the woman reached a critical stage. The nurses dragged her out of the van and carried her in on a stretcher. Sulaiman sat mopping his face and eyed the bottle of water – if only it had some country liquor in it! It had been such a trying journey. He heard faint cries coming from inside the maternity ward. Flies were circling round his head and drowsiness soon led him into another world.

When he woke up, the sun had crossed its zenith and the hospital was quiet. He jumped to his feet. What had happened? His stomach cried out in vexation. He had not even fed his bullocks. He imagined them mooing forlorn and hungry and half made up his mind to cycle back. Maybe he could return the next day. Who knew how long this business might take – hours, days? He looked around for someone to talk to. Then he realized he had not even asked the woman's name. How in the name of Allah would he locate her, and take her back? He kicked himself for being so stupid, for falling asleep, for answering Badal's call. His proud cycle van stood under the banyan tree, the cause of his present troubles! He heard footsteps and turned. A nurse in a white sari and head covered with a white starched cloth approached, a baby in her arms. She handed Sulaiman the baby and walked back to her desk. He had never in his life seen a creature so pink and so fragile. He took it in his hands, mesmerized, looking into the face, faintly human – two eyes closed tight, a bump for a nose, a strip of mouth, and a lot of pealing skin. He could also see the hair on the cheek and ears, it was disgusting and yet terribly attractive.

The nurse picked up a pen, looked at him and smiled. She had seen so many young parents completely unprepared for this moment. She saw the taaweez dangling from his neck, and, unsure whether he spoke Urdu or Bengali, chose Urdu, her own mother tongue. The language used by Muslims was heavily influenced by Urdu anyway. They would call an older man chacha, where the Hindu Bengalis would say kaku. A young man would be mia for Muslims and babu for Hindus.

"Baap kaa naam?" [Father's name?] the nurse pointed her pen at Sulaiman. Not quite out of the haze, the man heard "Aap kaa naam?" [Your name?] "Sulaiman Ali," came the answer. The nurse gestured to him to follow her, as she took back the swaddled infant.

He entered a room where families had crowded around beds. In a bed with no soul around, was the lady he had driven that morning, now like a deflated balloon. When she saw the baby she got up and took it in her arms fondly. The nurse continued her duty asking the lady her name. She replied "Madhumati." The nurse poised her pen one moment over the paper, then tilted her head in acceptance. These Bengali Muslims are funny – they have Hindu names. She turned to Sulaiman and asked, "Son's name?" and waited. Moved by the sight of the mother and the child, Sulaiman sent up his words of profound thankfulness – "Bismillah, Ar Rahman Ar Rahim, in the name of God, the compassionate, the merciful". He had not heard the nurse's question, and, during a long yawn of exhaustion, she had only heard the last word of Sulaiman's prayer, "Rahim." The pen scratched the paper. Thus, on the 8th of July, 1971, Rahim Ali was born to Sulaiman Ali and Madhumati Ali, at the Dayamayee Hospital of Sonargaon, East Pakistan.

The journey back was much more pleasant with mother sitting up in the van, nursing her baby, and the moon slowly rising from the horizon. The coconut trees were becoming their phantom silhouettes, and the river shone silvery white like a giant hilsa fish. On the way, Sulaiman stopped by his hut. The bullocks were mooing as he had expected. He rushed about his task of attending to them while Madhumati waited, now all danger passed. Sulaiman called over the bramble wall, "Amina chachi, do you have some food you can spare?"

"Why didn't you cook? Are you getting your father's bad habits already?"

"Chachi, can you come closer? I don't want to shout, but I will tell you everything." He whispered into her ear the events of the day, and disappeared into the barn. Amina chachi brought a plate of food and went to the van. She saw the baby and burst into a sing song tune, "Alle le le, come here my beta, my little boy." She took the baby and gave Madhumati the plate with some rice and spinach curry. Madhumati was very hungry, but she hesitated. She knew these were poor farmers, tenants her family would have fed with their extras in the old days when they had the means. "Chachi, have you eaten?"

"Arre beti, my daughter, we have also had babies. I know you must be hungry. Eat. Allah will provide for us. This is my good deed of the day. Besides this spinach is from my own plot, I can always pluck some more."

It was almost midnight when Sulaiman cycled Madhumati to her part of Sonargaon, the Hindu area. But from half a kilometre away they knew something was amiss. A stench assaulted their senses. It was the smell of the funeral pyres of dead bodies, as if the whole village was a Hindu graveyard. Madhumati covered her nose with her sari. The baby started coughing. She was whispering in terror, "Hey Bhagavan, O Lord, what is this terrible smell?" The closer they got, the worse was the odour, and it mingled with the pungent smoke of burnt wood and tyres and clothes. Why was the village so dark and forlorn? Even at midnight usually you could hear snores, coughs, babies crying, a lamp flickering in a window, a dog scratching itself. The big house was dark, and through the moonlight it rose like a phantom fist from the ground. Sulaiman parked the van at the iron gate and jumped down to open it. With a shock he realized the house was burnt, some embers still flying in the night. Not a human sound could be heard. Madhumati sensed his hesitation at the gate, and cried out in panic, "Has something happened? Come back, where are you?" Sulaiman returned speechless and slowly drove the van inside. Madhumati gasped, "No, no, no!"

They searched the house for traces of her in-laws, but the smell of cooked flesh told them more than they were ready to accept. Sulaiman picked up a smouldering piece of wood of what could have been the bedpost and jumped around the floor littered with charred remnants. Madhumati also stumbled from room to room calling out in a shaking voice, "Ma? Baba?" a distant cry of a jackal was the only answer. After roaming the house from porch to kitchen garden and finding nothing that could be claimed from the flames, Sulaiman suddenly remembered the baby. Where was it? The jackals were crying louder now. They would have smelled the burning human flesh and the live ones nearby. He rushed out and found the ball of cloth on the van – wriggling, alive. He picked it up and gave it the warmth of his chest. The woman was turning things around, scorching herself, screaming in pain, then calling again "Ma? Baba?" Sulaiman could take it no longer. The baby too was scared and started its elemental cry. He went in, found Madhumati walking dazed, her sari dragging on the ground, the ends black with ash. "We need to leave from here." She turned her wild eyes on him. "Ke tumi, who are you?"

"The rickshaw driver, Sulaiman. Here, take your son. We need to go away from here. Those people may return." Those people were the ones who were torching Bengali houses around East Pakistan. They were the army personnel flown in from West Pakistan, who had no law to answer to, who were in fact given special orders to extinguish the last Hindu kitchen fire in this land. The same land which had once seen hundreds of years of Hindu rajas, Buddhist kings and Muslim nawabs, none forcing their religion on the common man.

It was the longest day of his life for Sulaiman, and he was ready to fall asleep standing. But his chores were not yet over. He ripped out the bed cover from his mattress, replaced it with a fresh one, and led Madhumati to it. She sat there, dazed, her son on her lap asleep. He knelt beside her and looked around for a word with which to address her. Finally he thought of the word Badal had used. And the thought of Badal alarmed Sulaiman. Was he burnt too? But he had other things to worry about right then. "Boudi, please sleep here. I will be on the porch. If you need anything call me. Here is a bottle of water. I am sorry for what has happened, but we have had a long day. Tomorrow we can think about what we should do." He unfolded the mat on the porch, laid his aching body on it and was gone to the other world.

The next morning he woke up late, stiff from sleeping on the hard floor. Yesterday came back to him and he wished it was all a bad dream he could forget about. But how could it be? The baby was crying. The mother was leaning against the wall wild-eyed, muttering to herself. Could she not hear the baby cry? The whole neighbourhood would come around asking what had happened. Sulaiman picked up the baby "Boudi, he needs to be fed." She looked at him in surprise, "Ke tumi? Who are you?" This time he did not stop to introduce himself. He marched to the bramble barrier and called out, "Chachi, are you awake? I need to talk to you urgently."

Chachi's grumbling came haltingly from the other side. "Awake, you ask! Some baby kept me awake most of the night. What is it now? You and your old man have such a knack of getting into trouble. I am thinking of changing my hut to some place far away from you."

"Chachi, please come fast," begged Sulaiman. "I am in big trouble."

"There, did I not predict it?" said Amina chachi, and waddled to the peephole in the bramble. Then she held her hand over her mouth in disbelief as he told her all about last night.

"The planting season is on in full swing, as you know very

well. I did not do any work yesterday. Now I need to go to the field."

"And leave me to manage your household, you fool?"

Sulaiman had run away, before Amina chachi could finish swearing at him. Nevertheless, she took charge of the Ali household for the next few days as Madhumati recovered from her shock. Sulaiman stayed out of the way as much as he could, especially when she was nursing the baby. Amina chachi teased him, "Did I not tell you to get married a long time back? Now Allah has thrust that duty on you."

Sulaiman just laughed at her womanly jokes – always trying to bind the men to family duties! It was not easy to bind one as free as him – he had it all planned out. The next day, he had returned to the big house, and found Badal in the garden. Badal had seen the soldiers come swaggering into the village that fateful night. The old man was too sick to move, and they killed his wife before she could protest. Then they set the house on fire. Badal was small and dark as a shadow. They did not even see him; he had escaped far away and stayed up the night on a tree. In the morning he returned to his kitchen garden and continued tending to the brinjals and beans. Sulaiman found him lighting the earthen chulha – the clay furnace – with the wood he got from the smouldering furniture in the house. The structure of the house had survived, though black with soot. Sulaiman lit a bidi, and tried to sweet-talk Badal into accepting boudi and the baby. He did feel a little guilty about it – Badal was a mere boy! They bargained at length, and finally Sulaiman got a handful of fresh vegetables every day, and a promise that Badal would call him as soon as any man came to the house. Sulaiman was hoping her husband would return to take charge of whatever remained of his family and property.

Madhumati went about her daily acts like a puppet – ate when she was fed, drank when water was offered, took the baby when it was given to her, and spoke not a word. Days passed, and Amina chachi grew more and more petulant as the lady was still unresponsive. One day she handed a bag of massoor dal to Sulaiman. "Here, feed her this dal – it will help dry the blood." Sulaiman wondered, "What blood?" but dared not ask.

"I am going."

"But where are you going, chachi? What do I know of women and babies?"

"Why? Were you walking with your eyes bandaged all these days I was helping? I noticed you slipping out early and returning late. Is she my responsibility?"

"Is she mine then?" argued Sulaiman.

But Amina chachi had already waddled away. He knew she was right. But he did not have any answer for his question. Why was her husband not returning? Did he not get the message, that his parents were cooked alive? Maybe Madhumati was the only live person who knew of his whereabouts. He had to bring her back to this world and ask her these questions. He tried to talk to her, but she seemed to have gone deaf. When the baby cried he handed him to her, but she did not respond. He then fed to the baby cow's milk diluted with water. He was furious with Amina chachi and with his own misfortune. He used to be a free man, singing in the open field until a few days back, and now he was torn between waiting for a man and his mad woman.

One month passed, two passed. The man at the grocery stall handed him the rice with a lascivious smile, "Sulaiman mia, looks like you have got married? You buy twice the quantity of all the stuff. Was there some hanky panky? Tell me your little secret, mia." He returned to find her delirious, rolling on the mattress, shivering. Now this was the last straw. He marched straight to the front door of Fatima chachi, the midwife. A protesting Fatima was dragged to the house by Sulaiman, and made to see the patient. This experienced lady struck her forehead after a brief second's inspection. "Her milk is poisoned. Does she not feed the baby?"

"No, she does not react to anything. She is unhinged."

"The baby looks quite fat though."

"I feed him cow's milk."

"You fool. He needs her milk."

She massaged the sour milk out of her, took the baby and gave it to the mother. Sulaiman turned his face away and was slipping out, when Fatima's strong hand – the same that pulled babies out of their chambers – grabbed his wrist.

"Did you see what I did?"

"Let go, chachi."

"No, I am not going to return for this again. You will have to force her to feed the baby, understood?"

"How?"

"Like I did. Undo her blouse and let the baby do the rest."

Sulaiman held his head in his hands and sighed. "Allah, you bring me down this far? Why can't that dandy city babu of a husband return?"

Nonetheless he did his duty and with trembling hands touched her blouse, undid the clasps and brought the baby to her breast.

* * * * *

Then one day Badal came running in the evening. "The men are here." They rode on the cycle van, and as cautioned by Badal, hid it a little far. Sounds of a bawdy merrymaking came from the house. Sulaiman had not expected the husband to return with friends and set up a feast in his own destroyed ancestral house – in fact his parent's funeral pyre! Surely it was not the man he was waiting for then who had come. They crept in the darkness towards a window that showed a flickering firelight inside. Men in army uniform were drinking around a fire and cooking meat over skewers. They spoke in Urdu as they were from the West Pakistani military divisions. Sulaiman thought to himself, "So here are the men who are killing Bengalis all over the land." At last he understood how the Bengalis could be singled out from these broad-shouldered, sharp-nosed hulks. A diet of rice and fish produced fishlike bones and soft features. The West Pakistani people ate wheat and meat and so the body structure was like a solid door. Their country was much colder too and mountainous, making them hardy and fair-skinned. Here the land was on the equator at the edge of the sea. The skin was sun-burned and features smooth, to the extent of being mongoloid in Chittagong, like their Arakanese cousins in neighbouring Burma.

From another room shouts of terrified women could be heard. The two stealthily inched their way towards the window and peeped in. The scene was chilling. Men were kicking women and pinning them down with their knees. Then they were being raped, and their screams forced shut with hands and mouths.

Sulaiman hissed, "Ya Allah!" Badal's small face had bulging eyes. In one night he was yanked out of childhood into the dark side of adulthood.

One of the men was talking, "Brother, there is no need to be so tough on her. You will as though kick her very spirit out of the body before you get to it."

The man sniggered, "If you have no stomach for it why don't you go and cook for us? I say, what do we gain from this war? This is just a job – a job where I don't even know if tomorrow I will live. Can't I enjoy meanwhile?"

"If you don't care for your country, why did you join the army?"

"Because there was no better paying job for me out there. And with such perks." He sniggered loudly.

The men boasted about how many Bengali women they had ravaged. From Dhaka University to remote villages, the army boys had picked women and had raped them. This was war. This was the revolution the Bengali leader, Sheikh Mujibur Rahman, called the "fight unto freedom". "Let every house become a fortress."

A simmering dot of fire landed on Sulaiman's bare chest as one of the soldiers threw out his cigarette end. Sulaiman gasped and immediately shut his mouth with both palms. The soldier walked to the window but the complete darkness outside made it very hard for him to see anything. The two humans crouching there held their breath. Then they saw the ominous shadow move away and declare "Some street dog must have smelt the cooked meat. I stared it out of here."

Badal and Sulaiman silently crawled back to the van and Sulaiman drove them to his house. Badal was shaking in fright.

"Will they uproot my garden? The potatoes are freshly planted."

"They don't care about such things. But Allah forbid, they should find you."

"If I were Muslim, maybe they would not harm me," ventured Badal.

Sulaiman thought for a moment. "If you are Bengali they will hurt you, whether Muslim or Hindu, man or woman."

The boy was crying. "Then where will I go? I am an orphan and have nothing but only that hut and patch of land."

Sulaiman had an idea. Pretending to be Muslim may earn some clemency. He went to his treasure chest and brought out his father's old fez. "Wear this at all times, and when you see the soldiers wish them Assalam Alaikum before they start suspecting you are Hindu. That's our greeting. It means 'let peace be with you'. And if someone wishes you those words, reply with Walaikum salaam, 'let peace be with you too'. Then if they are close by, kneel in prayer and they will not disturb you. Wear that fez all the time – don't neglect that detail."

"And how should I pray? I have seen it is quite long and complicated."

"That is too much to teach now. Just face towards Mecca and kneel."

"And where is Mecca in my hut?"

"I will show you tomorrow." All this help to Badal was to make sure he did not plan to run away from the big house. Who would then inform him when the renegade husband turned up?

The next day they went back to the big house. Fortunately it was deserted. Sulaiman entered the hut and was struck by a wooden statue standing by the wall.

"What is that?"

"Lord Gopal, the Chakraborty family heirloom."

Sulaiman laughed, "You little fool. If they enter your house they will cut your head right there. Don't you know Islam does not believe in idol worship? All your fez and salaams will not convince them you are a mussalman."

"But this is not just a wooden doll. I worship it."

"Worship in your heart and throw it away."

Badal reeled as if he was punched in the stomach. "Throw Gopal away? The greatgrandfather brought it from far off Brindavan on his head, walking barefoot all the way."

"Where is this Brindavan?"

After the great battle of the Mahabharata that purged the hundred evil Kaurava brothers, the only survivors were the five good Pandava brothers, Lord Krishna and some of their allies. The dynasty continued through Parikshit, grandson of Arjuna, one of the brothers whose charioteer was Lord Krishna himself. In one of his expeditions King Parikshit made an enemy of a powerful snake, Takshaka, who vowed to kill Parikshit within seven days. The king was then placed in a walled tower protected by many sentries. Each morsel of food was checked for poison, each person was scrutinized. Believing his last days had neared, Parikshit called upon the sage, Shukadeva, to hear about the life and works of Lord Krishna. The story thus uttered by the sage became the Bhagavata Purana. It is the foremost text among the followers of the bhakti movement – those who seek union with the Lord through devotion. To complete Parikshit's own story, a little worm inside an apple that was offered to the king grew into the monstrous snake, Takshaka, and the king was bitten to death.

"Brindavan is on the banks of the River Yamuna, in northern India. That is where a long time back, the Chakraborty family's greatgrandfather, Haridas, went for a pilgrimage. It is where Krishna spent his childhood, grazing cows with other young boys of the village – thus earning the name Gopal – the Cowherd. Krishna was actually the grandson of the king of Mathura, but his evil uncle Kansa had usurped the throne. The divine child grew up in the safe haven of Brindavan. His pastimes with the village folk – their adoration for him, his pranks and their mutual love – make up an important chapter of the Bhagavata Purana."

"Is that the gospel?"

"Yes, for us Krishna bhaktas. There are wandering storytellers, kathaks, who sing out the Purana seated in the temple dais."

"Badal, will you tell me the story of your Lord?"

"Yes, listen, the story goes like this. Kansa had imprisoned his father, the king of Mathura, taken over the kingdom and had unleashed a reign of terror. A prophetic voice warned him that his newly wed sister's son would kill him. So he threw his sister, Devaki, and her husband, Vasudeva, into a dungeon. Every time Devaki had a child, Kansa smashed the baby on the stone walls. Then Lord Vishnu, the Preserver of the creation, blessed the couple by taking birth as their son, Krishna. Vasudeva's shackles were snapped miraculously on the night Krishna was born, and the father was able to take the child to the other bank of the Yamuna – to Brindavan. Krishna grew up there as the son of Yashoda and Nanda, in a pastoral family, in the beautiful surroundings of the lyrical countryside. Kansa thereupon sent several demons to kill him, but they all failed in their mission. When Krishna was a youth, he and his foster brother, Balarama, killed Kansa and brought peace back to Mathura."

Haridas Chakraborty bought an idol of sandalwood, sweetly fragrant, three feet tall. Gopal played the flute and stood with one leg folded before the other. A cow behind him looked up in adoration at the enchanting face. Haridas laid flowers at the feet of the statue and after an elaborate worship started his journey back home on foot across the Gangetic plain. At night he slept with Gopal on his chest. The statue would touch the earth only at the final destination – its sacred pratishtha, its established spot. And that would be the Chakraborty villa in Sonargaon, a few kilometres south of Dhaka. He crossed the confluence at Allahabad, where the Ganga flowing out of Lord Shiva's locks meets her sister, Yamuna, saturated with the pollen of Lord Krishna's feet and the invisible mythical river, Saraswati. Then placing Gopal on his shoulder he traced his steps past Gaya in

Bihar, city of Buddha's enlightenment. In Bengal he stopped at Kenduli, where devotees gather in throngs for a spiritual fair, called Jaydev mela, after the thirteenth-century poet, Jaydev. The song compositions in his Gita Govinda describe the passion of the cowherd girls, the gopis, for their beloved Gopal. From Kenduli he walked to Mayapur, the birthplace of Sri Chaitanya Mahaprabhu, the wandering saint who spread love for the Lord all over India.

"Sulaiman mia, I have heard this from my grandfather, who was himself a little boy when Gopal came to Sonargaon. Listen. Haridas Chakraborty crossed the Padma River by boat with the idol on his lap and finally reached his home here. That temple, you see there, was then just completed to house the Lord. Here he placed the statue on the ground. Gopal touched the earth of Sonargaon after Brindavan. The spiritual connection was made. Bells pealed through the village and women blew conch shells. The tenants of his zamindari had assembled to witness this momentous event. They were each given a bag of rice and cash. Women got a sari and men a dhoti. Ever since Gopal has looked after us as he did the rural people of Brindavan, saving us from droughts and harsh rains and everything evil from men and nature."

"I wonder if my greatgrandfather was there too that day."

"Yes, he surely was. The Muslim and Hindu peasants together celebrated the planting of Lord Gopal on the soil. And you are asking me to throw Gopal away! I saved him that night when they came to burn the house."

"How? You must have taken a great risk."

"Yes, I was just on time to run out of the temple. Otherwise Gopal and I would be ashes too."

"What else did you save?"

"Nothing. I climbed a banyan tree and waited all night with Gopal in my arms."

Sulaiman now understood the importance of this delicate statue. It was indeed exceptionally beautiful, of a rare workmanship. The Lord had a peacock feather tied to his crown, and wore ornaments all over his body, all carved in great detail. His smile was charming, mysterious. The more Sulaiman looked upon the face, the more he adored it until he was baffled as to what they could do to hide it.

Badal had the idea. "Shall we dig up a hole in the garden and plant it there?"

"What if they take away the land?"

"This land was given to my grandfather by the Chakraborty grandfather. Now it is mine. One can't steal land, it is not moveable."

The two of them made a wooden box for Gopal from the planks that had survived the fire. Then they wrapped the idol in the freshest clothes Badal could find, his father's silk dhoti used for religious ceremonies. They dug a big hole near the mango tree, and placed the idol there. Badal was crying – as if he had returned from the funeral of his own father.

Chapter Eight

Debjani

The bell rang, and Raja answered it. "Sir, what are you doing here so early?"

"Hello, Raja." Anand was embarrassed.

"No, you can't take my sister out today. It is my turn."

"I had an off-period and so thought I would come and say hello."

Raja laughed, "I was just teasing you. Bina-didi, someone has come to see you."

Binapani and Anand came out of the house, and he called an autorickshaw.

"Where are we going, Anand?"

"You will see. Are you scared I am kidnapping you?"

"No, but I don't like surprises. No, really, I insist you must first tell me."

"I am taking you out for a nice tea. Happy?"

"Yes, I am happy." she said in Hindi, which sounded like "I am you" – mein Anand hoon.

But the "out" turned out to be "in". Binapani entered Anand's house. His mother was prepared for her guest of honour, and Binapani understood the surprise was only on her side. The mother was wearing a starched and ironed sari, and had arranged every table with a vase of flowers.

"Bina, this is my mother, and if you don't mind she will speak in Hindi as she does not know English."

Binapani liked the cosy house and its colourful setting – floral patterns on curtains, Gods on wall calendars, and furniture with embroidered covers. It seemed Anand had not planned to shock her all the way, because his sister and father would not be back till late. His mother looked Binapani up and down and declared,

"You look better than your picture. But then there you were all wet."

Binapani looked at her and then at Anand, a question mark on her face.

Anand stared at his mother without batting his lids for a whole minute. The lady was undeterred.

"What, Anand did not tell you anything?"

"No," responded Binapani.

"He rescued you on that Ganapati immersion day from the sea."

Suddenly Binapani could put two and two together. So it was Anand, and no wonder he had pretended to know her from before. At least, if anyone knew her dire secret, it was the one person who also cared for her. She was relieved, but pretended to be hurt.

"No, he did not tell me anything. How secretive of you!"

"So Binapani, what did you do in Calcutta?" his mother continued chatting.

"I was studying English."

The mother chuckled. What was funny about studying English, Binapani wondered.

Anand was smiling too, "Bina, you are a girl, so conjugate the verb with a feminine gender."

That was the whole problem with Hindi. Every word had a gender. You were reminded in a hundred ways that you were a female, and not only you, but the road and the window and the notebook were female too, whereas the chair and the table and the door were male. Adjectives, adverbs and verbs followed the gender of the noun, and they also morphed when they described a singular object or a collection. Bengali was genderless, plural-less, egalitarian, non-biased, perfect. Binapani lost her confidence and stumbled on every word, in the process adding both masculine and feminine endings. The mother was laughing uncontrollably, much to Anand's embarrassment. Binapani concluded her life's story in Calcutta,

"Gypsy, she is a he dog, and Haradhan-da is a beautiful driver, and my mother a handsome cook, and Bhupen-da she is a gardener and I miss my friend who are all kind-hearted. Therefore I was studying a gender-less language for my master's degree."

"Splendid," cried his mother. "You will continue your master's programme here, won't you? I want an M.A. daughter-in-law."

Binapani closed her eyes to think. Who was this daughter-in-law?

The mother's tongue buzzed like a bee on a flower. "Did Anand not tell you? He wants to marry you."

Anand jumped, "Aai, go and make tea for us."

His mother was like an agile she-monkey. "Tea is already made." She held up a flask standing on the table. The three plates of snacks were also ready. She poured out the tea and uncovered the snack plates before them.

Binapani was stunned. "No, Anand did not tell me."

The mother pondered, "What else did he not tell you? Let me see."

"Aai, stop playing the fool," came Anand's professor-like tone.

"I just remembered. Did he tell you he was a gold medallist in school? He was good in sciences and arts and won the all-rounder's medal. But he chose Sanskrit."

Binapani smiled at Anand. "No, he did not tell me that either."

She looked at the big brown laddu, a sweet shaped like a ball. She had never seen any laddu as smooth as this and as big. What was it made of? She picked it. When it had almost reached her mouth it vanished out of sight. She looked at her empty fingers which had met each other in astonishment. Where was the enormous thing? It was all over her lap in millions of crumbs, some rolling down to the floor!

The mother was laughing and clapping her hands like a little girl.

Anand rushed up to get a towel. "Wheat laddu, Bina – you can't pick it up like that. Now get up and dust it off gently. Careful it has ghee and will stain your sari. Aai, stop clapping! It is not a comedy show on TV. Help us clean the mess."

Binapani had blushed red, "Anand, what else should you have told me that you did not?"

"Just one more thing – your tea is now cold."

On the way back Anand was pink in shame. "I apologize, Bina, my mother was a pest today. She is not..."

"I loved her, she is a child within. You should let her be. It is such a joy to see a spontaneous, unpretentious person of her age."

"Really, Bina, you are not joking?" Anand cradled her hand between his palms. "So what do you say?"

"Yes."

Back at home Anand took his mother to task. "What kind of behaviour was that? Telling her all those things about marriage all of a sudden?"

"Hey, mister professor, if I did not tell her, you would roam all the gardens of the world and never propose. Let it be known that your marriage was fixed by your parent. This is what is called an arranged marriage – Marathi style."

* * * * *

Binapani and her uncle went to pick up her mother from the railway station. She looked at her mother's forehead and saw the sindoor. The monster was alive then, that was all she wanted to know about her father. Then she saw her mother's jaw was not well aligned. She held that dear face in her hands to inspect it better. Her mother tried to snatch herself away, "Oh, you are looking at that jaw. I got such a lockjaw the other day, it will go in a few days, don't stare at it so much."

Binapani turned the face back at her so their eyes met. "Ma, you cannot lie to me, I am your daughter." Her mother sat down and braced herself. "That day when you were spotted in the morgue, your father had rushed home to meet you. He was storming up and down stick in hand. He screamed, 'It would have been less shameful if she had become pregnant.' He had some knotty answering to do to his superiors – his own daughter spying on him from his own house! Quite a shame!"

"Maybe he should have resigned," countered Binapani.

"I told him a boy was killed – the boy who mattered most to his only daughter – and here he was thinking of his career, his honour. So he slapped me hard." Binapani was now shaking in anger, and hot tears poured out of her eyes. Her mother patted her, "He apologized afterwards."

"What if I were there that day before him? Wouldn't he have killed me?"

Her mother nodded. "Bina, don't judge him harshly. He too believes in his duty towards his nation. Just like those boys."

Binapani screamed, "Ma, don't compare them!"

Debjani had brought two trunks from Calcutta full of wedding gifts and Binapani's clothes and books from home. There were five Benarasi saris and a whole dinner set in silver. For the women in the Deshmukh family, she had bought Dhakai, Tangail and Taant saris, specialties of Bengal's weavers. And for the men she had brought silk dhotis, already pleated. Some jewels were made in Calcutta, and she meant to buy more from Bombay. Except for Binapani's father, she had brought everything.

"Your father is not well, as I said, Bina. And the trouble in Calcutta has only aggravated." Binapani did not want to see her father. Yes, it was better to think he was busy than wonder if he cared for his only daughter's big day, especially since she was not marrying his choice, not even a Brahmin. She did not care, Anand was a Brahmin in spirit, more a brahma gyani – knower of truth – than any man he could have found for her. Her mother believed in her choice. Nothing else mattered.

* * * * *

Her uncle performed the part of the ceremony meant for a father. He repeated the mantras after the priest, he handed over the girl to her husband – kanyaadaan – he put the ring on Anand's finger, and blessed the couple. On the night of the ceremony, they had a baashor ghar, Bengali style, where close friends stay up with the newlywed all night to play games. Raja's football team was well equipped for the teasing session, and in Anand's camp he had Savita's college army. There was a pot of coloured water with one ring in it. Binapani and Anand thrust their hand in together to get the ring. Their hands just swam around each other without finding anything.

Then Bina held Raja's ear in her free hand. "You little monkey, is there a ring in here at all or not?"

Raja escaped from her grasp tossing the ring on her lap. "Bina-didi wins! Jamai-babu, now you have to sing."

Anand protested, "I can't sing, I can just chant shlokas."

"No Sanskrit hymns today. Nothing serious is permitted. You have to sing."

Savita whispered in her brother's ear. Anand cleared his throat and started singing a love song from a film. *"Yeh chaand kaa roshan cheheraa,* a face full of moonbeams ..."

A roar of cheers went up in the air. Binapani blushed. Anand sang and everybody else clapped in rhythm. Then they got a bowl full of cowry shells and covered it with a handkerchief. Again Anand and Binapani had to dig in with their hands and pick the cowries one at a time. His side counted for him and her side counted for her, each making so much noise that the counters all made mistakes and skipped numbers. At the end, when no cowry was left his side screamed louder and beat her side down. So she had to sing. She chose a Bengali Rabindra Sangeet, the frothiest of Tagore's love songs. *"Praan chuae chokkhu naa chaae,* my heart desires, but my eyes are shy."

The reception arranged by Anand's family was civilized compared to the wild wedding revelry. They were a more erudite clan, concluded Binapani's mother, or maybe the Marathi's sense of humour was different from the Bengali's. Raja was yawning after the two days of excitement. He could not even kick imaginary footballs in his frilly dhoti. Men had grouped together in clusters like grapes and were discussing politics. Binapani's uncle sat with his sister, and a group of Anand's colleagues gathered round them. The college principal was curious about Bengal.

"Mrs Banerjee, how far do you think we are from resolving the Naxalite issue? You must be really close to it with your husband in that position."

"My husband was saying the biggest fear is the Chinese involvement with the Naxalites, who, you know, are Maoist Communists. Chairman Mao did assure them of support verbally when it all began in Naxalbari, in 1967, but luckily no weapons followed."

"For sure we do not want another slap, like our 'Hindi Chini Bhai Bhai' deal."

Nehru had signed a treaty of cooperation with the Chinese in 1954, and called it optimistically Hindi Chini Bhai Bhai, a slogan which meant "The Indian and the Chinese are brothers". That was mainly to resolve the border disputes with China. But, when in 1959, the Dalai Lama escaped to India and India gave him refuge plus a district in the foothills of the Himalayas, relations with China were strained. In 1962, for a month, two disputed border territories were under fire from China. The Arunachal valley, at the eastern edge of the Himalayas, was one theatre of war and the other was a province, Aksai Chin, as big as Switzerland, the north-eastern tip of Kashmir.

Someone brought in Kulkarni, a retired army general, to the table.

"There are many problems with high altitude warfare, and unfortunately most of India's disputed territories are in the mountains."

"Thank God we have oceans on the other sides," someone added.

"The Himalayas were a very good natural border too, and they still are, but the passes were discovered and adventurers came in."

Desai was a businessman, "There was also a healthy trade through these passes, and an offshoot of the Silk Route came into India from the Nathula Pass in Sikkim. Another came into the Indus Valley from the Karakoram Pass. As an unfortunate consequence of the 1962 war, the Nathula Pass has been closed, and China now owns the Karakoram Pass."

Debjani said, "For me the Silk Route has always evoked romantic images, as if it was an adventure from the Arabian Nights. I blame Marco Polo. Sometimes I find it difficult to believe it really exists."

"Of course it does! The Silk Route is a three-thousand-year-old rugged pathway that connected the Mediterranean civilizations of the ancient world with the Indian and Chinese cultures. Silk from China was the greatest attraction for traders, but along the route caravans also carried other merchandise, including perfumes, jewels, glassware, and slaves."

"Desai, did you hear of the Spice Route? The famous spices of Kerala that Vasco da Gama discovered for the Western world?"

"Yes, the two routes were connected. The Silk Route had a maritime counterpart which collected spices, incense, opium, hemp from the Malay, Indian, Arabian peninsulas, and the islands of Indonesia. From south India the ships met the Sindhu River at the port of Karachi. The cargo flowed up the river and caught up the main branch of the Silk Route in Afghanistan. Merchants headed towards the Ottoman Empire via Persia and distributed the goods by sea to northern Africa and the Adrian Sea ports."

"And did you say there was a tributary of the Silk Route that came down from Sikkim?"

"Yes. From Java and the Malaya peninsula ships anchored at the Padma delta. Then ambling through Bengal, crossing the Nathula Pass, the route caught up the main branch. And, Mrs Banerjee, to satisfy your fantasy-like rendering of the Silk Route, it also facilitated the exchange of ideas and cultures, diseases and medicines, marauders and explorers."

Kulkarni continued, "As I was saying, those are the two precise points of contention between China and India, Arunachal and Aksai Chin."

"And the Dalai Lama," wedged in the principal.

Debjani's brother said, "Agreed. But Kulkarni, we have not heard what you had to say about the high altitude warfare."

"First of all, the Air Force cannot help, not even for reconnaissance. If at all visibility is good for a few hours, turbulence from helicopters and the echoes can cause avalanches. Then secondly the conditions are so harsh that soldiers die of cold before they are shot at. And then it is all about possession."

"Position you mean?"

"Position and possession, here it means the same thing. One who possesses the peak has the better position. In the Aksai Chin area, the one northeast of Kashmir, for us, Indians, to reach the peaks we have to negotiate the Karakoram Range. But the Chinese can drive in their jeeps. So they had the better position and built a road there, on Indian Territory. Same story in Arunachal Pradesh, they had the peaks."

"So why did they withdraw in one month?"

Desai tried to answer it using logic. "There is always a give and take of territory. That was the one instance the press highlighted because it was the longest of the skirmishes. But in reality border disputes happen all the time. Some hot-headed Chinese soldier threatens an Indian jawan, or the Indian side shoots at a passing Chinese as infiltrator and a little firing happens. A few soldiers get killed. Then they stop until the next incident."

Kulkarni smiled to the sherbet in his glass.

"Mr Desai, in general what you say is correct about all borders, not just Indian borders. But this one instance was different. The 1954 treaty that Nehru made was actually pro-India – we had both, Aksai Chin and Arunachal Pradesh."

The principal asked, "Didn't the Chinese call Arunachal the North East Frontier Agency, like the British did?"

"Yes, that is correct."

"Arunachal Pradesh is a much better name. In India, it is the land which greets the sun first, the land of Arun, charioteer of the Sun God."

Kulkarni resumed, "In 1961, India took over Goa from the Portuguese, one could say by force. Add to that granting asylum to the Dalai Lama and possibly encouraging Tibetan insurgency. So China declared India to be expansionist and felt threatened."

"How could that be? Even the borders were not well protected. Surely China could see that. Nehru concentrated all his effort on economic development."

"The Chinese are shrewd, I tell you. They knew it very well. At that time the United States was selling weapons to India. The Prime Minister, Nehru, had international prestige for co-founding the Non-Aligned Movement. So China decided to show its military prowess to the India-US nexus. Thus the month-long war in autumn, up there at fourteen thousand feet, was a demonstration. Even the ceasefire was pre-planned. India lost Aksai Chin but Arunachal Pradesh was returned."

"And that forced Nehru to increase the defence budget."

Kulkarni continued, "But the genius of the Chinese ..."

"Genius, Kulkarni?"

"Yes genius – strategically speaking, of course – was the timing. When the US and the USSR were busy in the Caribbean in October, China launched her attack. India would have no ally to help her. What am I alluding to?"

"The Cuban Missile Crisis."

"Exactly. From 1958 to 1961, the United States had installed nuclear missiles in the United Kingdom, Turkey and Italy capable of striking Moscow. The USSR was also setting up its nuclear missile bases in Cuba as a retaliatory measure, when in October 1962, a US photo reconnaissance plane captured pictures of the installation. One of the tensest of Cold War negotiations ensued between President Kennedy of the US and Nikita Khrushchev of the USSR."

"Yes, it read like a drama in the newspapers. The United Nations stepped in as mediator to end the missile crisis."

"Correct. The Cuban installation was dismantled, and the European missiles were deactivated," recalled the principal.

Kulkarni looked around theatrically, "Wasn't it clever of the Chinese to time it so well? The war exposed India's border patrol deficiency. In fact, Pakistan attacked us in 1965 thinking we were still militarily inept."

"I heard China thinks Sikkim is theirs?" questioned Debjani.

"That's the problem with small autonomous provinces. The big fish fight over them fin and gill. India too thought they had privileges in Tibet – assumptions carried forward from the British Raj."

"Shall we blame the British?" some wit made everybody laugh.

Kulkarni also laughed, "Here I don't think we can. They had been in as much of a quandary as us. Throughout the British Raj, there were lines drawn in the borders – the Johnson Line, the McMahon Line, lines over the highest peaks, lines favouring India, lines favouring China."

"But they were all grey lines in reality," quipped the wit speaking with Kulkarni's gravity.

"Well said, well said," encouraged the others.

Desai added, "What are borders after all? Just so you can teach school kids a number to remember – India x square kilometres, China y, Pakistan z. Give or take a few kilometres. People are a continuous blend of cultures and there is a daily movement back and forth. The farm is next to the pond, the market is beside the grove, call one India and the other China, what does it matter? That is how it used to be when people were sane. Now the whole area is a series of colourless border posts."

The principal reminded them, "All said and done, the Himalayas are our greatest protection. Otherwise a nuclear China could have routed us any day."

Kulkarni was at his gravest, "And who says that threat is not looming large?"

China had tested her first nuclear weapon in October 1964.

* * * * *

Rupali came to Savita's side, by Anand's throne.

"Ice cream?"

Savita was getting bored arranging the gifts as guests had

stopped trickling in. She pounced on the cup. Half way through she asked, "Bhaiya, do you also want a spoonful of ice cream?"

"Thought you would never offer. Yes, of course!" said Anand. He was famished.

"Rupali, get another cup, please."

Anand took the cup and gave it to Binapani. Savita eyed him jealously.

"Rupali dear, can you get another for my brother?"

"No, we will share," Anand protested, "Rupali, sit and give Savita some company."

Damini was passing by trailing an ornately embroidered dupatta that made every girl wild with envy. The two damsels fell upon Damini like leopardesses.

"Damini, where did you get this dupatta?"

The dupatta is a gossamer thin scarf, a few metres in length, worn around the neck or over the chest. The traditional Indian attire was not stitched – it was a long cloth that was wound round the body in various ways – the sari for women and the dhoti for men. The Muslim settlers brought in the fashion of stitched clothing. Both men and women wore a loose trouser tightened at the ankle – the salwar – and a knee-length tunic – the kameez. Women added the dupatta to this ensemble. Much cunning went in fashioning the dupatta with embroidery, tassels at the edges and bits of metal foil that shone like mirrors. A dupatta would often cost more than the rest of the attire as it was the most prominent part of a woman's salwar kameez.

Damini patted her dupatta, "Everybody loves this. Guess where I got it from?"

"Fashion Street?"

"No."

"Chandni Chowk in Delhi?"

"No. From Kashmir."

Rupali and Savita drew in their breaths. While living in a houseboat on the Dal Lake the Mughal Emperor Jahangir had remarked, "If there is a heaven on earth, it is here, it is here, it is here."

Savita asked, "Did you see any signs of the 1965 war?"

"No, we were there the year before. It is indeed as we hear – a most beautiful place, an enchanting fairyland. And guess who I saw there?"

"Some cricket star?"

"Sharmila Tagore and Shammi Kapoor."

"Kashmir ki Kali!" shouted the other two.

"Yes! We were standing on the banks of the Dal Lake in a crowd for one hour to see the shoot. But it wasn't boring at all. The other bank has the Himalayas dotted with palaces of the Dogra kings, and the lake has houseboats floating dreamily on it. Finally Sharmila appeared, dressed as a Kashmiri damsel, wearing the embroidered kaftan and heavy silver jewellery."

"It was a wonderful film. Shammi Kapoor was from the big city and there in Kashmir found his kali – his blossom."

"And she used to sell flowers from her houseboat."

"Oh, the houseboats are so much fun." Damini's cheeks dimpled in mischievous delight. "You can lean out and pick a bouquet from a passing boat."

"Oh, but don't try to walk over. Remember how Shammi crashed in the water?" laughed Rupali.

"You know, Damini, my bhabhi is also Bengali, like Sharmila. The other day after the wedding bhaiya sang that very song for her, the one where Shammi does his houseboat stunt."

"Sad, isn't it, that Kashmir has seen so many battles?"

Anand was eavesdropping, and he placed his comment at their service, "That is the main reason we are fighting for Kashmir I think. Its tourism can generate enormous amount of wealth."

A new member joined the group of men standing around Debjani and her brother. He said, "We, that is, India, China, Pakistan, are just small fry in a sharks' game." Anand would have recognized it as Lajpat's contribution had he been around. Sure enough Lajpat had turned up coughing up his Cold War conspiracy theory. Now that India had signed a twenty-year cooperation treaty with the USSR, he had a new bounce in his steps.

"As soon as China and the Soviets start quarrelling over east Asian supremacy, the eagle lands. So China becomes America's newest friend, and is urged to help Pakistan fight us."

"But Lajpat bhai, Kulkarni just told us the United States supported us against China."

"Listen, nine years is a lot of time. The tables are now turned. This is politics, my good friend! Now in this second war with Pakistan, we have to face China and the USA, both backing Pakistan."

Debjani added her impression, "China is not supporting Pakistan in this Bangladesh War, at least as far as we know. Of course, they are doing it verbally, but that does not really count."

The principal said, "Lajpat bhai, I must correct you there. We are not fighting our second war with Pakistan, but the third."

"Oh yes. I often consider the 1948 war as a continuation of the freedom struggle."

Right after Partition, in 1947, the many princely states of the Indian subcontinent were given the choice to join either India or Pakistan. The Hindu Maharaja of Jammu and Kashmir joined India, after some initial hesitation. But Pakistan did not like his idea, since its side of the kingdom had a majority of Muslims. Consequently Pakistan started supplying weapons to insurgents. This led to a war over Jammu and Kashmir that commenced shortly after Independence and lasted more than a year. This northern-most state in India is shaped like a ram's head. Its left horn is Aksai Chin, which India lost to China in 1962. Its right horn, plus the right eye was carved out in early 1949 when the ceasefire was called. The new enclave is called "Pakistan Occupied Kashmir" by India, "Pakistan Controlled Kashmir" by Pakistan, "Pakistan Administered Kashmir" by much of the world, and the people in a part of that region call it "Azad Kashmir", meaning "Free Kashmir". The truth is that it has ever since been a war zone active with military encounters.

The second war with Pakistan in 1965 was over this same piece of territory. It lasted from April to September and ended when the United Nations again brokered a peace treaty. Everybody knew there is no solution to the problem, so they defused the current imbroglio. Then the soldiers each went back to their barracks on the mountain peaks and resumed their vigil. An entry was made in the history books – "Second war between India and Pakistan ends in diplomatic truce". The Pakistani papers reported, "We still occupy a large section of Kashmir, like we did in 1949, therefore Pakistan Zindabad, long live Pakistan." Indians celebrated the ceasefire, "We have not lost an inch of our territory, so go back to your business, and Jai Hind."

Kulkarni finished the discussion, "Wars are terrible but they do unite people. All of India raised money to support the troops, patriotic films were made, the best men wanted to join the armed forces."

To which Lajpat added his sugar coating, "And it worked to digress people's attention from the internal problems. I say, wave your flag, but watch out for the pothole."

Anand looked at Binapani. "Hungry?"

She licked her lips, "I could eat an elephant."

"Oh no, you have smudged your lipstick." He leaned over and wiped the uneven edge from her mouth. A camera's flash startled them.

Raja grinned, "Thank you!" Later they would find the photo hanging on their bedroom wall.

* * * * *

Anand had rented an apartment close to his college in Dadar. It was newly built and decorated with furniture handpicked by Debjani. The Bengalis had planned the bride's homecoming in their rustic custom, and the Marathis had planned it in their more sophisticated style. So while the milk boiled over in the kitchen to symbolize prosperity, the Bengalis had brought along a pot with a fish swimming in it. If the bride did not catch the fish with her hand, she would be a bad householder. Binapani squealed as the fish slipped from her grasp again and again.

Debjani was ready to help, but her brother held her back, "This is so much fun. We shall see how well you trained your daughter to run a family."

Debjani whispered, "She does not know the difference between massoor dal and moong dal, leave alone cook or catch a fish. Take pity on her please, bhai."

"All your fault didi, now will you stay here to pamper her? Come on, Bina, get the fish."

Binapani was wet with water she and the fish were splashing together. Anand intervened. "We are vegetarians anyway, why do you want to force her in this fishy business?"

"Oh ho, look at him, so loving," cooed everybody after the red-faced groom. Binapani looked at her mother in despair. "I will probably be a bad wife after all. But it is too late."

Debjani embraced her and wept. At last she realized she was losing her daughter, the one precious gift from God she had protected with her life.

"Take the wretched fish away," she commanded in her tearful voice. The revelry ended and evening fell in the new house. Debjani bid a sad goodbye to her daughter and son-in-law. Binapani embraced Raja, and her aunt thanking them for all they had done for her. Anand touched her uncle's feet, and was blessed. Night fell with the smell of jasmine strewn on the soft new bed. Binapani collapsed in exhaustion. "Oh, I am so tired."

"Me too." Anand agreed. "Let's just sleep, for once, after three days."

* * * * *

The summer months gave way to the monsoons. Binapani joined Anand's college for completing her master's programme. She passed the exam with top marks, and Anand's family celebrated on a boat out at sea. Then life went on in the new house in its own rhythm. Anand returned from college and found the utensils in the kitchen undisturbed, the dishes and glasses untouched. He made tea, and they had it together in the balcony. He made dinner, and they ate it. She never complained about his cooking.

Often his mother came to visit with a basketful of food she had cooked. Sometimes they went to the old house and spent a happy evening watching a film on television. Binapani started finishing books from Anand's college library at an alarming pace. She would forget to eat lunch – the extra food that Anand kept for her from dinner. She was withdrawing again into her world of fiction. Anand could not spend much time with her as he had to do the household work too. A bai was hired who made just the chapattis. Since she cooked with too much oil and spices Anand had to do the rest himself. He wanted to encourage Binapani to talk, to be happy, but life was slipping past at a fast pace, ignoring her slower trudge. He took her to Matheran – the hill station in the Western Ghats. They did some horse-riding, and walked through a curtain of mist. Monkeys swung from branches and landed on the grass, naturally green from the abundant dew. He made love to her, she did not resist, nor participate. Sometimes he imagined he was still carrying her in his arms, unconscious, but alive. When some people saw them, a beautiful woman and a handsome man, they turned their envious eyes to follow them. Old folks smiled, "Aha, what a match – made in heaven!" And Anand looked at her face, but her eyes were far away, looking at a star that did not exist in their sky.

* * * * *

Anand got a phone installed in his office in college. He took Binapani there one evening and they booked a trunk call. In a few minutes the operator called and connected them to Calcutta. Anand heard his mother-in-law's voice.

"Hello?"

"Ma, this is Anand. I have just got a phone installed in my office. Can you hear me well?"

The receiver was snatched up by Binapani. She had decided not to talk first lest her father picks up the phone. But it was her mother.

"Ma, this is me, Bina. I am terribly sick. Help!"

Her mother's voice was tense immediately. "What has happened, my little moon?"

"They will not let me eat potato. I said it was the Bengali regional vegetable and it was medicine for me, but they would not believe."

"Bina, the Bengali regional vegetable is fish, not potato. But asking for it may be bargaining too much."

"Fish? Forget it. Ma, they will not let me eat rice at night. Nor for breakfast."

"Why do you want rice for breakfast? You never had it here. Now don't ask for too much. Hello, hello?"

The phone seemed to be passing through an air tunnel. Then Debjani heard Anand's voice. "Ma, how are you?"

"Why are you asking me? Ask your wife, she seems to be rather sick. The doctor says a sick person needs to eat whatever she likes."

"Not when she has no idea how to look after herself in this situation."

"Which situation?"

"Oh, did she not tell you? We are expecting a baby," laughed Anand winking at his wife.

Debjani relaxed on the chair and smiled. "Give her the phone."

Chapter Nine

Madhumati

Sulaiman washed his hands to purify himself before offering prayers to Allah. But he did not feel pure at all. It was because of the mad woman, Madhumati, whom he had begun to see as a natural outgrowth of his house, like a plant that flew in with the wind and grew roots. He felt he had to wash her up too. He dipped her hands in the bowl of water, and was shocked to find her nails had each a half moon of dirt. Then he saw her hair, tangled, uncombed and un-oiled for months. He became a whirlwind on a mission. Prayer forgotten, he took her to the washstand outside and pumped out water from the tube well. He poured water on her head. She did not resist. He scrubbed her hair with soap. Amina chachi heard the splash that lasted longer than the perfunctory Sulaiman bath and came to spy on him. She chuckled to herself seeing his efforts. Then she saw him struggle to get her sari cleaned while she was still wearing it. She could stand the joke no more, and came around to help. Together they cleaned the mother and then the child. A fresh sari was wound round Madhumati. The old one was soaped and hung out to dry in the sun. Two prayer times had passed with all the fuss. Sulaiman finally sat on his mat. Yet his mind was latched onto something, and would not open to the Lord. Then he remembered that he had not cut her nails. He got the knife from his shaving kit and applied it to her fingers one by one. It was so much harder to cut someone else's nails.

"What is your name?" Sulaiman jumped away. The knife clattered on the floor. She had spoken and was looking at him, her eyes focused, and as normal as on the day he was bringing her back from the hospital.

She spoke again. "Tell me your name. Do not fear. I am fine now."

He stammered, "Sulaiman. Sulaiman Ali."

"Sulaiman Ali, you have been very kind to me and my son. I have no words to thank you. I just pray the Lord is graceful towards you, always."

He did not know what to say for an answer. He went to his prayer mat and started thanking the Lord himself, "Bismillah Ar Rahman Ar Rahim, in the name of God, the compassionate, the merciful."

The next day, he stirred on his mat, which he had got used to, and was surprised to hear sounds from the porch. She was there lighting a fire in the chulha. His instinct said she knew nothing of housework, being herself a big-house lady. He jumped up, "What are you doing? You will burn yourself."

She laughed back, yes, she did laugh. "I know all the household work. You can rest a little more if you like, and I will have some food ready for you."

He lay back in disbelief.

"Really? I never thought the ladies of big houses knew these things. Don't they have servants to do such chores?"

"We just had a big house, but inside it there was no money. We have had no servants for a generation now."

He went back to the mat, watching her fussing around with pots and pans. He laughed to himself, all he needed to do was to pour some water on the head.

That day, out in the field, he ate with great relish the meal she had cooked with the vegetables Badal had sent from the big house. He could get used to this life, and then he caught himself fancying such a possibility, and gave his bullock an extra tug. In the evening he wanted to ask her about her husband, but felt too shy. The next day again he ate the khichadi, rice and dal cooked together, and wondered why he could never make it so well. Then, the third day, she was up before him, and was sweeping the patio. He observed she was dusting clean the red hibiscus flower petals. He returned home to the smell of fried fish and warm rice. What more could a man ask? Then again he slapped himself. He had to know about her husband's return.

The morning's meal was a piece of onion and a chilli with last night's rice cooled in water. It sucked all heat out of his body and he was as placid as his bullock, both ruminating in ankle deep water. Such too could life be. He would never ask her about her past, they would run away somewhere far, a land of cool showers and warm rice, firefly sunsets and palm rimmed pools. Then he shook his head. It had to be done.

So, one evening when the baby had been put to sleep, he walked up and down on the porch, unable to enter as he knew not how he should ask. Madhumati stepped outside.

"Sulaiman mia, is there something you want to say?"

"No," he said, and pretended to lie on the mat. She had not gone back and he could feel her presence, tingling the hair on his neck. He turned back and met her eyes, waiting for him.

He sighed and sat up on the mat. She sat on the stairs.

"I have asked Badal to keep an eye for your husband's return. It has been two months now. Did no one tell him about all this?"

Madhumati stiffened. Sulaiman's heart sank – maybe this was not the way one talked to married women. Oh, he was such a fool! Will she go back to her withdrawn state? But she answered him calmly.

"Did Badal not tell you anything?"

Sulaiman thought she was asking about what else happened in that house. He did not want to share that night's experience when the soldiers had come. He shook his head, "No, Badal did not tell me anything."

"Sulaiman mia, look at me and tell me yourself where my husband is."

He looked into her eyes, but could read nothing there. He shook his head in incomprehension.

She touched the parting on her forehead.

"When a Hindu woman is widowed, she does not wear sindoor here. Even that first day, did you see the red mark? And look at my white sari and my bare wrist." A thunderbolt struck the simple Muslim. So all this while had he been waiting for a dead man?

"We, Bengali Hindu women, wear a red powder in the parting of our hair, white bangles made from conch shells and a red bangle of coral. These are the signs by which a married lady is identified from an unmarried one when her husband is alive. A widow goes back to her unmarried state with the addition of the white sari, as a perpetual message of mourning for her dead husband."

Sulaiman whispered, "I am so sorry for you."

Madhumati looked at the darkness and talked on, "He was a student of engineering in Dhaka University. You know the university has, or at least had at that time, a hostel for Hindus. It was called Jagannath Hall. In one night, 25 March, this year, 1971, there was a great massacre in Dhaka. Students were killed, any man who spoke Bengali was killed, even the Bengali soldiers were disarmed and shot at. All the students of Jagannath Hall were murdered. There were more than seven hundred of them. The bodies were thrown in a pit and covered with dirt."

Sulaiman's eyes widened in disbelief.

When Pakistan was created in the two enclaves separated by a thousand miles of Indian territory, one assumption was made – that a nation could be created with people of common religion. Within months the assumption was proven to be false. Power was concentrated in the West, and thus the development projects and contracts remained localized there, including the military leadership. Urdu was made the official language although much of the East spoke only Bengali. The rift was brought to a bloody head in the language demonstration on 21 February 1952. Hundreds were killed but eventually Bengali received the status of a state language. Then, in November 1970, a cyclone devastated the eastern province, but there too the government dragged its feet to provide relief. In March the following year, when the party of Sheikh Mujibur Rahman in the East won the elections, again the West did not allow him to form a government. This worked as the last straw and Mujib declared East Pakistan to be an independent country – Bangladesh. Pakistan flew in battalions from the West. When the navy reached the port of Chittagong, the Bengali porters would not unload the ships, and the Bengali soldiers would not open fire on them. The mutiny in the armed forces had begun. These Bengali soldiers would soon join the Mukti Bahini – the army formed by the East to fight the West. On the night of March 25, 1971, Operation Searchlight was launched by the military of the West. Atrocities began against East Pakistan. Hindu sections of Dhaka were burning, Bengalis were being massacred all over the land, irrespective of religion. The next morning Mujib was arrested and thrown in a prison in West Pakistan. Major Ziaur Rahman of the East formed an army base in the district of Meherpur, and from there the armed struggle was being conducted.

* * * * *

Sulaiman could not sleep that night. The images of mangled bodies came up like vomit in his mind. Inside the room Madhumati too was tossing in her mattress. Finally he went in and sat beside her. "Where are your parents?"

"My own house is, or maybe was, in Khulna. But now I hear the Hindus there are leaving for India in thousands. I tried to send a letter to them, but I think they had already left."

Sulaiman wondered what she wanted to do now, but had no heart to ask. It was enough of reality for a night.

The next day he went to meet Badal in an angry mood.

"Badal, why didn't you tell me about your elder brother? I was foolish enough to ask your boudi about her husband."

Badal was surprised. "Did you not know it? She does not wear sindoor or the conch shell bangles."

"Well, of course not. Why else should I ask you to keep an eye on any man who comes here."

"I thought you wanted to catch the men who come to squat on the property. That is why I called you that night when those horrible soldiers were here."

* * * * *

After the harvest Sulaiman went to sell his rice to the wholesaler in Sonargaon. A group of young men were having tea from earthen pots and discussing the war. They called out to him,

"Sulaiman mia, want to join the Mukti Bahini? Here, take a look at what is written in the pamphlet." Training of civilians had gathered strength in Meherpur district, close to the Indian border. From August active operations had begun. The Mukti Bahini had bombed West Pakistani ships in the port of Chittagong. They had captured two airstrips which were crucial for the Indian army to fly in ammunition. All able-bodied men were called upon to join in the freedom effort. India helped Bangladesh train and strategize.

The men tossed their clay tea cups on the ground and heard them crack, "We will show them if the Bengalis can fight or not."

Sulaiman was surprised at the comment. "Why? Don't they believe we can fight?"

"They think we are smaller in stature, and so weaker. But fighting is not just physical strength – it is also tactics, the guerrilla style. And that's what our Bahini is trained for. Don't we have the fire of freedom burning in our hearts, the shame of being looked down upon?"

One of the men patted his beard thoughtfully, "You boast about the Mukti Bahini, but not all have confidence in it. The Hindus are fleeing into India like ants out of a trampled anthill."

The Hindu pickle vendor joined in, "Yes, we will also leave soon. Given the way we are being treated here, it is better to face an unknown future than a known destruction. Arre, I should have gone during the Partition itself."

"Good thing you did not go then. Whoever tried to cross over was gambling with his life. There was no safety on either side of the border."

A man reading the newspaper snapped it shut with a clap. "Who says people were killed at our border with India?"

The other man defended his position, "We read in the papers.

A whole train came to the station, and inside were only legs and arms and heads and bodies, all in separate pieces."

"That was on the western front. Not here. We Bengalis don't distinguish between Muslims and Hindus. Families were allowed to choose where they wanted to live, and they moved, like they always did from time immemorial. That is why there are millions of Hindus here just as there are Muslims in the Indian side of Bengal. Don't we love Rabindra Sangeet as much as Nazrul Geeti? They are written by poets of different religions, but in the same language, about the same heritage."

Sulaiman nudged his neighbour, "Who is this gentleman – seems to know a lot?"

"He is a history professor at Dhaka University. I heard he is writing a book too. Better keep quiet and listen to what he has to say."

The professor continued, "And now that this exodus of Hindus has begun, the world will think we too are intolerant. But no, it is not us Bengali Muslims chasing our Hindu relatives away. It is the West Pakistani military. Would you introduce yourself first as a Muslim, or a Bengali?"

"A Bengali," echoed the others.

"Bengal has seen a myriad religions, and they have never been a cause for disharmony. The Buddhist kings who spread Buddhism to Tibet, Burma and Bhutan were from Bengal – the Pala dynasty. Then the Hindu Rajas and Muslim Nawabs ruled the same people for centuries. Bengal was so united that the British feared her and divided her – as part of their Divide and Rule policy. They cut her up on the basis of religion. But there were so many protests, patriotic songs, political marches, strikes, bomb blasts, murders too – that in seven years they had to revoke it. It was at that very time that they moved the capital from Calcutta to Delhi, which they felt was more manageable."

"But that would have been a long time back," mused aloud a man in the crowd.

"Not so long. The year was 1911. And thirty six years later we got divided again on the same erroneous grounds."

The crowd assented to all he said, "Yes, we are Bengalis first and foremost."

The professor addressed one of the boys. "Hey you, go down to the river and get me a handful of Ganga and another handful of Meghna. Mind you, don't mix them."

Everybody laughed. Ganga, the sacred river from India, and Meghna in East Pakistan joined their waters at the Padma delta.

"Go tell your Hindu neighbours not to lose heart. The Mukti Bahini will liberate Bengal, and our family will be reunited."

Sulaiman was so inspired to join the Mukti Bahini that he did something very impulsive. He met the moneylender and asked if he could loan out his bullocks for a while. He would forego planting the winter crop, and then by the next season, surely the war would be over.

The shrewd man polished his whiskers for a long time, then said,

"I could take your bullocks and loan them for you. Will five rupees work for a week?"

Sulaiman sensed he was being cheated, but he did not himself know anyone who would take his bullocks and pay for them. So he left with a promise to bring them to the market the next Saturday.

Back at home Sulaiman was nervous. How could he tell Madhumati about his plans? Where would she go? Madhumati had just recovered her sanity, and he did not want to burden her with these tribulations. While the bullocks munched their cud, he chewed the fish bones and thought about Madhumati's life. It was a tumbling downward, from one tragedy to another. Now he understood why she had gone half mad. Suddenly he heard gunshots far away, coming from his village. He jumped to his feet and ran. Was the West Pakistani army back, were they going to burn down their village like they did Madhumati's? He remembered the cries of the raped women and ran faster. His legs moved as fast as his mind. What if they were after Hindus and they were tipped off about her whereabouts? He ran over gravel, bruising his foot, turning muddy puddles red with his blood. Gunshots could still be heard. She was a woman, Bengali and Hindu, the worst possible combination. Then he had no energy left to think, he just ran for his life, or more for another's life he had come to care for.

Sulaiman reached his house breathless. She was there inside. Sitting on his prayer mat facing Mecca, her head covered with her sari like Amina chachi. He collapsed there on the threshold and looked up at heaven clutching the doorpost. "Ar Rahman, Ar Rahim, the compassionate, the merciful". In her hand the Quran shook hearing the panting breaths. She turned slowly, not sure who had arrived this time. Her baby was on her side on the prayer mat. They were as if inside the Lakshman Rekha, where no one could hurt them. In the epic Ramayana, the prince Lakshman had drawn a line around the hut where Sita, his boudi, would be left alone. It was a magical line of protection – nothing inside it could be harmed. The army had indeed come to scavenge for Hindus, and particularly women. But she had the presence of mind to leap on the prayer mat. She had hoped this posture would save her. They had come and ransacked the house, not finding anything valuable, but had left her to her prayer. Her eyes were closed and her lips trembled, "Gopal, help!" Then she heard steps receding and angry voices calling out, "There is nothing in this bastard's house and his woman is too thin." When she thought they had all left, she felt the breath of a person close to her, very close, and she opened her eyes in reflex. He was one of them, the last one who was still in the house. He held the Quran that was opened in her hand and slowly rotated it around. Urdu was written right to left and since she did not know how to read it, she held it as her instinct told her – aligning the left margin. He had seen through her. For a long moment they looked at each other, transfixed. Then she whispered, "Shukriya" – "thank you" in Urdu. In one quick gesture, he held her face, kissed her on the cheek, and walked away briskly.

When Madhumati saw it was Sulaiman, she dropped the Quran and ran to him. She had embraced him and was crying in his chest like a lost child. She was also saying something that sounded like "Take me to India, please." Again and again, "Take me to India, take me to India."

He soothed her, "Enough, enough of crying." He was weeping too in utmost gratitude.

"Don't leave me again Sulaiman, please take pity on me and my child."

Sulaiman promised in his heart never to leave them. They were his family now. That night he touched her as a lover, no more the doctor or the father. He knew he was not free any more, but he preferred this bondage.

* * * * *

"Sulaiman mia, give me the key to this treasure chest of yours." Madhumati asked Sulaiman a few days later.

"It is behind the mirror. Are you looking for something?"

"Yes, legal papers of your land."

"I have never seen them myself. It has come down from my grandfather, who acquired the land when the Zamindari broke up. I doubt if my father has seen them himself."

Madhumati looked through the treasures. It included an embroidered veil from Sulaiman's mother's wedding. There was a pair of silver tumblers, now black with age, and one piece of gold – a necklace. At the bottom Madhumati found the papers she was looking for. And below the whole pile she found another paper, crisp and new. She was curious. She read the contents and started laughing.

"Mia sahib, did you see this one?"

"Yes, I put it there. It is from the hospital that day when you were ..." he did not want to remember the end of that horrific day.

Madhumati was still laughing. "But did you read it?"

"How do I know what is written? I can't read English."

"It says on 8 July a son, named Rahim Ali, was born to a father, Sulaiman Ali, and a mother, Madhumati Ali."

Sulaiman's ears turned red hot. He had no idea how such a

thing could have been recorded. Madhumati put him at ease. "Don't worry mia, we will go to the hospital and set it right."

At the hospital after a bit of haggling, they parted with some baksheesh and got a new birth certificate. Partha Chakraborty was born to Balaram and Madhumati Chakraborty. Sulaiman was about to tear the first paper, when Madhumati grabbed it out of his hand. "Mia sahib, let me keep it as a souvenir." She had other plans he had no idea about – simple peasant that he was, without a perspective of the shifting times.

Sulaiman tapped the shoulder of the boy watering his plants.

"Badal, we are going to India."

"Going away to India, just like that? Will you leave your field?"

"No, I will sell it and go – if I can. Otherwise too I will go."

"And boudi?"

He did not say it was for her he was leaving. Her safety was his responsibility now. She had lost more than him, so he should face his losses too. But they had each other, and that was worth any amount of land or wealth. Badal was too young to understand the bond between a man and a woman, that transcended religion, language and whatever else human beings imagine segregate them. But there was something Sulaiman too did not know about Badal. Sulaiman hesitated, then broached the subject.

"Badal, I think your boudi and I will get married in India."

Badal was silent for a long time. Maybe he was struggling with the question of his boudi's religion. Sulaiman sat with him.

"She wants to become mussalman too. Yes, it is true, after the Quran saved her life. Really, I am not forcing her. She will be Mumtaz. Mumtaz Ali," he added proudly.

Badal spoke at last. "What about the boy?"

"She named him Partha."

Badal clapped his hands, jubilant. "Good, boudi. The family tradition is to name everyone by his relation to Gopal. And Partha was the Lord's best friend and disciple. It is for him that the

Bhagavad Gita was sung in the battlefield of the Mahabharata. One of Gopal's names is Partha Sarathi, charioteer of Partha."

"Badal you are not angry that your boudi will be with me then?"

"No, not at all."

"You know we have another name for the boy too. Rahim. It means 'the merciful'. We recite his name in our daily prayers, Isn't that special?"

Badal was happy, he concluded, "Partha Chakraborty is then Rahim Ali?"

Sulaiman caught Badal in an embrace. He really was the only living relative his Mumtaz had. "Come with us, Badal, you are my brother-in-law now."

Badal shook his head. "I cannot go anywhere."

"The army will overrun the country any time now. We don't even know which army. If it is the West Pakistani army, who knows if they will keep you alive."

Badal still shook his head. "No."

"But why?"

"Because Gopal is here in this soil."

Sulaiman was amazed at the boy's faith in a wooden idol.

"Don't worry, Sulaiman mia. I will grow my vegetables and live happily here selling them in the market and buying rice and fish from the money. And I have learnt your lessons well. Assalam-Alaikum."

Was life that simple, Sulaiman wondered – maybe it was for a child. "Let your Lord Gopal take care of you, always."

Badal helped Sulaiman pile their things under the thatch of the cycle van. Rahim lay on a hand-woven mattress placed on the treasure chest. The sacks of rice and lentils were stacked along with milk powder, sugar, pickles and a tin of cooking oil. The hurricane lamp dangled from the bottom ledge filled with as much kerosene as it could hold. Badal had brought a basketful of cucumbers for the journey, easiest to eat as they did not need cooking, and they contained fresh water. The two bullocks and the field were sold at the best price the unstable times could fetch. Madhumati insisted on converting the money to gold, even if that meant losing some in the process. Amina chachi had come to stand by, and she was holding Rahim till the end. Badal's face was sad as he looked at his boudi going away. She tried to take him along once again, but he shook his head. He was holding the fez Sulaiman had given him and was turning it in his fingers. "Why?" she demanded. He replied with one word "Gopal." Then she knew no more coercion would work. She held him to her heart for a moment, then grabbed his hand and put a wad of notes in it. Sulaiman's eyes patted every object he saw from horizon to horizon, imprinting in his heart the sights of home, one last time. Amina Chachi was crying, "Inshallah, God willing, all will be fine and you will reach India safely." Some other villagers trailed them as they picked up speed. Sulaiman rang his bell as a goodbye note. Badal ran till his legs would carry him no further. Then he cupped his hands around his mouth and cried, "Khuda hafiz Sulaiman mia, khuda hafiz Mumtaz begum." Let God be your guardian.

The pools covered with a green carpet of lotus leaves, palm trees waving like flags, orange pumpkins hanging from brown mud huts, cows returning from the field, women bent down planting rice saplings, banana trees overhanging with fruit, ducks quacking, piglets squealing, hurricane lamps in windows – all, all the sights of their homeland made Madhumati and Sulaiman's heart cry out. Any moment they would give in and return. No matter what the future had in store for them. This was their mother, and even if she was poor and kept them badly how could they abandon her? And yet day after day the legs worked like pistons on the pedals, and the cycle van advanced raising a trail of dust. People were walking westward, all towards one destination. People with bundles on head, children and old men, goats and cows, throwing their burden on the way as legs got weaker. The trains were jammed to the point of suffocation. Those who could not pay a strong man to secure them a seat hired a bullock cart. Those who did not have any means for wheeled transportation chose to walk for miles, shelterless, hungry, exhausted, to be in a place that would provide shelter and food and rest – India.

The closer they got to the banks of the Padma, the more crowded did the streets become. At a well, Sulaiman stopped to mop his sweating body. There was quite a line for drawing the water, and all were talking about reaching the riverbanks before nightfall. Women wore their vermillion marks, men spoke in a Bengali that had fewer Urdu words. Sulaiman laid his prayer mat, and was the only one praying. Madhumati asked everyone she could find from Khulna about her parents. But no one knew anything. Hindus from all reaches of the country were escaping to India. Some had passed by a well that was jammed with dead bodies. Another had seen a mass of rotting flesh floating down a river. Madhumati heard about other villages being burnt to the ground like hers. Yet most people were hopeful.

"I hear the borders are all open for us. They have made some refugee camps too."

"Ten thousand people from Rangpur have entered Assam, and from Sylhet and Chittagong, they all have reached Tripura."

Madhumati lit the stove and cooked some rice and dal. They ate it with the pickle and the extra rice was stored in a pan of water, which would last another two days before she would have to cook. Kerosene was getting dearer as they approached the border. They slept under a tree on a mat and when in the morning the dew drenched them they crawled under the van's thatch. The next day was again the gruelling drive beside a line of sore-footed, cracked-lipped marchers. Madhumati was grateful for the cycle van and Sulaiman. She saw women with children and no men helping them. She saw men carrying their pregnant wives on their backs, sons bearing their mothers in rickety palanquins. She saw grandparents bidding goodbye to their family, too weak to continue. Some died on the way, some dusted themselves up and resumed their march.

At the banks of the Padma commotion broke out. The cycle van was too big to be transported as every bit of space was used to transport humans, chickens, goats and cows. The nearest bridge would add four days to their journey and their food supplies had dwindled. Sulaiman would not abandon the van. A fist fight was imminent. Madhumati wedged herself in the middle of the quarrelling men and dangled a trinket before the boatman's livid face. He inspected it and nodded his assent. It was a gold locket she had saved for just such an occasion. Sulaiman took her aside and chided her for parting with it.

The ferry lurched on the waves and people vomited more in fear than motion sickness. Children fainted, suffocated by the wall of bodies around them. Animals were stamped on and bit whatever came close to their teeth. On the other bank the earth was slippery with thousands of feet pressing it down in their rush to get out. Bodies slid on the mud and people walked over them. They were yanked up and crashed back together. Eventually all were out of the bog into land and safety. Each one prayed in his own way to his own deity, since every minute in the boat promised to be the last in their life. The cycle van was shoved ashore with many helping hands. The worst of the journey was over. Thus Sulaiman's prized vehicle crossed the river and was fated to reach India along with the nine million refugees.

Chapter Ten

Aleya

Madhumati and Sulaiman took charge of their dearest possession – the cycle van. He pulled it and she pushed it up the sandy beach to the line of coconut trees. Then they heard sounds coming from nearby – distressing sounds. Holding the trunk of a tree a woman half bent, was retching her guts out. Her small frame shook at every thrust. Madhumati went to her and patted her on her back to ease her pain. She was very weak from exhaustion and could hardly walk. Madhumati indicated with her eyes to Sulaiman that they had to care for her till she was strong. They lifted her into the van and there she fainted. Madhumati walked beside Sulaiman holding Rahim. After a few hours they heard a faint voice calling from inside the van, "Didi."

Madhumati found the woman was no more than a child, hardly eighteen at the most. She had a sweet face set in a halo of dark skin, like a Krishna in female form. Her name was Aleya, and she was travelling from Dhaka alone. On that fateful night of March 25, her family was killed before her eyes, and she was taken in as a sex slave. The army cantonment in Dhaka was full of the cries of such broken souls as hers, whose families were killed or who were kidnapped from universities. During the day they washed and cooked, during the night they slaved with their bodies. Day after day, she and the other girls planned to escape, but were captured and raped even more mercilessly. Once when the barber had come to shave the soldiers, she had found a way to steal his scissors. She cut her hair like a man's, and pretending to be an errand boy, slipped out. The streets of Dhaka were unsafe, not any less for men than women. Any able-bodied man who looked like a Bengali was shot on the spot or beaten to pulp. Students and intellectuals were targeted the most. During the day, she sat among the beggars of the mosque covering her face, pretending to be a leper, so that none would come close. At night she ran as fast as her legs would carry her, out of Dhaka, westwards, towards India. And then she started throwing up in the morning, and knew one of those rapist soldiers had impregnated her. She would never know which one of the hundred or so men it was. Madhumati recalled her own close brush with the soldiers and shuddered.

When she was strong, Aleya took her turn to walk by the van while Madhumati rested and nursed Rahim. At night the tired Sulaiman collapsed in the sand, or on the mud, or wherever they stopped, his whole body sore and aching from the incessant fatigue. They were inside Meherpur district now. The last cucumber was eaten and still Rahim sucked at his mother uncaring about her privation. She could bear her hunger no longer and asked Sulaiman to make a little detour into the village nearby for some provisions – kerosene for the stove and some dal and rice. Thanks to the wheels they had made good progress, pedestrians would take weeks to cover. Many were too drained to walk, and just gave up on roadsides, erasing the dream of India and safety. Every day they hoped it would be the border, but that elusive line was yet another day away. India faced a major refugee crisis – itself not rich enough to feed its own population. The war needed to be concluded soon because India could hold no more the spate of dispossessed, hungry and tired asylum seekers. Did these people, crossing the border every hour, believe they would find shelter and food in India? How would an impoverished government suddenly feed millions of people, and where was the space to create shelter for them in the densely populated cities?

It was late in the night of December 3, 1971, when Operation Chengiz Khan was kicked into action. The Pakistani Air Force started shelling a dozen Indian air bases in western India. Their tactic was to divert India's troops from the eastern front and cripple the Indian Air Force. But India had already received intelligence of the covert attack and had removed her aircraft to safer zones. At midnight the same day, the Prime Minister, Indira Gandhi, declared open war on Pakistan as a result of these bombings. The Indian Army rolled its tanks into Bangladesh, and with the help of the Indian Air Force and the Mukti Bahini, advanced rapidly. The Indian Navy paralyzed the Pakistani naval fleet in the Bay of Bengal.

The stream of people moving westwards through Meherpur saw the Indian tanks moving in eastwards, to help their country win independence. The Indian troops could be recognized by their camouflage uniforms. Many of them spoke Bengali as they were from the other half of the united Bengal state, before the 1947 Partition. They were in army jeeps and waved at the people. "Ebarer shongram muktir shongram, this time the struggle is for freedom." The refugees recognized the slogan of their leader, Sheikh Mujibur Rahman, and they shouted back the same words, full of energy, all of a sudden. Some plain-clothed troops also passed by them – the civilian recruits. These soldiers talked to the fleeing people, "All you strong men, come fight for your country. You don't have to go to India. You will be able to remain in the free land of Bangladesh. Stay and help liberate the Bengali people." There was excitement among the men. Sulaiman looked at Madhumati, and she shook her head. The women knew if they separated, there would be no chance of reunion. Who knew what really lay at the border? Ominous instances from history still sent shock waves through their psyche.

But Aleya was obstinate about joining the Mukti Bahini. At first the couple thought she was just fantasizing about it, but then she walked out of their protection and started talking to the soldiers. She returned determined to leave. Madhumati protested, "After coming so far after so much hardship, you turn back a day before we reach India? What kind of folly is this?"

"Didi, they will take me in the army as a medical helper. I can at least do the first-aid job for the wounded."

Madhumati reminded her that she should not lift any weights, given her condition. Aleya ignored the advice. "Do you think I want this child to be born? This war bastard?"

"Shh, sister, one does not say such things about life. It is not the child's fault."

But Aleya would not listen. She was in her last mission, had seen enough of life and death, and was preparing for her own ambush.

"I wish to be in the frontline of the offensive. Then it can be quick and easy."

Madhumati was firm now. "Aleya, you have no right to end the life that is growing within you."

"Why should I bring a child into this wretched world? Have you heard the heart wrenching cries of ravished women? Your ears will not hear temple bells or the victory call of conch shells any more. Only the piercing cries of women in pain, in fear, in shame. This is my one way to shut out that sound."

Day had hardly begun for her, and she was ready to enter into the dark night. Madhumati tried very hard to convince her about the privilege of motherhood. But Aleya had started despising herself and the child in her.

"I have seen enough of the cruelty in human hearts. I do not want to show it to any child. And now I can at least prevent one from seeing it, and *that* I shall achieve."

"Aleya have faith, the Mukti Bahini has India as its ally. The war will be over very soon and then we will all start afresh – a new life in a less cruel world."

"Where men will respect women? Don't show me vacant dreams, didi."

"Aleya, have I not found God's messenger to help me through the rough passage of my life? I know you have suffered enough. Now he will send you his angel too."

She smirked. "You want me to believe in God, in Allah, Krishna, Buddha – after all this? I believe only in Yama, Lord of Death, the only compassionate, the only merciful, the Ar Rahman, the Ar Rahim. Let me go, didi."

The next day while the Ali family headed towards the border, Aleya lifted her cloth bundle on her shoulder and her other bundle hidden in her belly. They hugged for the last time and Madhumati held her close to her heart.

"Aleya, go to Sonargaon, south of Dhaka. There, ask for the banyan tree, everybody knows about it. It is hundreds of years old, and they have a shrine at its foot. Opposite the tree is a big house, burnt down, but its walls stand and it is still a shelter. It was my house, and was called the Chakraborty family house. I and my son are the only survivors and I am off to India. Claim it on my behalf, my sister, and live there happily."

Aleya shook her head in denial. She could not see beyond a few weeks, or she hoped, a few days. Madhumati held her tighter.

"Aleya, repeat after me, just to make your elder sister happy."

Aleya looked at the horizon. Madhumati turned her face. "As a parting gift to me will you not repeat what I said, just once? Think of all we went through together in this journey."

Aleya said, "Didi, I cannot express how grateful I am to you and mia sahib."

"Then say it for gratitude's sake."

"Sonargaon, banyan tree shrine, Chakraborty house."

"One more thing. A gardener lives there. His name is Badal. He is even younger than you. What is the gardener's name?"

"Badal."

Then Aleya was gone like the will-o'-the-wisp she was named after, the sudden methane gas fires that light up in marshy patches and burn briefly, till they exhaust their own energy. Thus she would be consumed by her own iron will.

In thirteen days the Pakistani General surrendered, and the war was over. On December 16, 1971 a new nation was born. Her name was Bangladesh – country of the Bengalis. Indian and Pakistani leaders met in the hill town of Simla, in India, and signed the Simla Agreement. Ninety thousand prisoners of war were handed over to Pakistan, and the expanse of land on the western frontier India had occupied during the thirteen days was returned. For a brief period the subcontinent had become an intense action theatre in the Cold War drama. The United States had sent an aircraft carrier to the Bay of Bengal to help Pakistan, and the USSR had trailed her with its submarines, both equipped with nuclear missiles. Sheikh Mujibur Rahman was released from jail in Pakistan and returned to lead the new country of his dreams. Bangladesh soon after signed a friendship treaty with India. Henceforth, for India, the Padma valley and the Sindhu valley would be neighbours of very different character.

* * * * *

Anand returned from college and found Binapani in bed with a book in hand. "How are you feeling, my dear?" She had the same one word reply most of these days.

"Hungry."

"Have you eaten?"

"Not since you left."

"What Bina, you must be very hungry! I told you to ask Chhotu to get whatever you like from the shop opposite. Did he not come today to give you tea?"

"Yes, he did," she said lazily.

He rushed to the kitchen and found the fridge, stove and sink untouched. The baby in her was not going to be happy with such a mother. He did not ask himself if he was happy with such a wife. He just took a few deep breaths and returned, joyful as ever, the indefatigable Anand.

"Come Bina, let's go out today."

At the restaurant, Anand asked Binapani,

"So Bina, what shall we name the child?"

"I want it to be a character from ancient India."

"You mean, not just a quality, like my name, but like yours."

"Yes, then we will get a whole story from the character plus the meaning of the name."

"Good idea, because a name goes a long way to define a person. Every word has a vibration of its own, that's what is meant by mantra. Sanskrit is a mantrik language. Its power begins in its very utterance, even before we impart a meaning to the word. When we express the sound we are releasing a certain vibration in the atmosphere. And if it is our name, then people are directing that vibration towards us, and we have to be able to receive that vibration."

"Is that true? I never thought naming a person could be so profound."

"That is why I don't want the name to be a God's name. It is too much responsibility to bear, since if one cannot catch the vibration, one may succumb to undesirable forces that will prey upon one's weakness."

Binapani smiled, relieved. "That rules out the thirty-three crores of names of Gods. Now I can see names in the range of a constellation, instead of a galaxy."

They laughed. It would still be quite a task to pin down a single star from a constellation.

Anand said, "How about a name of a sage, and for a girl we will pick a wise woman."

"Such as?"

"Shall we play a game? You will guess the names I choose."

"All right sir, I am ready for your viva test."

The dinner was served, and Binapani's mouth was full of food, so the best she could do was listen to his story.

"When the mountains could fly, once the Vindhya Range became too arrogant and lifted her head high enough to block the sun's path. So the people prayed to a sage who had enormous powers. The Vindhya peaks bowed down for the sage to pass, and he extracted a promise from her that she would remain bowed as long as he did not return. And so he never returned from the south of India."

Through a mouthful, Binapani said, "Agastya."

"Very good. And if we have a girl we can name her Lopamudra, his wife, an erudite woman."

"But Anand, what do they mean?"

"You are right, Bina, the meanings are convoluted, we should explore some more."

"Tell me about other famous couples."

"There is Yajnavalkya and Maitreyee, Vashishtha and Arundhati, or Janaka and the wise woman in his court – Gargi."

"How about a heroic character, a king, a princess of action?"

"Then we should seek refuge in the Puranas."

"Shall we look in the Mahabharata, in the age of the brave?"

"Yes, what better warrior than Abhimanyu, who fought a battle single-handed against enemies surrounding him and engaging him all at once?"

"But Anand, he died in the fight at a tender age. Next please."

"The most skilful prince – Arjuna – or one of his other names – Partha, Dhananjaya."

Binapani was thinking of girls' names. "Among women of course there is Draupadi. Now that is a character for a women indeed! She was born from a blazing fire – a sacrificial rite – for one purpose – to set the stage on fire. She was insulted so deeply that the only course left for her to avenge herself was to start the great battle of the Kurukshetra – once for all, to purge evil from the face of the earth. Even if she did not fight with weapons herself, she was the fountain of inspiration of her valiant husbands."

"Yes, but Bina, nobody names their daughters Draupadi, precisely because she had five husbands."

"But these were not just men, these husbands of hers. They were each son of a God. We can worship five gods all at once, can't we? All of us Hindus worship many more than five. Your house has a shrine with a hundred Gods and Goddesses. So what is wrong with five such husbands? Besides, even if you consider it socially, she did not choose to marry them all. It was a misunderstanding that landed her in that situation."

"But Draupadi had too much of revenge in her blood. A girl cannot bear that responsibility. Her whole life had just one purpose, and she flew at it like a predatory eagle. How many moments of enjoyment did she have? None. Despite those five husbands, she was insulted by men, even manhandled several times."

"Sometimes one person is used by a whole generation to set up a new yardstick. Draupadi was that unit of measure."

"Bina, she will be chased by her own fate to accomplish something big. Why disquiet her with a perpetual struggle?"

"Because ultimately she will triumph."

"There was no real victory in that war, speaking for human sentiments. Draupadi lost all her sons, remember?"

"But her purpose was not in the human scope. It was a battle to re-establish dharma."

"Bina, I still don't think a girl, our little girl, could have a name that will give her no peace. She will have admirers, but no lover."

"Draupadi loved Krishna, and he was always there to help her."

"But she wanted a human lover too."

"There was Arjuna for her."

"No, she could not love him as she wished because she had to love all the five brothers impartially. Her love for Arjuna was thus compromised. She had to dilute it by force."

"Anand, if Draupadi is not so common a name, let us choose her other name – Panchali – princess of the kingdom of Panchal."

"Bina, if you want a fiery woman, consider the matriarch of the clan – Satyavati. She was also mother of the great sage, Veda Vyas. Or choose Ganga, mother of Bheeshma – the one with the unshakable oaths. How about Kunti, mother of the Pandavas?"

"Kunti is good, and her other name too – Pritha – mother of Partha."

"For boys we have innumerable choices. The Pandava brothers, their martial arts teacher, Drona, their family teacher, Kripa, then the elders of the family, Bheeshma, or his first name Devavrata, Vidur, then the sage father of Vyas, Parashar, Vyas himself, Bheeshma's father, Shantanu, the generous Karna, the valiant Parashurama, and so on."

"I like the character of Arjuna best of all."

"Yes, he was specially blessed by Krishna, because he could surrender like no other human being."

Before the battle Arjuna and the Kuru brother, Duryodhana, went to seek alliance from Krishna, who was the king of the

Yadavas. Krishna divided his help to both parties but they had to choose. One would have the whole Yadava army, the other would have him alone, and that too as a charioteer. Arjuna gratefully chose the latter, while Duryodhana merrily picked the former. Of course, the divine wins. The wisdom of the Gita was taught to Arjuna in that battlefield. It is one of the greatest gospels of the Hindus.

"Looks like we have a boy's name – Partha?" asked Anand.

"Yes, Partha is short and sweet."

"And for the girl we have Satyavati?"

"No." Binapani made a face. "I am not satisfied."

"All right, we will think of some more names for her. And if we can't find one, we will name her Anamika – the nameless one."

"Satyavati is better than that!"

"Yes, you will like the name eventually. It means one who is truthful. We have satisfied both our original premises. Come now, my pet, you are going to fall asleep in the taxi, I can see."

Shortly afterwards, Anand's mother came with a suitcase to take Binapani with her back to the Deshmukh family home. She was a hard-working woman, who chased Savita out of the kitchen back to her study room. She was determined to have an M.A. daughter, and was proud of her professor son and his M.A. wife. The lady fussed around Binapani, and annoyed her a wee bit. She was banned from reading racy novels, and had to do her daily quota of prayers. Had the Brahmo influence gone so deep in her that she saw these rituals as paraphernalia? Anyway, she succumbed to the pampering and hardly went hungry – after all their grandchild was being born, and she was just the vessel.

Anand spent all his free time telling Binapani stories from the Upanishads, or reading her the Gita. She heard about the discourses in King Janaka's court, about the wise Gargi challenging the greatest of sages, Yajnavalkya, about him leaving for the forest along with his enlightened wife, Maitreyee. His famous words to Maitreyee were: "Not for the sake of the self do we love the wife, but for the sake of the Self". The first self is the selfish self – the ego. The second is the higher Self. When one has discovered the Self, one has also found the Self to be the All. In that state, one is irresistibly drawn to all. One becomes the quintessence of love, since there is no 'one' or 'other', everything is the Self. Binapani saw the beauty of Sanskrit. It was not just grammar when Anand spoke, but a body of spiritual truths. He said the baby was listening to everything, like Abhimanyu, like Ashtavakra.

When Abhimanyu was in his mother's womb, his father, and the greatest of warriors, Arjuna, was explaining a strategy in warfare called the chakravyuha. Here soldiers stood in concentric formations to trap the enemy inside. Arjuna knew of a way to penetrate the chakra, the circles. He had finished describing the way to pierce the enemy ranks, when he was called upon for another duty and had to leave. So the baby heard just part of the warfare secret. In the Kurukshetra war, Abhimanyu penetrated the chakravyuha, but could not get out of it. He fought till his last breath, even whirling the wheel of a chariot when his weapons were felled from his hand.

"The other story is about Ashtavakra. His grandfather was the great sage of the Chhandogya Upanishad – Uddalaka. He said the famous words to his son, Shwetaketu, '*Tat twam asi Shwetaketu,* You are That, Shwetaketu!' Anyway, Ashtavakra's mother used to attend her father, Uddalaka's classes, when she was carrying him. Her son was thus wiser than his own father, Kahoda, before he was born. Once when Kahoda was teaching, the baby corrected him again and again, eight times in fact, talking from the womb. The enraged Kahoda then cursed the boy to have eight deformities in his body. Therefore ashta vakra, meaning 'eight bends'."

"Poor son, what a punishment for being knowledgeable!"

"The story goes further. In short, Ashtavakra wins in a contest of spiritual debate, and his father pardons him, thus ridding his body of those bends."

"Good, I like stories with a happy ending."

"Bina this is not a story. It is history. Some day we can read the Ashtavakra Gita, literally, 'the song of Ashtavakra'. His mellifluous words will touch a chord deep in your heart."

* * * * *

Shortly after Christmas, Binapani got a letter from her mother, full of exuberance.

"Dear Bina,

Our lady prime minister did it! She should be honoured as queen of Bangladesh. Thirteen days, only thirteen, and the Pakistani General, with almost a lakh of troops, surrendered. Aren't we proud that a new country with our language as its national language is born? They call the rupee, taka, same as we do in Bengali. It is now an international currency. And do you know what song they have chosen for the national anthem? Our gurudev, Rabindranath Tagore's *Amar Shonar Bangla*, 'O my beloved Bangladesh, I adore you.' In 1905 when the British Viceroy had split Bengal, indignation broke out across the province. Leaders organized mass movements, writers inspired with their words, it was a powerful awakening. Tagore led a public march to protest the government's decision. At that time, he composed this song. There was such a show of solidarity that within seven years the partition was resealed. And again we have helped our Bengali brethren. Rejoice, and imagine I am feeding you a big sandesh. I miss you so much today. They are lighting fire crackers all around. But without you I don't feel like celebrating. That's why I am writing to you instead."

Binapani felt sorry for her mother and for all the people of the Indian subcontinent, the Bharat of the epic Mahabharata. Now her one nation had become three countries. The only consolation was that Pakistan did not sit astride India like a jockey on its horse.

* * * * *

Miss Lilly, the principal's secretary, knocked at the classroom door and without waiting for Anand's permission poked her head in. She indicated a phone with her hand, the thumb touching her ear and the little finger her mouth. Anand leapt out of his chair, "Anand, your wife. Go go go! I will tell your students." The phone sat in the principal's office, and the whole staff knew Anand's big day was arriving. Anand and his mother waited at the hospital. His father was in the office and Savita in her college. They had left hastily with a note stuck on the door, "Going to Hospital. Baby on the way." Anand walked up and down the corridor sweating in fright. His mother caught up with him and made him sit once in a while. She tried to tell him how it had been with her, and that all would be fine.

But all was not fine. A nurse with a staccato walk approached him. "Mr Deshmukh, can you follow me please? No, madam, you can wait here, nothing to worry." She continued while Anand strode alongside, benumbed in fright.

"There is very little time, so I will have to be honest. Your wife is passing out. She will not listen to our instructions, she will not breathe as we say, she will not push. Now her blood pressure is very low and at any moment she will become unconscious. We cannot risk putting her on anaesthesia. So we want you to encourage her."

Anand winced. The nurse thought it was because men were not allowed in childbirth operation theatres.

"Don't worry, we have made an exception for you. Now wear this, it is sterilized."

Anand had winced because he knew why she was passing out. She was actually passing away. Again he had to lift her out of the water in his arms. He held Binapani's hand, and came close to her ear. The other half of her body was behind the curtain with three nurses clustered around.

"Bina breathe, see, like I am doing. And every time you exhale, push hard. Let's do it together."

He made a big sound while exhaling, but she was half asleep. He massaged her forehead and started crying.

"What will I do without you? Please, my dear, don't go. You are my dream girl, aren't you? I cannot live without you."

The nurse pointed at the screen which recorded her heart

rate – it had not changed, it was very weak. Anand continued to plead with her about his destitute state, about the baby's lonely future. But Binapani had decided to leave. Then he was possessed like a man falling from a cliff, snatching at the last rock, even if it were unstable.

He raised his voice and did not care if the whole world heard him. "Bina, listen, the girl that will be born will live even if you choose to die."

The nurses all looked up at him. One of them shook her head and shrugged her shoulders, indicating, "We don't know if it will be a girl or boy."

But Anand had to clutch at the last rock. "One day, she will grow up and face me. Then how will I ask her to fight? What right would I have to impose on her the zeal to live? When her own mother did not fight for her? What shall I tell her? Your mother did not want you to live? Your mother did not love you for a single day because she was gone? Your mother did not cry for you, did not teach you anything, your mother bore you for nine months but did not care for nine crucial minutes for you? Your mother did not respect womanhood? Your mother did not do what her own mother did for her?"

The pulse rate on the screen had increased. Binapani was wide awake and listening.

"So Bina, here is your chance to show your daughter how to live. Be the example. Let her drink life to the lees. We will call her Panchali, the one born from a sacrifice – your sacrifice. Abandon your madness for death, that she and you may live. All you have to do is push, push, push!"

And push she did. She screamed and dug her nails in Anand's hand. He swallowed his pain and kept repeating "Push, push, push."

Then they heard the baby's cry and Binapani exhaled a long, tired and happy breath. Anand was now the victim of his own trick. He looked wide mouthed and wider eyed at the opaque screen. A nurse popped out her head and her lips moved, but no sound reached Anand. He frowned hard at her. Then she held a bloody squealing baby above her head, and Anand saw his child for the first time. Bina was panting and her eyes were closed. She asked weakly, "Is that Panchali crying?"

A fainting voice reached her from the ground below, "Yes."

Part Three

Chapter Eleven

Raja

Lilly from Anand's college, and her husband, George, came to visit the newborn. Panchali had a perfect round face, and was nicknamed rasagulla, the ball of homemade cheese floating in sugar syrup, the Bengali regional sweet, as her mother labelled it. By now there was a Bengali regional proverb, swear word, spice, fruit, flower, animal, bird, hairstyle, and so on. So here was Lilly, the flower, holding rasagulla, the sweet, and asking the inevitable question, her name. All the visitors so far were surprised by her unusual name, and some who knew the significance congratulated the couple's audacity. But Lilly and George, being Christian, did not know anything about Panchali. Anand gave Binapani the pleasure of explaining. "Have you heard of Draupadi? Panchali is another of her names."

Lilly said she had read the Amar Chitra Katha, the comic books recounting stories from the Hindu mythologies. Draupadi rises out of a fire, has a big contest for her marriage where Arjuna wins her, and she would have continued if George had not intervened.

"Cut, cut, Lilly, you are racing ahead. I was a poor Christian boy from Goa kissing the Holy Cross and reading Jesus' miracles. You will have to introduce me to these characters."

Lilly gave him a little punch in his ample belly. "Poor boy indeed! He played street cricket while we girls read those wonderful picture books."

In India, these comics are as much a part of a person's growth as pimples and wisdom teeth. "Long live the Amar Chitra Katha!" Binapani waved the verbal banner.

Anand came in with a tray of lemonade. "Rightly said so, Bina. Shall I explain why? 'Amar' means 'immortal', so they will live long. 'Chitra Katha' means 'story in pictures'. You know what I loved most about these comics was suddenly coming across a fine piece of artwork. Some of the artists, anonymous and unrecognized, not big names who can rent art galleries for their exhibition, are very skilful. The expressions they conveyed were touching. Shakuntala pining for her husband who has forgotten about her, Mirabai worshipping Krishna, Draupadi angry and insulted, Bheema swearing, Yudhishthira head bowed."

Lilly agreed, "Yes George, we must get you some Amar Chitra Kathas now that you are big enough not to play in the street."

"Lilly, I am still a sportsman though, I play carom."

"By the way, that is the Bengali regional sport. Am I right, Bina?" asked Anand teasing his wife.

She denied it. "Go tell it to Raja. The Bengali regional sport is football, not finger ball." Carom is a sitting billiards game where the balls are coin-shaped wooden pieces struck with a similar piece, but stronger, made of plastic.

"Anand, tell them the Mahabharata," requested Binapani.

"Sorry, that will take me months. The composer, sage Veda Vyas, had to ask Lord Ganesh to be his scribe as he realized the story would take ages to recite."

"What if you stick to the trunk of the narrative, and keep the branches for the Amar Chitra Kathas?" suggested George.

"That will work." Anand started the story. "It happened a long time ago, beyond the earliest mists of history. India was united by King Shantanu of the Kuru dynasty. He fell in love with a woman on the banks of the river Ganga. She was actually Ganga personified, Goddess Ganga. There are some temples dedicated to her, and as you know we believe taking a dip in the Ganga purifies us of past wrong deeds. She was actually invoked from heaven to earth..."

"Anand, don't digress, they will get confused." Binapani brought him back to the trunk.

"Good point, keep a vigil on me, Bina. We don't want to steal the comic book's task."

"Shantanu marries Ganga and they have an extraordinary son, Devavrata."

"They have other sons too who are sacrificed, but that is another story." Binapani added her footnote.

"Then Ganga goes back to her home in heaven, and Shantanu finds himself another wife, Satyavati. Devavrata vows to relinquish the throne and never marry because Satyavati, or rather her father, wants her son to be king. Since he makes such a powerful promise, Devavrata's name is changed to Bheeshma, the keeper of a 'dreadful' vow."

Lilly nodded, "I recognize him now. He was the grandfather, the pillar that held the structure of the feuding parties as long as it was possible."

"Yes, he was a most respected elder. We now fast forward to Satyavati's two grandsons. The older boy is blind, so the able-bodied younger boy, Pandu, is crowned king. But he unfortunately dies very soon, of a curse. So the blind brother, Dhritarashtra, ascends the throne. It is decided that half of the kingdom would go to Pandu's sons and half to his."

Binapani explained, "The five Pandavas are the sons of Pandu, but they are not actually his seed. They are each a divine blessing from a different God."

Anand went on, "Dhritarashtra starts plotting to keep the whole of the kingdom for his eldest son, Duryodhana. By the way, Dhritarashtra has a hundred sons, and one daughter and they are called the Kauravas, after the clan name, Kuru. The rest of the story is a series of stratagems to oust the Pandavas from their rightful kingdom, including murder attempts, gambling tricks, lies and allegations, insults and ruses. The Pandavas can bear it no more, and the great war of Kurukshetra ensues, which literally means the battlefield of the Kuru dynasty. Dhritarashtra's sons are destroyed, and the Pandavas reign supreme."

"Why Anand, that was rather short! We did not even hear about Panchali!" complained George.

"This is just the skeleton. The struggle between good and evil, filial competition, clash of colossal egos, spiritual anguishes, all begin from the birth of the Kaurava and Pandava brothers. And that part Bina will recount while I make some poha for you."

"Unfair!" cried Binapani, "You hand the difficult task to me."

"Oh, all right, then you make the poha and I will continue." Anand pretended to be nonchalant. Binapani frowned.

Anand gave in. "I will tell you some more. The Kauravas are terribly jealous of their skilful cousins, the favourites of the family. So they send the Pandavas to live in a palace made of inflammable material. However, warned of the impending danger, the brothers escape, setting the wax palace on fire. Their evil cousins believe that the Pandavas have been dispatched for good, and secretly rejoice. For a year, the five live in obscurity as Brahmins with their widowed mother, Kunti, biding their time to return and surprise the merry Kauravas. Then they learn of the contest that is to be held shortly in Panchal, the winner of which would marry Panchali, the princess. Now Bina, your turn."

Anand left for the kitchen and Binapani called after him,

"Add some potatoes, please, Anand. The contest has been specially planned by the princess, Panchali, so that only the best archer can win it. And, of course, she has just one man in mind, or rather in her heart. Arjuna is the best archer in the land, and only he can pierce the eye of a fish rotating on a wheel. As if that were not hard enough, one had to look into a basin of water below to aim at the fish on the ceiling above. Duryodhana and his brothers fail as do many other princes. Then finally Arjuna, in the guise of a Brahmin, succeeds in hitting the target, and wins Panchali, much to the humiliation of the warrior clan. One more insult is added to the Kauravas' store. But how can one compete with cousins who are divinely endowed?"

"And so Panchali marries the most valiant hero of the age. Beautiful name, congratulations, Binapani," concluded George.

"Don't you rush, that's hardly the end of Panchali's story."

"Please go on then."

"The brothers return with Panchali to the hut and want to surprise their mother. So from outside they call out, 'Mother, see what we have brought back today.' Kunti answers without waiting to see what it was they had got, 'Whatever it is, share it amongst yourselves.' And, of course, the mother's wish is the sons' command. So Panchali gets five husbands!"

"But isn't she already married to Arjuna?"

"Yes, poor Panchali had heard about his feats and had fallen in love with him. But now she has to love four other brothers equally. And that's not the end of her troubles. The Pandavas are welcomed back to their kingdom, and Panchali becomes queen. Then, Yudhishthira is challenged to a game of dice, a proposal that cannot be declined. One would think it is all about luck, and I am sure the Pandavas thought so too. But in the palace it turns out to be quite another game. It is a gambling bout with enormous stakes. Duryodhana's uncle, Shakuni, is a champion dice player. Actually he is a cheater who uses black magic to control the dice. Anyway, Yudhishthira loses his kingdom first, then he starts staking his brothers one by one, himself, and ultimately his wife. Panchali is dragged to the court by her hair, and in front of all the elders, the younger Kuru brothers and her five husbands, is insulted, the worst insult a woman can endure in public."

Lilly said, "I know that part. It was shocking when I first read it as a little girl. One of the Kuru brothers tried to strip her."

George was surprised, "Looks like the Mahabharata dealt with adult topics in that era."

"It was not a story, you see. It really happened, whether children should know it or not, it happens even today. That is why the Mahabharata is considered a mirror of society, an eternal mirror wherein events repeat cyclically. Panchali prays to Lord Krishna for help, and, miraculously, she remains fully clothed even after Dusshasan has fallen exhausted, having pulled off yards and yards of Panchali's garment."

George asked the uncomfortable question, "You said the elders were also present, including the grandfather Bheeshma?"

Binapani sighed deeply. Just then, Anand entered with a large platter of steaming poha, and handed her a plate with a pile of potatoes on it. He looked around the silent crowd and asked, "What happened?"

Binapani answered. "The vastraharan, the snatching of Panchali's clothes."

"Ah, of course. Well, to complete the story, the Pandavas are not made bond slaves this time round. But after the next game of dice where they lose again, they have to spend twelve years in the forest and one year in disguise. During this period Panchali suffers other agonies as well. She is not recognized as the queen of the country, but is taken to be a beautiful slave girl. The strongest of the husbands, Bheema, protects her every time. Denied their kingdom even after the thirteen years of exile, the Pandavas accept the inevitability of war."

Binapani finished the story with the last details, "After the court scene Panchali vows to tie her hair only when she can apply Dusshasan's blood as hair oil. And Bheema vows to break Duryodhana's thigh as he had asked Panchali to sit on it, like he would have a courtesan."

"It is certainly a story of strong vow keepers and feminine exploitation," shuddered George, not used to the gruesome detail the Deshmukhs had supplied. "I can see this Panchali was an adamant character. Watch out for your little girl!"

Anand laughed, "If it just obstinacy we can deal with it. We hope she will not set a hundred chariots on their fatal course!"

* * * * *

One day Binapani received a small parcel from Calcutta. She plucked the letter from its envelope, and ran her eyes down the page. It had Aparna's name. She was alive then! Tears slid down Binapani's eyes and blurred her vision. Memories descended like dew drops – the carefree college days, the Coffee House meetings, Bidrohi, gun shots, the morgue, dead bodies, Tushar, Tushar ... It seemed aeons had passed since she heard from her friend. So much had happened in between.

"Dear Bina,

Remember me as one with high fluting voice singing from the topmost branch of life. Not as the wingless goose I am now. Charu-da, you might have heard, was captured from his hide-out and was tortured to death in custody. He died on July 28,

1972. All the dreamers are permanently put to sleep. The rich will get richer and the poor will suffer ever more. Unfortunate me, I am alive, as you can see. I have taken up a job as a teacher in the Loreto girls' convent school. I long to see you, but I know life has floated you away on another course. I heard you have had a daughter. I am happy for you, and I wish I could remould my life as you have done."

Binapani shook her head. How wrong poor Aparna was! She herself was a sleep walker, a drugged puppet. People made her act, they pumped air in her lungs so that she could breathe. She was a husk waiting for a strong breeze to blow her away. Aparna's letter had one last line. "The police have returned some of the things they had confiscated. I chose this one for you. It was his."

Inside the parcel she found the gospel of the Satya Yuga, Savitri, by Sri Aurobindo. She opened the book slowly as if it was a door into a temple of peace. A sheet of paper fluttered to the floor like a feather. She picked it up and read. It was in Tushar's handwriting, the same she had seen under Che Guevera's portrait.

My love, if ever it happened, I wanted you to know,

"O man, the events that meet thee on thy road,

Though they smite thy body and soul with joy and grief,

Are not thy fate; thy touch thee awhile and pass;

Even death can cut not short thy spirit's walk:

Thy goal, the road thou choosest are thy fate."

"There is a truth to know, a work to do."

Binapani pressed the book to her heart and cried tears of gratitude. She had found a dear friend.

* * * * *

Raja was back from the football tournament in Delhi trailing clouds of glory. He was now in the Maharashtra state team and still the star of the game. He picked up Panchali and gave her a spin in the air and caught her back. His father was shocked, "Raja, she will hit her head in the ceiling fan. If you must continue your monkey tricks, go do it in that corner."

Binapani was arranging the many small bowls in the big silver plate. "Raja, that girl loves to fly, even if it is for a second. At the rate Anand bounces her up, one day he will not be able to lift his arm to write on the blackboard."

It was Panchali's annapraashan, the food ceremony. She was now six months old and would begin to eat solids from today. The presence of her mama, maternal uncle, was necessary. There was a lot of symbolism attached to the ritual, and Anand wanted to bring his family together to officiate over it. The protagonists, Raja, the maternal uncle, and Panchali, his niece, were finally pinned down before the plate. Binapani's aunt had made the Bengali dishes and Anand's mother had made the Marathi ones. Every kind of food of myriad hue and taste was arranged on the plate in little bowls, colourful like a miniature painting of a spice shop. Panchali wore a red frock and sat in the lap of her uncle, who could not be persuaded to wear the traditional dhoti, but wore the kurta churidar – an acceptable compromise. Anand was the grandmaster of the ceremony.

"Before we begin, let us understand what annapraashan means. This Sanskrit word is used by the Bengalis and there is a similar ceremony in Maharashtra called ushtaavan. Every person is like an onion with layers of being around him. The innermost layer is matter, the one maintained by food. Subsequent layers are life, mind, truth, bliss, conscious force, absolute being. Anna, prana, mana, vijnana, ananda, chit, sat."

"I don't like the onion image, Anand," said Binapani. "Let us make it more appealing, closer to the human form. Shall we imagine it to be a Russian doll?"

Anand felt a vacuum in his belly. Oh no, not Russia again!

Raja nodded, "Yes, I like the image. What, Jamai-babu? Have you not seen a Russian doll? It is hollow inside, painted on wood, in two pieces, joined at the stomach. When you open a doll, you find another inside it. And so on till you have a cute little human figurine smaller than Panchali's hand."

"I see, it is a wonderful analogy. The smallest doll is the

annamaya layer, the layer of matter. Since our body is matter, and it is maintained by food, food is also called anna."

"Yes we know, the Goddess that provides food is Annapurna, the fulfiller of material needs."

"So annapraashan means literally the 'sacred consumption of food.' Anywhere you see the prefix 'pr', you can guess it lends a sacredness to the word that follows it. 'Anna' plus 'pr' plus 'ashana', which means 'to eat', gives us the full meaning."

"Crystal clear," commented Raja, "But why do I have to feed her?"

"Yes, Anand, why does the maternal uncle have to perform the ceremony?" echoed the others.

Anand scratched his head, which Binapani thought was in mock deference, "Why don't we all brainstorm about it?"

Raja's father threw the first marble in the court, "It must be related to some custom from ancient times. I say the woman went to her father's house for the delivery and returned only after this ceremony."

"Really? Did her father allow her to stay for that long in his house? I thought the husband's family would need her help. I would like to call for a retake on this. Your turn, aunty," Anand turned to Raja's mother.

"Let me see. So far the baby was drinking her mother's blood..."

"Ma, don't be crude," was Raja's cool advice.

"No, it is true, blood becomes milk. But agreed, it invokes a Kali-like image to our minds. So this is the first day she will eat something other than what her mother's body provides for her. That something should then come from the mother's brother. But I can't explain why, my instinct says so."

Binapani continued the train of thought. "Now we know there is something called genetics, but in those days they did not know it in detail, but they knew its significance. Why else were marriages with relatives banned?"

"What a preposterous idea!" exclaimed Anand's mother.

"No, Aai," Binapani tapped her gently on the shoulder, "There are communities that respect such unions. In Karnataka, I heard girls marry their maternal uncles, their mother's real brothers."

"We are back to the maternal uncle. Let's solve it quickly," prompted Savita, "Raja, you are the point of contention. The burden of proof rests on you."

Raja ventured, "Is it because he is closest to the mother genetically?"

Anand helped him on, "And since for the baby it is a shock to eat food of alien taste, given that she has known just one flavour for six months, her shock will be minimized if she is fed by one who is closest to her mother, whose body she has been literally eating."

"Jamai-babu, then to ease her shock, they should give her milk items, like rasagullas." He was looking around for the Bengali sweets on the plate.

"No, on the contrary she should taste all that's available. You know the first impression is very important."

"I know that. If my first game before the committee was a flop they would never have chosen me in the state team. Don't laugh Bina-didi, I have bad days too. One wrong kick and the toe gets stubbed; then for the rest of the game I am a lame duck."

"So Panchali's tongue will get her first impression today and the brain will classify these as acceptable acquaintances," finished Anand.

Raja's mother complained, "You are right, in Raja's annapraashan we did not make any bitter item, and ever since I have not been able to make him eat anything even slightly bitter. Only when he gets diabetes, which he will, given the amount of sweets he eats, will he be forced to eat bitter food."

Raja could defend himself easily, "Strangely ma, I asked my classmates, and none of the boys eat bitter."

His mother gifted him one of her grimaces. "Bina, I have made bitter gourd for Panchali. So don't worry, she will not be food fussy."

Anand's father poked his head around trying to decipher

the food without tasting. "Anand, there should be all the six types of foods, those which are classified in Ayurveda. I can see some mango chutney as sour, of course sweet and salty, and the bitter gourd, how about some pungent dishes?"

Binapani's aunt answered, "I cooked with mustard oil, so she will taste a lot of pungency."

"What about astringent?"

"Astringent? Baba, I have never heard of that flavour. What are the foods?" asked Binapani.

"Fish?" That was from Raja who would have liked some non-vegetarian dishes in this mix.

"Astringent is when we eat raw fruits like guava, you know how the tongue becomes sticky. That is an extreme case, but lentils have the same property."

"We have plenty of dal."

"All right then. Anand, the stage is all yours."

Anand picked up a book. "Now I will read a passage from the Taittiriya Upanishad."

Everybody sat in silence. Panchali felt the difference in the atmosphere and whined on Raja's lap. He brought his finger to his lips and with a severe look uttered "Shhh."

"The Sage Bhrigu approached the great one, his father, and said, 'Teach me father what is the Brahman'." The father enjoins upon him to concentrate his energies on the Brahman, thus can it be comprehended. Bhrigu then sits to meditate and realizes anna is Brahman, matter is the supreme. He then returns to his father and is told to continue his introspection. In this fashion he discovers the other layers of the being to be the Brahman also. Life, mind, truth, bliss, are all That. Anand concluded in his own words,

"I promise to honour food, this material layer of my being, this clay pot that holds the divine spark, this chariot upon which I journey. Om shanti, shanti, shanti, let there be peace in all three regions."

Then Panchali sat on Raja's lap and he picked up a bit of cauliflower in his hand. She watched his hand and followed its path to her mouth, but when the food touched her lips she wailed.

"She does not know this is food. She thinks it is some punishment. Raja, why don't you eat so that she can copy you and gain confidence?"

"At last!" said Raja, and started eating from his plate next to the big ceremonial one. Then again he brought the food to her mouth, and this time she smacked her lips enjoying the novelty in every taste."

After a meal with the twin ethnic blends, everybody was satisfied. The cooks were amply complimented and they started exchanging recipes. The men were lounging and Anand's father, who was a banker, said,

"Talking about food, the Green Revolution that Indira Gandhi started is commendable. We have become exporters of grains, can you imagine, despite our exploding population? I wonder how?"

Binapani's uncle replied, "Now we have two harvests per year, we import hybrid seeds and have improved on catchment of monsoon waters. In fact, as a side effect of irrigation techniques, we have dammed rivers and get hydroelectric power."

"Yes, there is ample food. But what about the other necessities of daily life? I mean education, housing, sanitation, hospitals?" Anand was worried about the quality of life.

"Anand, let us tackle one issue at a time. Besides, population control is a huge sociological problem that needs expert handling. It is not as easy as buying some High Yield Seeds and planting them."

Anand's father was interested, "Yes, I have heard of these miracle seeds. Are they really good? I mean, yes, we get more rice from the same plot of land, but don't these need more fertilizer, more water and pesticides? I cannot believe all those chemicals are good for the soil. And don't they climb up the plant stems and lodge themselves in the foodgrains?"

"Sir, we should have faith in scientists. You and I are the common man. Do we have an option to oppose government decisions?"

"But we are a democracy. We can question the decision making through the press, through the opposition party. We can write to our elected representative."

"You need a loud voice for that."

Anand answered them, "If you have a genuine concern, the microphone will be provided. You have to start speaking, and you will find many more are sitting on their sofas and are pondering over the very same issues."

"Is that so? Anand, you give me hope." Binapani's uncle was impressed by the enthusiastic new generation. He remembered the war-time famine in Bengal. People knocked on doors, emaciated and agonized by hunger, "Sahib, do you have some phèn to spare?" Phèn is the starchy water thrown out after rice is cooked. That watery waste had become precious nourishment for the poor. Reports said three million people had perished in one year, which meant about ten thousand a day.

There was a famine in Bengal during the Second World War, in 1943, which is recorded as one of the world's worst ever famines. Bengal at that time included Bangladesh, Assam, much of Bihar and parts of Orissa. The reasons were complex, but a big factor was the War. In the previous year a cyclone had flooded the paddy fields, rice, whatever cultivated, was exported to the war front in the Middle East, creating a severe domestic shortage and the loss of Burma to Japan cut off the supply from that region. To add to the woes, traders hoarded whatever was available from present fear and for future profit, driving up prices beyond the purchasing power of most people. Ever since that nightmare, the government of India had decided to control the stocking of grains and their release in the market. The World Bank had loaned funds to many developing nations for the Green Revolution, and some of the best results were seen in India. Within a decade from 1967 when it started, agricultural yield multiplied several times. Canada invited Punjabi farmers to come over and share their techniques with them. There were two harvests per year, one from the monsoon, the other from the water collected during the monsoon.

"Ice cream anyone?" came Savita's cheerful cry.

"Savita, I am bursting now." Anand held his belly.

But Raja was ever ready. "Yes!"

Some other voices followed, feebly though, "Me too."

"Bhaiya, you are the only exception."

"All right, come let us all go for a walk to digest this lunch that Bheema, the vrikodara, the one with a wolf's appetite, would enjoy." So they walked about in the garden downstairs, ice cream cup in hand. Panchali was on Anand's father's lap and he exclaimed, "Look Anand, your daughter loves ice cream."

"Yes, baba, she recognizes it is milk."

Savita ran ahead and faced the ambling group.

"I have a question. If this annapraashan ceremony is finally cutting the umbilical cord, the psychological severance between mother and child ..."

Anand was impressed by his sister, "Savita, that is an insightful observation!"

"And if the doctor has to be the mother's closest blood relative, then why not her sister?"

Now they were all face to face with Savita and the indignations of feminism. "Why was the Indian cultural history so patriarchal? Why did women not go to the gurukula, those schools where a student lived in the forest hermitage with his master and learnt the Vedas from him, and all other knowledge? Why did women not become priests? The only place a woman had in a temple was as a devadasi. She was offered to serve the deity in the temple, to bathe him, and to sing and dance for him during the festivals. So that she could not be teased into marriage, she was palmed off early in her life, in a token marriage. Her husband could of course remarry afterwards. Or sometimes she was wedded to the deity. The most beautiful flower of a poor family, which could not afford to marry the daughter, was offered to the Gods. In reality she often ended up being the concubine of the king, or whoever else was the temple patron. Surely some of the devadasis wanted to lead a normal family life, with a husband to herself and children to look after? But others always made the important decisions in a girl's life. Why did women suffer this treatment for so long?"

Binapani turned around and joined Savita's camp. "Yes, tell us why?"

Her uncle dismissed their predicament, "Often the mother's sister was in her own husband's house and could not appear for the annapraashan ceremony. She may herself be a mother with many responsibilities. But about suppressing education for women I wholeheartedly side with you. It was a corruption, and that is why the Brahmo Samaj and many others tried to fix it. Women now go to school and even have good jobs these days."

"But they are not allowed to officiate in ceremonies. The sacred hymns of the Vedas cannot flow out of their lips in public." Binapani was not appeased.

"And I hear some temples don't allow women to enter when they are in that state, you know what I mean."

"Yes, they are impure at that time," her uncle turned to his wife, "Explain to these young girls."

"Bina, you know that blood is impure blood. Why are you questioning such basics?"

Binapani retorted, "So why don't they ask people to purify their minds too before they enter the temple? Because it is harder to do? That is hardly a justification for keeping the woman out of the temple."

"You feminists should realize you have the lower castes in the same boat. So it is not just about women and temples. We all agree it was a corruption."

Anand came to placate his wife, "Bina, I told you the stories of the erudite women of ancient India. Surely they went to the gurukulas. Only later when Brahminism was on the rise did such divisions creep in. And now in modern times, amends are being made. There is a quota for women in medical colleges, as well as for the backward castes."

"There are women's football teams in every state and at national level Bina-didi, and teams for hockey and volleyball too." Raja was trying to help Anand.

"And yet female foetuses are killed. And girls' fathers are chased years after the wedding for replenishing the dowry. And if he cannot comply she is tortured, and sometimes killed." Savita continued the tirade, "Girls are sold into houses of ill repute to fund the family coffers."

Binapani's uncle shook his head, "A social stigma is difficult to erase with government policies. Tell me, Martin Luther King Jr in America fought for black equality just the other day. How many years was it after the actual abolition of slavery? A hundred years. People's sentiments had not endorsed Lincoln's signature. But in time the structure will change, as more and more outstanding examples of women and persons of backward classes make their mark. Consider Ambedkar."

Anand's father continued, "That's an excellent example. We know Dr Babasaheb Ambedkar as the chief architect for drafting our Constitution. But do you know where his story begins? He was from the untouchable caste, which is a notch lower than the shudra."

Anand explained, "His classmates shunned him and even when he wanted to drink water the peon poured it from a height into his palms. The cup or the peon would not risk being contaminated, and of course none of Ambedkar's kind could touch the tap. But he was so brilliant he passed all the entrance examinations and became a lawyer of great repute."

"And he remembered the pathetic treatment he had suffered. So he fought for creating reservations for women and backward classes in educational institutions and government jobs. The decree was ratified into the Constitution."

"A few months before his death he converted to Buddhism, a religion he had admired from childhood and which did not have the caste system. He then officiated in the conversion of thousands of untouchables. They adopted a new name for themselves – the dalit, a word that means 'those who are trampled upon.'"

Anand caught up with the ladies and turned them around. "At least middle class India has realized its folly, and there are millions of us now. Every year educational institutions have more and more students and these modern gurukulas are multiplying too. Watch and be patient, many changes will happen in one generation." The ladies strode ahead, noses in the air.

"Oh, did I tell you I have bought tickets for Ghulam Ali's concert?"

Two sweet voices chimed in, "Ghulam Ali, king of ghazal, you mean?"

"Yes, love songs, do you think you tigresses will enjoy them?"

Ghulam Ali was a singer from Pakistan with an enormous following in India. His songs were on the immortal theme of love, the heartbreaks, the vigil, the reunion, passionate love, reciprocated, unrequited, devotional love, dead paramours, martyred emotions, defiant and shy, lost and regained. The ladies had turned into purring cats and each gave Anand a pat with a clawless paw. "Ah women!" he thought, "At least they were easier to placate than men."

Chapter Twelve

Mohan

The celebrations had ended in the refugee camps, and hard reality was creeping in. There were people everywhere, and queues for the toilets, queues for a plate of rice and dal, queues for drinking water.

Madhumati shivered under the blanket, "I think we should travel deeper into the country to find some work. We have been here long enough and I am afraid an epidemic will break out. I don't think medicines will reach on time. As long as we have our van we are much better off than most people here."

Sulaiman agreed, "Shall we go to Murshidabad? Imran chacha from our part of Sonargaon had once said there is a silk factory there where he was going to work. Maybe he is still around and could help me get a job."

So again they loaded the van and started towards Murshidabad. From 1206 CE India was ruled by several dynasties of Turkic warlords and Afghan chieftains. Then from 1526 the Mughals from Central Asia made India their home. They chose Dhaka as the capital of Bengal – the state which also included Bihar and Assam at that time. When the Portuguese had landed in the port of Chittagong, they were repelled by the Nawab, the Mughal deputy of Bengal. The British too were forced back in the Anglo-Mughal war. During the reign of Aurangzeb, a few years before the Mughal empire dissolved, three villages were sold to the British East India Company. They were Gobindapur, Sutanuti and Kalikata – the latter pronounced "Calcutta" by the Europeans. It is from this foothold that the Company enlarged its presence and eventually ruled India. After Aurangzeb died, the Nawab of Bengal, Murshid Quli Khan, cut off ties with Delhi and shifted his capital from Dhaka to a small town closer to Calcutta, which he renamed Murshidabad. In the battle of Plassey, a location near Murshidabad, the East India Company ousted the last Nawab in 1757. Then in a series of engagements, they gained the rest of Bengal from the Portuguese, the Dutch and the French.

Sulaiman was right about Murshidabad – his willingness to work hard earned him a job in the silk industry. He would have preferred to pull a pair of bullocks and make the earth yield a staple diet, but one could hardly complain since they were lucky to find shelter and subsistence within weeks of their arrival. At least this work with the silk worms provided him proximity to nature and fresh air. Madhumati also worked to reel the silk, while Rahim lay on her lap.

It is believed the rearing of silk worms and the extraction of silk from their cocoons was kept a secret in China for a long time. Demand for this delicate fabric created a trade route that connected the Far East to the Mediterranean world. The Silk Route bifurcated from Tibet and slipped through the Himalayan pass into India. On its way to the ports of the Bay of Bengal, it passed through Murshidabad. Silk was dearly sought after in Japan, India, Russia, Korea and these countries eventually developed their own flourishing industries giving China stiff competition. Depending on the climate and the food given to silk worms, different species thrive, thus creating different textures of the cloth. In Bengal, Karnataka, Kashmir and Uttar Pradesh mulberry plants are cultivated to make the mulberry silk. Other silks in India are the muga of the Brahmaputra Valley, the tassar is grown in thick jungles of Bihar, Madhya Pradesh and Orissa, and the eri is cultivated in Assam and Orissa. The female deposits about 400 eggs, each the size of a pin head. In six weeks they become three inches long, are fed continually, and shed their skin four times. The larva secretes a thin filament, which is the silk, and in a week makes a cocoon. Some cocoons are kept for breeding and the rest are boiled and the thread is rolled around a reel. It is a very labour-intensive industry, which is a blessing for India since she has ample hands looking for work.

Madhumati had set up a chulha in their hut and she was

kneading the dough for the flat breads, rotis. "Mia sahib, I am tired of lying to these innocent women."

"What are you lying about?"

"That I am Mumtaz, but in reality I am still Madhumati."

"Oh that!" He had almost forgotten about it. "That can be fixed in an hour. All we need is to find two witnesses."

"Is that all? When we get married, it is a long process. We call upon Prajapati to witness the union. He has to be invoked with much supplication."

"Who is he? Some priest of the temple?"

"No, no," laughed Madhumati, "He is the creator of the universe. He is also known as Brahma. You know we have three main Gods, who were not born, that is, not conceived in a womb. They are the original three principles that rule everything that is born – the jagat. One creates the universe, another preserves it and the third destroys it."

"Why is the third needed?"

"Because it is a cyclical process. Again and again these creations are made and remade."

"How many times?"

"There is no end to this process. Every cycle has four stages; we call each of these a yuga. After the four yugas there is complete destruction and yet again the four yugas begin. Thus the universe goes on forever."

"How long does a yuga last?"

"It lasts as long as it takes the Father of the Creation, literally the praja pati, to blink an eye. In our human terms, it is thousands of years."

"Oh, then it is all an imagination. Nobody has lived that long to witness the change of yuga or the return of the cycle."

"There are seers who have that perception. They can see beyond time. Can you fathom timelessness, or a time before Time? Everything we can hold in our thoughts has a beginning."

"No, I don't think the sky has a beginning. It just stretches on and on from the western horizon to the eastern, neither with a beginning nor an ending."

"That, mia sahib, is in terms of space. But time is another concept. All this we touch – the mud, the grass, this pot, Rahim, the tube-well – each has a beginning. Can you believe that there is any one thing that is eternal?"

"Allah."

"Yes, we recite in our prayers, we know the word 'eternal', but we cannot grasp it."

"Mumtaz begum, you make my head spin. Let me set up our plain and simple nikah."

Life goes on smoothly until a thorn called aspiration or ambition pokes us in the seat. "There would be more money working as a miner," said a new recruit. He himself was tired of the stuffy mines and had a breathing problem. "But Sulaiman, you are strong, why don't you go to Asansol? There is a better paying coal miner's job waiting for you there. And don't be a fool to go cycling in this rickety van." Yes, she was fast wearing out with the long journeys and like a grandmother wept her complaints at every pedal stroke. So Sulaiman sold his mute companion and went on to meet a new challenge, travelling by bus.

In Asansol it rained coal dust from the sky. Clothes on lines became black, faces were powdered with the soot, roads were tarred with the flakes and the earth was peppered with chunks of coal. This was the coalfield. Five times a day the azan, the call to prayer, blared from the many mosques. Throngs of miners lived in the slums. Many spoke Hindi as this town was on the Bengal-Bihar border. They lived with their goats and chicken in shanties that used the cement walls of big houses as backbone. When the house owners yelled at them for dirtying their walls, they fought back thrusting their rolling pins in the air like swords. The women swore and spat, the men went under the earth and choked themselves in foul air. They coughed black lumps from their throat, they breathed with difficulty below in the moist holes, and soon above too. Mumtaz caught Sulaiman's hand rubbing his eyes red, "We will die here. Let us return to Murshidabad."

"So soon? No, they will laugh at me. Let us go further. I hear there is a better mining town in Bihar."

Thus they reached Jamshedpur. An industrialist from Bombay wanted to create an iron and steel factory and came to Bihar, rich in all sorts of minerals. Here on the dry earth beside the mines, he planted a tree. Within years that tree gave birth to a whole township arrayed with shaded avenues and houses with gardens. Scientists and engineers from around the country settled here and made it a thriving city ringing with the cheerful cries of children. A school was set up, then a hospital, a police station, a cinema hall and soon Jamshedpur was a coveted place to live in. Men worked in the Tata Iron and Steel Company, TISCO, and came up with the best formula for making steel out of the iron ore. The steel held bridges and electricity pylons throughout the vast country, and at home water filters and pressure cookers had their origins in the iron ores of Bihar. On the darker side of the moon there were the miners' quarters. But the Ali couple agreed that brown earth was better than black coal. The iron ore was hard to dig, did not flake off like coal, but here the air was easier to breathe. Mumtaz tied a cloth towel on her head and carried the dolly of heavy clods. It was hard labour that broke backs and made the skin raw with sores. Bihar was drier than Bengal too. Once in a while they reminisced about that land with red soil and banana groves and water, lots and lots of water, in streams, in ponds, in the delta, in rivers, falling generously from the sky. Here the only moisture was sweat and spit.

One day a man mingled in their crowd and enticed them to yet another labourers' adventure. "Not another mine!" grumbled Sulaiman. He longed to work in fields, to touch the living earth, to plant a sapling in the soil and see her grow. But Mumtaz had already packed their small belongings and was headed towards her new destination, back on the bus. It was as if they were returning to a new place, same as the one before. Or was it? To all superficial viewers, Jaduguda was just another mining town, craters and supervisors, women balancing dollies and men with pick axes. Every day new workers joined the existing crowd. "What did they dig for here?" wondered Mumtaz. On the first day they were made to queue up, all the newcomers. As the line inched closer to the desk of the man chewing a paan, Mumtaz saw every person repeated the same action.

"Name?"

The labourer mumbled his name, which was written down. Then he pressed his right thumb in a pad of ink and marked it on a paper.

"Next!" The man spat out some betel juice for every fourth person.

Mumtaz's forehead was creased in doubt. This custom was new. Why would the mine owners make the workers sign? Did they care about the workers? Was this some new injunction that the owners had to provide medication for an injured man? Maybe that is what it was. They cared for the poor. When they reached the desk, she slipped ahead of Sulaiman.

"I can sign my name. May I borrow your pen?"

The man looked her up and down and scowled. "If you are educated, why then are you working in a mine?"

"We have come from Bangladesh during the recent war. And we have not found any other job."

"Oh, I see. Here, use my pen." Mumtaz turned the page around to sign but took her time to read the contents. The man was getting irritated. "How long does it take you to sign? Do you have to draw your name or write it?"

She ignored him and kept reading. It was in English.

"I hereby declare to have understood the full impact of the hazardous nature of this occupation and absolve the Government of India of all consequences that may befall me upon this undertaking." So this was different because it was not a private company like Tata, but the Government of India. But the word "hazardous" made her wonder. She had to know more. She pulled Sulaiman aside and told him about her presentiment. The man at the counter did not understand what they spoke, as it was in

Bengali, but he was trained to catch the offbeat notes. He snatched the paper from her hand and waved the two of them away. "Next."

Mumtaz wanted to do her own investigation. They walked among the crowd of men and asked them,

"Do you know why you had to put your thumbprints?"

"We did not ask. Who asks such silly questions? Do I need to earn my daily wage or waste time in talking?"

"What are you mining?"

"Who cares, there are so many kinds of metal. For us it is all the same, lumps of obstinate earth."

"But no, this is different. That thing you signed said it was harmful to your health."

One of them bared his black teeth. "I have worked in coal mines. My lungs are worse than a cigarette smoker's. This kind of mining hardly comes close to it."

One man straightened up. "No, brother, maybe we should find out what we signed for. My uncle once signed for something he could not read, and he was pauperized. He used to own a plot of land, and now his wife is a maidservant and he pulls a rickshaw."

Some more men had stopped working and had crowded around Sulaiman and Mumtaz.

"So what are we mining?"

"I don't know, it is my first day here, but we did not sign the paper. What if there are explosions? What if the thing you touch or breathe is like some poison?"

The supervisor walked in, shouting in his querulous voice, "None of you will get paid today. Get back to work, dogs. And you two, come with me, creating trouble! You must be from Bengal. We have no miners' union here, and we don't want the Communist nonsense in our mines."

They were marched to the main building. Mumtaz looked up at the sign above the entrance. One word she did not know stuck in her mind – uranium. Whatever this "uranium" was, it had to be known. The man in the office stretched his legs, threw back his arms and yawned. "You two, what do you want here? Seems like you were distracting those hard-working men?" The supervisor pointed at Mumtaz. "The lady here knows English. They are from Bangladesh. Refugees."

The man sat up and placed his hairy elbows on the desk. "Achha, is that so? Why, we could do with a school teacher. Would you like to teach?"

Mumtaz looked up at Sulaiman beside her and his eyes were as bright as hers. "Yes, surely. Give me one chance and I will show how well I teach."

The slouching man looked her up and down lustfully. "Yes, I can imagine that. So how about you meet me here in the morning? Come before noon. A bus leaves at that time, and mind you, it is not a city bus that runs every few minutes. It runs once a day. And you," he looked at Sulaiman, "You can start tomorrow. No, just come, we will see to the signing business later. You have an educated wife, you are a class apart." He laughed emitting a blob of betel juice that trickled down his chin.

The next day Mumtaz nursed Rahim and handed him to Sulaiman, "If Gopal wants our fate to change he can pull the reins and the chariot horses will run in a counter direction." She wore her best sari. She had been a diligent student at school and was married based on her good education, rather than her family's wealth. Her father had hardly any money left after marrying off his two elder daughters, even to entertain guests with the feast, leave alone producing a dowry. Luckily the in-laws in Sonargaon, although poor, believed education to be a person's real wealth. And now at last she was about to embark on that sacred journey. She touched Sulaiman's feet, much to his embarrassment, and went out to meet the man. He was there lazing around and got up when she came in. The bus picked them in a few minutes. It shook like a tin of powdered milk and the conductor banged on its side, increasing the noise. Surely, its nuts and bolts would have marked its path back. A calf was mooing for its mother close to the entrance. Chickens flapped their wings at every jerk. Many sweaty bodies were packed tight like paddy in a sheaf. Mumtaz stood holding the bar above and he was behind her, pushing her with his body. She felt terribly uncomfortable and when his hand started touching her stomach below the blouse, she hissed, "Behave yourself!"

"To get something, you must also give, begum, haven't you learnt this simple principle of life?"

A man wearing a clean shirt and trousers, perhaps the only polished man in the bus, was sitting within earshot. He heard her and immediately got up. "Behenji, sister, you can sit here." She thanked him and quickly slipped into his vacated seat. He took her place and towered above the lascivious factory middle man. "Where are you going?" He asked her in Hindi. The man behind answered, "Hey mister, don't you get too cosy with strangers."

Mumtaz answered him in English. "This man said he will take me to a school to be a teacher. And on the way he wants to take as much advantage as he can get away with."

Mohan, for that was the name of the gentleman, was surprised. "What school? Do you know the name of the place?"

"No, who is going to talk to this lout! He will think I am trying to familiarize myself with him. I don't want to step on his shadow any more."

Mohan thought for a while, "The bus is going to Ranchi and it will be evening when it reaches there. In between there are villages, but these are the poorest of the poor. I doubt if there is any school."

She looked up sharply. Her escort, who was itching to stop this conversation he did not understand, now felt it had gone too far.

"Come, time for us to get down."

She looked out. There was nothing to be seen around, no telegraph post, no well, no field to indicate human habitation close by.

He was shaking his hand in an irritated fashion. "Come,

what are you looking at outside? The bus has not stopped yet, it will stop in a proper place."

Mohan accosted her crude escort, "Hey, where are you taking her?"

"What is that to you, mister?" The man raised his voice, "Fellow wants to steal my woman, watch out, the rest of you!" he guffawed, at the same time prodding Mumtaz towards the exit. She protested, but he kept nudging her. Finally she was holding on to the door handle desperately, asking herself if the bus would stop at all. Then she heard a cry behind her, and the next moment she was flying out of the bus.

Mohan had sensed foul play and had followed the ruffian to the exit. Then to his surprise he saw the man getting ready to push Mumtaz out of the door. The bus showed no intention of slowing down, but something had to be done immediately. Mohan raised the attaché case he was holding and brought it crashing down on the mischief-monger's head. The next events happened in quick succession. The man screamed in pain, but managed to shove Mumtaz out of the bus. The push was weak as the bus lurched – the driver had jammed the breaks on after hearing the cry. All eyes were now turned on the man at the doorstep, and some necks did impossible twists to look outside the window. Cursing away violently, the rowdy stretched his arm and banged on the bus's side, signalling the driver to pick up speed. Mohan leaped out of the moving vehicle expertly, and ran alongside to slow himself down. The bus with its commotion of questioning voices disappeared behind a cloud of dust. Mohan rushed to the fallen figure. Mumtaz had hit her side instead of landing head on. Her arm was bleeding and her forehead was bruised, but she was conscious.

Mohan helped her up and made her sit on a rock, "By the Lord's grace you have survived. This wound is nothing compared to what was intended." She was breathing in quick bursts of shock and fear. The landscape was barren, not even a blade of grass grew here. He clicked open his attaché case.

"Are you a doctor?" she asked hoping he had some first-aid kit tucked in there.

"I wish I was one, for your sake." He turned around the attaché for her to inspect. She saw a jumble of wires and some plastic pieces shaped cunningly. "This is a radio. Now I will call the jeep from the factory to pick us up."

Mumtaz could have cried with joy. This was better than first aid. "Hey Gopal, hey Jagannath, hey Krishna, hey Mohan, I thank your infinite compassion." She had spoken aloud without knowing it as her ears, still in shock, could not grasp what her mouth had said. Mohan joked, "How did you know my name?"

"I do not know your name!"

"Yes, you just thanked me. I am Mohan."

"Oh," she said, wondering at the coincidence, which her mind said was not a coincidence at all. Who else but He comes to help His devotees. *Na me bhakta pranashyati.* That is what He told Arjuna in the Gita. One who adores me shall ever be protected.

"I am Mumtaz."

Mohan interrupted his radio setup and looked at her. "Are you Muslim then? I thought I heard you pray to Krishna?"

"A bit of both you could say."

"Then you are like the saint, Kabir – both at the same time. You know I don't like to differentiate either; it is all the same whatever name you give it."

"Yes," she agreed it was all the same. Her real story was too long to relate to him. He called headquarters. She was fascinated by this method of communication, out in the middle of nowhere, but not lost at all.

"The jeep will be here faster than it took the bus to come."

Mohan leaned on the rock. "Now tell me the real story. Why did he try to kill you? I suppose you know he tried that. At first I thought he was going to sell you to a ...," he hesitated, "Well, you know what they do with women." Mumtaz told him about the form she had read. Then of course he asked her how she was educated and very soon she had conveyed her life's story in gist.

"You are a lucky woman, you know, because I will tell you what uranium is." He jumped back to his attaché and got out an instrument which looked similar to a radio. It had a needle too. "This is a Geiger Counter. Come let us take a walk, if you can." She had wrapped her sari round her wound. Mohan remarked, "Ah, the many advantages of the one-piece Indian traditional clothing. Use it as bandage, as blanket, as handkerchief, to collect fruits, to wipe yourself, to shade yourself, to veil yourself, all the while wearing it too." If needed, she could cut the sari in half and still be well covered, for it was six yards long. They wandered around the barren surface, Geiger Counter in hand. After a point they heard the instrument make "cluck cluck" sounds like a chicken. Then it started as though flapping its wings and clucking louder. Mohan stopped and noted the readings of the instrument in his pocket notebook. Then he started walking around the place and noted where the Geiger Counter became silent.

"So what is uranium?" reminded Mumtaz to Mohan.

"This fellow here, Mister Geiger Counter, tells us that under this earth there is uranium. In a few months miners will come here to ease it out. It will be shipped to the laboratory in Bombay. There they will extract it and send it to the Tarapur reactor to generate electricity, and to Kalpakkam and the other nuclear reactors under construction. They will also keep some of it for research."

"But is then uranium like iron, or copper? Why did we have to sign that declaration?"

Mohan decided to start at the very beginning. "Do you remember how the Second World War came to an end?"

"The Axis powers surrendered – Germany, Italy and Japan."

"Yes Japan. Two atomic bombs were dropped there. Atomic bombs are bombs made of uranium and its cousin, the element, plutonium. The Hiroshima bomb was of uranium and the Nagasaki a plutonium one."

"I see, uranium is the name of that element. So are you making bombs here? And therefore are scared that some may burst?"

"No, we are not making bombs at all in India. The world has

seen the enormous amount of energy a nuclear fission can release. Fission is what makes the bomb explode. We in India want to control that power and use it to light our tube lights at home."

"But I still don't understand why it is more dangerous than coal. People get asthma in the coalfields."

"Mining is a very difficult job. A man can take it only that long. Then he has to find some other occupation."

"Mohan sahib, you are still not telling me why we had to sign."

"That is because after that incident in Japan they found people who lived there got cancer. And then children born after the war had twisted limbs and other internal deformities."

"What are you saying? How are you hiding this from the miners?"

"Asthma can kill, but cancer kills faster. It is a question of months or years. But then coal dust can also cause lung cancer, and cigarette smoking does it too. There is something in uranium that could cause cancer if a person is exposed to it for long."

"How long is 'long'?"

"Mumtaz, you ask too many questions. But I am a nuclear scientist and I will tell you something. Life is hazardous, whether in an iron mine or a manufacturing factory, or in the streets. People die in the heat with no water to drink, they die of mosquito bites, they die of wrong medication, they die of broken limbs, they die in wars, they die in factory accidents, in laboratory mishaps. We all take risks. And the plain truth about making the mine workers sign is that the government has collaborated with other countries in this project. You know the USA and Canada are helping us with the reactors. The first reactor at Tarapur, that is now supplying so much electricity, was built by an American company. So we want to keep our papers straight."

The nuclear programme in India began shortly before Independence. Homi Jehangir Bhabha, who was schooled in Bombay, continued his education in Britain, and did his research in theoretical physics. He was a brilliant scientist who had worked alongside the pioneers of quantum physics in Europe. He was vacationing in India when the Second World War broke out in 1939. The war changed many fates. The men he had worked with, Enrico Fermi in Rome and Niels Bohr in Copenhagen, who themselves were close friends, were called by the American scientist, Robert Oppenheimer, for a top secret research project. It was nicknamed the "Manhattan project" which produced the world's first atomic bombs. Bhabha stayed back in India to create the nuclear research centres in Bombay with funding from Tata. The Tata Institute of Fundamental Research (TIFR), was born. A few years later he founded another facility that is now named after him, the Bhabha Atomic Research Centre (BARC). After the war the United States wanted to erase its image as the nuclear weapons state, and so started a programme called "Atoms for Peace". They provided expertise and low interest loans to several developing nations to set up reactors. It was also a way to ensure the Soviet Union stayed out of these fledgling states. The understanding was that these countries would not manufacture weapons, but would use nuclear energy solely for generating power. The first Indian reactor, at Tarapur, close to Bombay, was constructed by General Electric. Then came the research project CIRUS, a Canada, India and US collaboration, CIRUS being an acronym for the three countries and the word "Reactor" inserted in it. It is because India had international partners she wanted to keep her record books clean in the nuclear programme.

Mohan continued, "I have to map this whole region and recommend setting up mines. Bihar is very rich in minerals." Mumtaz nodded. This was already their third mining experience.

"So can India make a bomb too?"

"Yes, she can, but she does not want to. You know, our first Prime Minister, Jawaharlal Nehru, championed the CTBT at the same time as he was founding the Non-Aligned Movement."

"CTBT?"

"Comprehensive Test Ban Treaty. It means no country can manufacture bombs, since we have all witnessed the danger of such a bomb. An atomic bomb has a long-range effect. If it is dropped on Delhi, the whole city will become ashes within minutes. Then the waters of the Yamuna and the air will be polluted with radioactive elements. They are the ones that cause cancer. They will travel in the air around the whole globe, of course getting dilute, but eventually their traces will be found all over."

"Do you mean we are affected by the bombs that were dropped in Japan?"

"As a layman I would say 'yes', because the air cannot be trapped around the earth. But as a scientist I cannot prove it because we cannot determine the source of individual atoms. Some of the radioactive elements went out in outer space, but how can one guarantee none of it is still in our atmosphere?"

"This atomic bomb sounds much worse than any other bomb. I hope nobody ever uses it again."

"That is why Nehru wanted all the countries that had nuclear power to sign the CTBT. He envisioned a world in peaceful harmony."

"And who are these countries that have nuclear power? Did they all sign it?"

"These are the five members of the Security Council in the United Nations. Why they have maintained their supremacy over the other hundred and fifty is another story, or rather history, or perhaps mystery. All these five have nuclear energy facilities. So they signed a partial version of the CTBT in 1957, but created another treaty called Non Proliferation Treaty, NPT, where it said no one can test nuclear weapons any more. But here is the catch. These countries had already done their tests, and now they could just manufacture the weapons. But the rest of the world was being prohibited from having weapons, that is, if they agreed to sign the NPT. India objected to this privileged treatment, and did not sign. But many other countries signed it in 1968 when it was finalized."

Mohan was talking about nuclear disarmament, knowing well that at that very moment some others were extracting plutonium from the used-up uranium in the CIRUS reactor. China had tested her nuclear device in 1964, the Bangladesh War had brought the US and the USSR navies, both loaded with nuclear weapons, into an eyeball-to-eyeball confrontation. Nehru with his vision of a harmonious world was dead, Bhabha's pacifist successor to the department of Atomic Energy, Vikram Sarabhai, was also dead. The bomb lobby in the Indian parliament wanted to use nuclear weapons as a deterrent, which meant, not to actually drop a bomb, but to wave it in the face of enemies as a threat.

The jeep had come and picked up a wiser Mumtaz. She had made two promises to herself and she would fight tooth and nail for them. One, she would make her son a scientist, like Mohan. Two, she would earn money by teaching. And for these she would work every hour of the day if necessary. For Rahim's education she would not stay in this dust bowl for long. He would go to a school that taught English and learn about the ideas that shape the world. That very night the Ali family packed to leave. Some asked, "Is it because you didn't want to sign that paper? Is there something wrong in this mine? Tell us. We want to be forewarned."

There is something wrong in being poor and illiterate and helpless. That is what she would mend. But to these labourers she said, "This mine is like any other, unhygienic and back breaking. Don't linger here till you are sick and broken in spirit. Find something else to do other than mining. But rest assured it is no worse than any other. We are Bengalis and pine to return home." And so back they went to the humid clime of Bengal, stopping at no mining town this time, all the way to Calcutta, the big city with good schools and urban dreams.

Within days good luck struck the Ali family. An aged man pulling his rickshaw was found coughing on the roadside, and Sulaiman tended to his needs, becoming his adopted son. They looked after him as they would have looked after their own father, and when the old man died, Sulaiman continued to live in his shanty and rode his rickshaw. Thus the many streams that mingled their waters formed a delta. Human lives were stitched together in a patchwork that created a roof, a shelter, a home. Mumtaz went from school to school to find a job. And finally in a small primary education school she was made a teacher. It was a beginning. She dressed well in a clean sari so that none could guess she lived in a canvas hut. She rationed her food to buy soap, and woke up in the early hours of the morning to pump water from the tube well. She was as good as any middle class, educated, confident young lady of the metropolis. Women had just started moving about freely alone in the streets and applying for jobs. Of course, there were families that considered a working wife an insult to the husband. They said such a woman had bartered her honour for money. But there were women who wanted to become independent. They pointed to the lady prime minister and went about their task of finding a niche in a man's world.

Mumtaz soon became a favourite teacher and parents approached her for tutoring their children outside of school hours. The added benefit of Mumtaz as tutor was that she would take private lessons in people's homes, where the children could be supervised by their parents. She was willing to walk long distances, squeeze herself in a crowded bus and reach the home of the little girl or boy who needed to learn English. They gave her an inexpensive sari for the pooja, feeling apologetic, not knowing how much their kindness meant. She accepted all the gifts as given by Gopal himself. He was consenting to her zest for life, her sacrifice, her hard work, and her aspirations. She listened to the English news on the radio and practised correct pronunciation. She noted down words she did not know and at school looked them up in the dictionary. More and more students who wanted to escape the Bengali dialect of English often taught in schools sought her help. Sulaiman left the rickshaw and graduated to the position of a taxi driver. They worked day and night, saving money to rent a flat and educate Rahim. They were like so many young couples dreaming to launch a ship from their roadside gutter.

Chapter Thirteen

Savita

On holidays and often after college, Savita came to her brother's house and kept herself busy tidying up the place. She disposed of the old newspapers, and haggled with the vegetable vendor when he passed by ringing his bell. The bai was made to dust and scrub while she cooked a grand meal. Anand always complimented her cuisine and then they went into cyclone speed Marathi, and Binapani slipped into her own dream world. Savita bathed Panchali after a long oil massage. Binapani peeped in while the elaborate process was on and sniffed the air, "My mother says mustard oil is good for the skin. It helps in the circulation."

A reply bounced back, "Good, then in the mornings you should give her a mustard oil massage." Savita was at best curt with her sister-in-law. She observed Binapani reading a novel while she folded the clothes. "You should read Crime and Punishment. It is a Russian author, too. Don't you adore such novels? Or maybe you should read the existentialists. Have you read The Outsider, by Camus?" What she really meant with such comments was too much trouble for Binapani to comprehend. She had to at most re-read the lines Savita's words interrupted.

One day, Savita was in a particularly vicious mood, maybe because it had rained and the clothes hanging outside got wet, without Binapani realizing it. She hissed, "Bye bhabhi, and thanks for ruining my brother's life." Binapani was incensed. She sat up and tossed the book aside. "Savita, what did you just say?" The answer was a crash of the main door.

When Anand returned, his cheerful humming self, Binapani told him. "Look, I think Savita should spend some more time with her friends instead of running our household. I can manage the cooking, washing, and bathing Panchali."

Anand explained, "I know you can do all that. It is not for you that she comes."

Binapani wondered if she could really pull off what she boasted. She had not stepped in a kitchen all her life.

"Savita needs to be occupied in some work to keep her mind off ... besides what good are her friends? They go to see films to be teased by those loafing boys outside the hall whistling tunes for them."

"Like *Chaudhavi ka Chand*?" Reminded of their own little escapade in the early days of their courtship, they both laughed. But that was not the last of the bloodletting between the non-blood relatives.

Another day Anand was out and Savita was her chirpy self flying around the house. Then Panchali started crying and Binapani called out for help, "Savita, why is the baby crying?" Savita came in and she was a ball of fire, some mother Durga in salwar kameez. "The baby is hungry. Oh, don't bother, dream girl, I will get her to you."

Binapani aroused herself from the bed.

"I have been bearing enough of your nonsense, Savita. Why do you come here if it is such a burden?"

"Because otherwise you will neglect my brother and end up killing your daughter. No, correction, the baby."

"Listen, just because I did not need to cook so far does not mean I cannot."

Savita paused in front of her sister-in-law, "All right, how many whistles for rice? How many for dal?"

Whistles? Wondered Binapani. Savita's nostrils flared like a mare's.

"Pressure cooker whistles! Tell me, sapno ki rani, dream girl, why did you marry my brother?" Binapani was about to speak. "Oh, stop it!" cried Savita, "I know what you will say – I did not, he married me. I will tell you why. You had nowhere else to go and my brother was the kindest, stupidest man to fall in this trap."

Binapani sat up defiantly and answered back, "Yes, I had one place to go and your brother forced me back. And I am ready to depart any moment. The train does not seem to arrive."

Savita gasped. What was she talking about?

"Really Savita, I mean it. It can be quick and easy. I will write a letter, no one will suspect you. Don't you have a pharmacist uncle somewhere? He will surely know of some method. You will have done your beloved brother a big favour too."

Savita stared at Binapani in horror. Is this what Anand had warned her about once? This must be why he treated her like a china doll, delicate and easily breakable.

She softened, "Bhabhi, I am sorry. I did not mean to be rude. It is just so warm here, and Panchali has been crying the whole day. I think she has prickly heat. Let me get the powder." Savita was scared now. If Binapani did something drastic, her brother would drown himself in sorrow. She loved her brother so much it was not love any more, but fear. She was afraid fate would snatch her only brother from her just to play a nasty trick on her. Maybe, just maybe, Anand loved Binapani that badly, and he too was scared to lose her.

Savita returned with a cup of tea. Binapani let her take Panchali and tuck her in bed with pleasant baby talks. Her daughter giggled and responded with little cries of joy. When Panchali would start talking she would call Savita Aai, and know her, Binapani, distantly as her wet nurse.

"Savita, sit. No, not on the chair, sit here on the bed beside me. Listen, I love your brother."

"Bhabhi, please I am sorry. Don't tell him about it, let's forget what happened."

"Will you teach me to cook?"

"I will be here, bhabhi. I am not going to abandon you three. Besides, I love to cook."

"Savita, what are you hiding? Or is it some person you are hiding from?"

Savita sat like a clay idol. Then slowly tears started trickling down her eyes. Binapani put a clumsy hand round her shoulder, trying to be a sister she had no practice being. "Aren't we sisters? You can tell me."

Savita just cried and shook her head. After all Binapani had hardly won her confidence.

By the time Anand returned home sunshine was flooding in. Binapani was bathing Panchali under Savita's supervision, which meant the sacred Bengali formula of mustard oil was dismissed. That night Binapani asked Anand,

"Is Savita escaping from some event in her life?"

Anand replied absentmindedly, "Not that I am aware of."

"Oh, so you won't tell me. Some family secret, and of course I am the outsider."

"No, Bina, it's just not a pleasant story. And we want Savita to forget about it."

"But you know she hasn't."

Anand was alert, "How do you know? What did she tell you?"

"Nothing. That's the problem. She just kept crying."

"Why Bina, why did she start crying?"

"Because she was sad and I thought someone had broken her heart."

"Bina, don't talk to her about love, please. You know maybe I should have warned you before. All right, I will tell you what happened. Sit." Anand began his sister's story.

"About a year back she started going to a college in Churchgate, you know the one close to the Gateway of India, the most exciting place in Bombay. Opposite the bus stop there was a photo studio. She used to frequent that stop, sometimes with friends, sometimes alone. Twice a day, in the morning on the wind running, in the evening on the water, waiting."

A photo landed on the open page of the book Savita was reading. She saw herself in it, balancing on one foot in the act of hopping off the bus. The surrounding was blurred and she was in clear focus. She had never seen such a beautiful picture of herself. She looked up to find a young man beside her, looking rather shy. They talked and kept meeting at the bus stop. He worked as an assistant cameraman in the film industry and developed his photographs here. He took her to a tour of the studio and there she was aghast to find more of herself – ringed by friends, smiling at her book, her face in a sepia tint, her looking up at the sky, with the clouds reflecting in her iris. He was no ordinary photographer. He was a real artist with a fantastic future ahead. He lived with the camera in hand and often saw the world through his lenses, his filters, his framed harmonies. They roamed around the city. He clicked away while she talked or laughed or pondered. They walked on the beach, under the arch of the Gateway, cooped up under window shades during sudden showers, sat on rocks facing the sea watching the clouds sail by. "Chirp chirp" clicked the camera's tongue immortalizing the Savita song bird. She and Shaan became the talk of the other girls. When they teased her, she just played along with them to give them some pleasure, for she herself was safely nestled in Shaan's heart.

Shaan handed Savita a strip of paper.

"Shaan, I thought this was another photograph of mine."

"You are getting greedy, jaan-e-man."

"Today it is jaan-e-man, yesterday it was dilruba?"

"Don't they mean the same things? Yesterday you were my sweetheart, today you are my heartthrob."

"Flatterer, you pick these up from the songs you are shooting."

"Sorry, I did not know education happened in sleep. I have a conventional way of learning, from what I hear and see."

"Pardoned, I like the way you apply your knowledge. So what is this paper?"

"It is better than your picture. Now don't get upset, I can take your photo any day, but this is valid for just a day. It is a pass into the film city."

"Pass? Why do we need a pass to enter the film city?"

"Otherwise a million people will crowd there, waiting for some director to discover them. Everybody wants to be a hero. But getting a chance to act is not easy. Connections matter, and of course, talent and looks too. Directors don't just pass by school year end programmes to pick up good actresses; they go to the performing arts' institutes and handpick the best. Of course if you are part of the family, then you have better chances, same as the tradition of the classical music. If you are born in a gharana, musical family, then you are automatically trained into its culture."

"So are you going to shoot some Kapoor family offshoot?"

"No, this man is fresh on the scene – your favourite hero."

"And mister, how do you know my choice?"

"Now let me guess ..." Shaan pretended to scratch his head, then blurted, "Amitabh Bachchan?"

"Wrong."

"Not possible. Every girl loves his angry young man attitude. Even when he is the underworld don, you love his righteousness towards, say, his mother. When he is drunk, it is because he was ditched. When he is fighting it is to save a girl he did not know till that minute. When he is dancing involving all his six feet, of height I meant, that becomes the style for the next Ganapati procession."

"But I must admit Amitabh has the best voice. Remember that last dialogue when his friend, Anand, died, anand marta nahi, meaning 'happiness does not die'? It gave me goosebumps."

"Yes, the film, Anand, launched Amitabh Bachchan like a comet into the starry sky. It helped that the seasoned actor, Rajesh Khanna, played Anand, who was dying of cancer. People loved the film and it created a lot of awareness for the disease. And yes, that famous bass measured tone of Amitabh! Ten girls in a row can get pierced by his single arrow. Through the heart, out of the back, into the next one's heart and so on. Bam bam bam, all ten dying for him."

"You are so jealous, all you men."

Shaan was lost in the crowd of electricians, prop setters, makeup girls rushing in and out, the man holding the umbrella during breaks, the director sweating, Amitabh towering above all. Savita saw the wooden plates that were clicked on every shoot with the name "Abhiman" on it. Two people were talking business, throwing up astronomical figures. Maybe they were from the financier's office. She caught the words "Pakistan channel" repeated several times.

Shaan walked to her seat and showed her a piece of coffee-coloured glass.

"What is it? Does someone need a monocle?" she asked.

"It is a lens filter. Look through it. Do you see the sky overcast? Now if I throw some water on you like this, won't you believe it is a rainy day?"

"Shaan, you rascal, give me the jerry can." He had picked it up from the props after the scene was finally shot. He brought lemonade, with some soda added to it to make it fizzle. Then they got the Marathi regional snack, vada pav, a bun with a ball of fried vegetables in it served with pudina and tamarind chutney. She mentioned what she had overheard.

"Savita, the Pakistan channel means smuggling films to Pakistan. You know the people there love Hindi films, I mean it is all about our common culture, but their government has banned Bollywood. Many films are from the Mughal period, which is as much Pakistani as Indian history. Most often the language used in these scripts is pure Urdu, Pakistan's language."

"Why is Bollywood banned?"

"After the 1965 war, only Doordarshan, the Indian government's television channel, was allowed; I suppose because that is controlled by our government and it will not have anti-Pakistani sentiments. Also our women are a little too liberal in their clothing, speech and behaviour for Pakistan's comfort."

"Doordarshan then has to maintain a conservative censor board."

"Yes, but not Bollywood. It is all private. It could make war films, Partition films and show the Pakistani government in poor light. A film is a very powerful tool for education, or propaganda."

"Maybe they are scared we would make anti-Islam films."

"Why would we? India has as many Muslims as Pakistan, and besides, popular culture has nothing against Islam. We have so many blends of Hindu-Islam religions. In many villages religious poems invoke Allah as well as Rama. The greatest of the Mughal emperors, actually one of the greatest emperors of all time, Akbar, had a Hindu wife and many Hindu ministers, and he promoted harmony among all faiths."

"Yes, I remember his new religion, the Din-I-Ilahi, a blend of Hinduism and Islam, with additions from Jainism, Zoroastrianism and Christianity."

"And if you consider the persons who make up Bollywood, you will not be able to separate the religions at all. Playback singers, actors, directors, lyricists, the whole range of staff, from my role to the producer's, are a mix of Hindus and Muslims and other religions too. Mehboob Khan directed a film called 'Mother India', showing the greatness of our country, India. Did he say he was Pakistani because he is a Khan? 'Mother India' travelled the world and ran for decades."

"Shaan, if you were to make a film, what would you do?"

"I would make a film on how films are smuggled into Pakistan. And smuggle that film to Pakistan."

Savita laughed, "Very smart idea. That will give Pakistan more reason to ban Bollywood."

"No, that will give Pakistan's government a moment to consider the cultural reality, miles away from its politics. If they want votes they should keep people happy. One sure way is to allow Bollywood."

"Shaan, do we smuggle films to other countries?"

"No other country has such a ban. Hindi films have travelled around the world and have bagged prizes too. And this was even before colour films were made. The script, storyline, songs are so poignant in some of Guru Dutt's and Raj Kapoor's films, that they will never gather any dust in some forgotten archive. They are subtitled in Arabic for much of Middle East, in Pashto for the Afghans, dubbed in Chinese, English, Russian. You know Raj Kapoor's film, Awaara, about the life of a tramp, did its tour in 1951 and became a big hit in China. And of course Russia loves our family values, socialist bent of mind, conservative outlook, sharing and sacrificing with pride, the aspirations to grow out of an oppressed era. They have banned Western films and welcome ours. Many countries in Africa love Hindi films. They don't even dub or subtitle them. They just drink neat. Posters of our heroes can be found in their cars, restaurants, tailor shops, saloons. In Nigeria theatres showed 'Mother India' for more than ten years.

"Why does Africa resonate so well with us? Is it because there is a large Indian Origin population over there?"

"Even in countries with hardly any Indian expatriates there is a big demand for Bollywood. I think it is because they are like us, developing nations, recovering from a bloody battle that was not theirs to start with, trying to erase a colonial past, women balancing water pitchers on head, peasants tilling the land with a pair of bullocks."

"Shaan, you must try your hand at script writing. My brother writes plays and I know it is such a satisfying hobby."

"Savita, I love photography. Besides, to find a niche in this competitive industry is a blessing. There is already a queue of script writers begging for a minute of a director's attention."

Savita had star dust in her eyes. She could hardly wait to meet Shaan to ask him about his day, about all he learnt. He had a penchant for educating, whatever he said was novel, and he lived actively and soaked up every droplet of information that could be converted to knowledge.

"Shaan, have you been to Kashmir?"

"Of course. That is where the songs are shot. Where else would you get such lavish beauty? It suits our temperament perfectly since the Bollywood songs are mostly fantasies, dream sequences with extravagant landscapes, picturesque trees, flower gardens dappled with rich hues, breezy cascades, lakes mirroring the sky, clouds caught in the mountain's crown. Kashmir is all that."

Savita had reached her own dreamland in her mind, as if she was in her own film with Shaan by her side in Kashmir. He opened the window of her eyes and peeped into her soul.

"Savita, I will take you to Kashmir with me."

"Promise?"

"That is one thing I would love to do more than photography."

"But Shaan, that is possible only if we elope."

"Why can't we do it the right way?"

She was afraid of the right way. Even the heroines in films were not allowed that much freedom.

Shaan continued. "You said your family was unorthodox, and that your brother was seeing a Bengali girl?"

Savita sighed, "Shaan, all in good time. Let them call you home first."

Anand reminisced, "At home we observed she was brighter than usual and smiled to herself a lot, and of course we guessed. So my mother caught her one day." "Savita, you come home late from college these days. Madhu said you don't chitchat with them anymore. Do you sit in the library? No, I don't think so. What is happening, do you want to let us in your little secret?"

Savita brought out one of her exquisite photos.

"Is that you? You look like a film actress. Coloured photos too! I see, you have found a photographer admirer."

"He is a cameraman in Bollywood. They are shooting an Amitabh Bachchan film now."

Aai looked through the other photos. "He is quite an artist, my sweet Savita. Will he take my photo too? And I want it in colour."

"Aai, do you want him to photograph you? Surely he will do it."

"Then ask him to come home."

Savita glowed like a full moon. Aai called to baba "Are you listening? Savita will bring..." and she asked Savita, "What is his name?"

"Shaan."

"She will bring her dilruba here."

"Her what?" asked baba. You know aai, she won't miss a chance to use filmy dialogue.

"Her dilruba, her sweetheart, Shaan. He will photograph me."

"Why should he take your picture when he could take mine instead?"

Savita was enjoying this situation very much. Shaan would take both their pictures, she assured them.

"Savita, tell baba all about this Shaan of yours." Shaan means pride as you know. "Arre pagli, my sweet one, don't forget to show these charming tokens of love."

Baba smiled at the photos, and teased her. "These are such top class photos we can use them for your marriage prospects." Savita blushed and ran out of sight, "Oh sorry, looks like you have done the job yourself."

Shaan walked in, wearing formal pants and a long-sleeved shirt as if he was coming for an interview. Savita could hardly keep herself from biting her nails. They sat far away on the sofa like two nervous rabbits. Slowly he warmed up to the work he did and we could see his heart and soul were in it. He described the many techniques resorted to during filming. They were fascinating; the positioning of lights, the imitation of day during night, the many angles from which the same scene is shot. We could see he had a bright future ahead of him in the film industry. Not only did he have the requisite skill but also was so amiable, well endowed to be in the entertainment business. My parents were happy, their hardest task solved with ease by their daughter herself.

"Everyone has seen the famous song, mere sapno ki rani ... How do you think it was shot?" quizzed Shaan. It was from the film Aradhana, released a few years back. The hero sang out to "the queen of his dreams" riding in a car parallel to a running train. The heroine in the train looked out of the window at the serenading hero and his driver friend. The train is the slow toy train that goes up to Darjeeling, a hill station in the Himalayas.

"The camera must have been in a vehicle running in front of the hero's car."

"But it would have shaken then. You will get a headache if you watch such a shaking scene."

"Then the camera was in the engine room of the train, it will not shake when taken from a train."

"You get one point for that as an acceptable technique, but sorry, it was not used in this case. There is no shot of a curving train, which is where the camera in the engine room helps. This train had just four compartments. All give up? Here's the answer. The hero and heroine were never in a real train or car, nor did they go to Darjeeling. Long shots of the vehicles were taken in Darjeeling. In the studio the car stood on one spot and on either side the roadside scenes were projected on two screens.

"And I suppose for the heroine it was simpler. You had to just create a window from where she looked out."

"Yes, as simple as that. If you get to see the film again, observe how the driver rotates the steering wheel at his heart's content. If he were actually driving on that narrow mountainous road, he would be in a ditch very soon. At one point he even takes his hands off the wheel to play the mouth organ."

When we were all laughing and eating suddenly baba tapped himself on the forehead, "So Shaan, I forgot to ask you your full name." Our family, as you know, is among the most progressive of the Marathis, which says a lot about its free-mindedness. Look at me, I pursued a career of a language professor, when everybody else rushed to become an engineer or a doctor. People ask about the surname first and there is an encyclopaedia of opinions founded on that last name. Now with education most people should be classified as Brahmin. But if you take the original meaning, one who seeks the Brahman as his main duty in life, then very few will qualify. My father did not even care to know what language Shaan spoke at home. Look at our marriage, did he ever question it? It was enough that Savita was happy with this man. So he was being playful and said, "Let me guess what Shaan stands for. Shantanu, or maybe Ishan?"

"Shaheen. Shaheen Khan." Came the reply. Suddenly we had all lost our voices.

If he were Albert Pinto I would escort my sister down the aisle of the church. If he were Jeremiah Ezekiel I would dance linking hands with his brothers. If he were a Sardarji or Pestonji I would learn their custom and rejoice in Savita's joy. But poor Savita, why did he have to be a Khan?

Shaan looked from father to daughter and saw both had their eyes cast down. A minute back the family was thanking its stars, and now the day had dawned obliterating all trace of stars. My father folded his palms, his face crumpled in embarrassment, "Shaheen, pardon us. I hope you understand why we ask it of you. Please leave alone our daughter." Shaan sighed as if he had halfguessed this would happen. Savita had started weeping softly covering her face. There was no better person I would have liked for my sister, but he was a small man with a big shadow. They were surely a joint family where women lived indoors managing the household. Savita would not have a single friend as their traditions are very different, and the women would not be as educated as her. She would have to wear clothes that would cover her body from crown to toe, and look through a veil. She would be suffocated. Her elders would decide what books she could read, what friends she mixed with, when she visited public places, who escorted her.

Shaan got up without a word and I followed him outside. It pained me to see him leave sullen faced after the evening of entertainment he provided. And who knows how many intimate hours he had spent with Savita. I had to explain, "Shaan, don't get us wrong. We are not orthodox Hindus. We have absolutely nothing against Islam. In fact I would be happy if my sister prayed five times a day. We believe in a supreme and let him be called Allah. But we do object to your customs with regard to women. We know even if you were strong enough to defy these rules for some time, all the other members of your family would sooner than later pin you down. It may seem normal to a girl brought up to expect it, but Savita here has all the freedom I get. She comes and goes at will, wears whatever she likes, she reads anything that pleases her, and has friends we don't even know of. We would not want her to be caged."

Shaan nodded, "It is one of those inescapable realities of who I am. And you are right; I cannot fight it all alone. It would mean abandoning my family. That I cannot do since they rely on me. Khuda hafiz."

He leaned closer and whispered, "Take care of Savita, she deserves the best, better than my own circumstances can offer."

I pressed his shoulder overcome with emotion. He was the best man I had seen in a long time.

"What happened next?"Asked Binapani after absorbing the sad story.

"We changed Savita's college closer to home. She was a wilted flower, and it hurt us all to see her. Luckily for our little daughter, Savita has started life afresh."

Chapter Fourteen

Nirmal

Zamindar Shashi Bhushan was returning home in his carriage when the horse reared up, and sent him lurching backwards. The driver cracked his whip in the air and screamed, "Move, you scum of the earth!"

Parting the wooden shutters he saw two bare-chested peasants standing with hands folded, holding on to a wheel, risking being crushed by its weight.

Shashi Bhushan called out to the driver, "Stop the carriage." He addressed the two bedraggled men, "What do you want?"

"Zamindar babu, we are tenants of Nihar Lal up there beyond the hill, but we request your largesse to buy the land from him where we cultivate our crops. Please, sire, we pray to you. We and our entire family will serve you as long as we live."

Shashi Bhushan thought to himself, this was becoming a nuisance now. From where would he get so much money to buy his neighbours' lands? To these two he said, "Go to my dewan and write your name in his books. But no promises, understand, and don't go announcing it to all the others."

"Sire is very gracious," and they lay prone in the sand, arms outstretched, believing this kind-hearted landlord would save them as he had rescued Rakhal and Abdul. It was the year 1858 in the Hooghly district of Bengal south of the big city, Calcutta. Shashi Bhushan went to his dewan's office and looked at the names. There were more than two, in fact about twenty names, a thumb imprint beside each one, with the same petition, requesting him to buy their land, from various zamindars. The dewan, his book-keeper, shook his head. "No, Shashi babu, we cannot afford all this. Besides we will make enemies of our neighbours if we try to buy all their land."

"Dewanji, we already have more enemies than we can handle. Today in the market I met the sahib from the Indigo Company.

He all but threatened to ruin me if I did not convert my plantations to indigo within three months."

The cotton mills in Britain were spinning out cloth for the fashion markets of Europe. Whoever wanted to wear drab colours when the rich blue dye was freely available? Didn't the motherland, the empire over which the sun never set, have tropical fields where the dye could be planted? From various colonies in Africa and Asia indigo leaves were unloaded in the ports of Bristol and Liverpool. It was a cash crop, but it did not mean all pockets were enriched by it. And neither did indigo grow free. It cost much, for a simple reason, that it could not be eaten. Farmers were paid a pittance for the sacrifice they made. They were given spurious loans that bound them to the British planters for generations. The native landlords got a shaving of the large profits to keep their hookahs bubbling and both parties were happy. But there were a few unhappy landlords, Shashi Bhushan being one. He saw an ominous cloud stretching out to the horizon, above the rippling indigo plantation. One peasant, Abdul, approached him, and Shashi Bhushan bought the poor man's land. Abdul could then plant rice. Soon another came with the same supplication, until every day there were these hungry hard-working bodies obstructing his path, crying out for mercy. Already in the 1830s all the food crops of Bihar were converted to opium plantations. And where did this most lethal narcotic go? To the immense market of China, where people were sucked up by the fumes and spiralled down the irreversible slope of addiction. The East India Company had fought an opium war with China and had won privileges to set up shop there. This time it was indigo in Bengal.

But in the case of opium, it was the business establishment, a trading company with just one motive – to maximize gains. This time around, the imposition of indigo cultivation was by the government, run by a people that had taken upon themselves the onerous task of civilizing the brown and the black races. Surely this was an exception to their benevolent fatherly solicitude? In 1857, an event occurred that would go down in history as the first Indian war for Independence. The Company's army generals tried to split the solidarity among the soldiers by creating religious tension. But the ruse backfired, and all the Indian sepoys turned instead against the masters. Prominent leaders of some princely states planned to unite their armies and along with the sepoys challenge the Company military. But the British were quick in quelling the uprising. Nevertheless, the lesson drove home, all the way to the Queen's palace. The control of India was transferred to the monarchy from the East India Company.

Shashi Bhushan met his neighbours one at a time and tried to reason with them. But reason and conscience had parted ways. Indigo meant more profit than rice or dal. And what about the peasants? Who cared, they bred like dogs. One man dead would be replaced by three of his sons. "And Shashi babu, we warn you, these British planters are not going to pardon your arrogance." Compassion was termed arrogance these days. Shashi Bhushan borrowed money to buy a few more acres of land and won over a handful of grateful tenants. Then the Indigo Revolt happened. The peasants themselves got together to avenge their decrepit state. It sparked off when one of them was beaten for not planting other people's cash crop. The angry peasants set the indigo mills on fire, raided the houses of zamindars and destroyed the hated crop. The timing could not have been better, for it was the age of the Bengal Renaissance. A prominent playwright, Dinabandhu Mitra, wrote Neel Darpan, the "Indigo mirror", exposing the atrocities perpetrated against peasants. Another son of Bengal, poet Michael Madhusudan Dutta, rendered it in English. The play was soon read by the populace in Britain and it shocked them to learn how their superior civilization treated its lesser brethren. To save face in the homeland, the indigo plantations were abandoned in Bengal, and some planters were executed. Africa was still supplying the dye anyway.

The peasants' wishes were fulfilled, but Shashi Bhushan had more enemies than he could handle. The moneylenders encroached on his peace, his zamindar neighbours encroached on his land, and the remaining planters set their lawyers on him. For years he struggled to keep his land. Eventually he had to sell it to pay the lawyer's fees. His philanthropy was punished with poverty. Just before he was pauperized he went to Calcutta and bought a house to provide some refuge for his family. Such was the law of the land that it could prove white to be black to support the rulers. At this very time, a Bengali magistrate was sitting in his house admiring the statue of Durga, the ten armed Goddess of power, the mother who protects her children. He was inspired to write a poem, dedicated to his other mother, suffering India. He envisioned that one day she would regain her grandeur like Lakshmi or Durga, once again she would be *shyaamalaam sujalaam*, dense green, flowing with rivers of delight, *suhaasini sumadhura bhaashini*, the ever-smiling mother with honeyed tongue. This was Bankim Chandra, another powerful voice of the Bengal Renaissance. Little did he know that in less than twenty years his "Vande Mataram" would become the mantra of victory for freedom fighters, and thereafter his motherland would adopt this poem as the national song of free India.

Shashi Bhushan roamed the streets of Calcutta in search of peace. And that he found finally at the feet of Sri Ramakrishna. The enlightened saint was then living in a temple in Dakshineshwar, spreading wisdom through his divine words. The great master taught that true joy came from deep within and not from the ephemeral touches of kamini kanchan, objects of desire. A salt doll went to measure the ocean and became the ocean. Unite with the Eternal that you essentially are. The sage, Avadhoot, had many masters – one of them a bird. A kite had once caught a fish and was flying away with it in his beak. A flock of crows started chasing him. Wherever he flew the crows cawed after him. Finally the kite dropped the fish and saw the crows were now all chasing the fish. He sat peacefully on a branch and pondered, "So it was the fish they were after, and not me!" Such is desire. As long as we have it we are chased by all sorts of troubles, but once we let it go, we are free. In the Hindu pantheon, all deities have a creature as their vehicle. The swan is the vehicle of Saraswati, Goddess of learning. If milk is given to a swan mixed with water, the swan can drink just the milk and leave the water aside. This is symbolic of the faculty of discrimination. Life is a mixed bag; the one with discrimination can lighten his weight by making the right choice. Sri Ramakrishna was called Parama Hansa, the supreme swan. And his disciple who spread his eternal message of dharma around the world was Swami Vivekananda, named after the word for discrimination, viveka. Sri Ramakrishna often used to pass into a state of ecstasy. His face would glow and he would start dancing with childlike abandon. Once a drunkard saw him and said, "Give me the wine he has drunk, and I shall touch liquor no more."

After the sage passed away in 1886, Shashi Bhushan moved on to become an ardent follower of the Brahmo Samaj, those that did not discriminate between rich and poor, priest and peasant, brahmin or shudra. They worshipped the eternal One, Ekam Adwitiyam, one without a second. He tried to teach his children to love all creatures. Then he passed away to the next world. His widow took up a last pilgrimage to Ganga Sagar, the island at the tip of Bengal where the holy river meets the Bay of Bengal. People believe that if a person drowns at this sacred confluence he is assured of a heavenly abode. There, like many other aged kinsmen, Shashi Bhushan's widow offered her body to the current of death.

The son, Ashish babu, disillusioned after a childhood of regal pampering, could not reconcile himself with his fallen circumstance. The First World War had begun and the British government was in dire need of weapons, tanks, ships and planes. Ashish babu had some capital left from his inheritance and all his well-wishers urged him to invest in the iron industry. A cotton mill owner from Bombay, Jamshedji Tata, envisioned an iron company in the ore rich area of Bihar. A barren piece of earth sprang into life, a city was born, named after him – Jamshedpur. Along with his son, he started the Tata empire with the Tata Iron and Steel Company. But while these enterprising businessmen from west India rode the wave, Ashish babu flailed his limbs about in vain. He tried to wake up in time to meet the brokers in the trading house. But his pleasure-filled upbringing hadn't prepared him for the harsh realities of life. His mornings coincided with the sun's midday march and his night began when the moon set, clearing the stage for the sunrise. Money slipped out of his hand like water. He still went to the theatres in his borrowed luxury car, and brought back a dozen thirsty friends who drank his imported whiskey, ate mutton curry, and lay around in his guest chambers until the revelry of the next day. The war passed by without him making a paisa. The family treasures were dwindling and more heads were crowding the same house. Sisters-in-law duelled with words, brothers turned out their empty pockets, parents boasted of past glory.

Nirmal Kumar, the eldest son of the family, borrowed money from his father and set off for Burma. His plan was to stick a foot in the lucrative teak business. But while the elephants were moving logs from the forest to the factory, he heard a voice on the radio, "Ami Subhas bolchhi, this is Subhas speaking". The great leader, Netaji Subhas Chandra Bose, was calling upon his people to fight for India's independence. He had returned with Japanese backing, and was forming an army in Singapore, another British colony. Nirmal Kumar abandoned his lumber enterprise, and jumped on a train that took him through the Malay countryside to Netaji's army headquarters. He joined the Indian National Army, and was trained in guerrilla warfare. There the youth, Nirmal Kumar, looked upon the comet from heaven, Netaji, and offered him his blood, sweat and tears. But what should have been a decisive campaign ended in failure. The soldiers were lost in a swampy jungle in Burma and no Japanese army came to their aid. Subhas Chandra Bose himself was reported to have died in a plane crash shortly afterwards.

* * * * *

"Have you heard the news, didimoni?" asked the boy handing over the ink pot to Debjani.

"Nothing to make me happy, but you seem to have a dimple in your cheeks today?"

"The war is over."

"What? What did you say? If you are lying, I will bring all my friends, and skin you alive."

"No really, I swear." He called out to the store next door, "Jhulan kaku, do you have the newspaper?"

A newspaper came sailing and landed in the stationery shop. But Debjani was not there. She had not even taken the ink pot she paid for. He saw her disappearing form, hands holding up the sari and running as fast as it would allow her.

Debjani burst into to the girls' hostel. "Jharna, Chaitali, arre, where are you all?" Tara came panting down the stairs and carried Debjani out with her. "Where is everybody?"

"They are all in the assembly hall. Where were you? The principal has called for a gathering. The war is over!"

The hall was packed with students, teachers, peons, secretaries, and their families. A hum rose up like smoke from a bonfire.

"Quiet, quiet, please." The principal had come in flanked by the professors. "Sit."

"But there is no place, sir." Everybody was shaking with excitement. None could sit still at this moment.

"All right, keep standing."

"As you may have heard, the war is over. Hitler has disappeared, killed himself most probably, and now Japan has surrendered."

Applause rent the ears, and the windows of the upasana hall shook in response.

"But we are not here to celebrate the victory of the Allied forces. Two bombs were dropped on Japan this month. They are no ordinary bombs. Not a blade of grass survived the atomic bomb blast. Just a crater was left where once roamed cars and rickshaws, soldiers and children. It happened in Hiroshima, then again, in Nagasaki. And these places are far bigger than our home, Santiniketan. We have amongst us great artists and scholars from Japan whom Rabindranath himself invited to contribute to this university. They are our family. Therefore today's gathering is not to celebrate the end of the war, but to concentrate for one moment in honour of the dead, those millions of civilians in Hiroshima and Nagasaki." A gong was struck and all stood silent. Tara looped her arm around Debjani.

Rabindranath Tagore started a small school in a district north of Calcutta, after moving there in 1899. But in his mind this was the seed for a vast and cosmic tree. All around him society was fragmented by religion, sect, caste, territorial boundaries, political identities, colonial masters and their oppressed subjects. The individual himself had been reduced to an insignificant spoke of the giant wheel of machinery. This new faceless world had just factories to produce goods and markets to consume them. Tagore thus saw a need for a place where the human being and his society could be remoulded in the image of the cosmic man, visva maanav. Shortly after the World War I the school became a university. Tagore travelled to Japan, Europe, Russia and America, inviting leading philosophers, artists, virtuosos of music and other scholars to participate in his dream. They assembled there to cultivate universality, through an unending expansion of the mind and spirit, through a communion with fellow-beings and nature. Santiniketan, the sylvan harmony, was true to its name — "the abode of peace".

Debjani was stringing an earring of jasmine buds. She wore bracelets of rose petals and a garland of marigold. The girls dressing up for the dance were like a bower of flowers. It was the poush mela, the winter harvest festival. All ornaments were made of flowers, and each girl compared her neighbour's design chattily. Debjani's younger sister came prancing up to her, a letter in hand.

"Look what baba has written. Your betrothed has returned from Burma. Actually he was not in Burma for long. He had escaped to Singapore and had joined Netaji's army."

Debjani felt bashful to hear the word 'betrothed'. But she was proud too, he had served Netaji then! It did not matter that his campaign petered out in the swamps of Burma, that the Japanese help he had expected was not forthcoming, that he himself disappeared from the war theatre. He was still a leader of incomparable courage, whose one aim was freedom for India at any cost.

Debjani wrote to her father that she would not give up her studies when she was so close to completing it. Some of her friends were married off in their first or second years at college. What was the hurry? One crucial year in a person's life was worth more than a decade in later life. But fathers were patriarchs of the family, and they sometimes valued their word more than their daughters' education. So Debjani wrote with much supplication. After all, the final exams were just five months away. Then she tore up the letter. She was thinking of Ritu's father and writing to her own. He was different. He had sent his daughters to Santiniketan so that they could imbibe good values living in close proximity to the best men of the age. She was right too. He had arranged the marriage after her final exams.

The Second World War was over, and Britain was finally ready to grant independence to many of its colonies. The Viceroy of India, Lord Mountbatten, was given the task of overseeing the Indian Independence. The prisoners of war and Netaji's soldiers caught in some surreal tropical nightmare woke up in their hometowns. Nirmal Kumar returned to the family house and was suffocated to madness. He sat for the civil service exam, passed it and started his new life in a rented house, wearing the khaki uniform of the Indian Police Service. His father had already fixed his marriage with the daughter of a fellow Brahmo Samajist. Thus when Nirmal Kumar marched into his old house wearing the shining badge of the coveted IPS, Ashish babu prepared for the concluding act of his fatherly duty. Nirmal Kumar married Debjani, to whom he had been engaged for years. They looked at each other for the first time, when Debjani parted the two betel leaves from her eyes.

*****

Binapani and Savita were having their kala khatta while Anand took Panchali to wet her feet in the water. Kala khatta, the "black and sour", is a chunk of ice on a stick dipped in a black juice that tastes sour and sweet at the same time. One has to eat it fast; otherwise the juice will drip down the sides of the mouth and make the person look like a rakshasa, a demon. Panchali tottered on her feet but ran into the water screaming in delight. Anand followed and scooped her up throwing her a few inches in the air and catching her back. His parents were sitting on a sheet of cloth on the beach and watching the horses pass by, raising the spray with their hooves. The Deshmukh family was having a picnic on Juhu beach. Then Anand brought Panchali to the little party assembled on the mat. Binapani bared her black tongue at her daughter, "A...A...A". Panchali screamed and started climbing on her father in fright staining his shirt with her sandy shoes. She had never seen a black tongue. Anand's mother whispered to her husband, "What a thudd class mother! She is frightening her own daughter." A few Westerners passed by in colourful shirts and shorts. They had long hair and wore the flip-flop sandals from the local market. Two women accompanied them wearing necklaces of beads and not much else. Anand's mother made a face, "Look at those women. They have come out in their undergarments!"

"Aai, that is a swimming costume. It is called bikini." Savita corrected her mother.

"They can wear all that in their own country, why do they want to corrupt our boys?"

These aforementioned boys had already made a human chain and were staring at the feminine pieces of work. They had also started singing, "Dum maaro dum" – inhale my friend, inhale." It was a song from a recent film on the fast spreading drug problem in India. A sister gets sucked into a gang of addicts and the brother follows the hippie trail to rescue her. He locates her, but it is too late, she has just died of an overdose. This film made every sister yearn for a caring brother like Dev Anand, the hero. But it also had a warning note for those who were trying to experiment with narcotics. For a decade Nepal sold hashish and cocaine in the retail stores, like any consumer good. In 1973, with pressure from the US government they banned these drugs.

The hippies of the USA, England and Australia were thronging to the beaches of western India. Goa was a cheap place to stay in and had the warmest beaches lined by coconut trees. Drugs were also peddled for them along with country liquor. They usually passed by Bombay causing a stir among the youth. Some young people in India too wanted to experiment, come what may afterwards.

Savita explained, "Narcotics and hallucinogens became popular in the 1960s in Europe and America. But soon people realized that some of these, particularly opiates, did not just get people high, but brought them down very low too. And every time they were in the dumps they were desperate to get out of that pathetic state. The effect of the drug wore out faster and they had to take more of it to get to the same stimulus. In no time it became a vicious circle from where some perished, literally died of an overdose, or did something desperate."

"Yes, that is what the film shows. Dev Anand's sister cannot handle the impasse she had landed herself in, and commits suicide," commented her father.

"But then why do people take them to start with, especially now that all its dangers are known?" asked Savita's mother.

"Aai, for the same reason we practise religion. For freedom, moksha."

Anand protested, "Come on Savita, don't compare the spiritual state of moksha with this temporary illusion of freedom."

"From what I've heard it seems to be a foretaste."

"Savita, have you been experimenting with something?" asked her father seriously.

"Oh no, not me. But, you know, some do in our college. And they talk about their experiences. One fellow said he felt he was flying, another said he saw brilliant colours and the world was all fluid, something about things melting into each other, people free of all inhibitions, laughing together."

"What inhibition?" her mother eyed her suspiciously.

"All sorts of inhibitions. Aai, imagine you are not an Indian mother with two children who look up to you for guidance. You don't have to follow customs like listening to baba, you don't have to wear this sari that makes you sweat. There are lots of happy people around you dancing. You hear some music with terrific beats, and you want to abandon your body to its rhythm. So you just do it. You don't own anything any more, not your body, nor your past, none of your ideas and conventions. You are free of your body's aches, its cravings, your mind's prejudices, its ignorance, emotional wounds, jealousies, desires, insecurity. You are free to love whosoever you like, not just one person, but many, all."

"Savita, stop right there. Free love as you know does not mean emotional love only. Don't scandalize aai." Anand was teasing his sister.

"Savita, losing one's ego is all very good, but if they know that same climb will plunge them deep down, why should they do it?" asked Binapani.

"For that enigmatic experience! Besides, not all drugs make you plunge deep down. When one is in the zone, I heard, one does not think of the future, time itself does not exist. So it does not matter, nothing matters. There is no tomorrow. There is no yesterday either."

"But Savita, this is only an escape, not freedom. Moreover, a sense of freedom which slow-poisons the body and brain . . . is it not dangerous?"

"Yes, bhaiya, I know it."

"Sage Ashtavakra tells the Rajarshi Janaka, who was both, a sage and a king, that he is already free. His only inhibition is that he does not know it. He thinks he is bound, he looks through a veil, the veil of ignorance, and imagines himself to be trapped. The sage tells the king to remind himself again and again 'I am already free, I am forever free, I am free, I am free'. And that thought itself has the power to make one realize how free one is."

Binapani added, "Sri Ramakrishna also said if you consider yourself to be a sinner, you will become one. Therefore imagine yourself to be pure."

* * * * *

"There is a courier shipment for you, Bina," called out Anand from the doorway. The delivery man spoke Bengali with no "sh" sounds, all was "s", like the Bangladeshi classmates she had had. He was indeed from Bangladesh and had crossed over during the war. Thanks to his job, he had an opportunity to see the big cities of India. She gave him a sweet and some water, in the style of the Bengalis, never water alone. He left gratefully and she opened the package. It was from her mother and disturbingly brief. "Your father is very ill. Please proceed home immediately."

"What does this mean, Anand? She has sent some notes, one two three, why, it is actually seven hundred rupees!"

Anand came round and asked her to translate every word her mother had written. Binapani tossed the letter on the table and counted the money again.

"I think ma wants us three to go there and that is why she has sent so much money. She fears I will not go to Calcutta if you don't come along. And right she is, I am not going to Calcutta ever in my life."

Anand was thoughtful, "Bina, I think she sent the money for you to book a plane ticket. Her tone is urgent. Why else will she spend the money to courier this?"

"How can she assume I will go there? Just like that ... after they kicked me out, putting me on drugs and packing me off? I am not going back, and not for him in any case."

Anand's voice was very sad now, "No Bina, your father is dying, and you need to go. Nobody punishes a sick man, one's own father the least."

"But, Anand, you have no idea what that place means to me. I can't handle it."

"Go, Bina, just go. Do it as a sacred duty."

"Anand, are you asking me to go, all alone, just like that?"

"Every minute you are out of sight I will live a hundred years in utter terror. What if you do not return? But yet I will risk it. Because in a few days this chance may never come. He loved you once, Bina, and for memory's sake do it, please, Bina, please."

* * * * *

Panchali waved to her mother from Anand's lap at the airport unaware of the great turmoil raging in the heart inches from hers. Binapani held her little hand till she heard the last call for her flight. Anand said very few words as he was holding down a lump in his throat. Was this going to be his last sacrifice for his beloved? Handing her over to Calcutta, her old haunt, her past, her future?

"When will ma return?" asked Panchali.

"Soon, very soon, and till then you and I will play doll house together."

"Yes, I will comb the hair of the dolls, you will put them to sleep."

* * * * *

Binapani opened the door of her house and was met with a deathly silence. "Ma?" She called hesitatingly. A woman looked out of the window and she exclaimed "Bina, I am so glad you have come." The next moment Gypsy was covering her with his frenzied licks and her mother's sister was patting her head, tears in eyes. "They are in the hospital, Bina, your mother practically lives there and comes home late at night to catch some sleep. Have a bath and eat something. Then Haradhan will take you there."

Binapani went to her room, and found her aunt's sari hanging from the clothes rack. She slipped out and left her suitcase in the storeroom. Gypsy was complaining in his doggy language, and stopped whining only when she patted him. In four years he had grown slower and did not place his paws on her shoulder. But he remembered her and was now telling her about all that had transpired from the day she was gone suddenly from his life.

Haradhan had aged too. He spoke very little, or maybe because his master was sick he wanted to show respect. She asked him tentatively, "So what has happened to my father?"

He answered vaguely about not being educated and not knowing certain difficult words doctors use. Then he wept for some time quietly and finally said, "But one thing I know. He is not returning."

At the hospital, Binapani was shown a room, and Haradhan left her outside the curtains. "I will return," he said, his eyes moistening again. She parted the curtain and her eyes met her mother seated beside the bed, her hair unkempt, her eyes red. They ran into each other's arms and wept. She indicated her father's almost lifeless body hooked up with tubes and sacks hanging from above and below. "He is slipping into unconsciousness, Bina."

"Ma, you look so tired, go and rest, I will sit here. Shall I call Haradhan-da to pick you up? And here, mashi has sent some food." She extracted the stainless steel carrier from her bag.

Her father had woken up, "Ke, who has come?" He looked around slowly. Was this the man she had left four years back? What had life done to him? Was it the Naxalite raids, her own desertion, the Bangladesh War, or simply disease? Or maybe an inner call to leave this borrowed pot of clay and sunshine.

She heard a voice coming from far back in time, an energetic youthful voice "Ke, who was singing on the radio?"

Binapani sat by her harmonium, smiling smugly.

Her father entered the room, "Was that Sandhya Mukherjee?"

His daughter shook her head.

"Then surely it was Arati."

"No baba, it was me!"

"You?" he exclaimed, still playing the game, "Wonderful! Sing it again."

Binapani's voice was tender, "Baba, it is I, Bina."

He stretched his shaking hand and she grabbed it trembling with emotion. "Bina, is that really you?"

"Yes," she whispered breaking down, placing that cold hand against her warm cheeks.

"So have you pardoned me, ma?" He had called her ma, the most precious of names, "My darling daughter".

"Yes, baba, yes, yes," she forced her throat to speak.

One day a fifteen-year-old Binapani wanted to surprise her mother by making her an omelette. But after much labour all she had was a ruined pan and a houseful of burnt smell. When Debjani returned, before she could begin to scold, Binapani's father declared he was the culprit. Then there was that time during a vacation when daughter had partnered with father in Ludo and had cheated to win. And once when she was even younger...

Binapani took her father's hand and placed it over her head.

"Baba, bless me that I may lead a good life."

"Arre pagli, silly child, who am I to bless? There is a God above who watches our every move. He giveth life, he preserveth and taketh when the time comes."

* * * * *

A week later they returned from the burning ghats. Very few words were spoken, all hearts mourned in their own way in silence. Binapani watched her mother remove the white bangles, the red coral one, the iron plated with gold, and place them in a jewel box. Aparna had come to be with the family the last few days. Debjani gave her coloured saris to her sister, Binapani and Aparna. Haradhan drank himself to stupor for two whole days, and then asked for a long leave to visit his home in the village. There was no home that Debjani knew of. He was forbidden to drive and was granted his retirement, a room in their house, and the task of walking Gypsy.

"Now Bina, we need to settle you too."

"Ma, I cannot leave you here alone. Come with me."

"I have been thinking of going to Jorasanko. You know for some time now, the Tagore family house in Calcutta has become the Rabindra Bharati University. It is possible they need a librarian. I have always wanted to read books, yes, English books too. The kingdom of literature stretches before me, and I do want to run in that field plucking wayside flowers, admiring butterflies, hiding under toadstools."

"Bina, shall we go to the Coffee House?"

"No Aparna, I cannot go there."

"I understand. At first I felt the same. Then I decided to rid the storeroom of its cobwebs. We cannot escape from our own past. We have to face it. You'll see those chairs are not left vacant. Other dreamers are weaving their dreams."

"Aparna, I am not escaping. I am merely allowing the past to remain pristine in my heart. And the long shadow it cast upon me – that I have cremated."

"Let's at least go to College Street and meet Kanai-da. He may have a Russian romance for you."

Binapani smiled at her friend's effort to dispel her gloom, "I have read so many novels, Aparna, but have neglected the one story I know best of all – the story of my own life."

And so Binapani passed by the white marble Victoria Memorial, the grassy expanse of Maidan, the new advertisement boards rising from the disappearing tree line, the sooty electric wires with a family of sparrows on them, the packed vegetable market with onions rolling onto the street, the red brick office buildings, the tram chugging placidly through the avenue of trees, into the railway station.

* * * * *

Anand opened the door and before he could say a word, Panchali had leaped on Binapani like Gypsy would in the olden days. "Ma is back, ma is back!"

Tears slid down Anand's eyes. He wiped them hastily. "Panchali, ma is tired, now run along."

Binapani crouched and caught the girl in a large embrace. "No, Anand, I am not tired any more." Panchali lisped the words, "Ma, what have you brought me from Kol, Kol Taka?"

Binapani realized to her dismay, she had not even thought about her little family here. She hugged Panchali tighter and kissed her on her cheek. "I have brought you a mother!"

Anand had turned to hide his tears. Binapani held his hand and pulled him down close to her. When their faces almost touched, she spoke through her tearful laughter,

"And for you I have brought a wife!" Anand gave up all resistance and fell on her clutching her like one at last allowed to rest. They were all three a pile near the door. She put her arms around his neck and whispered,

"Aami tomaake bhaalobaashi. I love you."

Chapter Fifteen

Atul

On a full moon night in May 1974, in the desert of Rajasthan, close to a village called Pokhran, a nuclear test was conducted. A telegram reached the Indian Prime Minster with the words, "The Buddha is smiling." That night was Buddha Poornima, the birth anniversary of Gautama Buddha. The United States and Canada, India's collaborators in her nuclear programme, called foul, although the government tried to plead it was a peaceful nuclear explosion. From then on India would be on her own. No country would supply her uranium, or technology or loans for her atomic energy programme. India shrugged off the accusation, and called upon her scientists to continue independent research, whether for electricity or otherwise. A new generation research reactor, Dhruva, was designed indigenously at the Bhabha Atomic Research Centre, and many new reactors would mushroom around the country in the coming years. Pakistan had already known from 1971 about India's nuclear readiness. The Prime Minister of Pakistan, Zulfikar Ali Bhutto, declared that even if the Pakistani people had to eat grass and leaves, they would sooner create their own nuclear facility. He promptly sent a worldwide invitation to all Pakistani scientists to return home, and they answered to his call. The two countries had yet another toy with which they could play snatch-and-grab.

* * * * *

Savita sat demurely bedecked in her silk sari and pearl jewels. Her whole family kept vigil around her, while the groom's father paced around the room, looking out of the window every few minutes and checking his watch.

"That boy will be the death of me. Malavika, give me another tablet."

"No," replied his wife decisively. "You have had one just a

few minutes back. Trust your son, he will be here. He is not like the saint who suddenly got cold feet before his wedding and ran away. Savita dear, don't worry; he is as good as any of us in keeping time. We Indians are not famous for that and we all make allowances for each other. On his wedding day he will be on time, I will myself see to it. Here there is no muhurta, so we did not press him to come earlier."

In an engagement no priest is required, nor any astrologer to calculate an auspicious time, the muhurta. Atul was the groom, who grew up in Bombay, was a civil engineer, and now worked in the capital city, Delhi. Atul's father threw up his hands, "There he comes, the ullu ka pattha." Binapani suppressed a giggle, and she and Savita exchanged confidential looks. Ullu meant owl, not a savoury epithet for anyone, but not as derogatory as the shuor, pig. Pattha is offspring, so the whole meant 'son of an owl'. If the father used that abuse on his own son, he was actually calling himself an owl. But most people forget the meaning of the phrase and use it as a gentle rebuke, like some Christians swear using the name of Christ, hardly meaning to invoke the image of the Saviour.

Atul came in with a suitcase in one hand, wiping his sweaty forehead. "Hello everybody." He leaned over his father's frame, a little smaller than the door frame, and waved at Savita, "Hi darling!" Savita put her hand over her face and pressed her lips together to hide her smile. Through her fingers everybody could see her face turn rosy pink. The patriarch was unimpressed by his son's nonchalance. "You!" Atul and he said the next words together as if they had rehearsed them for many years, "Ullu ka pattha." Then the father was on his own, "How dare you insult me and your mother in front of our new relatives? You made the bride tremble in concern, and her father was all but ready to call off the alliance. I will skin you, and I don't care if you are an engineer or a ..."

"Stop, baba. Here your train is running full steam, but the real trains are cooling off in their yards. Don't blame me for any of this. If you have to, blame George Fernandes."

His mother sighed. "What has happened to our country! Another railway strike, was it?"

"Yes, from Thane I came on bus, not one, but five. For a little stretch from Pune, it was on the top of a lorry with just about two hundred other stranded passengers. We had to literally strap ourselves with our luggage not to fly out."

His father had stopped steaming and grabbed his son's handkerchief to wipe his own face. "What a smell! Now don't you dare go sit with the bride yet."

From the tail end of 1974 there were more holidays in factories, colleges and government offices than working days because of strikes. Seasoned politicians like Jayaprakash Narayan, who had been a freedom fighter alongside Gandhi, called for a no-confidence motion against the prime minister. A four-year-long case accusing Indira Gandhi of using government utilities, the police force, bribing the electorate during her 1971 election campaign was being heard in the Allahabad High Court. George Fernandes of the opposition party had called for a railway strike in Bombay, others had joined hands in Bihar, and slowly the unrest was spreading. Of course, the general elections were approaching and the opposition, the Janata Party, was itching to occupy the throne. Ever since Independence, the Congress, the largest party during the British Raj, had had control of the government. When Nehru passed away, for about two years, Lal Bahadur Shastri became prime minister. The day after the peace treaty with Pakistan was signed in Tashkent, in 1965, he had a fatal heart attack. Indira Gandhi, Nehru's daughter, was voted to power, and had already won two terms, a resounding victory in the Bangladesh War, and had proved quite capable, with agriculture and nuclear programme as additional achievements.

Atul was talkative, "The famous Indian punctuality in the railways reminds me of R.K. Laxman's cartoons of the Common Man." The Common Man was the quintessential Indian, usually speechless, just an observer of the socio-political mood. He wore a dhoti, a checked shirt, and was a middle-aged, balding, nondescript person, who had captured millions of hearts by just being around.

"Oh, I love those cartoons," said Savita, "Even during exams, when I had no time for the newspapers, I never missed the cartoon section."

"In a sense, that's all you need to know, a pictorial gist or a political jest. So once a train entered the station on time, and people garlanded the driver. The embarrassed driver says, 'Oh, please don't honour me, the train was supposed to be here yesterday at this time'." The evening passed pleasantly with exchanges of R.K. Laxman's insightful jokes.

"Remember the one where a fat politician is speaking from a podium. And someone whispers to the Common Man 'when he was an aspiring youth, he had a broad mind and narrow waist. Now that he is a politician, he has a narrow mind and a broad waist'."

"So, Savita, how do you like the ring?" Atul asked her in private. She had written him a few letters but was still shy to talk. She just nodded. "And how about the giver of the ring?"

She was amused, this young man, her future husband, was really too fast for her. He laughed and gave her a little slap on her shoulder. "Don't worry, I can talk for both of us. But I don't swear like baba. No really, I swear it." He laughed at his own little joke, and Savita smiled too. She indeed liked the giver of the ring.

During the family dinner when the guests had left, Atul let his bowl of rice pudding rest with a thud on the table. "All right, now is the engagement pukka, solid, final, irrevocable?"

His father answered him looking around benevolently, "I would think so, what do you say, Deshmukh bhai?"

Atul was looking at Savita. "Baba, I did not ask you the question." He gestured with his chin, and Savita nodded, "Yes."

"Good, now I can quit my job."

"What!" exclaimed all voices. Savita suspected he was being funny again. She was beginning to learn his mannerisms.

"By that I don't mean I will not work. I meant I will take up another job. In a private firm. And I know 'private' is a bad word in the middle-class setting – no provident fund, no pension, hard work, fewer leaves and all those calamitous punishments. But I am tired of working in a sarkari firm where people have droopy eyes in the morning and read newspapers till tiffin time, then go for a smoke, and return when the peon has made tea. I did not study civil engineering to design a chair that will hold me while I doze in it. I want to build hospitals and suspension bridges and hydroelectric power stations."

"Wonderful speech," Atul's father applauded, "But you are not serious. There is no job security in a private firm. You can no more play with your life, henceforth you are not going to be alone."

"That is why I languished in that government office for so long. Just to get a good wife. None of the middle-class folks will marry their daughters to private firm employees. I think you should revise your beliefs, or rather non-beliefs about private companies."

"In that case, Atul, join Tata or Birla. Nothing smaller."

Atul joined his palms. "Thank you, aai. I will join Birla. They should have an office in Delhi. As if one day the Tatas and Birlas were not small!"

"And don't stay for too long in Delhi. I hear there are strikes every day in front of the prime minister's house and the Parliament. Come back to amchi Mumbai." Amchi Mumbai were the Marathi words for 'our Bombay', like she was a dear family member. Bombay was the financial capital of India, where politics played but a secondary role, and people loved to get back to business as usual. Delhi was altogether different with her chequered history of conquests. During the Mahabharata era, when the Pandavas were ousted from their capital city of Hastinapur, they built a new city called Indraprastha. The magician demon, Maya, had constructed it by clearing a forest. The palaces were enchanting, as if studded with gemstones, with stairways and balconies playing hide and seek, the floor as polished as the surface of a lake. Delhi was Indraprastha five thousand years ago.

* * * * *

Savita's wedding was arranged with much pomp. It was during the Ganapati festival so that Atul could attend the worship and his wedding during the same leave. Savita went with her friends to buy the saris for herself and her new family. They were all very sad she was going so far away to Delhi, but some of her other friends had already spread like spores in the wind all around. Atul had come on time, and he had not even changed his job. The country was under a state of emergency, which meant the prime minister had unlimited power and the parliament stood dissolved. In mid-1975, Indira Gandhi decided the internal situation in the country was unstable with the many strikes that had begun to affect the economy. The court had found her guilty, her election was voided, and she was barred from standing as a candidate for the next six years. Within a fortnight of the verdict she applied a clause hitherto unused in the Constitution – Emergency. As chief of the police force, she arrested many opposition leaders, especially agitators, censored the press, even used the government television channel, Doordarshan, for propaganda messages. Some of her keen opponents went underground, were hunted down and sent to jail, like George Fernandes. The last bastion of hope for democracy, as the parties in Punjab called themselves, were finally curbed and forty thousand party workers were jailed. She had a long agenda; to spread literacy, clean up the bureaucracy, crack down on bribe-takers and lazy government officials, increase agricultural productivity. Atul was upbeat, "I came on the roof of a lorry the last time, and this time I arrived in a train, dot on time. Whoever said we Indians cannot be punctual should eat his words."

"Atul, why did you not join a private firm?" asked his mother, teasing him.

"Because the government office functions now like a private firm, with the added benefits of pension and more leaves. All latecomers and slackers will be thrown out. Projects are now getting implemented. You should see how much life it has pumped in us. Personally, I think people are happier applying their knowledge than taking advantage of the lack of policing."

His father agreed. "Best is the crackdown on corruption. To get any job done, you had to warm your way bribing every small official, starting from the gate keeper, who will not announce your arrival unless you give him money for tea. Ridiculous state of affairs! It needed a strong slap and that is what it got."

Savita's father reminded them, "But Atul, this is not democracy."

Binapani was vehement, "Baba, why does India need democracy, especially if some other system works better?"

"Because when there is no vox populi it is the end of accountability. Indira Gandhi has gagged the press. Now she can do anything she likes and no one will know it or be able to oppose it."

"What does the opposition achieve anyway? They just retard the carriage. And now we have proof that it is not rusted, it is the workers who were pulling her badly."

Savita too added her observation, "I hear teachers have started teaching again. They are all scared of the sudden visits of invigilators. Hitherto in government schools they used to sit in the classroom and read novels, then call the same students home for private lessons, for a double income."

"Savita is already siding with her husband," complained her mother.

Savita answered her back smartly, "Like you are siding with yours."

"Look at this girl's cheek. She has found a new staff to lean on!"

During the reception, Anand was busy greeting guests, but came around ever so often to ask if his sister or wife wanted something, stuck as they were at the throne and pedestal. He brought them pakodas, the vegetable snack deep fried in a batter made of powdered pulses. Binapani gestured to Savita she had to vomit and ran away. When next Anand came around Savita called him. "Bhaiya, I think the pakodas have too many chillies. Bhabhi may not be used to such spicy food. Get her some sweets.

She has gone again to vomit. Why don't you talk to the caterer?" Anand leaned close to her ear and whispered something. Savita brightened, "Really? Congratulations, Bhaiya."

The crowd gravitated to Atul's throne, and Lajpat was back with a bang. "Why do we adulate democracy so very much, may I ask? Is it another American export?"

"Why not? America is a resounding success in democracy."

"But the idea they export and impose on other countries is a resounding failure. In the name of democracy, it is pure and simple trade. Consider Guatemala."

Binapani caught the allusion from Che's involvement in Guatemala. Lajpat elaborated, "When the socialist government, elected to power by the people, wanted to take away land owned by a foreign investor, all hell broke loose. United Fruit had large land holdings where banana was planted. And the banana was being exported to the USA. Did the people in Guatemala starve for that? Maybe they did, but why would an American company care for the Guatemalan poor? Anyway, this new socialist leader did, and weapons were supplied to insurgents by the American owner of United Fruit, who, by the way, was a defence contractor in the USA. An American stooge was replaced as head of state."

Binapani completed her own thought, "And Che moved on to the next capitalist victim, Cuba. Similar other countries, also, or rather, alas, blessed by nature, were Panama, with the canal linking the Atlantic to the Pacific Ocean, South America with her rich minerals and coffee, Saudi Arabia had natural gas, the Philippines was the Indian Ocean base, and so on."

Talwar said, "Lajpat, democracy is not a post World War II phenomenon. People have fought for freedom since time immemorial. Let us not blame or credit America for it."

"Talwar sahab, all I am saying is that the people have to decide for themselves what kind of government they want. It cannot be a foreign import. Look at our neighbours, our other selves in reality. Sheikh Mujibur Rahman, yesterday the hero of the Bangladesh War, today murdered by petty army officials.

Now General Ziaur Rahman has imposed Martial Law. If democracy does not work, so be it."

"Agreed, Pakistan too has had phases of democracy and Martial Law. General Ayub Khan, then Yahya Khan ruled in the last decade. Only after the war was lost did people clamour for civilian rule again. But in the long run, Lajpat, I think the three countries want people's rule, even if many complain that a true democracy cannot function with so many illiterate voters."

"Talwar sahab, let me ask you one question. What idiom do we use to describe the best possible government? We call it Rama Rajya, the rule of King Rama. A monarchy!"

Some others laughed at Lajpat, "We suppose in the absence of a king, we have to live with Queen Indira."

Someone a little more serious continued, "But Lajpat bhai, she has banned opposition parties, censored the press and is putting people in jail without trial. Is that fair?"

Lajpat, the dogged underdog, had an answer, "That is because everybody has not accepted her queenship. Yes, laugh at me, but are you all not happy that your letters reach their destination? And as an added bonus they reach on time?"

* * * * *

After a tearful farewell, Savita was gone to Delhi. Atul brought her into his flat. A new bed stood with strands of jasmine garlands hanging from all sides. She inhaled. "Atul, these are fresh jasmine flowers. And look at the heart sign made with rose petals. Who has done these?"

"It must be Sakina. I had given the keys to our neighbour and the maid, Sakina, was told to come this morning and clean up. She is really scared you will dismiss her."

"Why should I?"

"Because I complain all the time, look at that corner, and the ceiling has cobwebs."

"Atul, don't worry about these details; I will handle them from now on."

"Oho, I forgot I am not a bachelor any more! It feels good.

Now my bride, fan me. He spread his arms to feel the wind on his chest, as if the ladies in the king's palace were going to wave their hand fans for him. Savita went to the switchboard,

"As you say huzoor, your lordship." The fan started rotating showering them with marigold petals. They were both covered with the thin orange strands, and spent joyful moments picking them out of each other. Sakina was very thoughtful indeed.

The maid came in the next day, and looked at Savita with a guilty smile. The bedroom was strewn with flower petals of three kinds. Savita observed as she cleaned and made small talk to put her at ease.

"Sakina, last night the fragrance of jasmine kept us happily awake for a long time. And the trick of the fan was simply magical."

"That is why we plucked jasmine buds. We knew they would bloom last night."

Sakina was moving off to the next room when Savita found she had overlooked some petals. She helped her playfully, being very careful not to scold the lady who had worked hard for her welcome. Maybe she had to save up for days to buy the flowers. "Sakina, look there in that corner, there is one marigold petal." Sakina bent low and sighed, "Ah yes, didi." She picked it up and continued her prattle. "And so these women in my slum, they all planned to give you both a surprise. Your husband is a very good man, you will find out. When Amanat's son broke his hand, sahib took him to the hospital. Look outside the window, didi, you can see a bit of our slum there. So we all plucked the flowers from the garden, yes at night, and we strung them together."

"And no one saw you?"

"No, we were all wearing our burqas, the black gowns, covered from head to toe, and were as dark as the night herself. Even if they saw us they would run in fright. We had planned to press our nose and start making sounds like ghosts, like this." She made a nasal "A...A...A" sound.

"Sakina, you make me laugh! One minute, stand right there. Can you reach up to that corner and get the cobweb down?"

Sakina looked up and swung her broomstick all around missing the cobweb. Savita now understood Sakina's problem with cleanliness. She could not see well.

"Sakina, can you see the jasmine flower in that corner?" Again the maid bent down and brought her eyes close to the spot indicated.

That evening when Atul came home Savita said, "I have solved your cleanliness problem."

"Savita, don't let her go yet, give her one more chance. They are really poor, these people. You could train her surely?"

"Ahh, listen first to me. You go off like the street buses during our wonderful Emergency era – nonstop. Sakina has poor eyesight. All she needs is a pair of new glasses."

Atul was relieved. "Savita, you are a real Lakshmi in this house." The next day Savita took Sakina to the eye clinic and got her prescription glasses. The maid came extra early before Atul left to show him her glasses.

"Sahib, look what your wife gave me – eyes. I can see everything so clearly now. I did not even know things could be seen so well. I knew you will get yourself a wife just like you. Mubarak ho, congratulations. I am so grateful to the two of you I have no words to thank you."

"Atul, what is that place from where little specs of ashes rise up in the air, like someone has stroked a fire with a hand fan."

"Yes, imagine it to be the homa, the sacrificial fire of a temple. It is indeed that, but those little specks are birds, pigeons in fact."

"Amazing how many they are. Do you have binoculars?"

"Why do you need to spy on them? I will take you there this evening after office. We can have some chaat out there."

Savita's mouth had begun to water in anticipation. Chaat was the roadside Indian snack that had the added taste of the dust and dew, the guilt of eating spicy food, and the sweetness of doing it together with so many unknown co-conspirators. That evening, Savita saw a building that blew her mind, three domes in white marble, arched gateways, minarets topped by a cupola, inlaid walls, a vast courtyard. It was a palace of Allah, the Jama Masjid. Pigeons landed to peck at the grains and flew back to their nests tucked under the minarets' eaves.

* * * * *

Savita was a child lost in a factory that ground spices. The stones pressed against the cumin seeds and made a deafening sound. She cried for her mother, but her call was lost in the din. She woke up restless. Atul was already awake and he was staring out of the window towards the Jama Masjid. The grinding sound was very real.

"What is that awful noise, Atul? What time is it?"

"It is about five thirty now. I think something big is happening around there, in that slum area where Sakina lives, near the mosque. Shall we go and see?"

"Atul, I want to sleep some more, you know I was dreaming I was lost ..."

"Savita, I think I will go and find out." He sounded nervous.

"Wait, I am coming." They went out and aroused an autorickshaw driver on the road. Some early dogs were barking and the footpath dwellers had started brushing their teeth with neem stick. The milk man called out. "Namaste Sahib, where are you two off this morning?"

"We want to see what is happening there."

"What is there to see? It must be some new road they are constructing. The tar rollers must have started work early. Now we are in Emergency, everything happens tataafat, snappily."

The autorickshaw dropped them near the commotion. In one second they knew it was not a routine road construction. As the daylight lifted the curtain of night, a strange sight revealed itself. A big bulldozer was rolling right into the line of shanties. These huts were made of woven coconut leaves, roof and wall. They fell without protest and were gobbled up in the machine's jaws. People were scattered all around, scrambling to hold on to the belongings they could salvage in the melee. Savita wrapped her dupatta over her nose as the dust rose up in the air. A crunching sound was heard, and she saw the remains of a chulha pulverized to dust. Women were weeping and children, many naked, clung to their mothers, frightened. Savita saw the film poster of last year's super hit, Sholay, above the whirling dust. She recalled the scene where the dacoit kills every member of the police officer's family, including the children. Within seconds of the shooting, all human voices are silenced, but the swing upon which mothers and children were seated, still sways back and forth, the only inanimate heartbeat left. Savita pointed at the poster,

"Atul, they are destroying these people's lives, like in Sholay."

"Yes, I heard about this scheme. It is another of the maverick son's brilliant ideas."

"Sanjay Gandhi?"

"Yes, beautification of the city. Slums need to be cleared and these people resettled outside Delhi."

A splintered mirror fell off the bulldozer's mouth. It reflected the sky in fractured bits, like a poor man's dream. There was a bindi stuck on it, the little dot used as facial decoration. A woman would have planned to wear it on her forehead when she went out to do her maidservant's chore this morning. But some mornings are not like the others.

A bus came screeching and stopped close by. Some strong men with batons in their hand were catching hold of the slum dwellers, only the men, and driving them into the bus. If they resisted they were prodded in with the stick. Atul turned to see this new development. Savita found a bottle of nail polish rolling on its side, having escaped the damaging crunch of the jaws. She picked it up, and suddenly she wanted to cry. It felt like her dream, the grinding sound and no mother to hide into. She turned, but Atul was not there. "Atul, Atul!" she cried frantic, her voice hardly audible over the din. Then she caught a glimpse of him, his neck thrust forward mouthing her name, but no sound reached her. Then he was shoved into the bus, and they went past her almost grabbing her dupatta off her shoulder.

She had to get home. Parting the people as if they were a thick jungle, she started jogging back from where she had come. Now it was broad daylight, but there was not a single autorickshaw, or any kind of transportation. They were all scared to get picked up in that bus, whatever it meant. Savita walked all the way home, keeping her eyes on the tall building where she lived. The muezzin called out from the Jama Masjid's minarets in his customary fashion as if life went on despite all. At her doorstep, she realized the key was with Atul. She went up one flight of stairs to Atul's friend's flat. The Arora family welcomed her and tried to make her feel at ease with hot tea. Savita bit her nails like a little girl and tried hard not to cry in fright. This was the capital, with all its political turmoil and she did not know many people.

Mr Arora said, "This time our young acrobat, Sanjay Gandhi, has gone beyond limits. This breaking down of slums is not like a Maruti stunt, which exposed his inexperience, but was relatively harmless. This is serious. I say did they think of resettling all these thousands of people? And it is not just this slum, there must be others in the plan."

His wife replied, "It seems these folks were forewarned and asked to move. Who knows how, maybe flyers were dropped. They cannot read. They might have made toy boats and airplanes of the papers. Or perhaps announcements were made, like they do when a new film is released. A man passes by in an autorickshaw and screams out the news in a mike."

Sanjay Gandhi was not an elected Member of Parliament, but being the son of Indira Gandhi, had enormous power over her and therefore the country, in this Emergency era. There was a plan to make an affordable car, a people's car. The industrialist, Birla, had built an empire by selling the Ambassador car, which was the staple of the Indian roads, from taxis to the President's fleet. But this huge contract was awarded to Sanjay Gandhi, one who had no entrepreneurial experience, only a love for racing cars, and was a stunt pilot himself. He dashed to Germany's Volkswagen, of the German "folks' car" fame, and at the same time contacted the Japanese Suzuki. The two potential partners fought to outsmart each other, and finally the Suzuki design of Maruti 800 stuck. Then Sanjay Gandhi started interfering with the cabinet ministers, dictating their task, until they resigned, and one of his loyalists was awarded the spot.

Someone knocked on the door, and Savita ran to open it. She had pasted a note on her door letting Atul know where she was. It was the milkman. Mr Arora assured her,

"Savita, don't worry about Atul, he will not return so fast. Only after he can participate in a good episode will he return. I am willing to bet he went off in that bus on purpose for some adventure."

"What if they took him to jail?" Savita nibbled a nail.

"Then right now he is having tea with the warden. You don't know him as well as we do."

His wife shaded her mouth with her hand and whispered, "He is jealous of your husband. Atul seems to run into so many adventures just like that, and then he comes and tells them like they were stories of Sinbad the Sailor."

Finally, after three hours Atul did turn up, sweaty but beaming. Savita fell on his chest and cried a little.

"Now what?" asked his friend turning up his nose in defeated pride.

"You will not guess where I was."

"In an oilfield they just discovered near the Parliament House?"

"Hah, you must be seething now. You jealous little monkey. I was in a health clinic where they were performing vasectomy."

His friend chuckled at last. "Is the job done, did they nab you for being so nosy!"

The ladies could not follow, "What is that 'vasec' thing?"

"It means neutering of men."

"What?" cried Savita.

"Oh no, they could not get me. It was easy. I just had to speak some English to prove I was a bystander who got picked up by mistake."

"So now they are neutering! And do these men know what it is they are undergoing?"

"I doubt it, but it is a question of hours when someone guesses."

Atul's friend was being sarcastic, "I suppose they call it vaccination! Now who is such a fool? Why do you need to vaccinate there, and what about women? Don't they need vaccination?"

"Dinesh, on the contrary I think at last Sanjay Gandhi has struck upon a good idea."

"What are you saying? Forcibly neutering these people is a good idea? He should be tried in Nuremburg."

"Don't overreact. All men with two children were notified to get vasectomy done. But I am sure none turned up. We all know India has a huge population problem. And these people have no idea about family planning. Education will take a few generations. We know Sanjay is a pilot who flies at breakneck speed. He wants the results now."

"Atul, a social issue cannot be solved with bulldozers and syringes."

At Savita's doorstep, Sakina's whole family was waiting. Her mother-in-law held her two kids while she held the baby suckling her. Savita whispered, "Sakina has three children! I thought she was my age."

"She is. Now you see why vasectomy is necessary?"

The family did not want to resettle in the outskirts because she was working here. They were hoping the big engines would pass by and then they would surreptitiously return and set up their homes again. They were elastic in their dwelling habits having so little to lose. They were willing to pitch tents in the corner of the garage. All they needed was a small place to lay their blankets. They had lived without toilets and running water all their lives, and would feel privileged to be able to share the watchman's facilities. Only Sahib had to put in a word for them. Atul spoke to Sakina's husband, "Adil, why don't you go and get the simple operation done? They are doing it for free." Adil looked at his feet. Savita took the women away with her out of earshot.

"It is not painful, and after this you will not have any more children. Do you agree, look at me while I speak. The women have left, you don't have to feel embarrassed."

"They say you will lose your manhood."

"That is nonsense. Surely you don't want more children? What will you feed them? Can you send them to school? What if they get sick?"

"Then why don't they do it for women?"

"Because the operation for a woman is not easy. She has to take rest for a week, and henceforth she has to be more careful too. But men don't have any such problem. The whole thing takes minutes. Thousands are getting it done."

Adil kicked the wall and grunted.

Atul felt frustrated. "No wonder force was needed." He went inside his flat.

"Savita, you had better talk to Sakina and explain about family planning."

"To urge her to send Adil for the operation? Will he listen to her?"

"I doubt he will. What I meant was teach her how to prevent having children."

"They don't have money to buy contraceptives!"

"Just teach them about timing."

"Ah, that I can try, but you know it will mean many days will be prohibited, about a third of the month, and frankly I don't think disciplining husbands will work."

"Does not sound like a solution then ..."

"Maybe we should tell her about the law they passed a few years back."

"The abortion law?"

"Yes, Atul, I think women in our country will look upon it as a salvation. How many know they can walk into any government hospital and ask for an abortion, and that it will be done free of cost, and the whole business will be kept secret?"

"Yes Savita, I think our kind of democracy is more about educating women than men. Most of the women in that slum are the main earners for the family. They have a steady job. Their men stand in streets every morning to be chosen by the Public Works Department or a construction project, to lay roads, mix cement, and the like. They often waste the money on booze and sometimes grab the wife's earnings too."

"Just bad habits?"

"No, the work they do makes them ache in the body. And with poor nourishment the only way they can ease the muscular pains is by alcohol. And, of course, it has the pleasure factor too. But at the same time it is addictive."

"Why don't they use the money to buy better food?"

"They can, and that is where education comes in. Their role models have drunk themselves to sleep, not eaten good food. Someone has to stick a boulder in front of the cart that is running downhill. From childhood, before they get into the bad habit of making wrong choices, they have to know what is right. And also that the right way is available for them."

"Atul, will this thing blow out of proportion? I mean if they picked you, surely they have neutered some men who have fewer than two children?"

"And some who are not married? Yes, possibly. There is always a price to pay."

"And the other thing is why did they choose this slum, full of Muslims?"

"Savita, Delhi was under the Muslim rulers for five hundred years. Even the common men who settled here were mostly Muslims or converts to Islam. Non-Muslims had to pay the jizya tax. But if a person converted to Islam he got land, cash and better job opportunities. What could a poor man do, but align his faith to his purse? Therefore the biggest slums in Delhi are Muslim ones. But this is not to say Hindu slums are any different. We have seen enough of them in Bombay."

There was a cartoon by R. K. Laxman showing a space research centre with the banner "Man on the moon project". The Common Man stood at the entrance of the busy laboratory. One of the scientists pointed at him and said, "This is our man; he can survive without water, food, light, air, shelter ..."

Part Four

Chapter Sixteen

Jalal

"Didima, where did baba and ma go?" asked Panchali. Debjani opened her mouth to answer and dropped the rubber band pinched between her lips.

Panchali picked it up laughing, "Third time! No, first tell me, and then tie my hair."

"They have gone to the hospital to get you a toy, a live and kicking one."

Panchali clapped her little hands, "Oh, I will have so much fun!"

"So tell me what kind of playmate do you want?" Debjani now fiddled with Panchali's shoe straps.

Her granddaughter tilted her head to think, "I want a horse!"

The question had two options, boy or girl, not an animal. But Debjani remembered children's tantrums and just played the game. "All right, let's see if your parents have also the same plan for you."

At the hospital the Deshmukh family was waiting for them to arrive. "How is Bina?" asked Debjani, worried that she would have a hard delivery this time too.

"How are they you should ask, it's all over."

Debjani picked Panchali and ran panting, forgetting the girl was not a baby any more.

Anand took over Panchali, but she squirmed in his arms. "Where is my horse, where is my horse?"

He placed her on the ground and looked at his mother-in-law wearing a mock frown.

"This is not a horse, didima. Where is the tail?"

"Panchali ma, don't touch him, he is asleep. The tail is ... tucked inside the towel." Debjani patted Panchali's hair disrupting her own hard work, and asked her daughter excitedly, "So what's the name?"

"I don't know, Ucchaishravas maybe?" laughed Binapani as best she could after the battle she had undergone. "Remember, that is the celestial white horse of Indra, King of the Gods. He can fly like the winged Pegasus of the Greek mythology."

Anand rescued Debjani, "Ma, we were thinking of naming him Yuyutsu, since his sister is Panchali. You know he is not as well known as the other characters in the Mahabharata, but that is a shame."

"Anand, I must confess my ignorance. Enlighten me."

"He was a half-brother of the hundred Kauravas."

"I thought all their names began with Duh."

Anand laughed, "That is hardly possible. Will parents name their children with that prefix? It means 'bad'. Yodhan, is a warrior, and Duryodhan, a bad warrior. Dusshasan, a bad ruler. Their actual names all had the prefix 'Su', which means 'good'. Good warrior, good ruler, Suyodhan, Susshasan, and so on. When the story was written they had already proved themselves to be the bad fruits of the family tree, so their names were changed in the narrative. But Yuyutsu, the youngest brother, was different. In that infamous court scene when Panchali's sari was about to be pulled off her, and nobody tried to intervene, Yuyutsu was furious. He could not protest because that would mean insulting the elders, his grandfather, Bheeshma, and his own father and brothers. But when the deed was done, and Panchali asked her elders why they had sat mute as if paralyzed by the spectacle, Yuyustu also spoke up. He expressed his disappointment and walked out of the court. In the Kurukshetra battle he fought in the Pandava camp, and afterwards he and the Pandava brothers shared the land as local regents, while the eldest Pandava, Yudhishthira, became the emperor."

"Anand, this is a very good name. I hope our Yuyutsu will not wait that long to help his sister, if such a situation arises, and I pray it does not."

Binapani added, "The name means one who is enthused to fight."

Raja came jogging into the room and picked up the baby. Everybody wondered how one individual could change the atmosphere from the serene to the chaotic within seconds. He handed a Five Star chocolate bar to Panchali, who suddenly wanted to touch her horse because her uncle would deny her nothing. The baby had started crying and called in two cooing nurses. Raja's parents squeezed into the compact room, and in the confusion, Raja embraced his aunt, Debjani. "Pishi, I have a surprise for you too. No, it is bigger than a Five Star bar. I am going to join the Mohun Bagan team."

What's and Oh's followed and then were shut up by laddus in mouths. "But, pishi," said Raja pulling a long face, "Here is the bad news. I will have to relocate to Calcutta. I was thinking since you are alone, maybe I could disrupt your peace."

Debjani held her heart. "At last I will be able to unlock some of the rooms, and get a driver for the car." She was so happy she had to wipe her tears. "Oh, and the pump shed needs a new door, and the façade could do with a coat of paint, oh my God, we could get a dog too, oh my God, the garden needs fresh plants. And when your father retires he should come right back to the house. Bina, I have so much work!" she wiped some more tears.

* * * * *

Anand settled in his favourite chair and Binapani reclined on the sofa with Yuyutsu at her breast. He opened the letter from Delhi. "So let us read what Savita says.

Dear Bhaiya

Atul has found a new job in a private firm. You can tell aai and baba right now. They will know it anyway when they come here for my delivery. Looks like Rama Rajya did not last very long. And now the monkeys are ruling. I see only banana skins tossed all around and people slipping over them. You must be smiling at me, how unlike baba I have become. All right, I admit I am under Atul's influence and I am glad he joined a private firm. When our baby grows up a little, I will also start working, maybe as a teacher, or in the human resources department of a private firm. These have started mushrooming all over in Delhi, and I am sure in Bombay too. Why should I rest at home when the country needs hard-working people? Is it not sad that we have millions of job seekers, and yet potholed roads, and people using streets as toilets? Atul has done some calculation; if the money that is funnelled out of a project could be collected, water tanks could be constructed in every neighbourhood, and public toilets built with a pukka sewage system to solve hygiene problems."

When the jails were full of political prisoners, some hundred and forty thousand of them, and clandestine pamphlets flooded people's desks as much as pro-government newspapers, Indira Gandhi called for new general elections. She had become unpopular with her iron-fisted so-called dictatorship. She risked the elections in 1977 and lost them. The Janata Party coalition rose to power, and for the first time Indian democracy learnt an important lesson – the precariousness of a coalition government. Any decision had to be blessed by multiple factions, each working solely for its own future, not the country's. No bill could be passed in the Parliament without protracted negotiations. Tribunals were set up to investigate the Emergency misdeeds, but they functioned irregularly. The government machinery went back to its inefficient ways, and there was a leadership vacuum. The Prime Minister, Morarji Desai, resigned, gave way to Charan Singh, who also could not steady the sinking ship, and within two years fresh elections were announced.

* * * * *

Binapani was buying vegetables from the vendor who sold his produce on the hand-cart, when a lady smiled at her, "Are you Panchali's mother?"

"Yes. I am Binapani."

"I am her teacher in kindergarten. They call me Asha Ma'm."

Binapani wondered for a second if Panchali had done something naughty.

"I know your husband well, Anand Deshmukh. He is very active during the Ganapati poojas. What I wanted to tell you is that Panchali has good organizing abilities. We are very happy to have her in our school."

"Really? Can you see it already? What did she do?"

"Piyali, one of our junior teachers, is getting married soon. We told the students about the special event in her life and that she would leave us. On Piyali's last day at school, the students prepared a surprise for her. They held hands and sang nursery rhymes she had taught, circled around her and performed quite a few dances. Then at the end they sang 'Happy Birthday To You!' We laughed our heads off. They thought the special event was her birthday. Anyway it seems the whole show was planned by Panchali. We were impressed that a small girl could control so many of her age and put together such a performance."

"That's her father all over!" Binapani said brightly. She was very proud of both of them, her husband and daughter.

At home she told Anand about Panchali's first report card from a teacher. He was as excited as her,

"We should celebrate, and what better way than a performing arts treat! Let's take her to the new film, Gol Maal. I hear it is the funniest ever made so far."

"I would love to see Utpal Dutt. What an actor!"

"And comedian! We can have some dahi vada on the way to the theatre, and bring some back for uncle, aunt and Yuyutsu." Road food sizzled, smelled and tasted much better than home food. Some thought it was the special ingredients of dust and bus exhaust, and some accused the spicy chutneys. But when the snack vendor came by ringing his bell, small and large feet came scurrying down to halt his progress.

Panchali trembled in excitement. She wore her birthday dress, a gauzy blue frock and matching shoes. Binapani tied a white ribbon in her hair and the three of them left for the theatre hall in an autorickshaw. Every experience darted into her consciousness – the pitch dark theatre, the smell of carpet, a hundred aunties wearing lipstick, their saris swishing like angels' wings, the beam of light stabbing the screen, the loud sound that pierced her ears, everything was new, thrilling. Panchali absorbed the moving scenes, the colours, the dialogues and songs, the facial expressions, the clothing, the scenery. Her mind was bursting with questions when the curtain dropped for the interval. Her parents answered them in as much detail as they could looking around embarrassed at their neighbours who were eavesdropping unashamedly and even laughed at some comments. At last Binapani caught the old man on her right, "You answer this one, sir." Anand also invited his neighbours and soon none had to pretend they were not listening.

The family walked out of the hall with a bouncing Panchali. She was too excited to walk. She skipped ahead and then retraced her steps to join her parents. "How long ago did Urmila and Lakshman get married? Do they have children? Can I meet them?"

Anand looked at Binapani bewildered, and then he explained, "Urmila and Lakshman are not in real life as you saw in the film. This is just a story. They even have different names, Bindiya Goswami and Amol Palekar."

Panchali stopped dead, "You mean they did not love each other?"

"No, they were just acting!"

"But they went through so much trouble to get married!"

"Films are like that. Bindiya and Amol have their own families and their own separate lives."

"It was all lies then!" Panchali started crying. "And I thought they were happy with each other."

In the history of Gol Maal, nobody had ever cried. In fact people laughed themselves to tears. And when they felt depressed they recalled scenes from the film to dispel the gloom.

"Bina, do something," whispered Anand.

"Shall I say you lied, and that they are together now?"

"Why rope me in? Think of something better."

They passed by the candy vendor. He takes one little blob of coloured sugar and fluffs it up into a pink cloud that melts in your mouth. Binapani pointed at the air-filled giant lollypop,

"Panchali, look what we have for you." She handed her weeping daughter the stick.

"No!" Panchali pushed it away. "Don't fool me with that. Why did they not love each other, why did they lie to us?"

"Bina, stop eating it yourself!" Binapani had no idea she was nibbling at the cotton candy.

"Panchali, but Urmila and Lakshman are happy. They both love somebody, if not each other."

Panchali eased her crying and stretched her hand for the candy.

Anand leaned over her head towards his wife, "I am beginning to feel scared for her already. She has too soft a heart."

* * * * *

Panchali adjusted her mittens with a lot of fuss. She had never worn these knitted woollen things in her hands and they kept slipping out, or so she thought. The family was visiting Delhi during Anand's winter vacation. Yuyutsu pointed at every passing horse, "Ghora, ghora!" he was discovering proper use of his tongue and the euphoria of communication. Binapani smiled, "He does not realize we are sitting on a horse-drawn carriage ourselves." They passed by the Red Fort, its walls serrated and imposing, as if even now some cannon's nose was hiding behind one of the red shoulders. This was not Bombay or Calcutta, but a city that had seen sieges and battles, city of secret tunnels and gallows, city of bazaars where ladies came to shop wrapped from head to toe in black cloth and monkeys danced around little girls performing acrobatic tricks. This was where women drove their private cars and went to cocktail parties in skirts, cigarette in hand. This was where the Savitas worked hard to keep the family steamer chugging, and the Atuls laid out nation-building blueprints. This was where the Sakinas living in the slums rowed their raft on a choppy sea, and the Adils held up the wheels on their backs.

Yuyutsu and Savita's son, Prahlad, touched and tasted each other for the first time, consciously. Then they discovered a scented eraser hidden inside a dog of red plastic that opened at its belly. Each wanted to possess the treasure, and proved that they had not received their names in vain. When the parents came upon the scene, they found the two halves of the eraser in the two mouths, each with an incomplete set of teeth! The dog's body had been partitioned likewise. Within minutes the two boys realized the folly of the division. Yuyutsu handed his half to his sister as he had no use for it, and Prahlad did the same, copying his brother, older by a few months. So Panchali thanked them both. She found herself richer by a full dog.

"Didi, what does Prahlad mean?" asked Yuyutsu.

"Yes, didi tell me also," Prahlad came and sat beside Yuyutsu. The two boys faced Panchali. She began, clearing her throat, like one of her teachers. "Lord Vishnu rests on a coiled serpent in heaven. When on earth there is a lot of fighting and we, human beings, cannot handle the situation any more, Vishnu comes to help us. Every time he comes down, we say it is an avatar of Vishnu that has arrived. Of his ten avatars, nine have already come and gone. In his first avatar, he appeared as a giant fish, and saved the good people from a terrible flood. In his second, he took the form of a turtle and helped in the churning of the ocean that produced nectar. He appeared as a boar in his third avatar, and rescued the Earth Goddess from the depths of the ocean with his tusks. In his fourth avatar, he revealed himself in answer to the prayer of Prahlad. Prahlad was the son of an asura king named Hiranyakashipu."

"What is an asura, didi?"

"A very cruel person. He scares children at night, and wants everything for himself. Big things, not just little toy dogs. This particular asura had been killing all the good human beings who were worshipping Vishnu. His son, Prahlad, disobeyed him and kept singing Vishnu's praise. So the asura got angry and tried to kill Prahlad, his own son."

"Oh, he was indeed a bad man," pondered Yuyutsu.

"A very bad man!" echoed Prahlad.

"First weapons and poisonous snakes were unleashed on Prahlad, but they could not even touch him. Then a mad elephant came running to trample him, but it saw Vishnu with Prahlad and dashed away. Then Prahlad was dropped from a high cliff, but Vishnu caught him in his palms. He had a witch of an aunt who had a boon of not getting burnt. She sat in a fire with Prahlad on her lap, but the fire did not touch him. Then Hiranyakashipu got very angry and asked Prahlad why he was praying to someone he could not even see. Was he not supposed to pray to his father, the great conqueror of the world? But Prahlad said, 'Vishnu is everywhere'. The asura mocked him, 'So is Vishnu in this pillar also?' Prahlad said 'Yes'. Then his father was so angry he kicked the pillar and broke it. From the shattered pieces, Vishnu really came out. And what a form did he have this time! He had legs like a man, but his face and arms were of a lion, that is why this avatar is called Narasimha, man-lion. Oh, I forgot to tell you that Hiranyakashipu had prayed a lot at one time. Brahma gave him a boon, and he asked for immortality. But Brahma could not grant it, so the asura asked that he should not be killed by man or woman or beast, by day or night, indoors or outdoors."

"Is that why Vishnu was half man and half lion?"

"Yes, and it was twilight, which means neither day nor night. Narasimha sat on the threshold of the palace and killed the asura. Then Prahlad became king, and peace returned on earth."

Binapani and Savita exchanged remarks, "For children, it is so easy to believe that someone can change forms like that; fish, turtle, boar, and then half and half."

"Yes, they catch the essence better than us; they don't get stuck on unimportant details."

"I am King Pallad!" lisped the little boy, looking proudly up at his mother.

"And I am King Utsu!" screamed Yuyutsu.

Panchali saw them get up and start sparring with their arms as swords, just when she was getting into a story-telling mood. "But Vishnu has six other avatars. I have not finished the story, come back you two." Nobody was listening to her any more, the story session was over, and now it was battle time.

* * * * *

The two families went to Amritsar in Punjab. Atul asked, "When are you sure you are in Punjab?"

Binapani was the first to raise her hand to answer, "When you see people in turbans with flowing beards and huge loose pyjamas."

Atul shook his finger, "You will know you are in Punjab when people start getting more friendly, not just by their turban, or the Bangali."

"What is a Bangali?" Binapani had never heard of any attire called the Bangali. She was a Bengali from Bengal, but how could a dress too be it?

"The same thing that is called a Punjabi in Bengal."

"Is that so? How very interesting! We Bengalis have used that word as a household name for ever without associating it with Punjab. It is the loose-fitting kurta worn over a pyjama. Fair enough, I should admit. But Bangali sounds so funny. I must share it with my mother."

People were friendly, especially if you passed by a line of tea stalls or snack shops. It was hard to pass one and choose another, you were called with endearments and gestures of welcome in those big bodies beckoning you with their fan-like palms. They smiled and joked. You knew they spoke from the heart. There was no hypocrisy, no slyness, no calculation for personal gain, no sarcasm to hurt another, just plain and simple good-heartedness.

At the entrance of the Golden Temple in Amritsar, visitors leave their footwear in the care of the volunteers in charge. All cover their heads in deference to God. Binapani pulled her sari over her head, and Savita wrapped hers with her dupatta. The men placed a handkerchief on their head and had to keep a check on them every few minutes. The children pulled up their sweaters from the back and blatantly showed their unpreparedness to visit the temple. Binapani had heard about the Golden Temple, but she had not expected to see it actually covered with gold, shining blindingly in the midday sun. A few feet from the ground up, all the way to the dome, the structure was plated in solid gold. The two families washed their hands in the sacred pool that surrounds the temple. The children splashed around playing with the reflection of the temple. Panchali exclaimed with delight, "Look, there are fish in the water!" And so there were; huge fish one foot long, white and orange and speckled, swimming close to the surface. People fed them crumbs from the sweets they got as prasad. The prayer hall under the dome was packed with devotees. Someone fanned the Book, the Guru Granth Sahib, with a soft white whisk, and another read from it.

Sikhism is a blend of the religions that were practised in Punjab at the time it was founded. Sufism from Persia, Islam of the rulers, and Hinduism of the native people fused together. The Guru Granth Sahib has writings of saints from all spiritual paths, including the words of the ten Sikh gurus. Sikhism emphasizes the brotherhood of man and equality in God's eyes, and respects the right of people to practise their own religion. For centuries, Punjab was the gateway to India. The adventurers had slipped through the Khyber Pass of the Hindu Kush mountains between Afghanistan and India. They crossed the wide-banked Sindhu, and reached the land of the five rivers, Punjab. Many conquerors stopped right there and did not proceed deeper into the hinterland. Alexander the Great did come a little further inward, but then withdrew back to Afghanistan. A form of Graeco-Indian art developed from that confluence of cultures, called the Gandhar art. Afghanistan was called Gandhar during the epoch of the Mahabharata. The much revered queen mother of the hundred Kuru princes was from this kingdom, and thus her name was Gandhari. Guru Nanak in the fifteenth century gathered his people under the aegis of the Sikh religion, and started compiling the gospel, the Guru Granth Sahib. They rejected idol worship, as did the Islamic people, but they had art depicting human forms like the Hindus. Their gurudwaras had the mosque-like domes, and ornate pedestals and interior decors like Hindu temples. Initially a pacifist religion, but eventually under Guru Gobind Singh, the last guru, they had to turn militant to defend themselves against the Mughal rulers. Two of their ten gurus were martyred in an attempt to protect religious minorities – Sikhs and Hindus. In 1699 the Khalsa was formed, the group of pure ones, who vowed to protect themselves, with force, if the situation demanded. They would be on constant alert, and carry the five Ks on their body. These were the dagger, kirpan, the iron bracelet, kara, hair they did not cut, kesh, the comb, kangha, and the under pants, kachera. Men added to their names a "Singh", which means lion, and women added "Kaur", meaning princess.

After a frolicsome hand wash, Prahlad slipped and fell on his back on the marble floor polished by thousands of feet. Some others were also performing the stunt, but since Yuyutsu giggled, he raised a tantrum. Atul was stranded outside till the boy was calm and returned to find the rest of them eating halwa, the cracked wheat sweet made with a generous helping of ghee, Punjabi style. Prahlad felt deprived and would have gone into his second tantrum. But quickly Savita stuffed his mouth with a ball of halwa.

In the afternoon, they took a rickshaw to the India-Pakistan border. Lahore and Amritsar were once twin cities, in the middle of Punjab, one of the largest provinces in British India. The line that split the nation in 1947 hung above these two cities for a period of months, undecided where it would fall. The suspense broke one fine day with the dismal news that the line had split the twins in the centre. Lahore went to Pakistan, and Amritsar to India. The Muslims marched westwards, and the Sikhs and Hindus eastwards. Both governments had made a promise to compensate with land those who were giving up immovable property. But the promise got lost in the chaos of the Partition. The Punjab of the ten gurus, the fertile land of the skilful farmers, was still called Punjab in both countries, but a fence was erected between the two halves. By the time the families visited, in 1979, the border line had a row of armed personnel looking at each other over a stretch of no-man's-land.

A couple of army jawans approached the little boys and started chatting with them, enjoying their kids' talk. The parents met another family which had come to visit from Rajasthan and they started their own serious conversation, about the recent

Emergency, and a lot of adult talk that bored Panchali. She started walking on the path that lay ahead, that grew drier and had fewer flower pots until there was none at all, as if that part of the earth was orphaned from human kindness. The Pakistan Rangers across on Lahore side detected movement in the adjoining zone in no-man's-land, and focused their binoculars. "Nothing to cause panic, it must be a civilian's child. She had strayed a little beyond the line." But the child kept advancing towards them steadily.

Binapani suddenly looked around, "Where is Panchali? Yuyutsu, where is didi?" Then she saw her, already far ahead on the road to Pakistan.

"Anand, look where Panchali has gone!"

They called her name, aloud, then together. She did not turn back. The army officials now had gathered, and one man had hopped onto his perch. He switched on the microphone.

"Attention please, there is a civilian's daughter walking towards you. Please do not retaliate. We will make her turn back."

Panchali heard the microphone call out her name, then her father and mother's voice begging her to return, in supplication, in panic, in anger. She turned for an instance, and wondered why they were calling out to her in that curious fashion and not coming to get her. This was different from wandering off on the seashore, then. There her father would have run into a wave and lifted her out. Surely this was less dangerous. Maybe there was a bit of fun on the other side of the road. And now she could see the other side of the road, with a similar line of army personnel. The only difference was that they wore green uniform instead of the brown. A different flag was flying from the pole. It was green with a sliver of a moon and a single star and there was a white band on it near the pole side. She walked right into the line of uniformed men, many of whom had knelt as if to greet her and be at her height. She smiled at them and pointed to the road behind, "Why did they call my name but not come to get me?"

"Because they are scared of us," joked one of them, "See we can become tigers." He made paws out of his hands in front of her face. She pushed them away.

"Who's afraid of a fake tiger?"

He picked her on his shoulder and they all stood up, "Look, that side is India, and here, where we are standing, is Pakistan."

Panchali shook her head. "No, my father says that is Amritsar. 'Amrit' means nectar and 'sar' means river, the place where nectar flows."

"You are a smart little girl." They looked at each other and nodded.

Panchali went on "What does Pakistan mean?"

A soldier answered, "'Pak' means pure and 'stan' means land, so Pakistan is a pure land."

"Then why don't they come to fetch me? Why should the nectar not flow into the pure land?"

The men looked at each other. "Does anyone have a toffee or something to give to this little girl?"

"No, I don't want a toffee. I know that trick. You will not answer me then. Tell me, did you fight with Kuldip uncle on that side?"

"No, not us," the men shook their heads in mock fear.

"Then it must be with Hari Singh uncle."

"No, we don't even know these people."

Anand assured his wife, "Bina, trust them. Nobody will have the heart to hurt a little child. You know Panchali, she must be asking them a dozen questions. Please Bina, don't make a scene here. I will request them to call her back again."

"Panchali, you are asked to return right now. This is a question of national security." The microphone blared from the Indian side and called her again.

Panchali asked the men, "What does that mean?"

"It means your parents must be worried for you. Now run along, Panchali."

She shook her head and her lower lip stuck out, "No, uncle, I am not going to walk back, I am tired." The men raised their eyebrows. Then the soldier who was holding Panchali, Jalal, put her down and switched on the microphone. "She says she can't walk back, she is tired." There was silence from the Indian side, which meant they were consulting with each other. Jalal continued, "I can bring her till the midpoint. I will come unarmed. One of you can pick her up from there. Come unarmed."

"Agreed," came the response after a few seconds.

Jalal removed his holster and handed it to his colleague. "Jalal, careful!" said the man. Jalal nodded and picked up Panchali in his arms. She waved at the men in green uniform. "Phir milenge Pakistan, will meet you again, Pakistan." They waved back cheerfully, "What a sweet little girl."

Jalal carried her on the road he had not walked on since his childhood. He was born in Amritsar, and when he was seven his parents discovered they were on the wrong side of the new International border. Two days after Independence the line that was to demarcate India from Pakistan, Radcliffe's hasty one-and-half-month labour, was handed down to the prime ministers of the new nations. They stared at it in disbelief. The jute fields and the jute mills lay on different sides. The power grid and the power station would have their connections snapped. Crops would dry cut off from their irrigation wells. What if this was shown to the leaders before Partition? Would they have given it up? Perhaps they could have shared it with the people whose lives it was going to change forever. And then who knows ... .

On the morning of July 18, 1947, the newspaper boy came screaming, a paper in hand. "They have decided! Lahore will go to Pakistan, Amritsar to India." Within two hours their neighbours had left. Jalal's father hesitated as he did not want to leave his property, but from his window he observed people were already taking over the deserted houses. They were Hindus and Sikhs, and some had journeyed on bullock carts from the other side of the border. He saw a glimmer of hope. Maybe he could go to Pakistan and grab one of the houses these same people would have abandoned. Jalal's family gave up the home they had lived in for generations and the plot of land they farmed, like fourteen million other people.

"Look, Panchali, right here, thirty-two years back I was on a bullock cart with my father and mother, my sisters and brother. We passed by so many other carts coming from the opposite direction. We called out 'Assalam Alaikum'. They answered 'Sat Sri Akal'. Let peace with you. Truth is Eternal. But ever since we have neither found peace nor truth."

"Where were you going on that bullock cart?"

"To Pakistan, and Kuldip was going to India. Then on the way someone swore at Kuldip's uncle because he had lost all he had laboured for, for sixty years of his life. And Kuldip's uncle too saw how his land was snatched up by those who had not mixed their sweat with the rain water to irrigate it. He answered with a stone that hit my uncle. And my uncle jumped down from the cart and ran towards the stone thrower and cracked open his head with a stick. The dead man had three strong brothers with a stick each, and what a fight there was! Bodies lay gasping for air on this very road."

"Right here? Near that rock?"

"Yes, that rock has seen so much it is mute with shock. This road is paved with bones and the trees that stood were watered with blood."

Kuldip Singh had come to pick up Panchali. He shook hands with Jalal and introduced himself. "Thank you for bringing her."

"Jalal-ud-din Saleem ... Kuldip, why are the Indian rifles pointing here?"

"Jalal, turn around and see the Pakistani side. They are also on alert."

Jalal shook his head. "Arre, we don't have proper answers for a child. Isn't it sad?"

"Yes, I agree completely. We just keep hoping some leader will have an answer, even for our questions."

Binapani was so angry she wanted to slap her straying daughter, but Atul stepped in front and picked her up. "Tell me your adventure in the foreign country. I have never been to one and I would love to step outside our perimeter."

"Is Pakistan a foreign country?"

"Yes, no, I mean, I don't know. You are right, Pakistan will not qualify."

* * * * *

Savita's letter read, "Indira Gandhi is back wearing a soft glove this time. She has apologized to the nation for the Emergency. Can you believe it? Is this what the Indian people want? Slackness in work, and an apology for efficiency? She has also roped in some of her former foes in her new government. Atul says he had overestimated people's sentiments. They did not want to work, they were just responding to fear. No whip, no work. So he has joined a firm that has great potential. They are going to build a temple for a religion called Bahai. I had never heard of it. But India being India, a soil fertilized by all faiths in the world, could not stay away from planting this Bahai way of life. Atul says, in the eighteenth century, Bahaullah in Persia founded a new religion based on tolerance for all religions. Teachers from other paths, Buddha, Christ and Mohammad, were all considered prophets. He has shown me some drawings of the temple. It will be magnificent, a modern wonder of the world. Imagine a white lotus with many petals, some closed and some spread out. Now blow it up a thousandfold. The delicate marble is coming from quarries in Greece. It seems some other Bahai temples around the world were also built using the same stone. The interior will be a huge hall with no religious symbols, nor any formal worship, or sermon. Men and women of all religions and cultures can meditate in their own way. What a wonderful idea! There will be nine pools around it and a beautiful garden surrounding the lotus temple. The whole area is a sprawling twenty-six acres. I just can't wait to see it done, but it will take years to complete. The architect is from the land of Bahaullah, Iran. But can you guess who has helped buy the land? A single individual, Ardishír Rustampúr of Hyderabad. He passed away in 1953 and bequeathed all his life's savings for it."

Sanjay Gandhi was elected to the Parliament, but could not contribute much. In June the same year, 1980, he was performing an acrobatic loop in his small plane over the Safdarjang Airport in New Delhi when it crashed killing the pilot. India had regained democracy, and Pakistan had lost it. The prime minister elected after the Bangladesh War, Zulfikar Ali Bhutto, faced a military coup by General Zia-Ul-Haq in July 1977. Bhutto was charged with an attempted murder of one of his opponents, was found guilty and hanged in April 1979. General Zia converted Pakistan into an Islamic Republic imposing sharia as the civic law. Iran followed soon, led by a political aspirant who was also the head of the religious order. The Shah of Iran had fled the country in January 1979 amid massive protests and street demonstrations. The exiled religious leader, Ayatollah Ruhollah Khomeini, returned to Tehran and was given a red-carpet welcome. A Shia Islamic Revolution swept across Iran making its neighbour, Iraq, nervous. Saddam Hussein in Iraq led a Sunni minority government in a Shia majority country. In September 1980 Iraq attacked Iran over an old border dispute, expecting Iran to cave in. But within months Iran won back the lost territory and was on the offensive.

By then Iran's other neighbour, Afghanistan, was rocking with shellfire. On December 27, 1979, 700 Soviet soldiers dressed in the Afghan military uniform took over government buildings and the media in Kabul. The Communist government in Afghanistan had requested its ally protection from insurgents – the Mujahideen, the Islamic army. The United States launched itself in the battle against the Soviet Union as part of the ongoing Cold War conflict. Pakistan became the Mujahideen base camp for arming and training recruits. Saudi Arabia and some other Islamic countries supported them. What India needed most at this juncture was internal stability. The Iron Lady, Indira Gandhi, who had proved her mettle in the Bangladesh War, put a strong government back on its feet. Very soon, she nationalized the banks and revoked the "privy purse", a privilege of cash allowance the British had conferred on the Maharajas of the princely states for surrendering their sovereignty and joining one of the two countries, Pakistan or India. There were 565 such kings who forfeited the grant from the government's exchequer after thirty-three years of enjoying these perquisites.

Chapter Seventeen

Sukhvir

Maan Singh entered the room trailing his long dripping hair that wet the ends of the kurta. His eldest son and his nephew were engrossed in a game of chess. From the room upstairs his brother's wife could be heard singing with the women of the neighbourhood. She played the harmonium while another played the pakhawaj, the side drum. Praan Singh came in, "Maan, this year the rains will come early, I can smell it in the wind. We must plan the harvest in advance. You two boys, we will need your help for sure, understood, time you learn some of our trade. Playing chess all the time will not do."

"Uncle, we are not just playing chess, we are playing Radcliffe chess," declared Sukhvir as if he was destiny incarnate.

"And what may that be?"

"See, I get Multan," said Sukhvir, picking up his cousin's knight. Preetam smiled, "But I take Gurdaspur." Sukhvir's rook disappeared on Preetam's side.

Maan Singh snorted while combing his hair. "Boys here are playing being lawyer Cyril Radcliffe."

Praan Singh was impressed by the youngsters, "Well, that is what it has come down to, I hear. There are two persons from the Muslim and two from the non-Muslim side to assist Radcliffe, but it seems they disagree on all proposals. So, finally, it is left to the lawyer to pick and drop this city here, that city there."

"Oye Sukhvir and Preetam, where have you put our home, haan, Rawalpindi?"

"Papaji, Rawalpindi is not decided yet. It is still on the board," replied Sukhvir.

Sukhvir's younger brother pretended his fingers were a flock of vultures over the chess board. "Here goes the Chenab river to Pakistan, and Sutlej to ..." Sukhvir pushed his hands away. "Go away rascal, this is not a game for children." He snatched Chenab and Sutlej back and placed them on the board.

Maan Singh twisted the cloth around his hair into a turban. "Pra-ji, do you think Rawalpindi will be in Pakistan? I mean there are so many of us Sikhs, will they ask us to leave?"

His brother was almost sure because he had heard it from the police station. They would give Gurdaspur to India, which had a Muslim majority. In this way the barter would go on painfully city by city.

"Listen, it is not easy to decide, given that most of the provinces have an almost equal number of Muslims and non-Muslims, which is Hindus and Sikhs combined. Who knew some day we would be segregated by religion? We have lived in close proximity for hundreds of years. If they chose strictly by majority, you would have a border which ran across the countryside like a snake. And what kind of majority is 51%, 52% anyway?"

"You are right. One has to be practical too. On the eastern border, Khulna district is Hindu, and Murshidabad is Muslim, but I hear, to keep the border sane, they have bartered the two."

"Hey Maan, if Rawalpindi does go to Pakistan, will you migrate to India?"

"No, how can I drag these twenty bullocks all the way? Besides here there are so many Sikhs; we will give each other company, what do you say? You will stay, I hope."

But in July 1947 they had hoped for too much. One night they heard a knock on the door; not a gentle tap, but sticks rammed on it, angry sticks. What wrong had they done? Nothing, only they wore turbans in the Sikh fashion. They too believed in a book, but the wrong one. Maan Singh ran up to the terrace and peeped over the parapet. There were at least ten of them. In the neighbouring house he could hear cries of women, "Please, please leave him. Take me." The child screamed, "Mummy, mummy, help, help!" Where was the father? Was he killed already? Maan Singh slipped out to the barn and with a steel blade cut the tethers of his cattle. The animals started lowing and rushed out in confusion. The door was creaking on its hinges ready to give way. Maan Singh, his wife and the two boys ran out through the back door past the crowd of bullocks towards the field. The moon was just coming out and they could see the silhouette of Praan's house. Just one more field to wade through and then they would be at his brother's house. Maybe the two men could defend themselves. Maybe there would be more people assembled at the place, the biggest mansion in this region. Maan lifted the smaller boy on his shoulder and held his wife's hand. She skidded every few steps, and her lips repeated the Lord's name.

Close to Praan's house they were stopped by a small man, "Sahab, don't go there. The family and those who were hiding inside ... they are all dead. People are waiting to kill whoever reaches that house. Come with me to my hut."

"Who are you?" One could not trust anyone any more.

"I worked in your field. Mansur is my name. Either trust me, or die."

For several days following, the family squatted in a small room with hardly any space to stretch. When they heard voices outside they ducked low under the charpoy. Sunlight never penetrated the oily curtains, and after two days their lungs were so foul with their own waste that they would have died of asphyxia. Then one night dressed in black they escaped on a bullock cart towards Lahore.

"If I live through this, Mansur Ali, I will pay you back for your kindness."

"Inshallah we will all live through this nightmare."

"And some day tell our children that adults make graver mistakes than them. And we were of that generation of foolish adults."

In Lahore, Maan Singh met his friend who was hesitating about leaving for India. Shambhunath had a huge house on a hillock overlooking the city, and he already had five families under his shelter. "In rough times we help each other, what is there to thank me for? Now let us pray Lahore goes to India." Maan had lost his brother, like so many others, and his friend patted him sympathetically,

"Before the Rawalpindi massacre I did not care where Lahore would be. I had the simple belief that my estate would remain intact. How can anyone steal land? But no more, the biggest theft in world history is happening right now. A nation is being robbed."

In mid-August the news spread like a wildfire. Not only was Lahore in Pakistan, but whole villages were being torched in communal violence. Shambhunath and his protégés packed what they could grab and made for the border, eastwards.

"Why is there so much of hatred? Did we not stay here together in peace before?"

"It is revenge, my friend, revenge! Nobody knows who flung the first stone. But once that deed was done, the rest followed like a threshing mill, a seesaw back and forth."

The five rivers of Punjab were split, two and three. An invisible live wire called the Radcliffe Line passed through a nest and sent its twigs flying. What remained was a train full of refugees, a village full of dead bodies, vengeance and cruelty, half a million dead, fourteen million displaced, an abandoned past, and an unknown future, in a new homeland.

* * * * *

The two boys, Sukhvir and his brother, were quarrelling for the window seat in the train. The floor was packed with bodies bending this way and that to let people pass by. They held tight to their only possessions – a bag, a suitcase, or a child. Sukhvir hit his younger brother, Balvir. A resounding slap from his mother fell on his cheek. "You two rascals think this is another pleasure trip! Do you know we have lost everything? If not for your father's friends we would be dead by now."

Balvir started crying and kicked Sukhvir continually.

"Sukhvir, get up and let your younger brother sit by the window. Now, be a good example to him."

The train started and the cool breeze quelled some tempers. Then it slowed and people looked at each other in terror. It came to a complete stop in the middle of nowhere. A rumour rose and panic chilled the hearts. The driver was shot and was falling off the train. The man leaning out of the exit screamed, "They are coming, they are coming!"

Passengers moaned, "Oh God, are they going to kill us like this, all jammed up. If we try to escape we will stampede each other to death." Some people near the gate jumped out and tried to crawl away hugging the wheels. Stones landed on the metal body of the train and sticks could be heard cracking bones. A horrific scream rent the air. Thousand prayers of succour rose up from the weeping multitude. Then suddenly the train started moving. Someone would have jumped on the dead driver's seat. Coal was being shovelled into the furnace and the train was picking up speed. Sharp stones tore past the window bars, and angry curses accompanied them. The train had escaped their grasp. Suddenly a stone crashed inside, and Balvir's body slumped on his brother, splattered with blood.

* * * * *

"Hey Rahim, are you there?" came the fakir's voice. Mumtaz was quick to answer, "He is studying now." The fakir was the old bachelor, the madman of Metiaburz, where the Ali family lived, a Muslim neighbourhood of Calcutta. He sang songs, composed poems, spoke about truth and beauty. Also he had an unhealthy habit of distracting the youth. Mumtaz kept a tight hold on Rahim. Nobody remembered the fakir's name, just fakir was enough. Fakirs were adherents of Sufism, wandering philosophers who cared not a paisa to earn their living. The man called aloud, "Oh, all right. They were showing Rakesh Sharma's space mission on television. But if he is studying, maybe he should not be disturbed."

The fakir started his ascent. Three figures pushed him aside and ran up the stairs to the landlord's flat. The last of them, Mumtaz, turned briefly with a smile of apology,

"Shukriya, thank you for letting us know."

Every bit of space in the landlord's room was occupied. Mumtaz sat under the dinner table, almost on Sulaiman's lap, and Rahim jumped on to the table. His friends were already perched on top. Rakesh Sharma was an Indian Air Force pilot, who had flown the fighter plane, MiG-21, during the Bangladesh War. The screen showed the Salyut-1 space capsule, and Rakesh Sharma with the other two cosmonauts posing in front of it. For months, he had trained in the zero gravity facilities in the USSR, and then for six days he was in space photographing the earth. On April 4, 1984 they returned to earth. The television showed Rakesh Sharma in his air force uniform shaking Prime Minister Indira Gandhi's hand. Mir declared,

"I will join the air force too, or at least the army."

Rahim slapped him on the head, "Then who will play the mouth organ?"

"Shh!" whispered Liaqat, "The elders should not know ... yet."

The kids had decided to start their own band, the "Bangladesh Diaspora". They would sing songs in their sibilant dialect, the words that flowed like the many streams of their old country, the sweet Urdu emotions romancing the brave Sanskrit ideas.

Indira Gandhi asked him, "So what did you see from up there, Mr Sharma?"

"*Saare jahan se achha Hindostan hamara!*" was the spontaneous answer. "I saw our nation, Hindustan, the best in the world." It was the first line of a song that accompanied the marching army on Republic Day. They saluted the tricolour, and displayed the missiles, tanks, guns, fighter planes. It was a song written during the freedom struggle, one that reminded people there was a nation to fight for, to die for, and that was their motherland. The composer was Allama Muhammad Iqbal, a lover of his land, the united India that had one enemy, the colonists. Then the word "enemy" was redefined in August 1947. The British Viceroy attended a celebration in the new country, Pakistan's first capital, Karachi, on 14 August. He then flew to celebrate India's independence the next day in Delhi. Iqbal became the national poet of Pakistan, and *Saare jahan se achha* remained with Hindostan, India.

Mir had started drumming on the dining table. Rahim took a deep breath and sang out in his full-throated voice, "*Saare jahan se achha.*" Liaqat looked around and found a Bournvita tin. He grabbed a spoon and applied it rhythmically on the tin's cover. The band was complete. Others joined in and what a chorus it was, spilling into the street and from the street many voices answered and soon a fire cracker flew up in the sky to look down at the earth, "Yes, indeed our nation is the best in the world." The whole country rejoiced, uniting their voices in one beloved melody.

The best in the world is our nation Hindustan,
We are its nightingales, and it is our garden land.
The tallest mountain shades us like the sky
It is our sentinel, it is our guardian.
Thousands of rivers play in its lap
Whose vitality makes our garden the envy of Paradise.
Religion does not teach us to bear ill-will amongst ourselves,
We are of Hind, our homeland is Hindustan.

* * * * *

Panchali picked up the newspaper from outside the door and exclaimed, "Ma, baba, look this is where we were, the Golden Temple! It is on the front page! It says something about the army fighting militants inside the temple complex, for one and half days. They call it Operation Blue Star. The Punjabi insurgents inside the temple are dead."

Anand took the paper. "After the militants were killed in the operation, the army entered the sanctum. And what do you think they found there?"

Binapani tried to guess. "Money, like the donation boxes in the Hindu temples? Gold? Smuggled something?"

"Yes, you got it, but what is that something? Guns. Stacks of them. Machine guns, self-loading rifles, anti-tank missiles. Also food and water to last months. Obviously they were prepared for a long standoff."

Binapani snatched the paper and her eyes sprinted across the front page. The Indian commandos entered the temple, and militants armed with machine guns and semi-automatic rifles fired at them. The operation began late on the night of June 3, 1984 and only when there was no recourse left did the army bring in the tanks. She imagined the tanks rolling on that smooth marble floor beside the sacred pool. Surely the commandos felt a tremor when they walked with their shoes on; but then they would have been as surprised to be fired at from the Akal Takht. It was a building on the periphery of the pool, a sacred place where the gospel, Guru Granth Sahib, is kept at night.

"Oh listen, Bhindranwale is dead, the leader of the insurgents. Shabeg Singh, the former Major General who had joined the Punjabi militants, also died in the crossfire. He must have put together the strategy as the commandos were being gunned down methodically, so much so that they had to finally roll in seven tanks! It was all over yesterday, 5 June, and we did not know this was happening. Let me read, maybe that mystery is also explained."

Panchali was getting taller by the day. She leaned over the paper and read it. "It says here. Punjab was under curfew, not even electricity was supplied for thirty-six hours. Communication lines were snapped. All journalists were picked up from their hotels and deposited outside the state."

"Let me drop you off at school today." Binapani was too excited to stay at home when for the first time such a drastic stance was taken by the government. A military attack on a sacred temple! But more intriguing was the fact that the temple had become a fortified armed camp. How was it allowed to happen? Didn't the Punjab Police know about it?

Throngs of parents had come that day to drop their children. They gathered in little groups in the school compound and exchanged news from the various newspapers. Teachers too were in no hurry to begin the classes. "Once in a blue moon or rather 'blue star', the first period can be sacrificed," joked a teacher. Every adult wanted to add his bit to the news.

"How were weapons allowed inside a temple? I can't imagine any in a church."

"At first Bhindranwale and his gang lived in a guest house

on the edge of the pool. Then he moved inside the Akal Takht. The head priest protested, but was overruled by the gurudwara's governing board. Every house around the temple was used as a stronghold or an observation tower."

"The chief of police force was gunned down some time back while leaving the temple after prayers. These renegades were above the law; the police had no power."

"Bhindranwale used to be a preacher, and had such a sway in Punjab that unless the central government took drastic measures Punjab would be a lost cause."

"But what do they want?" asked Yuyutsu to his mother.

"Khalistan, a free independent country."

"Why, did India treat them badly?"

"Oh they have so many resentments. Now, run along, looks like the principal has come herself."

The bell rang loud and clear, and cleared out the loud talkers. On the way out Mr Damankar was found shepherding the rest of the inquisitive parents. "I am sure they did not expect Indira Gandhi to ride straight into the sanctum to oust them. One needs some guts for that."

"Not acting at all was a bigger risk I think. If the Khalistan movement took wing, what should stop the others, say the Northeastern states? They too have harboured disappointments for long."

"Yes, correct. I am from Assam and I will tell you why there are insurgents there. There is a narrow stretch of land that connects the Northeast to the rest of India, just about twenty kilometre-wide at the constriction. Chicken's Neck it is called. When it floods we are cut off by road and sometimes telegraph poles snap. We are then a country of our own anyway. Often it feels as if Delhi treats us as an extra limb, not terribly useful, neither dispensable. Then there is the continuous influx of Bangladeshis. We believe the Central Government should allocate much more for development projects in the Northeast."

"But do you agree demanding a new country is impractical?"

"Yes, I am not for secession. I was merely pointing out how some people could want it. If Pakistan attacks us tomorrow, can any state stand on its own? We need a union and a strong leadership therein."

The parents clustered around the man they found wearing a turban. He had come to drop his son in school. They asked Hukum Singh to explain about the presence of ammunition in a gurudwara. "You know, Sikhs had to embrace the warrior's creed when the Mughals had started pestering them. Our last guru, Guru Gobind Singh created the Khalsa."

"Wasn't the fifth guru killed by the Mughals?"

"Yes, we call it the martyrdom of Guru Arjan Dev. The ninth guru, Guru Tegh Bahadur, met with the same fate, but this time he was fighting on behalf of the Hindu minority in Delhi. Anyway, I was saying we carry weapons on our person, the dagger, kirpan. So I would not say it was sacrilegious to store arms in the temple complex, which already has guest houses, the kitchen, and toilets. But the Akal Takht, that is a stretch."

"So when did the demand for Khalistan begin?"

"We Punjabis never wanted to split Punjab, in fact we opposed the Partition altogether. Then when it became inevitable we questioned why a Partition based on religion did not create a country of its own for the Sikh people?"

Sikhs had the 18th century Sikh Empire to look back upon. It stretched from Kabul to Aksai Chin, and included the whole of Kashmir. Jawaharlal Nehru asked the Sikhs to join India and he promised Punjab an autonomous status. But after Independence nothing was forthcoming. They were told Punjab had lots of non-Punjabis too.

During the 1950s the national language issue became a cause for much woe. India had thirty odd states, many of which had a distinct language. But since most north Indian states spoke Hindi, it was chosen as the national language. The pan-Indian ancient tongue was Sanskrit, but it was no more a spoken language for a century. One of the early British education ministers remarked that as long as Sanskrit was widespread it would be hard to break India's unity. So methodically Sanskrit was removed from schools, and the ancient texts were pedantically ridiculed. Within two generations, the culture was on the brink of extinction from the popular mind. Then came the great revival with the Brahmo and Arya Samaj, followed by the Renaissance. During Nehru's tenure when Hindi was included in the school syllabi all over India, in the official contract documents and as the language of the state assemblies, people started rioting. The government softened its decree and each state had three languages. Railway station names were written in English, Hindi and the local language. Contracts could be written in any of the three languages, Hindi was not made a compulsory subject in schools. There was also a rearrangement of state boundaries on language basis. Punjabi grievances accentuated when it was carved out in 1966. The southern Braj-speaking people formed Haryana, and in the north the Pahari people joined Himachal Pradesh. The capital Chandigarh was ruled directly by the central government. The three rivers Ravi, Sutlej and Beas did not flow exclusively in Punjab any more. So the central government took over the distribution of their waters, adding salt to the wound.

Hukum Singh continued, "Do you want to hear some more grievances? There were massive arrests during the Emergency, and then the arrests never stopped as Bhindranwale gained popularity. In November 1982 during the Asian Games in Delhi, the militant Sikhs had decided to protest. So all Sikhs, the innocents included, were picked from trains, buses and other vehicles and barred from entering Delhi."

"Tell us about Bhindranwale."

"Jarnail Singh Bhindranwale was a preacher to start with. But slowly he became the Khalistan movement personified. He told the people, in an independent Punjab, they would not have to give their crops to the central government or wait for water to be released for their fields. He convinced them they were discriminated against. They went to him to resolve disputes, not to the court. From 1982 he was living in the Golden Temple, and urging people to prepare for a battle ahead."

Binapani whispered to Mrs Talpade, "But the Sikhs must be doubly enraged that Indira Gandhi attacked during an annual festival. You know there were thousands of pilgrims inside the guest houses, many of whom were caught in the crossfire."

Hukum Singh overheard her. He clicked his tongue and shook his head. "It does not bode well, not well at all."

Mrs Talpade pointed out, "But she did not want the soldiers to fire. The army expected the militants to surrender. They called out over the Public Address system."

Binapani reasoned, "That explains why they chose this season. It would force the militants to consider saving the pilgrims' lives."

"But now that the deed is done the army will be blamed, and Indira Gandhi the most of all."

Binapani replayed her morning's conversation to Anand that evening. "It seems the Sikhs were also hurt that they were classified under the Hindu pantheon, for the marriage act, for example."

"Bina, as it is India is a diverse country, so to simplify matters two distinct social laws are recognized. In the Islamic law a man can have four wives, and in the other one it is monogamy."

"I think they object to the word 'Hindu'."

"The word itself is a misnomer, it means very little. When the British came to India they observed a lifestyle that was different from theirs, but it was difficult to find a single thread to reach to its source. Indian culture is as diverse as its many rivers, starting from mountains all over, emptying on all sides, and sometimes drying out midstream. There was no gospel these people followed, no one deity they worshipped, no identifiable master. Some did not even have a deity; they worshipped the nirguna Brahman, the featureless Essence. Every idea that was proposed was countered in a discourse of mutual enriching. The theses, antitheses and syntheses, all found their place in the culture. So the foreigners just called their bewilderment 'Hinduism', derived from 'Hindu' – a name given by the Persians to the people who lived on the other bank of the Sindhu. You would call yourself a Hindu, but try defining a set of customs and beliefs that makes you a Hindu and you will understand the folly of it. You cannot even say it is not Christian, because Christ is worshipped too. You will see him and Buddha on the same podium at the Ramakrishna Mission."

"Oh, that is not just a sign of religious acceptance. Sri Ramakrishna actually followed the various spiritual paths to their culmination – Christianity, Buddhism, tantra, advaita. And he concluded, in words that have become now a mantra, jata mat tato path, 'All paths lead to the Absolute'."

"Even when we say Hinduism is not Islam, we mean the Islamic social customs are different, not the philosophy."

"Islam came to Bengal through wandering Sufi saints, fakirs, and that mysticism blended naturally with the tantriks, the worshippers of the Mother Goddess, and later enriched the bauls, those free itinerant spirits. The wine of Sufism mixed with the country liquor of the tantrik and the baul and all drank the nectar of immortality. Hindus worship a deity called Satya Narayan who is represented by a wooden plank, not an idol. And that is because it is taken from the Islamic Satya Pir tradition. Folk poetry and mystical songs have the names of Hindu Gods and Allah in the same verse. Many Muslims participate in the pooja and worship the triune Goddesses – Lakshmi, Saraswati and Durga. Muslim artisans paint Hindu deities, beautifully, although strictly speaking, it would be condemned by the orthodox as idolatry. The Sikh culture must be similar. I heard they follow the custom of rakshaa bandhan."

"Yes and Sankraanti, the harvest festival, and they have sevaa, offering of work for the good of the community. This concept of helpfulness without the expectation of being rewarded, the unconditional sacrifice, the whole hearted devotion, respect for the ones who have taken on the mendicant's robe, veneration for the elderly, weaving spirituality in daily customs, belief in the cyclical nature of things, in reincarnation, the conviction that nothing is irreversible, a faith that the divine can be experienced ... these are some of the basic traits of the culture we call 'Hinduism'."

* * * * *

It was the last day of October in 1984. Savita was listening to the film songs on the radio while she cooked. Suddenly the programme was interrupted, an excited voice blared, "We have just had the report that Prime Minister Indira Gandhi has been shot. She has been rushed to the hospital and I am right now standing in front of the hospital main gate. You can hear the crowd that has gathered here and I will pass on the mike to one of them. We want to know who shot her."

"Two of her Sikh bodyguards turned around and gunned her down. This is a revenge for the Operation Blue Star." Savita froze.

The phone rang. It was Atul and he sounded tense although his voice was calm; she knew him too well. "Savita, go to the school and pick Prahlad right now. I am coming home. You heard what happened, surely?"

Savita took an autorickshaw and came up with a hundred excuses to get Prahlad out of his classes. None of them were necessary. Other parents were already there like ants searching for their eggs and dispersing in panic. She got home a minute before Atul came in with his boss, Sukhvir, his parents, wife and two children. Atul ran to the window and drew the curtains. They spoke in whispers and he conveyed his fears. The radio was turned on, but it was drowned by a furious knock on the door. Atul looked through the peephole. He rushed Sukhvir and his whole family inside the bathroom, then pushed Savita in with them. The men strode in when Atul opened the door. They were repairing the road nearby and had run up with the same hatchets they used to crater the concrete.

"We saw you taking those Sikhs with you. We need to get them. They have killed Indira Gandhi!"

Atul stood beside the frightened Prahlad. "I did not get anyone. It is possible those Sikhs living in the floor above came back at the same time I did."

The three men armed in their crude weapons opened the cupboards and looked under the beds. Then one of them asked, "Who is in the bathroom?"

"My wife. Savita, are you coming out?" Atul called pressing his mouth to the door.

Savita's voice could be heard from inside. "Just a few more minutes. Is it urgent?"

The men wagged their index finger at Atul. "If we hear you lied, one day that little boy of yours will be missing from school. If you give shelter to those traitors, you will be marked a traitor yourself, understood?"

"You think I will not miss our prime minister if she dies?"

"She is dead. We got the news from a friend standing in front of the hospital. Now watch how the Sikhs get massacred."

After Operation Blue Star, Sikhs resigned from civil services and the armed forces. Some gave up medals and honours they were awarded. Then on 31 October, their target number one was eliminated. In the next few days the mindless violence against anyone wearing a turban was terrifying. Their houses were burnt, dead bodies of Sikhs lay strewn in the streets of Delhi. The rage spread across the country claiming about five thousand innocent Sikhs' lives. Some escaped like Sukhvir's family. For weeks they had vanished from the face of the earth, tucked away in friends' houses, until the momentum of vengeance died out.

Sukhvir completed his story, "I did not get the window seat and survived. Poor Balvir. You don't want to know how the three of us came to Delhi. We lived in train carriages and were hunted down like rats, by the other dispossessed people, all hungry and dying. My father's friend had loaned us some money so we were the richest of the poor. At least we could buy food and a pair of sandals to walk on. We came to Delhi because father's instinct said if at all we get government help, it will be distributed out from the capital. The Punjabi Bagh in Delhi was a refugee camp in 1947. Now it has houses, schools, bazaars and film halls. Thirty years of labour, the same hard work we would have offered to Mother Nature in Punjab, was given to the township. The government gave us loans to set up businesses and started housing projects for us. We never went back to Rawalpindi and Mansur Ali, may God have mercy on his soul.

Even when we lived on the footpaths, we did not have to remove the turban. India had welcomed us Sikhs, Pakistan had kicked us out. And now this very turban is a hindrance. That which I wore as my crown is the cause of my downfall."

"Sukhvir, the mob has no mind. It is a machine that has been wound and will continue till its tension is exhausted."

"Yes, as you say Atul, I will cut my hair. My brother died and it was not his fault. I don't want to die a similar death."

"Yes, I know there are hurt feelings on both sides. It saddens me that today Sikhs and Hindus are split too. But we know this violence has nothing to do with you and me, with the common man. We are bystanders in a political game. Yet we get accused and punished. The massacre is still going on and these wounds will fester for many more months, maybe years. Be practical, yaar. Cutting your hair does not mean you are sacrificing your religion."

Sukhvir cut his own hair and his son's. The boy asked, "Papaji, did they burn everything, our photographs also?"

"Yes, son, the last memory of our home, Rawalpindi, is wiped clean. We look different, and maybe we are different people now. Is India our homeland any more? I wonder, after this senseless killing."

His father, Maan Singh, touched his shoulder, "Son, don't be so disheartened. Waheguru is in the heart, not in the appearance. We live; not like our little Balvir."

Sukhvir stood by his father, scissors in hand, his head bowed waiting for the old man's consent. Maan Singh removed his turban slowly. His long hair rolled out till his calves. He turned to Sukhvir and took the scissors. Every strand of hair he let drop gently into the turban, as if they were his childhood companions he was bidding farewell to.

"Khalistan is not our cause. We are Sikhs who wear the dagger for self-protection, not terrorism. We are Indians and the colony in Delhi is our home. If it is burnt, we will clean the debris and begin afresh. We know how to begin, because we have lived through an end before."

Chapter Eighteen

Tariq

"Dunya, Dunya, who is at the door?"

Dunya retrieved the plate and walked past her aunt, "Chachi, don't scream so loudly. They will feel embarrassed."

"Who are they? I have been observing you loitering at the door these days. Should I report on you?"

"Don't be melodramatic. They are Afghan refugees from the war, proud people who have lost much, but nobody came to beg. I invited them."

"Child, how many will you help? There are hundreds of them pouring into Peshawar."

"Chachi, aren't we of the same race? Don't we speak the same language, Pashto? They are our family. Why can't we help at least those we pass by? If we worry about the end, we will never get started."

"Tomorrow when there is a queue outside our door, then we will see you bite your nails, as if we grow money on trees!" The aunt sighed. "Here comes Nazia Hassan." Dunya's sister, Darya, entered, rubbing a towel on her wet hair. She was singing the song they heard a million times on the radio, Aap jaisa koi. It was sung by the rising star, Nazia Hassan, for the Indian film, Qurbani. The video was smuggled into the house under a woman's shawl from a cigarette shop with an interesting back room. In Pakistan the ban on Bollywood films continued. Chachi skirted around the bed and reached for the window. She pulled the shutter close, "The way you two carry on ... talking to strange men and singing at the top of your voice. Don't you know the Islamic Law frowns on singing?"

The girls exchanged winks.

"Yes, make fun of me. Your father is no better. He has been announcing in public that you, Dunya, will be a Waheeda

Rehman, and Darya will be Nazia Hassan the second. Some day the military will be on us to straighten you three. I don't care, I was just thinking of your poor mother."

Altaf Aziz was a big man, in breadth, height and audacity. He huffed and puffed against the restrictive policies of sharia in the market place, and those who did not give him furtive glances, whispered well-meant warnings. "I want my daughters to be actresses and singers. Is there anyone here who thinks my boast is empty?" Nobody challenged the big man. Those who had seen his daughters before they were forced to wear the black veils and barred from public performances, agreed with him. Darya and Dunya had all the best features of Afghan princesses. Darya's voice was famous in the local radio, and Dunya was a young actress directors had better watch out for. Nazia Hassan, a Pakistani pop singer, was in London and she could sing to her heart's content and dance openly on stage wearing any dress that suited her fancy. Girls fired by Nazia's pop songs saw her as an icon of feminine freedom, and Bollywood the greenroom for their talent. Altaf was annoyed with the military coup of General Zia-ul-Haq, then angry with the imposition of sharia, and now he lost patience when the Afghan War began. Peshawar, one of the biggest cities of the northwestern frontier in Pakistan, became a weapon trafficker's opportunity, training ground of militants and a vast refugee camp. American soldiers and the Mujahideen were seen toting their machine guns in the open. It was not safe for children to walk alone to their schools, and what could one say for girls? Altaf became paranoid about protecting his pretty daughters and his only day-dreaming little boy. India would be his destination, declared Altaf, although his friends clicked their tongues, "Deserting your motherland? After all the struggle the father of our nation, Jinnah, had gone through to give us a country of our own?"

From the beginning of the 1900s, the freedom struggle and the Indian Renaissance invigorated each other. Nationalism became a spiritual endeavour, the new dharma of life. Revolutionaries held the Gita in one hand the revolver in the other. In that climate of religious revivalism, some of the minority,

Muslim members of the Congress Party, felt marginalized and some saw political opportunity. They walked out and formed the Muslim League. In 1930 the League proposed the idea of a separate Muslim nation. Politicians whipped up mutual fear and Hindu-Muslim riots claimed thousands of lives. But not all Muslims believed in the two-nation theory. Allama Mashriqi of another Muslim party, the Khaksar Tehreek, and Mohandas Gandhi of the Congress Party tried hard to maintain religious harmony, pointing to the long history of mutual coexistence and syncretism that had prevailed in India among Hindus and Muslims. But by 1946, communal violence was in the danger of exploding into a full-scale civil war. Britain had no resources to deal with such a strife, and chose the quickest way of transferring power – granting it in two pieces. The Muslim League's leader, Mohammad Ali Jinnah, was sworn in, in Pakistan, and Jawaharlal Nehru took office over India, in August 1947. The borders had not been finalized and neither of the states was equipped to handle a population migration of that magnitude.

Altaf weighed his options. Applying for a passport, then for an Indian visa in the Indian embassy seemed the worst of them. If at all it had any promise of success at the end, it would take years.

"Altaf mia," said the cigarette vendor, "No, don't even try through Punjab or Kashmir; the borders are heavily patrolled. Same on the Sindh-Gujarat side. Border Security Forces are planted thicker than trees in an avenue. Taking a ship into Gujarat is also as bad since the port authorities will catch you and put you back on the next carrier to Karachi. I think the best option you have is through the desert. I can put you in touch with a friend who operates camels there."

Altaf pondered over it and discussed with his wife. He then surrendered to the cigarette vendor, who seemed to have prior experience. He and his circle of friends peddled foreign cigarettes, guns, films, narcotics, and of course smuggled immigrants.

"To make your task simpler, you can pay me here for the whole trip." Altaf could almost sniff the cuddy breath of the camel when this oily creature extended his palm. The deal was signed in thin air, and the Aziz family bid a secret farewell to their closest friends.

Tariq was a runny-nosed brat whose face was glued to the View Master. It looked like a pair of binoculars with a set of slides mounted on it. Tariq's universe was hidden inside that little toy. He travelled far away back to the 16th century during Shah Jahan's reign. He saw the Taj Mahal and his face beamed. She was his favourite. His eyes caressed the arches of the four stately doorways of the façade. He clicked on a handle, and there was Humayun's tomb in Delhi, pink and surrounded by Mughal gardens. Another click, and he saw the Jantar Matar, a complicated series of edifices used to read the position of heavenly bodies. He spiralled up the stairs, then slid down the cylindrical slope, proud as a pioneer. He visited the delicate marble temple of Salim Chishti, the Sufi saint. Tariq could imagine people sitting on the dais by the fountain, discussing about earth and heaven and the soul. Sufis, Hindus, Zoroastrians and Muslims assembled and read poems to the delight of the greatest of Mughal emperors, Akbar. Another click and here was the Badshahi mosque in Lahore, a twin of the Jama Masjid in Delhi, constructed by Shah Jahan's son, Aurangzeb. Tariq was lifted from his spot by his two sisters and lodged in a bus that jostled and made the Taj Mahal's four minarets look like fingers searching for the thumb.

When he was hungry he travelled back from the bygone age by lowering the View Master. Looking around he realized they were not at home. From the luggage stacked on his parent's laps he guessed they were going on a long journey. "Where are we off to?" He asked excited.

The bus made too much noise and his mother was shrewd enough not to announce to the world they would use an illegal passage. She poked her finger into the View Master, "There."

"Taj Mahal? Hurrah!" cried Tariq.

The bus deposited them in the city of Nawabshah. And from there onwards stretched the Thar Desert into India. They were not the only ones, and neither was the traffic from west to east alone. The guides knew the invisible roads on this waste of sand dunes which had wells on the brink of panic. Crossing the desert on camel back was bearable because Darya hoped to do the playback for the actress Sridevi. Dunya fantasized herself dancing with Rishi Kapoor in celluloid that would make her friends back in Peshawar green with envy. Altaf prayed they could live among the millions of Muslims in India in peace and prosperity. Tariq's camel walked a step at a time towards the Taj Mahal. His mother threw away her burqa and fanned herself. Then the heat got on her nerves and she started shedding the extra wraps she had on. The golden sand was marked with the black remnants of her past life. Then they saw a city shimmer in the horizon. "Jaisalmer!" the guide pointed ahead. They had made it! From the land of the Frontier Gandhi to the land of the Mahatma Gandhi.

Frontier Gandhi was the nickname given to Khan Abdul Ghaffar Khan, a freedom fighter from Peshawar, where the Aziz family lived. He was a close collaborator of Gandhi and a proponent of non-violence. When the Partition was approved by Gandhi's party, he was deeply disappointed. Several times after 1947 he was arrested in Pakistan for his pro-India statements and his open opposition to the dictatorial laws.

After a few days at Jaisalmer, they took a bus inland, to be better tucked away from the Border Security Force. The sandstone damsel, the pink city of Jaipur, threw an enticing tassel round Altaf's feet, which made him trip, and he knelt on the ground. He wanted to thank the all-compassionate, the all-merciful, the Ar Rahman Ar Rahim. His daughters saw the palace on a lake, the Jal Mahal, like a lotus frozen in space. The pink façade of another Rajput palace, the Hawa Mahal, was so charming Tariq forgot about his View Master. Their mother passed by the gullies where women sat outdoors and rolled out papad, chatting and laughing loudly. Altaf Aziz decided to travel no further. Jaipur was beautiful and his son had looked at the world for the first time, touching his View Master dreams with his little fingers. His daughters lived their reel life in real life. Not a person passed by on the road without noticing these two new doves in their alcove.

They walked arm in arm their faces and hair uncovered, like the other women. Money was in abundance among the people of Rajasthan, the businessmen of India. They knew how to multiply it faster than a Bengali could dribble out poetry or a Punjabi could grow grain or a Tamilian could compose a dance. The Aziz family would find a happy nook here in their new homeland.

* * * * *

Binapani and Anand sat transfixed in the front row of the auditorium. The applause crashed into their shore as though the audience was clapping for them. The last item in the school's annual programme was a dance performance by Panchali, with Yuyutsu as the singer. He was the child Krishna imploring his mother not to scold him for stealing butter. Panchali was Yashoda, Krishna's mother, the churner of the butter. Their relationship was one of the sweetest the Lord has with mortals, of playful love between mother and child, vaatsalya. Krishna provides many excuses proving that he could not have stolen. She melts like butter and gathers him in her arms. Then the divine prankster tells her that indeed he has stolen the butter. The song, *main nahi maakhan khaaiyo*, was sung by the bhajan maestro, master of devotional songs, Anup Jalota, who had immortalized verses of the ancient poet, Surdas. The language was Braj as spoken by the cowherds of Brindavan. At the end there was a pun where the words "I have not" become "Indeed I have", stolen the butter. Main nahi becomes Maine hi. When Yuyutsu sang it in his sweet childish voice it was as if the young Krishna himself was singing. Panchali wore the ghaghra of the cowherd ladies and a dupatta haloed her face. Her dance was delicate and her face expressed so much motherly love that no one believed she was just twelve years old. The curtains fell and the lights in the hall showed Binapani and Anand wiping tears of joy. This is what the two of them were doing locked in the room. They had planned a loving surprise for their parents, their own Yashoda and Nanda.

* * * * *

"Tariq, come, abba is calling us." The cricket game froze for a full minute as all the twenty-one players, except Tariq, stared at the sisters, Dunya and Darya.

Tariq tried to close the conversation summarily, "I can't. I am batting next."

"Tariq, we are leaving Jaipur soon. We need to pack."

"What? But I am in the cricket league!" Tariq at age ten played with boys of fifteen as he was as tall as them. The sisters had reached the gallery where he sat.

"Don't be so sad. We are going to your hero's state, Sunil Gavaskar's, the Indian cricket captain."

"He was, now it is Kapil Dev."

"All right, but don't you admire him? We are going to Pune, in Maharashtra."

"Why? I love Jaipur."

Darya pinched her sister's cheek. "Because Dunya will join the FTII, Film and Television Institute of India. That is where actresses and actors like Shabana Azmi and Naseeruddin Shah were trained."

"Really, are you so serious about acting?" Tariq looked at Dunya in surprise.

"Look Darya, this rat is teasing me." The two sisters pounced on their brother from opposite sides and chased him home.

"Abba, when are we leaving?" came Dunya's breathless voice from the doorway.

"Postponed, my jewel."

"No!" cried the girls.

"Just by a few weeks. This is the first time your mother and I will vote in our new country. They have registered us from Jaipur, so we will vote and take off the next day, promise."

"You don't need to vote, abba. Everybody knows the results. Rajiv Gandhi will win." After Sanjay Gandhi's plane crash in 1980, Indira Gandhi called her elder son, Rajiv, to join politics. He was a pilot in the Indian Airlines at that time. On October 31, 1984, when Indira Gandhi passed away, he became the interim prime minister. Within weeks fresh elections were arranged and his party, the Congress, was expected to win a landslide victory.

"But I want to vote; your mother too. It means we are accepted as citizens of India and are doing our duty towards democracy."

"OK, OK, vote." grumbled Darya.

"Thank you, ladies. Where is Tariq, I thought I saw him come in?"

Tariq was at that moment in the cricket pitch facing the bowler.

* * * * *

"Panchali, Panchali!" called out a voice from outside the classroom. "Your brother is fighting a bloody battle." Panchali dashed to the sandpit and found two boys wrestling like Bheema and Jarasandha. "Yuyutsu, stop it!" she cried.

The boys were not listening; so she jumped in the pit but could get nowhere close to the rolling mass of bones and flesh. Then a bigger boy, Amar, reached right in and pulled the boys apart. He was the elder brother of Yuyutsu's opponent. Amar turned on Umang and gave him a nice shake. "He beat me first!" cried the boy, perspiring.

Yuyutsu would not let it pass, "He cheated on us; he hid our marbles."

"Liar!" countered Umang and he took Yuyutsu offguard. Suddenly Yuyutsu had crashed on the cement wall of the sandpit. Everybody heard a crunch followed by a howl of pain. Panchali stooped over her brother. The arm was broken for sure. Amar helped her support Yuyutsu to the autorickshaw, which someone had called promptly. Panchali dusted the sand off the creases of his school uniform. Before any teacher could be called, the three of them sped away.

While they waited in the hospital, Amar pleaded with Panchali, "Please don't tell your father." Amar was scared as Anand was quite respected in the education circle.

"Of course I won't. It is a children's fight and they will sort it out. Thanks for coming with us, Amar. I would not have known what to do alone."

"Oh, please don't mention it. That's the least I could do."

The next day Yuyutsu came with his arm in a cast. Umang was waiting at the school gate. "Yuyutsu, I am sorry for yesterday." There was no answer as his target had turned away. Umang followed, "I got angry, I should not have made the last move. Here are your marbles."

Panchali turned her brother around. "He said something, or did I imagine it? He said the golden words."

"Yes, but he does not have a broken arm. He did not toss all night in pain."

"But you fought for two marbles! Don't you know there is something called dialogue? And if that does not work, there is something called involving the elders?"

"Elders are not interested in children's quarrels. He was being unfair. And if I had involved Amar or you, you would have patted us on the head and dismissed our case."

"You should have at least given us a chance. Not all problems can be solved, we must accept that. But a compromise could be worked out."

Amar had appeared and he whispered to Panchali, "This sounds like the India-Pakistan relationship and we two elders are the United Nations. Our clock starts from the first war of 1948, and all we can do is suppress the boil; not let it burst. Maybe these two have created a history of enmity between them, with little shoves and pushes in the bus and stubbing of pencil nibs, until this full-fledged fight."

"All right, let's try to solve it then, shall we, Amar?" She turned to Umang, "If you are sorry for what you did, you will help Yuyutsu during tiffin time."

Many students passed the strange sight of Umang pealing a banana for Yuyutsu. After class Umang offered to write down Yuyutsu's homework, much to the delight of the teachers. Amar and Panchali made the thumbs up sign to each other as conspirators. Very soon yesterday's feuding partners were talking amiably, and in the bus Umang reserved the window seat for his new friend. Amar scratched his head.

"How did it happen? Remind me, Panchali."

"The boil was allowed to burst and the skin healed itself."

"Ah yes. The key was to apply the right kind of healing. They found ways to collaborate."

*****

"Hello, abba," it was Dunya's voice. "Have you heard the news?"

Alarm bells started chiming in Altaf's brain. "No, what is it?"

"Retired General A.S.Vaidya has been shot dead here, in Pune. He was the Chief of Army Staff during the Operation Blue Star in the Golden Temple. Two Sikhs on scooter drew up to his car and pumped bullets in his body." It was August 10, 1986.

"There goes another target of the Sikh insurgents," sighed Altaf. Then he was nervous. "Dunya, how will you come back? Is there going to be a curfew?"

"No abba, don't panic. You really must take care of your blood pressure. I was just calling to let you know. And to tell you that Tariq should not go to play cricket in the field, in the open. You remember the massacre after Indira Gandhi's death? Of course, nothing happened in Jaipur, but now we are in a new state. But silly me, she was the prime minister. Though, caution won't hurt, will it? Can I talk to Darya? I hope she is back from her singing class."

Dunya was becoming a mother hen counting her eggs every time a drop of rain fell on her head. She and her father kept a close watch on the other three and teased each other of being overprotective. Altaf's wife was having too much fun to worry about anything. She had bought a new mixie, the latest phenomenon in kitchen care, and was experimenting on feeding it every possible ingredient. When asked how she could express so much joie de vivre, when Dunya, twenty years younger, was ever anxious, she replied, "Oh, I have so many people to worry about; I just don't know where to begin."

Chapter Nineteen

Swami

Panchali sat in the gallery and knew she was living through a profound moment. The left forward in the football team was a new boy who had joined that year. He flew like a bullet and kicked mercilessly. He scored a goal, he hit a shin, he tackled, he skidded, the audience cheered "Shreyas, Shreyas!" and Panchali sat mesmerized. During the break she replayed his moves in slow motion, and at the end of the match he had scored an important goal, squarely into her heart. Did they win the match? She did not care. All she cared about was to know this boy, to trail him, to snatch glimpses of his laughter, steal a mental picture of his profile, overhear his voice, listen to his brilliant words. Panchali befriended his classmate, a year senior to her, Saheli, and tagged along with her, just to get close to Shreyas. He entered the classroom, his chiselled face was frozen in Panchali's admiring eyes. She rehearsed talking to him in the bathroom mirror. It seemed so easy for Saheli and the other girls to tell him something casual, "Have you done that homework?" or "Have you read this comic?" as if he was one they could waste their words upon. He was precious, so precious one could but lay an exquisite verse at his feet.

After many upheavals, she found Shreyas one day passing by, alone. She stopped him, "Hey, Shreyas!" and took a deep breath that got caught in her throat and made her cough. "Sorry. As you know there is going to be a drama competition. Will you be interested to act in it?"

"You are Saheli's friend, right?"

"Yes, Panchali."

"I am going to participate in the quiz with the senior batch for the school festival. I can't do the drama too. Anyway, best of luck for it."

So he would not be her Prince Salim, and she his Noor Jahan. It would have to be Roshan then, her old partner in pranks. He was also her father's favourite, a spontaneous actor with not an iota of stage fright. In fact, the quality of his performance improved in direct proportion to the strength of the audience. For the romantic scenes if Shreyas had acted with her, hers would not be acting at all, but a statement of her life. She was more nervous for the quiz competition than on her drama day. Shreyas was brilliant, a star, a genius. Everybody in the audience whispered, "Who is that boy, he is simply routing the opponent." Panchali felt so proud she could have told them who he was. He was her sky, the tallest reach of her aspiration, her fabled prince, her king. She congratulated him, and he thanked her, like he did the many people who swarmed around.

"Panchali!" yelled a voice so close it made her jump. The history teacher snapped open her desk. He picked up the paper which his inattentive student was staring at and sneered, "Film poster!" All heads were turned towards them. He held up the picture of Aamir Khan, the hero who catapulted on the Bollywood stage and into Panchali's heart. The film was Qayamat Se Qayamat Tak, a love story that ended in a "Romeo and Juliet" style tragedy. He tore the paper across Aamir's face, after the others had a good laugh. Once, twice and then finished him up with some more mincing into tiny bits.

"You will write me an essay on the destruction of Buddhist manuscripts in Nalanda, tomorrow."

In the next history class, Panchali submitted her essay and sat down morosely. It was not easy to get that poster. She had to cut the paper deftly from the Stardust magazine, so that her mother could be fooled. Longing to peer at Aamir Khan's face, she looked under her desk and to her surprise there he was, smiling at her. Panchali looked deeply into that dear face she had begun to dream about. "Kaise ho, how are you, Aamir?" she conversed with him, and heard him reply, "Arre, I am first class, but you watch out!" How right he was. The teacher was standing over Panchali again.

"What have we got today?" He asked sarcastically. The desk was opened and again Aamir was found half winking up at the angry man. He waved the poster around and repeated the previous gestures. But the paper did not tear. It was laminated and as he fought with it, giggles filled the classroom. Aamir and Panchali each sported a benign smile. The teacher was furious, "You will leave my class at once, Panchali!"

The girl got up, "Excuse me." she pulled Aamir out of his grasp and walked out.

Sure enough a note was sent to her parents within a day. Anand called Panchali to his side.

"You cannot learn if you are arrogant about a subject. Approach it through humility."

"Baba, I love history. I don't go to soak up information and vomit it on paper – what happened when and give six reasons for it, and similar nonsense. History is our heritage, and they don't know how to respect it. They treat it like any other subject, like maths or geography, the empirical sciences. History is the story of millions of people like you and me who have lived through it consciously."

"All right, Panchali, calm down. I am a professor, and I know there are flaws in the education system. But it evolves too, gradually."

"I don't like the way he teaches. The other day I had to write an essay on the massacre of Buddhists and the burning of the library at Nalanda. I said it was because the Islamic invaders thought idol worship was the devil's act. And they found lots of idols in the Buddhist shrines. So it made sense that these should be destroyed and the people who espoused them, eliminated."

"Panchali, do you know some of the earliest writings were lost there?"

"I do feel it was a heinous crime. But one must admit that these people were being faithful to their own religion."

"Exactly where you and your teacher differ. It is not enough to be faithful to one's own religion when it teaches intolerance towards another's."

"The essay was not about critiquing Islam as practised in the thirteenth century by certain people. Is that true Islam? If so, how are the Sufi saints so very different?"

"I concede you have a point. The word 'Sufi' derives from the Arabic tasawwuf, which means wool, soft and airy. They would not harm a butterfly."

"In the exams if I write Buddhism was eradicated from India because of the Islamic hordes, I will get good marks. But how can that be true? When Shankaracharya came into the picture, a thousand years after Buddha, there was but a trace of it left in the subcontinent. It had travelled away to the East and Southeast Asia. And that was at least three hundred years before any Islamic conqueror reached the Indian interior."

"And yet that trace was vibrant. Monks were an easy target because they lived in monasteries, whereas the Hindu idolaters were householders, spread all over the land. Luckily some monks escaped to Tibet, Nepal and to the south of India. But Buddhism in northern India was effectively wiped out."

"If that is a judgement on the religion of Islam, why don't we accept Hinduism to be aggressive because Ashoka plundered and pillaged mercilessly? We just adulate his later deeds – embracing Buddhism, spreading it far and wide, constructing stupas and viharas. And he wasn't the last rapacious Hindu king."

Anand saw his daughter's nostrils flare in indignation. It was best for her to pour it out of her system.

"Then we say the Indian civilization began in Mohenjo Daro, now in Pakistan. Isn't that a contradiction? Textbooks in Pakistan will have 'the greatest fruit of Islamic architecture was the Taj Mahal, now in India'. The capital of Bengal was Dhaka, now in Bangladesh. Bangladeshis will learn the capital moved to Murshidabad, now in India. Pakistan gets its flag from the Mughal's banner, who ruled from Delhi, now in India. And India gets her name from the Indus River, now in Pakistan. What kind of farce in this?"

"All right, pretend you are the education minister. Now let's see you do it better."

"Can't we use the ancient name, Bharat, of the Mahabharata, which includes Pakistan, India and Bangladesh?"

"Immediately the greatest of our emperors, Ashoka, will take offence, for his reign extended to Afghanistan. And the Pala dynasty of Bengal too conquered bits of it but they did not have half of south India. At the other extreme, why not start from the days of fiefdom? Or the princely states?"

"Baba, are you teasing me?"

"No, Panchali, I am explaining. It depends on your frame of reference. You are outraged because of your choice. You chose a golden age, the textbooks chose post Independence. If you had picked the British Raj, you would have encompassed most of Asia."

"Surely a nation is more than a piece of land locked in by a boundary? Is there nothing deeper that binds people? We know it is not just religion, or race, or language, nor a common history. But there must be something else I cannot name, which I feel in my guts."

"Yes, there is." Binapani had joined them. "That something is what ignited nationalism, what inspired the best minds and hearts, what we feel deep within – a common psyche, a shared cultural heritage."

"Yes, the motherland we worship in the Vande Mataram."

"But Panchali, we have to live with what we have. Learn to compromise."

"As long as we cannot change it?"

"Yes, but not longer."

The three were quiet. Then Panchali looked at her father, "What are you smiling at, baba?"

"Oh, was I smiling? Sorry. I was reminded of a photograph I once saw of a man buried between two piles of books. On one side was a placard that read 'India', on the other, 'Pakistan'. It was taken in 1947. Can you guess what it was about?"

Binapani answered, "He was splitting a library during the Partition."

"Yes, in this way, painstakingly, all the national wealth was divided. The Priest King statuette from Mohenjo Daro went to Pakistan, and India got the Dancing Girl. Tanks, aircraft, ships, trains, buses, gold, silver, the treasury – every valuable moveable asset was thus set aside in two distinct piles."

"Ridiculous!" exclaimed Panchali and stormed out of the room.

* * * * *

Panchali was doing her homework when she heard one of her favourite songs from the same Aamir Khan film. *Gazab kaa hai din socho zaraa.* The lovers were lost in a grove of pine trees and in no hurry to get back to civilization. She pricked up her ears and heard Yuyutsu's voice singing it. Strangely it did not come from the bathroom, but from the outside. Panchali pushed the curtains aside and stuck her head out of the window. A boy was strumming on a guitar in the garden below. The bush behind was animated with the truant brother, serenading his own sister. It was night, but our guitarist hero was sporting a pair of dark glasses. Such a sophisticated touch could come from only one corner of the country, from Rajnikant, the Tamil films' evergreen hero. The same who could catch a flying bullet between his fingers, could stop a train with his arms, and shoot blindfolded. Neighbouring curtains flew open, and then all eyes turned towards Panchali, framed against her window. She had the presence of mind to switch off the light. Her parents had joined in absorbing the peacock dance. "You had better go down before the watchman comes running up."

"Hello, Panchali, recognize me?"

She sighed. He wasn't hard to recognize. It was Swaminathan, her classmate, and other than his dark glasses, he was the same in daylight as in the night. "I gave you the Aamir, the non-destructible one."

"Thank you," she said icily. He started swinging back and forth "*Tum ho akele hum bhi akele, mazaa aa rahaa hai,* you and I are alone, and aren't we having fun?"

She realized why he did not sing the whole song himself. "No, no, no, we are not alone; my brother is behind that bush."

She went round and got hold of Yuyutsu's ear. "Shall we go up, now that the pantomime is over and just about a thousand eyes are fixed on us?"

Swami stepped on her path, "Pantomime? No, no, Panchali, Romeo was singing to Juliet."

The two had walked out of earshot. Yuyutsu said he knew nothing about the plot, only that he would be paid handsomely for the feat. He did not even know the target audience. Would he have been serenading his own sister?

"And what was the payment, we beg of you to disclose." Swami had certain connections in Tamil Nadu and had promised to give his collaborator a chance to be a child playback singer.

They had reached home. "Ma, here is the culprit. You sing at night, and you have a bird-sized brain. From now on, I will call you ullu, owl. Ma, baba, he is joining the Madras film industry to become a Tamil playback singer."

Yuyutsu raised his collar proudly at the last comment. "Oh didi, he gave me this for you." It was another laminated poster of Aamir Khan. She threw it aside.

The next day Swami was grinning like a hunter who had trapped his bird alive. Panchali walked up to him and handed the two posters. "I think I am out of the Aamir phase. But thanks, they were very useful."

"Does that mean you are now in Swami phase?" She looked around hastily. Was anyone else hearing this?

"No, I am not."

He skidded beside her; "I know the other song too."

"Please don't sing, please."

"Then baby, will you meet me after school?"

"I will meet you in jahannam." Panchali opened her book and buried her head in it.

"OK, OK," Swami pranced up and down. When Aditi walked into the classroom, he gave his hair an extra flourish with his hand, in front of her face. She ducked away thinking it was an approaching slap.

"What's the matter with him?"

"Hormonal imbalance," answered Panchali without looking up.

Swami bunked the last period and hunted the precincts of the school for a restaurant called Jahannam. Then he looked for cosy nooks like tea stalls, or a chaat vendor, maybe a park with that name, or was it an ice cream parlour? He was tracing wider and wider circles and all the watchmen around the apartment complexes saw him pass by several times. Then one of them took pity, "What are you looking for, son?"

"Do you know of any restaurant called Jahannam?"

He chuckled in his beard, "A place with that name will get no customer."

"Why?"

"You don't know what it means then."

Swami's eyebrows parted company. One arched up, another ducked down, "And what does it mean?"

"It means hell."

Swami fisted his hands and gave the air a karate chop. Somebody needed to be put in her right place.

He barged into the group of girls saying their goodbyes. "Come Panchali, let us go to jahannam."

She clung on to Aditi's hand and tried to slip away with her in the autorickshaw, but Swami turned to Aditi, "Excuse us, please."

He twisted his lips like a film villain and advanced on Panchali.

"I have to take my brother home, mother is visiting ..."

"Oh no, remember you have to meet me in Jahannam?"

"You promised Yuyutsu something fancy, otherwise he would not be so foolish to sing for his own sister, and I would not have become angry. When people see me in my apartment complex now, suddenly they feel like singing that wretched song."

Swami was not listening, "Will you come on your own, or should I do it the old-fashioned way, like Dusshasan did?"

Far away Roshan was strolling past. He heard Panchali's enthusiastic call and as soon as he arrived she hid behind him. In racing Hindi she told him about her predicament and Roshan laughed pointing at Swami. "You used her brother?" He laughed some more, "Why didn't you take a tape recorder?"

"Stupid, because the song is sung by a female artist."

Roshan doubled up in laughter. "Arre, leave her alone. You can see she is so scared she is hiding behind me. I mean, look at me, can I stand up to a single karate kick from you? We are a bunch of drama folks, we don't fight. We use duplicates like you." He winked at Panchali. Swami felt flattered and his anger diffused. For the pleasure of his audience he demonstrated some of those famous kicks. And the day was saved.

Panchali played with the kittens in front of the school gate, waiting for Shreyas to walk by. Perhaps he would throw a word in her alms bowl. Another day had passed fruitfully, she had seen him. Once she was plucking mushrooms after the rains in the field, when the boys were warming up for the game. Shreyas asked her not to touch them as they could be poisonous. Sometimes during the recess they played volleyball and Shreyas joined in. She enjoyed seeing that face turned upwards, the smile when it made a good contact, his breaking into a mischievous laughter when he passed it to one who was not expecting it, his liquid eyes on her while he gave her the ball. She collected these butterfly moments in the secret chamber of her heart. During a kho kho game the monsoons announced themselves, rumbling and grumbling. It started raining and they were all cooped up under the storeroom shed. The wind sprayed water on happy faces, it blew in the promise of tender coconut, the renewal of life, the bursting forth of gaiety. The earth heaved her last sigh of summer and tasted the drop of paradisiacal nectar. It was a mad moment, and Shreyas was there with dozens of others stretching out his hand to touch nature's blessing. Panchali came closer and closer until she could almost feel his life flowing under her skin. She had to tell him something; otherwise the pain within her would make her burst open like a ripe pomegranate. Maybe he too wanted to tell her the same thing; he too was waiting for just such an intoxicating moment. When all were so close that none heard anyone but their own whirling thoughts, everybody planned to commit some life-saving misdemeanour. Harpoons of desire flew in the air and crisscrossed each other. Girls and boys were regrouping themselves driven by nature's mysterious mood. Panchali screamed a silent prayer, "Shreyas, I am dying of thirst on this weeping day. Give me just one drop of water you have collected in your palm. Say something that I may treasure forever." But she dared not disrupt his communion with heaven. His face reflected the dark cloudy sky. Stars of rain dew twinkled in his eyelashes. She watched him and knew she could not approach, not today. It was the fear of being rejected on such a day. It would have to be on a sweaty summer afternoon, not in this magical monsoon hour.

And so the hours flew and days passed by, reducing Panchali to a shadow. Sometimes she heard film songs and pranced around the greenery with Shreyas, like the heroes and heroines of dreamland. She imagined he loved her, and life was perfect. Then reality smacked her on the face when the song finished. With fumbling urgent fingers she picked the needle from the record and put it back to the start. Again and again she played those happy tunes to fill her empty heart. At least in her own world she was with him and nobody could snatch that away from her, not even Shreyas.

* * * * *

"Why am I making a face like a wrinkled handkerchief?" asked Prahlad.

"Oh, that is when you had just fought with Yuyutsu," replied Atul.

"No, that was in this photograph, with the Golden Temple in the backdrop."

"There too. You had slipped and Yuyutsu was laughing."

"We seemed to have pitched many childish battles? I can't believe it. This vacation I feel so bad we will not meet up."

"Yes, me too," said Savita, "But we should allow your aunt to visit her hometown sometimes."

"Baba, where shall we go for Dussehra this year? The Golden Temple?"

"Out of the question. The Golden Temple is a hotbed of activity with the insurgents still using it as a base. The Rajiv Gandhi government is trying various approaches to extricate militants. A tough police officer is now posted in Punjab who, it seems, has a green signal to arrest any suspicious person. I hear, men seen after dark, walking unaccompanied by women, are picked, questioned, and sometimes returned whole."

"Yes, we read in the papers – members of political parties disappear ever so often."

Atul sighed, "One reign of terror has replaced another and Punjab has been the last holiday destination, I would say, this whole decade of the 1980s."

"Atul, I have never been to Kashmir."

"Savita, that is the second worst destination right now. Militants infiltrate the porous border, bombs burst in market places, buses blow up. Innocent people are captured as hostages for barter with political prisoners. Harassed civilians continue to move out of Kashmir into Jammu and down south deeper into the country."

"And we cannot go to Tamil Nadu because of the LTTE problems."

"The Sri Lankan civil war has dragged India into it. What's the history there?" asked Prahlad.

"The island of Sri Lanka is inhabited by two ethnic groups; the Sinhalese, and the Tamilians – who are also in the Indian state of Tamil Nadu. From the mid-seventies, Prabhakaran, a Sri Lankan Tamilian, gathered an army to fight for an autonomous Tamil land in the north and eastern parts of the island. His cadets are called the LTTE, Liberation Tigers of Tamil Eelam. The ancient Tamil name for Sri Lanka is Eelam. Then Tamilians in India started providing sanctuary to the LTTE, a do or die militant group that even uses women and children as suicide bombers."

Savita explained, "The Rajiv Gandhi government wanted to end the turmoil in Tamil Nadu. So from July 1987, India sent the IPKF, Indian Peace Keeping Force, into Sri Lanka to defuse hostilities while the dialogue between the government and the Tamilians was under way."

Atul sighed again, "Unfortunately, a lot of peace keeping effort turned into warfare."

"It is not wise to visit the beautiful hill stations in the Northeast." Savita rolled her finger on that region of the map, "Secessionism seems to be the political fashion these days. Or is it the conflict with the Bangladeshi refugees?"

"Too bad we cannot see the rhinos of Assam. Shall we also go to Calcutta and meet up with didi and Yuyutsu?" Prahlad was looking for an excuse to join his cousins.

Atul considered the map of India. "We can still roam the wilderness on elephant back." he pointed close to Ranchi, in Bihar, "The Betla National Park. Anyone interested?"

"Yes!" called out two thrilled voices.

* * * * *

Rahim laid his school bag on the mat and sat beside the fakir. "You know, Bhola cornered me again. The other day I had told him Sufism was the mystical wing of Islam. He asked me to define it."

The fakir chuckled, "And did you define it?"

"Yes indeed," grinned Rahim, "I told him a Sufi blows with the fragrance of roses and flows like a leaf on the water."

"Poor Bhola."

"Yes, he was annoyed. He accused me of speaking in riddles on purpose. So I said, arre Bhola, why don't you first explain to me what hunger is. Then he understood. He admitted he could not define it, but could experience it, for sure."

"Yes, how can one measure the ocean standing on the seashore?"

The fakir added a handful of green peas to a bowl of puffed

rice. Rahim jumped up, "Wait, don't eat yet. Let me fetch some mustard oil from home."

His master held his hand and pulled him down. "Oh no, don't go now. Let's see the golden sunset first."

"But we see it every day. I am feeling hungry."

"Ah, such is the intoxication of love. Even for a day one cannot miss seeing one's beloved."

The fakir passed the bowl to Rahim. The mildly sweetened peas complemented perfectly the slightly salted rice puffs.

Rahim complained, "You keep talking about her. Today show me this beloved of yours."

"There she is. That tree with her branches spread out. She speaks eloquently to me. Look how those fingers are poised as an alif, alif for Allah. She is full of hidden clues."

The boy looked at the tree silhouetted by the sun's fading brilliance. And the more he saw, the more he marvelled. "How interesting! Isn't that a hamza, right there beside the re, re for rusool, the prophet? And I can see jīm for jamal, beauty, and over there a vanishing lām. And look, when we piece all those branches together a majestic aum gets written in the sky."

"Did I not say, she entices people? Every day she reveals a facet of the Supreme Mystery. Some decipher the calligraphy of life and some melt in the purple sky. One moment stretches into infinity and we forget she was once a single tree. As prince Dara Shikoh said,

> Like an ocean is the essence of the Supreme Self,
> Like forms in water are all souls and objects.
> The ocean, heaving and stirring within,
> Transforms itself into drops, waves, and bubbles."

The tenants of the tree had returned, birds of many voices, each eager to share the exploits of the day.

Rahim puzzled, "If Dara was thus large-hearted, tell me how did he have a brother like that despot Aurangzeb?"

"Dara was an exceptional man, an erudite scholar, a saint

almost. He translated the Gita and many Upanishads into Persian. Our Islamic history is replete with personalities of his calibre, those who assimilated the wisdom of all religions and left a sky-full of poems."

"Like Guru Nanak. Wasn't he a Sufi too?"

"Well, he was one of the sants, who were influenced by Sufism, and also by the tantriks and the bhaktas of Hinduism. At that epoch, in the sixteenth century, there arose a popular movement of Sufism. These masters broke away from writing in Persian and started teaching in the local language of the populace, using the metaphors from daily life. They wrote in Sindhi, Bengali and Punjabi and won followers from all rungs of society."

"The other day you said Sufis integrated with the Yogic practices of breath-control and physical postures."

"And emperor Akbar, himself a disciple of the Chishtiyah Sufi Order, invited scholars to his palace from all spiritual paths."

"But despite all these confluences there was an Aurangzeb. How?"

"Rahim beta, because of an unfortunate twist in our history. Sufism blossomed in India when Khwaja Muinuddin Chishti settled here, in the beginning of the Delhi Sultanate. Chishtiyah professed gentleness towards all, and soon it became an important movement. Other schools of Sufism also found a home here and blended cohesively with the existing culture. The tombs of Sufi saints were pilgrim shrines for Hindus too. During the reign of the Mughals a new Sufi Order entered India, the Naqshbandi. These were the orthodox children of Islam. They endeared themselves to the rulers, and a theocratic state started torturing non-Muslims."

"But not all Mughals were their adherents, Akbar and his grandson, Dara Shikoh, were two outstanding exceptions."

"Aurangzeb was a Naqshbandi and did not tolerate the other Sufis because of their liberal spirit. He killed his elder brother, Dara, usurped the throne and planted the seed of communal rift in the country. Some of his successors were tolerant, but politically too weak to turn the tide."

"Luckily Aurangzeb could not destroy harmony between the Hindus and Muslims from all spheres of life. Think of north Indian classical music. Great musicians like Amir Khusro of the Sultanate days and Tansen of Akbar's court composed songs venerating both Hindu Gods and Allah, songs which are sung even today."

The fakir ruminated, "The synthesis had a profound impact on the spiritual ethos of the people, no doubt. The sants wept for Allah and the pirs sang Rama's praise. Yes, that tradition has survived, though it was persecuted during Aurangzeb's reign. Musicians were prohibited from public performances, and they protested by conducting a mock funeral of their musical instruments on the outskirts of Delhi. Under subsequent rulers, classical music regained her wide pedestal."

"The musical families, gharanas, have always worshipped deities from both religions."

"That is why Rahim beta, sing. Sing to dispel gloom, sing when you are happy, sing to fill up your soul, sing to be free. Music is man's secret passage to reach the heart of the Almighty."

The shrill cry of birds died out. The last fingers of light wore their gemstone rings of stars and vanished from sight. The fakir knelt to pray, "Rahim, my beloved tree has now veiled herself with night. Let us also unite with the silence within and muse with the Sindhi Sufi, Sachal Sarmast –

Repeating the name of the Beloved,
I have become the Beloved myself;
Whom shall I call the Beloved now?
Separation and union – I give up both,
Whom should I belong to now?"

Chapter Twenty

Chitrangada

After Panchali was insulted in the Kaurava court, the elders felt ashamed and returned to her husbands all they had lost in the wager. But Duryodhana was furious with his father for spoiling his plans. Another invitation was sent to the Pandavas to play the notorious game of dice. In that epoch, the Kshatriyas, the warrior clan, considered it cowardly to decline such an offer. Although the Pandavas knew it would spell their doom, the challenge was accepted. They lost, and went into exile – to dwell in the forest for twelve years. In the thirteenth year they would have to live incognito. Smarting under the insult, Arjuna was urged to seek heavenly weapons for the battle that would surely ensue against the Kauravas. Arjuna travelled to the Himalayas and began his penance. Lord Shiva was appeased and gave him the magical Pashupata weapon. Then Arjuna, the most handsome man on earth, reached the far eastern reaches of the mountain range.

In Manipur, he found a band of royal boys hunting alongside, who dared to outdo him. He turned to chide the leader and to his utter surprise he was facing a woman. Princess Chitrangada was raised as a man and taught all the skills of warfare, hunting and politics. She was the only child of the king and a deserving heir to the throne. So far the woman in Chitrangada was hidden behind the armour, but when she looked upon the valiant Pandava, she felt bashful. What was this strange tribulation in her heart? Chitrangada worshipped her guest and Arjuna's fascination for the warrior princess turned to love. They married and lived a few months together. Then Arjuna continued on his quest.

When Binapani's cousin had a daughter, a year after Panchali was born, she was named Chitrangada, sisters of a special kind. Panchali was sitting in Chitrangada's house in Calcutta, reading a magazine. It was a monthly journal from the Soviet Union, New Times. It spoke about the new times that Gorbachev was conjuring. He was dismantling the KGB, opening up the economy, inviting foreign media and investment. The Warsaw Pact was floundering, states within the USSR looked forward to their independence, and the Cold War thawed. Two words became his slogan, Perestroika, restructuring, and Glasnost, openness.

Soft hands covered her eyes. Panchali threw aside the magazine and bounced up. "Chitra!" The sisters looked at each other instead of leaping like puppies. They stood back in admiration; they were both women now. Bathing under the same shower wearing knickers would remain a sweet memory of the past.

"Chitra, you still have the dimple in your chin."

"And you, Panchali, have you started singing like a nightingale? The mole in your neck is all but crying it out."

They laughed and embraced.

"Oh, I must make you hear the Russian record we got when we subscribed to the New Times."

"Wait, let me call Ullu. He has an eerie memory for tunes."

"Who is Ullu?"

"Think of the devil."

Yuyutsu walked in and sat on Chitrangada's lap as if it was his birthright.

"Get up, you rogue, you are full of bones now," ordered Panchali, feeling a little jealousy.

"And why are you Ullu, may I know?" asked Chitrangada peering around Yuyutsu's face.

"Because I am as wise as an owl. Happy?" The last word was for his sister smirking at his lie.

A soulful female voice sang in a language they did not understand, but the meaning was tangible. It was the cry of a trapped seed reaching out to the sun. There were tears in the eyes, but the heart was full of hope. Panchali was touched deeply, and asked it to be played again and again.

"She is a bird with broken wings but will not give up flying."

"Yes, that is Russia now, in the throes of change."

Yuyutsu pointed at an object that looked like a curio from the zamindari era, "What is that?"

"It is called a hurricane lantern. Just you wait for night to fall, and you will know what it is used for."

"You mean load-shedding? We have power cuts in Bombay too. But we use candles."

Their uncle walked in with a book which read Atlas of India. Yuyutsu swung from his free arm like a monkey "Mama is here, mama is here!"

Raja sat down on the bed. "The difference between a hurricane lantern and candle light is the same as between the Bengali load-shedding and the power cuts in the rest of India. You can reduce the flame in a hurricane lantern till it reaches nirvana, extinction in the black void. And then something within the human heart stirs into action." He raised his hand towards the sky and all eyes followed. But no magical bird came out of it.

The rest of the elders of the house joined the group. Chitrangada's mother said, "Load-shedding is a social glue. We sit at doorsteps or go to the terrace and talk to our neighbours over the parapet. You don't see gestures or facial expressions, but just hear the words hanging disembodied in the night air, pure and uncomplicated."

Anand added, "It is also essential for a student. Instead of learning formulae by heart, one is forced to really understand the law behind the equations."

"I like to play the game of catching faint sounds coming from faraway," said Chitrangada, "But baba gets inspired to tell ghost stories. Then for days cold fingers tickle me on the back, but I dare not turn around and stare into some hollowed skull. It's creepy to go to the bathroom alone at night."

"Oh, I must tell you what else it is good for." Raja was suddenly animated. "Once I was helping to set up the marriage podium at a friend's place. We were about twenty of us, men and women running around in all directions. Then suddenly pitch darkness. The conversation became relaxed. So many stars I saw that night. It was quite romantic. Now don't you two ducklings exchange smiles. Anyway when the lights returned a lady started pretending as if she knew me very well. So I finally asked her if she thought I was someone else. She was quite angry, 'Did you not propose to me?' Then she looked at my hands, 'Oh, it's not you, sorry. He had a ring'. So you see, one can hold hands in the dark and look at the moon and no one will know about it, not even the participants."

"Good story, Raja." This was the matriarch, Debjani. "We Bengalis don't work around a load-shedding; we integrate it in our lives; we welcome it."

Binapani agreed with her mother, "Yes life is too fast. We don't get the chance to witness ourselves running around, often in circles. During a load-shedding you can peruse on the diary of your life, read it quietly and make margin notes. It is necessary for a healthy livelihood, like jobs and monsoons. It pollinates the mind, and that is how ideas bear fruit."

Panchali was impressed, "Taalyaan, applause! Yes, there should be a place on earth where competition is replaced by contemplation."

Everybody cheered, "And let that be Bengal!"

After dinner Raja laid out the map of Bengal. "I was told a certain person here loves history, and so we will do a historical tour of Bengal." He winked at Panchali and assumed a teacher-like voice, "Write an essay on how the last Nawab of Bengal lost his kingdom to ..."

"The British in the battle of Plassey in 1757. Nawab Siraj-ud-daula, not even thirty at that time, was betrayed by his minister, Mir Jaffar, who was unwilling to give up the power he had had, while Siraj was still a minor."

Raja's jeer balloon burst on his face, "Bina-didi, I think Panchali knows some history."

"Of course she does."

"So we start from the British capital, Calcutta, and go to the present capital of the district of Nadia. In Krishnanagar, the best statues are made, in clay and plaster of Paris, and of shola, the white spongy wood you get in swampy regions. It is as soft as a bamboo core, used to make the delicate crown and other ornaments for Goddesses."

Chitrangada associated with Krishnanagar differently. "You would have heard stories of Gopal Bhanr, the jester in the zamindar's court?" After one graduates from the Thakurmar Jhuli Bengali fairy tales, one reads about Gopal Bhanr's wit. Her cousins shook their heads, "No."

Anand explained, "They heard the fairy tales from their mother, but when they grew up a little and could read, there were stories of Birbal, Tenali Raman, Mullah Nasiruddin." These were the various Gopal Bhanr counterparts across India. Birbal was Akbar's minister, the one who had a solution for any problem. Tenali Raman, born in Andhra Pradesh, was a scholar-poet of the sixteenth century whose practical jokes unveiled many simple truths. Mullah Nasiruddin was a Sufi teacher with an unconventional outlook couched in profound wisdom.

Raja continued, "Then from there we will go to Nabadwip, capital of the Sena dynasty in the mid twelfth century."

"Why is it called naba dwip, nine islands?" asked Yuyutsu.

"It used to be a collection of nine small islands on the Ganga. Now the water has dried in places, but we will still have to cross over it to reach one of the islands, Mayapur. Yuyutsu, what is it famous for?"

"Isn't it the birthplace of Chaitanya Mahaprabhu?"

"Very good. He was the founder of the Bhakti Movement."

Anand apologized for Raja, "Well, we don't know if we can use the word 'founder' in Hinduism, as these rise and fall in waves. The Bhagavad Gita could be considered the first text on adoration of Krishna. Then the Bhagavata Purana of Shukadeva has the stories of His play, leela. The poet Jaydev had composed Bhakti songs of Krishna in the twelfth century. Chaitanya Mahaprabhu was responsible for the last phase of revivalism, and yes, from that time onwards, from the sixteenth century, the fervour has only increased. And now it is a worldwide movement."

"All right, then we make a leap into the next century, to Murshidabad, the Nawab's capital. They have a palace with a thousand doors, therefore named 'hazarduari'. Here the river Ganga splits into Padma, that goes eastwards to Bangladesh, and Hooghly that descends to Calcutta. Then we will push northwards to the last place of our current interest, capital during the golden age of Bengal, of the Pala dynasty, a ruined city now, called Gaur. Later Pandua and Gaur alternated being capitals during the Delhi Sultanate. That makes five capitals, and Panchali, they should keep you busy writing your history essays."

"Mama, you forgot another capital."

"Which one?"

"Dhaka. Capital for two hundred years under the Mughals."

"Ah, Dhaka, of course. But how can we go there without some preparation? It is not India anymore."

Panchali smiled sadly. "Yes, the city of universities, pride of the Bengalis, now in Bangladesh."

Ishani, Panchali's aunt said, "I think I would feel insecure under martial law. We have grown rather used to freedom of speech and thought out here. In Bangladesh first they killed Mujib, then his successor, Ziaur Rahman was assassinated by the next army General, Ershad, who is now the president. That is the way of the army; Macbeth style."

"But have you heard about the great banking success in Bangladesh? I think that alone can make Ershad survive," remarked Raja.

"You mean the Grameen Bank, brain-child of Mohammad Yunus?" Chitrangada's father was an astute banker and he knew the pains of chasing farmers to recover loans.

"Baba, tell us about it." His daughter was interested.

"Mohammad Yunus, who had just completed his doctorate in the US, returned to his motherland, when Bangladesh became free, and started teaching economics. One day, while walking on the road, he spotted a woman in a torn sari sitting under a patched roof, knitting a bamboo stool of exquisite beauty. He learnt her story. A local moneylender had given her the money to buy the bamboo with the condition that she would sell her handiwork to him alone. She got a pittance for her whole day's labour despite her rare talent. Yunus wondered, 'If only instead of the moneylender it would be an organization less intent on making profits ...' Thus spun the mind of the economist. He tried to get a bank to grant her a small loan."

Chitrangada puzzled about it, "But a bank does not lend unless it is somewhat sure the loan will be repaid."

"That is exactly what the bankers said. She had to be creditworthy. The system does not allow a person without a history of borrowing to begin borrowing. But how then would she ever make a start? All she asked was a tiny amount. Yunus decided to fight no more the sceptical bankers, but instead start his own bank."

"Ah, now it makes sense. That is the missing piece in the puzzle."

"The Grameen Bank was born, the bank of the gram, the village."

Anand jumped in, "There is still the impasse of loans going bad. How did he hedge against it?"

"Aha, the Bank used a trick, for sure. It gave credit to five women at a time, who guaranteed each other's loans. You know, the Grameen Bank has become a social movement that has saved thousands of families from starving to death. All they needed was one sewing machine, a dozen silk worms, some bamboo, two cows, one husking machine, and they could improve their lot and their children's and grandchildren's."

Raja whistled, "Now, that is real impact at the grassroots."

Panchali summed up Yunus' saga, "He came, he saw, he conquered."

Chitrangada's father finished the miracle man's story, "A small loan is easier to repay, especially if five persons together shoulder the responsibility. In India we have given big loans and subsidies to the farmer. Water and electricity are free. Free means a bigger tax burden on the rest of the people. Free also means wastage. I have seen fields where the pump runs all night flooding the road and the crops. It is free from the government, but Mother Nature has a limited supply. All this can be fixed if there is a loan to be repaid."

Debjani continued, "In the long run, people would be better rewarded if they took responsibility and achieved something on their own. What do you say, Bina?"

"All very good, but I say we go to bed right now. Tomorrow is Mahalaya, remember, at four o'clock in the morning."

From the first sound of the conch shell, a deep peace settled on the listeners. Debjani lit the incense and pulled the curtains back. The powerful voice of Birendra Krishna Bhadra sped across the skies into the radio sets vibrating with anticipation. The Mother Goddess would descend on earth on this twilight of the new moon day. The Mahalaya is a collage of songs and chants to invoke Durga. It tells the story of the glory of the Goddess, Devi Mahatmyam, as recounted by Rishi Markandeya in the Puranic age. Panchali opened the text, the Chandi, and read Brahma's prayer, along with the chanter. After a pralaya, end of a cycle, Lord Vishnu rested on his serpent, the Ananta, the eternal. Two demons were born from his earwax, Madhu and Kaitabha. Immediately they plotted to create mischief. Brahma seated on the lotus that grew out of Vishnu's navel felt the tremor and looked down to see these two devils climbing up the stem, baring their greedy teeth. Who would set the next cycle into motion if Brahma, the creator, was devoured? He called upon Vishnu, but could not awake the Supreme from his own veil. He then started praying to the force that is the Veil, the Yogamaya. She answered his call and seeped out of Vishnu's body. He awoke and in a long battle that spanned years, killed the two demons.

The pale blue of the morning stole past the curtains mingling with the aroma of flavoured tea brewing in the roadside shop. The voice was as if weeping when it chanted the praise of Narayani, spouse of Lord Vishnu. Listeners were also touched to tears. Everybody sang the refrain of the last hymn. "*Rupam dehi, jayam dehi, yasho dehi, dwisho jahi,* grant us beauty, grant us victory, grant us prosperity, destroy our hatred." Conch shells reverberated from homes. The whole of Bengal was paying homage to the Mother. The intense worship would begin on the sixth day of the lunar phase. Durga was created by the concentrated energy of all the Gods, a Goddess with ten arms, each wielding a weapon given by a God, her clothes studded with precious stones and her hair bedecked with a jewelled crown. Durga is the short name for Durgati Nashini, destroyer of obstacles. Thus would she be worshipped by the Gods and sent forth to the earth to vanquish Mahishasura, the demon who could take on the form of any animal.

In her third descent to save the earth, the Mother would challenge the demon brothers, Shumbha and Nishumbha. Kali emerges from her body, a Goddess of fierce appearance and horrific deeds. She drinks the blood of the menacing Raktabeeja before it spills on the ground, and strings a garland with his severed heads. The Mother herself kills the evil brothers, and peace and joy are restored on earth. On the tenth day of worship she returns to her heavenly abode. Her idols are immersed in the river and people resume their life cleansed of the demons that reside within. There is love and amity everywhere for the ten days, and on the last day older folks are venerated with the pranaam, the bowing down, translated in a gesture of touching the feet. The elder person gives a sweet to the younger one, consonant with the sweetness of their relationship.

Yuyutsu declared after breakfast, "I am going to sleep."

"But you did not even listen to the wonderful Mahalaya," complained Dinapani.

"Of course I did. Yogamaya came right out of his body and killed Vishnu's sleep, as well as mine."

"All right, then what happened?"

"We battled hard ... to stay awake." He laughed and crashed into bed. "Didima help, it is vacation and ma won't let me sleep."

* * * * *

They crossed the river Hooghly from Nabadwip on a barge. The breeze blew softly and filled each ear with a bewitching tune. This was the song of the water, of fishermen, of slippery fish and enchanted nets, a song that flowed languidly downstream, a song that fell and rose with the waves, like the joys and sorrows of life.

"What are you humming, Ullu?"

"Didi, I can hear a tune but no words. Give me some verses to swell it up."

"The river wilful as a girl
Bid my folded sails unfurl,
She snatched my oars
And turned my course.
She chased my fears
And wiped my tears;
Brother let us play she said
Till the sky turns sunset red."

* * * * *

When Mayapur was still a cluster of little huts with round thatches, one boy saw a vision of Lord Krishna and knew his whole life would be the pursuit of that Lover. He abandoned his house, danced on the road in ecstasy, and very soon his madness became contagious. A following gathered around him and they heard the stories of Krishna, and fell in his snare like the gopis of Brindavan. They travelled across the country sweeping people into this sweetness of devotion. Now in Mayapur tourists pass by innumerable temples and guest houses. They admire the marble structure with a spiral stairway and a dome painted with constellations. The prayer hall has murals from Sri Chaitanya Mahaprabhu's life.

A huge crowd assembled to participate in the evening worship. A priest danced with frankincense in hand, while another fanned the deity and his consort, Krishna and Radha. The idols were hidden behind their flower garlands. Worshippers sat on the ground. Many of them were from the Western countries and wore saffron robes. The crowd chanted "*Hare Krishna Hare*

Rama". Drums beat and a thousand little cymbals tinkled. The heady aroma of the incense drenched the lungs and passed into the brain already filled with loud music. The effect was intoxicating, liberating, overwhelming. People got up and started swinging from foot to foot, their hands lifted above the head. Then they started clapping, and some clicked the thumb and middle finger. More and more people abandoned themselves to the momentum and the throng revolved around the drum players, the source of the beats. Panchali did not realize she was dancing. Her father too had a glazed look in his eyes, and tears of adoration. Raja had penetrated the crowd of the saffron clad ones and in spirit was a wisp of incense rising up to heaven. Yuyutsu pranced around his sister, singing till his throat begged him to go easy. Binapani and her cousin, Ishani, were holding hands and dancing a duet. Only Chitrangada was too shy to let herself drown in the moment. She stood smiling at everybody else wishing she could forget she had a body.

Then the drums performed the tehai, the three quick gambols of utter joy as the finale notes. The dancers relaxed and stood panting, sweating, slowly catching back the thread they had left dangling. Panchali and Yuyutsu steadied each other as their heads were still floating in outer space.

"What just happened?"

"I have no idea. I was not even here."

And they all laughed in a mad chorus and clapped. Every heart wanted to leap into everybody else's and embrace them. There was no more division of body and body, or soul and soul. There was just one Lord and one devotee, Krishna and humanity.

They ate bhog on the banana leaves, served by the young brahmacharis, the students of spiritual discipline. All the visitors sat in a line on the ground and ate with their fingers, the simple meal of khichadi and cauliflower curry.

"Ma, I have never eaten tastier food," declared Panchali.

"It is because they cook it in the chulha. The fire is from wood, which lends a different energy to food than our gas fire."

At night they saw how many stars one sky could hold. In the city lit with the neon-signs these stars were invisible, but here little dots of white bore holes into the black skin of the tight drum, called night. They visited other temples of Radha and Krishna, the two always together. In Mayapur Radha was allowed to love Krishna for eternity; in Brindavan she pined for him till the end of time.

"Until we unite with our Lord, the Radha within us will cry for him. That is the meaning and purpose of life. Everything else is the curtain that separates us from our Beloved, the Maya."

They arrived in Gaur on a van, a raft on three wheels, and as shaky as one on a rough sea. It was the most entertaining of all journeys. In one van sat the Deshmukh family, holding hands to counter the centrifugal force. The other one had Chitrangada's family and Raja. Ullu, the owl, tried to fly away several times and after a while Raja thought it was lesser exercise to run beside the van. When they had settled in the hotel, an auspicious sound passed by the road. It was the phuchkawalla's bell. In Bombay this snack was called panipuri, and in Delhi, golgappa. It is a fried puff the size of a ping-pong ball, the puri, stuffed with potato and spices, topped with tamarind juice. The vendor gave each person a palm leaf folded into a cone as they watched him make the stuffing. The mixture of potato and onion and lethal powders is unique to every region. Ishani and Binapani sucked in their saliva noisily, and got a severe look from their husbands. Then a dollop of the potato mix was stuffed into the puri; tamarind juice was cupped from a large earthen pot and the food bomb was placed in each palm leaf crater. It was so fiery Yuyutsu jumped up and down screaming, aau, aau. After each one had got his share Yuyutsu got one more, and then another, although he was the one who shouted loudest. At last the vendor wagged his finger, "No more phaau." Phaau was the free extra ones that the poor kid had to devour for shouting aau.

"Chitra, let's go for a walk, while these people laze around and have their siesta." The two girls started walking down the dusty lanes of the city that was all but abandoned. A few monuments and mosques under the protection of the

Archaeological Survey of India broke the monotony of shrubs. There was a watchtower, which could be climbed if one could get used to the smell of pigeon droppings. From the top you can see a vast checkerboard of fields stretching unbroken into Bangladesh. Ancient Bengal was called Gaur, and thus the Bhakti movement from Mayapur was termed the Gaudiya Bhakti movement.

Panchali asked her cousin, "Mashi was saying you are learning some form of martial arts. Is that true?"

"Yes, I became quite crazy after I saw Bruce Lee's film, 'Enter the Dragon'. I used to practise karate kicks in the terrace and dropped a few flowerpots. So my parents enrolled me in a kalari."

"What is a kalari?"

"It means, a school that teaches martial arts. It is a Malayali word, as this art form originated in Kerala."

"Ah, I have heard of it. Kalari payattu?"

"Yes, payattu means to fight. It is a traditional art of warfare, practised by both men and women, mostly for self defence, but can be used for offence too."

"Is it like karate?"

"Yes, a lot. It has sequences of steps derived from observing animals fight. They are the elephant style, cat, snake, boar, and many more, including even a peacock style."

They had reached an open barren land, and in the still afternoon not even a bee could be heard. Mango trees fringed the meadow, but were a blur faraway. Panchali observed her sister. She had poise in her very gait, as if she was dancing in her walk. "Very interesting. Show me what you have learnt."

"There are four stages of this training. People spend years in the first, where we learn the steps, kicks, jumps and aerial twists. The important lesson is to develop body consciousness; watch yourself from outside the body and see it flow with the rhythm."

Chitrangada tied her dupatta on her waist raising the edge of the kameez. "I have torn so many kameezs in this way. Now I wear a T-shirt over the salwar."

"Is that what the other girls also wear?"

"Yes, many of us do that and some wear the traditional Tamil or Malayali sari, the one worn as a dhoti around the legs to give maximum freedom. Men, of course, wear dhotis."

"I know that sari. It is called navari in Marathi, and is worn in that dhoti style. It is much longer than the regular saris."

Chitrangada started her martial art dance motifs, stretching every muscle of the body, stirring the air with her flailing limbs, striking the earth forcefully. One had to be very fit not to pant breathless after these energetic jumps and kicks. It also demanded great agility. If this was the first stage Panchali wondered what the others entailed. The choreography was artful and yet it could be imagined as a form of battle.

"You know, Chitra, what music would work with this dance?"

"The chants of the Mahalaya from the Devi hymns?"

"Yes, I can see Kali bending low to drink the blood off Raktabeeja's severed head. Also I am reminded of the hymns of Shiva's tandava dance."

"Panchali, you have understood the essence. We pray to a deity before we start practising, and it is an aspect, an avatar, of Kali, Bhagavati or Shiva."

"So what are the next stages of kalari payattu?"

"In the second stage we will learn to use wooden weapons; the long and short stick, and a curved one like the trunk of an elephant."

"I have never seen a weapon!"

"Yes, these are just the preliminaries for the third stage, where we will use metal weapons. The spear, the trident of Shiva and various kinds of swords; with curved and straight edges, a sword in each hand, and finally the curved flexible sword."

"Did you say curved and flexible at the same time? It sounds dangerous."

"And it is. Of course, it means very few adept students get to learn it. You know, I am very excited right now. I am practising for a workshop I am going to attend in Kanyakumari next year."

"Kanyakumari is not in Kerala, it is in Tamil Nadu."

"Kalari payattu is practised in all of the southern states, northern Sri Lanka, and places where the Malayali people have settled, like Malaysia. The British had to face these traditional warriors, who also used the bow and arrow. But gunpowder was superior, and then in the British Raj, kalari payattu was banned. But it did not die, it was just done in secret. When the khadi movement started in the 1920s, the cottage industries flourished, people started dumping foreign goods in the street and burning them."

"Yes, the boycott movement. Gandhiji marched to Dandi and made salt from sea water, so that we did not have to buy imported salt."

"Around that time kalari payattu was brought back to the mainstream and now there are many schools all over India. The best part of traditional art forms in their holistic nature. They teach Ayurveda along with martial arts. The workshop will teach us massage techniques to make the body more supple, and also cures of muscular wounds."

"Wow, you will learn all these when you go there?"

"And I will also spar with opponents of my level, with the stick. But listen to the last stage of training, strictly reserved for those who have great mental balance and control. It is fighting with bare hands."

"But how can it be superior to using swords?"

"Now I will shock you. Are you ready?"

"Do I have to close my eyes?" Panchali joked.

"Surely you remember Shushruta?"

"The doctor of the BCE age, who wrote a treatise on surgery?"

"Yes, besides surgery he knew a lot more; about Ayurveda and Marma Shastra. Marma means vital points, and shastra is the study of it. Shushruta found hundred and seven points in the body which, when struck with the fist or a stick, can paralyse a person, or cause an organ to stop functioning. Of these, sixty-four are fatal points. Imagine, just with the bare hand one can kill a person."

"No wonder it is taught judiciously. How many people do you think know Marma Shastra?"

"That is a secret an adept will not disclose. Nobody knows the count, but we know they exist."

Panchali pointed to a brick house in front. "Let's walk there. Who knows, it may be some king's treasure house in ruins, and maybe we could find something worthy in it."

"Yes, let's go there." The two girls had reached quite close when they spied some movement around the house. "Men, I think."

"Yes, men. Let's turn back."

"No, they are boys, our age, and they are wearing the NCC uniform." NCC was the National Cadets Corps, the boy scouts of India. Boys were trained to use light ammunition, they camped in the wilderness, sometimes they helped in the restoration of old monuments, learnt traffic control, rebuilt a village road; in other words became good citizens. The hardy ones enjoyed the outdoor life and the challenge of becoming self-sufficient; carrying their backpacks, lighting a fire, protecting it from the wind, cooking the simple meal, setting up tents, using as little water as possible.

Just as the girls were observing the boys, so were the boys observing their visitors. All activity of cleaning the ruins was replaced by scouring for a pair of binoculars.

"Chitra, turn around, they have binoculars. We will not show them our faces."

"Good idea!"

A few cries of disappointment reached their ears and they stood in the field bending forward and laughing, feeling very smart. The boys were queuing up to make them turn around. "Sister, this way to the city", or "Come give us a hand in digging this treasure", or simply, "Please, please turn around."

One pretended to have been shot; he uttered a cry of pain, but the girls did not turn. Then they heard the sound of hooves approaching from behind.

"What's that, Panchali?"

"Don't turn, some boys must be running after us pretending to be bulls."

"What if it is really one of those big black buffaloes? It could tear us to pieces. Listen the sound is coming closer."

"Don't go on like that. My back is tingling, Chitra."

"Run, run!" shouted the boys. "It's not us, it's a bull."

"Panchali, let's just run in front."

"No, wait. They'll laugh their heads off."

But the sound was so close they turned instinctively. It was indeed a bull, not the black hairy kind, but one with big horns and dilated red eyes. The animal was just a few metres from them when they yelled in terror and dashed forward. "Here, here," came voices from the nearest clump of trees. Panchali saw a boy in one of the trees ahead stretching his hand out to her, she grabbed it and he pulled her up, just on time to see the animal butt its horns in the tree trunk. Chitrangada was hauled up by another boy in the next tree. The bull was the only one on the ground pacing angrily. A bare-chested man wearing loose shorts came snorting after the beast. As if that was not a surprise enough on that otherwise empty stage, two men in army camouflage came lunging into the scene from behind the trees.

A soldier addressed the peasant, "Hey you, did we not warn you not to chase your bull here?"

"What can I do, sahib? Is there a way one can talk reason to a bull?"

The soldiers looked at the couples in each tree and smiled. "Sorry, are we disturbing you?"

Chitrangada and Panchali's faces reddened. "We were taking a stroll here when the bull charged at us. We don't know these boys..." Panchali's words trailed off as the soldier silenced her with a gesture of elder-brotherly indulgence. "Don't worry sister, we are all for free love."

That made her feel embarrassingly conscious of standing in the same fork, foot touching foot, with an unknown boy, his breath tickling her earlobes. The soldier pointed at the peasant,

"He comes every other day from the other side of the border to collect honey. And look over there." They saw palm trees each with a little slit and an earthen pot under the cut collecting the sap. "He and his co-conspirators fix those pots on the Indian trees and sell the toddy in Bangladeshi markets."

"Is the border close by?" asked Panchali, curious.

"Yes, right there where that brick house ends."

"Oh, I thought there would be a no-man's-land, border polices, sand bags with guns hoisted on them."

"Hey kid," the soldier addressed the boy behind her, "Tell your girlfriend not to imagine this to be the Pakistan border. The other day a fellow walked out because his kite had got stuck in a tree on that side of the border. There is no respect at all for us Border Security Forces. He was brought in by the Bangladesh Rifles, his ear an inch longer than when he left."

The peasant looked at the four kids, "The sahibs get a pot of free palm toddy and let us smuggle the rest out. All is good, children, we just enact this drama when strangers turn up, like you."

"Ei, you rascal, take your well-trained dog and disappear." The peasant whistled and the irate beast followed him, licking his shoulder like a dog. So this was the second international border Panchali was seeing! She laughed at the folly. And how did they draw the line over the river? Did a fisherman fight with another because the fish he had spotted swam into the other's net across the border? The boy behind her swung from the branch and landed on the ground. Panchali saw Chitrangada leap out in the air and steady herself on the ground. "That's a brave one!" said the boy standing under Panchali, arms outstretched to help her down. She chose to be another brave one and sprang up, held the branch he had swung on. But off went her body out of its grip and she in the air out of control. Nothing untoward happened. She landed on her feet, unhurt. The uncomfortable fact was that he had caught her in midair and brought her down, like a spotter for a gymnastic stunt. She thought, "If only he were Shreyas." And he thought, "If only trees had such fruits."

The four were joined by a dozen others, who did not need binoculars any more. There would be a bonfire that evening and the girls were invited. "Oh please don't say no, bring your parents too. It is just a little bit of fun talk round the fire." The girls winced. Not parents, but Raja mama would work. And so that evening the girls, escorted by their mama, came to the gathering. The fire was lit and one boy asked the guests, "So what are your names?"

Panchali shook her head, "Not so easy young chap, you will have to guess."

"Agreed, we accept the challenge. Then you will also have to guess all our names."

"Agreed," smiled Chitrangada and she winked at Panchali.

The one who had rescued Panchali started the game, "I am the Egyptian Sun God."

Panchali guessed, "Ra?"

"Yes, HIM."

"I see, Rahim?"

Some boys clapped. "Now your turn, young lady."

"You can win me only through the fish's eye."

"Meenakshi, fish-eyed?"

"No," remarked another, "Why would she say 'win me' then?"

"I got it! You are Draupadi."

"Close."

"Then Panchali?"

"Perfect."

"In that case," said a boy, "You should sit beside me."

"Are you Arjuna?"

"Close."

"Partha?"

"Try again."

"Sabyasachi?"

"Bull's eye!"

Now Chitrangada held Panchali back, who was complying with his demand. "Not yet, sister, he will have to fight me first."

The boys laughed, "That's easy, Arjuna fights one girl in his life, of course not knowing she is a girl. You are Chitrangada."

"Ah, then I get flanked by both," beamed Sabyasachi.

Panchali got up to sit beside Sabyasachi, but Rahim stopped her. "Yet, in this life, I rescued you, so you will sit beside me." Panchali shrugged in mock helplessness and sat beside Rahim.

"My turn now," said Chitrangada's mango tree hero. "I am a king, in Urdu."

"Nawab?" guessed Chitrangada. He shook his head.

"Badshah," said Raja.

"No. But let me give you another hint. I am the Soviet space station."

"Mir!" exclaimed the girls.

"Correct. Mir means 'peace' in Russian."

"Shall we have a song?" Panchali asked the assembly.

"Rahim, why don't you sing us something nice, something fitting." Mir produced a mouth organ from his pocket.

"A palli geeti fits this village setting. Let me sing one." As Rahim sang Mir played the harmonica, and Panchali imagined the village women dipping their jars in the pond, men stirring the pot of jaggery, life oozing from the palm tree, sweet and intoxicating.

She loved his deep thoughtful voice. "Rahim, is there a kind of song that fishermen sing? Song of the river?"

"Oh yes. It is called bhaatiaali, song of the bhaataa, the tide, song of the languid lakes and serpentine streams, of cascades rippling like a dancer's anklets, of lotus and hyacinth damsels bathing in the pool, of the sea embracing infinity." Rahim set himself afloat downstream, then rose up gently, melancholic at times, playful at others, mysterious like the bed of a dreaming ocean.

"O sailor of the deep sea

Do bend your ship towards me,
I arrived with my paper boat
To set her alone afloat,
But the bank crashed underfoot
Launching me on this mad route.
O sailor of the deep sea
Do make haste and rescue me.
You sail where she calmly flows
And I swim in the shallows.
Lift me from the whirlpool
Of this terrifying frothy ghoul."

Panchali could not keep herself pinned to the ground. She got up and abandoned her body to the snare of the melody. The fire light played with the shadows cast by her nimble steps. Rahim's song and Panchali's dance would remain in people's hearts for many years and they would reminisce, "Yes, that night was sublime."

"O sailor of the deep blue sea
Turn not a deaf ear towards me.
Her waves are like advancing walls
And I hear her bewitching calls.
I beg you sailor do come fast
Before she pins a wind to my mast.
I drown in her eddies
And scream out for respite,
Sailor of the deep seas
Why wait for the dark night?"

Part Five

Chapter Twenty-one

Shreyas

"Didi, are you going to make me a rakhi this year or not? Do you know Shravan Poornima is next Tuesday? You have to post Prahlad's." Panchali woke up with a start. The full moon day of the festival was approaching fast. Where was she these days? In Shreyas dreamland of course. She went to the embroidery shop and looked at the hundreds of silk threads to choose from. She found one like a peacock's feather, that looked green when she tilted her head on one side and navy blue on the other. This colour reminded her of Shreyas. Maybe he was wearing blue the first time she saw him, or perhaps his complexion would suit this thread. Then reality banged her on the head. Why was she thinking of Shreyas while buying rakhi thread for her brothers? She adored him as a lover, not a sister. This was one of tricks girls played on boys who trailed them. They put a big rakhi around the boy's wrist and sent a clear message. Sisters all over India were wishing their brothers good fortune by tying the raksha bandhan, in short the rakhi. The brothers in turn pledged to protect the sister, to do raksha, and therefore the two were bound by mutual goodwill, which is the bandhan. Panchali decided to make a red rakhi for Yuyutsu and a golden one for Prahlad. But she also bought the magical blue-green silk thread, and it would be for Shreyas, because that is what her blind heart begged her to do. Not because she wanted him to get a sisterly message, but because she loved this colour and she loved him, and thus she could love him doubly.

Tulsi came to Panchali's house to make the rakhis. It needed two hands to twist threads around each other firmly and tie them when they were taut. Once the tassel was made, the centre fluff could be done alone with an old toothbrush. Tulsi looked at her friend's palette.

"Panchali, why do you have three this year? Is there someone who is chasing you?"

"No, but there is someone I am chasing." she had almost said it aloud, but how could she? Shreyas was too precious and her love would remain locked in her heart till it found the right key.

"I could not resist buying this turquoise thread. But you know my brothers love acid colours. So I will just make a giant rakhi and admire it myself." Anand walked in and found the girls busy.

"Ah, the wonderful time of the year has arrived."

"Sir, please tell us the rakhi story." Tulsi loved to hear stories from Anand.

"It is one of the customs we have forgotten the origin of, but remember the many instances it was used. Once Lord Indra, king of Gods, was going on a campaign and his wife, Indrani, tied the thread on his wrist as a symbol of her good wishes. Then during the reign of the Mughal emperor, Humayun, Akbar's father, there was a Rajput queen of Chittor, a widow, who was on the verge of being attacked by a sultan of Gujarat. She sent a rakhi to Humayun as a way of entreating for his help. The emperor was so moved that he dropped the battle he was already waging and came to Chittor to save the queen. It is a powerful message from a woman to a man, that she wishes the best for him and he in return promises to protect her. Rakhi was used as a display of solidarity during the short-lived partition of Bengal in 1905. Hindus and Muslims put rakhis on each other and sent a dire note to the colonial rulers."

Panchali's intuition was rewarded. Not only did sisters tie the rakhi for brothers, but any girl who wished a youth well, tied it for him.

Anand continued, "And Panchali you should know the story of Draupadi and Krishna."

"No, what is it?"

"Once Krishna's index finger was bleeding, and Draupadi immediately tore her sari's hem and bandaged it. The lord accepted the gesture as tying of the rakhi and ever since he was the one who saved her – during the vastraharan, snatching of the clothes in the court, then again during their forest exile, from being cursed by the Sage Durvasa."

"Yes, that story I know." said Panchali.

"Then tell me." requested Tulsi, always ready for more stories, although she would have known this one herself.

"Durvasa, as we all know, had a notorious temper. Once he and his hundred disciples came to the forest hut of the Pandavas, sent by the cruel Duryodhana. He knew the forest dwellers had no means to feed so many guests, and hoped it would enrage the sage and he would curse the Pandavas. In our tradition, the woman eats last, making sure the men have had their fill. After she has eaten no more food is cooked for the day. When these hordes came to her, Draupadi had just finished eating. She sent them to bathe in the river and prayed to her saviour, Krishna. She had five husbands, but this task was beyond human ken."

"Isn't it nice that she had Krishna as the last recourse? One who could perform every trick on earth?"

"We too have him the same way," said Panchali.

"Yes, you would know," teased Tulsi, "You are Panchali after all."

"Anyway Krishna came to the hut ... oh, what luck to call upon our lover and have him turn up at our doorstep."

"Panchali, are you in love?" whispered Tulsi, avoiding Anand.

"Why? Can't I sympathize, without actually being in love?"

"You can, but there was something forlorn in your voice, as if you were giving up hope. Is there somebody, no really, after your father leaves, will you tell me?"

Anand cleared his throat to make his presence felt. "And so Krishna asked Draupadi to show him the vessel she had used. Luckily, it was unwashed. He found a morsel still stuck on the plate and ate it. Then he sighed in satisfaction, 'Ah, I am so full.' And when the Lord says it, the whole creation, being a little portion of his self, feels it too. The disciples held their full bellies, and did not even venture towards the hut."

Panchali at last understood why she had chosen the blue-green colour. Krishna wore a peacock feather in his crown. He was within every being, but for Panchali he revealed himself most through Shreyas. She had been given a living form to worship, a God in flesh and blood, a human her age in her little universe. These were her happy Brindavan days when Krishna and Radha swung together under the branch of a kadam tree, their cheeks coloured with pollen, the wind fluting hymns in their ears.

"Panchali, where are you lost again, twist the thread my dear, and stop fantasizing."

They made the gold and red rakhis and then the peacock one. Tulsi herself had a white rakhi intertwined with green. Then in solitude Panchali made a big flower for the blue-green rakhi, and at every stroke imagined herself getting closer to her Krishna – Shreyas.

On the full moon day of Raksha Bandhan the boys in school showed off their dazzling wrists, gifts from real and adopted sisters. Panchali had hatched a plan to catch Shreyas alone. She saw Saheli and her girlfriends pass by, then the boys came in a huddle, and he was there amongst them. Panchali caught up with him, and with a maths book in her hand asked him if he could explain a problem. The others left them alone and she suggested he use the board. They went into a classroom, and Panchali snapped shut the book.

"Shreyas, forget the problem, I wanted to give you something today."

He knit his brows then saw the delicate peacock-blue rakhi Panchali had handcrafted with utmost care. He laughed, "You want to give me a rakhi? And that is why you ambushed me?"

She had hoped to hear him say, "No, Panchali, I cannot be your brother, I love you."

But he said, "I am not promising to protect you."

She smiled sadly, "I am not asking you to. I have two brothers for that. A rakhi is the most tender wish a girl can give a boy."

"What are you talking about?" He was getting alarmed now.

"All I am saying is that I wish you all the best."

"Nothing more I hope, you are scaring me."

Her reply played only in Panchali's inner ear. "Nothing more and nothing less. If anything happens to you, I don't think I can live on. Ideally, you would love me. But I can reconcile myself with reality too. You don't have to care for me, just be happy, and I will live with that thought in my heart, that you are happy."

She said aloud, "No, relax. Show me your wrist, Shreyas."

Did her voice shake when she uttered his name, for Shreyas hesitated, "No, am having my doubts. I don't think I want it. I am sorry, Panchali. It is a very beautiful rakhi you have made." He was gone. Beautiful, but of what use? She tossed it on the ground in the empty classroom. Then knelt beside it and cried.

*****

It was the first day back at school. The flock of girls resembled a tree full of birds returning at sunset. Everybody wanted to talk about their vacation. Panchali had gone to Delhi to her aunt's house.

"Best was Agra. So my cousin from Delhi, Prahlad, blindfolded my brother and me with handkerchiefs. He helped us out of the rickshaw and walked us to the entrance, positioned us in the centre, then undid our blindfolds. Oh what a sight it was! We were facing a rust-coloured archway, tapered at the top, and through it we could see the white Taj Mahal, as small as this palm. Yuyutsu wanted to run in, but Prahlad held us back, walking in the centre holding our hands. He had been there before in school trips. Thus we marched forward keeping our eyes on the marble edifice that grew more magnificent at every step. The gate was like passing through a tunnel, but of course more spacious and ornately carved."

Aditi joined the group huddled around Panchali.

"And it went on and on and I wished it would never end. It just grew larger and larger on the consciousness till I was going to scream in delight, and almost beg him to stop, so that I may not go mad. I tell you all, this is something you have to absolutely experience. I held him back, 'Let's just stop right here and not go any further, I am too overwhelmed as it is. Let me regain my senses first'."

Aditi was shocked, "Panchali, what are you describing? Does your mother know it?"

Eyes turned towards her in bewilderment, then all the girls burst out laughing. Finally Panchali had dared to touch that manifestation of eternal love in the ephemeral world. Her voice was dreamy, "Everything about the Taj is grand. The architecture is poetry frozen. The marble walls have low relief of fruits and flowers and inlays in precious stones – red jasper, green jade, pink coral, purple amethyst, turquoise and others. The screens around the tombs are delicate pierce work on marble. Abstract patterns in contrasting colours dazzle the eyes, and the vine-like calligraphy flows like liquid."

Emperor Shah Jahan had built the Taj Mahal for his wife, Mumtaz, where she is still lying in an underground chamber, beside her husband's tomb. Panchali raised herself on the ledge and sat leaning against a minaret. A magnificent panorama opened up before her incredulous eyes. The playful waters of the Yamuna sparkled in the light. This is where Krishna floated his barge and the ladies of Brindavan accompanied him. She could almost see the silver track left by its passage, bearing the Divine Lover, Mohan, and his entourage of lovelorn gopis. She followed the shimmering path up river all the way to the frozen mouths of the Yamunotri, the cave in which the river was born. The Taj Mahal was a place to live for, a place to die in. Shah Jahan died looking at it from the other bank of the Yamuna, imprisoned by his fourth son, the youngest, who usurped the throne by killing his elder brothers and imprisoning his father and sister. Aurangzeb proved to be the cruellest of kings in the Mughal dynasty, reversing the tolerant policies of his greatgrandfather, Akbar. The Agra Fort where Shah Jahan lay sighing for the Taj Mahal, and Fatehpur Sikri, Akbar's palace, were all marvels. Atul had supplied fascinating details on architecture at every place. Yuyutsu decided to be an architect or a civil engineer, like his uncle. He would specialize in Mughal architecture, that happy fusion of the Hindu and Islamic styles, with its rhythmic curves of the cupola, the cusped arches, the tapering minarets, the delicate balconies for the damsels, the spiral staircases, the symmetries, the proportions, the angles, the choreography of gardens, the reflection on the pools – everything Mughal was superlative.

* * * * *

Panchali barely managed to get home and fall on the bed. A mad elephant in her belly was tearing down a forest. Her mother patted her sweating forehead as she tossed around moaning trying to find a single position of comfort.

"Are you going to do something or watch me die?" she gasped.

"Water has been set to boil. But what will really help is touching the body of the mother earth. She will suck up the extra charges that are coursing through your body."

"What charges?"

"Ions, electrically charged particles, that got aroused by the magnetic force of the moon. Let me see, today must be the new moon or the full moon, or thereabouts."

Panchali assumed it was one of her mother's quack theories, but it would not harm to stretch her fingers and touch the wall. How cool it was, almost shocking. Her mother was, for some secret reason, smugly happy. As if she had rehearsed for this event and at last she was on stage, performing.

"Girl, from now on you are on your own. I will be there, but you will choose not to be consoled by me. No man will understand your pain, because you will purse your lips and bear it."

Panchali screamed in pain. "Are you wishing I have not a soul round me when I am dying?"

"You are not dying. Childbirth is much more painful. This is just nature's way of building your muscles ... of the body and mind. This is a milestone where you have become a woman from a girl."

"Mother Nature is not sadistic. Besides I don't believe anyone can bear more pain. At least I can't."

"Is that so? Is it more painful than having your feet bandaged in a three inch parcel, and hearing your bones crack while you have to keep walking? Chinese girls from antiquity did it. Do you know why? To get a better suitor. For the same reason a tribe in Africa puts rings round the neck to elongate it. Some pull their lips and stick a coconut shell to shape it, all to look prettier. Here is some more. Did you hear of the Rajput practice of jauhar? When a defeat was certain, women jumped into a fire rather than surrender to the enemy.

"Why did they not have poison?"

"Because a dead body too can be defiled."

"Gross."

"In Japan they did that. They cut the jugular vein and convulsed to death. They call it Harakiri."

"Ma, you seem to be enjoying these gross tales." Panchali was in her "gross" phase. A few months back the paneer masala was "deadly" when Panchali was "deadly" hungry. The Anil Kapoor–Madhuri Dixit pair was "deadly", Kiran More was a "deadly" wicket keeper. Earlier, the traffic signals were "vicious", fresh paint smelled "vicious", the test paper was "vicious".

Binapani was undeterred by the allegation of grossness. "I am making you aware of what it means to be a woman, the responsibility Nature has imparted to you. And surely you know of the practice of suttee, where a wife sat on the funeral pyre of her dead husband."

"I know that."

"That's because her life would be worse as a widow, as a burden on her family. Who would protect her if she got assaulted, or restrict her if she fell in love?"

"I prefer the Muslim method where the brother-in-law takes her as his wife. She will get the respect she deserves." Panchali rolled in the bed holding her stomach. "Are you sure I am not dying?"

"Now, now, you can cry if you like. It helps release nervous tension. As I was saying, you will choose the best fruits for the people you care for, and eat the bad ones yourself. You will feed all, and if nothing is left you will fast in silence. You will not call it suffering, but sacrifice of love."

"It is a gross picture of slavery I won't succumb to. And neither do you do it yourself, ma."

"How would you know, I protect you by keeping secrets."

"Secrets? Women are notorious keepers of secrets. Wasn't that a curse Kunti brought upon herself and all women?"

"Yes, it was Yudhishthira's curse. His mother, Kunti, was given a boon as a young girl to be able to invoke any God for bearing children. This is how the Pandavas were born – of Gods. Anyway when she was given the boon she was unmarried and curious. She invoked the Sun God and to her embarrassment found herself with child. And of course it would be a big scandal if anyone discovered it."

"You mean, she was actually confined for nine months, and nobody knew her secret?"

"That bit is ambiguous. It is possible the child was handed over to her by the Gods she called upon. But the Mahabharata does not seem to think of it is an important detail."

"Then we too shall follow its lead."

"This boy, whom she named Karna, she sent afloat on the river. He was raised by a poor couple but finally his valiant destiny brought him to the Kaurava court."

"Time and again fate was grossly unjust towards him."

"Unfortunate Karna was befriended by the sly Duryodhana, and he fought in the Kaurava camp. After he was killed by Arjuna, Kunti disclosed the secret of Karna's birth. The Pandavas were shocked to learn they were fighting their own elder brother. Yudhishthira then cursed womankind to be henceforth bad secret keepers."

"There you go, ma, you say it yourself. Women cannot keep secrets."

Binapani explained, "Yudhishthira's curse worked partially. A woman cannot keep other people's secrets, but her own she will guard with her life. When a bride returns to her father's house, she says she is looked after as a queen. Then her mother sees the burnt elbow, but neither talks. It is a language of tacit complicity. If not for women, families would disintegrate. They are seed gatherers, peace makers, givers of the bowl of rice, Jagaddhatri, Lakshmi, Annapurna."

Panchali groaned, "This water is not hot any more."

"Place your palm on your stomach. With the other hand create grounding by touching the earth. You would have learnt in your science class about it." Panchali felt a current passing out of her through the channel of her arms into the wall.

"Talking about sacrifice. Look at Sita, after years of sitting under a tree surrounded by raakshasi sentries she is asked to prove her purity. And by what method? Self-immolation. Like the jauhar and suttee. And she does it with a prayer on her lips, not a complaint. And Savitri dares to venture in the kingdom of the dead to reclaim her husband's life. And Sati listens to her father insulting her husband, two men she has vowed to protect with her feminine strength. When she can bear it no longer, she does not strike the oppressor, her father, but jumps into a fire."

"Ma, you are romanticizing a woman's role. She does not make so many sacrifices, at least not without recognition."

"Nature compels her to, even against her wish. She will be drawn to these acts of selflessness. She will even guard from harm's way the thing she hates most – the male ego."

"Ma, I see you can be grosser."

"You know the male ego is like a cactus. Prickly outside and soft inside. And men carry one of these weapons to attack others. Women have to play the first line of defence."

"Is that what you do to defend baba's male ego?"

"Your father is different. He does not have a male ego."

"Taalyaan, applause, everyone clap. Well defended, ma! Why don't you finish the stories of the rest of these iconic women we worship for their fidelity – these satis?"

"Yes, on whose sacred path you have just started your journey today. The next sati is your namesake, Panchali."

"Are you joking? She had five husbands, all at the same time. How is she an image of fidelity?"

"That, I will let you discover for yourself."

"You have a gross sense of justice."

"You know when I was much younger than you, our Tamil neighbours set up a pandal for a feast. On it sat the girl, about your age, decked in a wedding sari. I was shocked that they practiced child marriage in the modern age. Gifts were given, a whole feast was prepared. Family and friends came from all reaches of the city. Then my mother explained what the festival was all about."

"It is gross, ma. Embarrassing. I would hate to publicize it."

"Well, she sees her elder sisters, she is told that her mother did it, and her grandmother all the way back in recorded time. It becomes then as normal as when boys have their sacred thread ceremony. Same pomp, invitation cards, gifts, relatives, and feast. I was young and I was angry at the unfairness of the creator. It is all right if men and women have different shapes and voices. But this imposition on the body, the rehearsal for a performance that may or may not happen, once or twice in a lifetime, was too much injustice. Only later when I observed how men have to shave their beards everyday I realized how lucky we women are."

"Does it pain so much to shave? I ask you, ma, what's wrong with your sense of logic?"

"Oh, no, my dear. It will not pain so much every time. But there indeed is reason to celebrate this event. You are entering into a sisterhood of secret keepers. From now on, you will suffer in secret and triumph in silence. You will spare the man you call your own from any trouble you can shoulder. You will shield him from the knowledge he may find hard to bear. You will bear it for him and filter truth to match his taste. You will water the garden of your heart with hidden tears."

"Still I think it is gross to announce to the world your weakness."

"And what makes you say it is weakness?"

"Because Draupadi was dragged into the court defenceless in that state."

Binapani was sure of some things. "She would have been dragged in the court and insulted in any state."

"Publicizing is gross and you cannot hide it. It is a polite way to warn society not to tamper with the woman any more."

"Well, of course. She will become more sensitive emotionally. Shouldn't people know how to behave with her? The soil of her heart will soften and words will sink deep inside. The sun's rays will have to burrow in further to loosen that pain."

"And she will have a bunch of restrictions slapped on her. Cannot meet boys without a chaperon. Cannot stay out late in the evening. This is just a way of getting societal cooperation. The imprisonment begins. I am glad we don't have such a ceremony."

"Actually I think these days they also don't have it. But looks like my stories have at least lessened your cramps."

"I found this awkward position where it hurts the least. And it also seems I am not going to die. Did Ullu return?"

"No."

"Good."

"See, like I said, your life as a protector of men has begun."

"At least the worst is over and he does not need to know I cried."

"What do you mean the worst it over? Childbirth is many times..."

"Oh, go away ma. I don't want to hear all that again."

A few days later Panchali returned from school all excited, "Ma, look what I have found. Where are you? Are you coming or not?"

"I can't – the milk will boil over."

"Oof ..."

"I will be there in a minute. Look at her impatience, as if the child is falling off her stomach." Binapani loved to use Bengali proverbs, and sometimes translated them in other languages, baffling her hearers with vivid images. Panchali was pacing about with an open book in her hand.

"Ma, I have found the perfect supplement for your excellent speech the other day. Listen to this. A well-trained woman needs to have sixty-four skills. She should be deft with her fingers, which means make dolls of various material, tailor clothes, do carpentry, pottery, make flower patterns in vase and on ground ..."

"Painting, embroidery ... I get the gist."

"She should know the art of disguise."

"The ones used in drama, make-up and masks?"

"Yes, plus she should be able to make cotton look like silk for example, anything coarse to look sophisticated."

"I can do that; you have no idea what I stuff in the cutlets you eat."

"I have some idea; it is day before yesterday's vegetables. And yes culinary skills are in the list. Then the whole gamut of mental and creative skills, like composing poetry, making riddles, even designing yantras, the esoteric spiritual symbols. Of course she should be a good conversationalist, singer, dancer, instrument player."

"What's left?"

"An important skill. What does Chitrangada learn? She should be able to wield weapons, like the bow and arrow and sword. Do gymnastics too."

"How about sciences?"

"Oh yes, that too is here. Knowledge of plants and their medicinal cures. She should be able to make perfumes, be able to construct buildings, make water catchments, know about mines and minerals. And there are some curious ones – she should be able to teach parrots to talk, perform magic, she should know gambling, and deduce the character of a person from his features. This is brilliant. I will change my education system and follow this chart. An all encompassing list of skills to become a holistic human being."

"Bow and arrow? What ancient document are you consulting?"

"It is called the Kama Sutra, written by Vatsyayana, about a thousand and five hundred years ago."

Binapani flared up, "I object to your reading that book. Give it to me. All those skills were for courtesans."

"No." Panchali protected the book from her mother's hawk-like talons. "All was admirable so far, until you hear the name of the book."

"Anand," Binapani called, "Look at what our daughter is reading."

"Ma, don't get him involved, I got the book from his office."

Anand came in and saw the book. "Oh that, it has wonderful language and keen insight. It's a classic for good reason."

"And mister, the content?" Binapani had her arms on her waist ready to tackle two at a time.

"I see what you mean, Bina ... Panchali, I think you should stop at that early chapter. It has a section from the ancient art, Kama Shastra, which gives tips about acquiring life skills."

"Exactly. Look no further to model your ideal woman," concluded Panchali.

Panchali had fatherly backing, "That is not just for women; men are encouraged to learn these skills too. It makes a person self sufficient and confident."

Banapani protested, "I don't like the word kama."

"Why, don't you desire to be clever, skilful, respected by others?"

"Kama is a baser kind of desire."

"Thus has it been tarnished in colloquial parlance. But its old meaning is desire for self fulfilment. Agreed, it does not talk about spiritual aspiration, but one should not neglect the material aspect of our nature either. *Annam maa nindyaat, tad vratam,* as it is said in the Taittirya Upanishad, 'We vow not to neglect matter'."

* * * * *

The sky was a jigsaw puzzle of white clouds lying scattered on the blue tablecloth. Panchali ran to the empty football field and gazed in admiration at the patterns above. One of the clouds had become a dog's face. She jumped to the next cloud; it was a bleating sheep. She found a cat licking its paw, a giraffe's head with the two pointy ears, and then a chariot's wheel, half stuck in the mud, like Karna's. This game was exciting; she turned around to span the rest of the sky. But her eyes dropped and fell on Shreyas advancing towards her. She had not spoken to him after the rakhi incident, that is, to the person of flesh and blood, though in her mind she prattled with him all the time. "Look, Shreyas, today I have a blister in my foot with this new sandal", "Do you like this hair band, it has a pink flower on it. My brother from Delhi sent." Sometimes her memory played tricks with her, and she almost forgot the real Shreyas. She had created her little duet of life without the second voice. Before him she felt nervous, shy and unsure of herself. But he was kind, or so she imagined. Shreyas had reached her, "Panchali, did you set another trap for me?" She was shattered. "No, I did not even know you were here. I was looking at the sky."

"Well, I hope I have made my stand clear."

"Yes, you have." she said, glassy eyes turning towards the grassy expanse. She walked past the bus stop, and the next, all the way home into the thickening darkness. She had settled cosily into the arms of the imaginary Shreyas and now the real one caused such a ripple, the image was destroyed. "What have I done to myself?" She asked with loathing. "I have longed for a cloud of white smoke, hoping for it to shower rain. As if dreams had the power to change reality. I have loved a stone-hearted person, wept for him, laughed with him, wished him all the luck fate would have apportioned me, lived just to know he exists on this same turf, called earth. All for this?"

The world answered her, "You have loved a deity of stone. Isn't that what your culture has done from time immemorial?"

She questioned the voice, "Have I no pride at all? He spurns me time and again and yet I love him? Is the world so barren of men that only one should cover it from horizon to horizon?"

"Panchali had five husbands, but she loved only Krishna."

She walked under the cheerful street lamps, by the humming tea stalls, past the garden full of merry-makers, across the street from the cinema hall, like Radha, with the garland of dried dreams in her hand and face strained with tears. Her Brindavan days were over. Now Krishna was in Mathura, king of the Yadavas, and she would pine for him, forever. In her heart even as Panchali raged, she knew it was not Shreyas' fault he did not love her. Love was a boon, or perhaps a curse that did not affect all. Some day perhaps he would find his Rukmini, hear her call and accept her flower wreath. And Radha would walk by the black Yamuna in the dark night. Once stung by this honeybee you can never overcome the pain.

Chapter Twenty-two

Roshan

Dawn sent her crow emissaries to announce herself. Panchali buttoned up her sweater and called out to her aunt, "I am going for a morning walk, will be back before breakfast." The roadside plants were balmy with dewy sleep, and the pavement sizzled with boiling water. "Chai? Tea?" Asked the man at the tea stall, clanking his tea cups, "Naashtaa? Breakfast?" called the frying kachauri from the skillet. Panchali filled her lungs with the scents of the city and walked on towards the dome that sprang from Aladdin's magic lamp. She strode under the arches of the Jama Masjid's gateway, past the pool, straight into the sanctum. Her sandals flew upon the existing pile of sandals. She rushed in and knelt down with the hundreds of kneeling worshippers. The sound of words she did not understand sent a thrill inside her. Surely they were singing praises of the Lord. The men stood up together, then they bent forward. Panchali followed their actions looking askance at her neighbour. Suddenly all the men turned towards her. She looked down self-consciously. Then in the next verse they looked away in the opposite direction. It was then part of the prayer routine! She breathed out in relief. They touched the ground with their foreheads, a posture she was familiar with, the sweet gesture of surrender, a humble obeisance. The muezzin's song rose up like incense and filled the chamber with its mystery.

The prayer done, they got up silently and filed out. Panchali looked around and found no women in the crowd. Then she looked at herself, wearing an orange salwar kameez, while the men were all in shades of white with fez on head. She fished for her sandals, yanked them up and walked away. It felt eerie to stand out so pronouncedly. It was only when she had gone past the pool and neared the gates that she turned back – three marble domes in perfect symmetry flanked by two pink and white minarets on a red sandstone courtyard. She had been driven by the spirit of beauty to kneel at her feet and worship. It did not matter that she was a Hindu girl and this was the Muslim men's prayer hour. Once you are in the house of God, there is no distinction between man and man or man and woman. Each is a child of the divine, equally loved, equally privileged. She looked at every detail of the Jama Masjid to etch it in the mental plate of her mind. She wanted to return again and again here to marvel, to pray, to bow down humbly at the grandeur of God's creation. Indeed it was true what the Upanishad claimed, *ishaavaasyam idam sarvam*, "All this is the habitation of the Lord".

* * * * *

"Didi, hold the spool tightly and when I throw up the kite unroll it just a little. Now some more. Feed the wind with the string." The kite swooped like an eagle on its prey then arched backwards.

Prahlad clapped, "Yes, that's right, now pull the string with your hand, no, not that way, watch out for the tree, lucky you missed it. Pull it the other way, quick."

Prahlad's white kite flew up to meet hers. Yuyutsu steadied his yellow paper plane with expert knowledge of aerodynamics. Many other such boats floated up from the terraces on the ocean of the sky and spanned it with white and blue and green and red and yellow sails. Birds landed on television antennas to watch these wingless creatures usurp their terrain. Binapani and Savita brought their cameras and clicked away at the children. Their faces were turned upwards, sometimes gleeful, sometimes in anguish, sometimes excited, sometimes dreaming.

Shreyas came from behind and put his arms around Panchali. He squeezed his hands beside hers holding the spool. She looked at him half turning and their cheeks touched. He was his dashing self, his eyes on the kite, lips parted in a joyous smile. He unrolled the spool and the kite gave a jovial leap in the air and took them along with it. Panchali saw her feet rise over the parapet, then skim over the coconut tree tops. Her back rested on his chest and their toes tickled the clouds. They were so high the Yamuna looked like a silver thread wound around the wrist of the city. Their kite was a flower bow with blue tasselled ends made of silken rakhi threads. Its spine was a flute, through which the wind piped a melody.

> Welcome aboard, I am captain kite
> Humble pilot of your present flight,
> Kick the ground and count to three
> From the earth's pull you'll be free.
> Loosen the thread, unroll the spool
> Blow me a kiss and I will swoon,
> Give me a wind to catch my tail
> And like an eighteen mast I'll sail.
> Through the cloudy palace of the sky
> Come, my children, we will fly.
> Climb up the stairs of vap'rous towers
> Slide down the slope of rainbow showers,
> Now let's float on the winding river
> Like arrows loosened from Kama's quiver.

"This is so much fun, Shreyas," she whispered in his ear millimetres from her mouth. They had spotted a boat on the river and the kite had landed them on it cruising at a gentle speed. The river's wet breath came dancing into their eyes, and they blinked the magical droplets away.

> The spray of rapture plays its game
> Setting the sinking sun aflame.
> Eyes become stars in paradise
> And lips rose-petals in disguise.
> A water fairy on a lotus sings
> Fanning herself with butterfly wings,
> Princely bees carrying honey loads
> Go galloping by on backs of toads,
> The dragonfly his whisker trims
> His mirror the moon disc as it swims.

"Shreyas, are you crying, my dear?"

"No, these are tears of joy."

"Really? Are you happy?"

"Yes, very much."

"Shreyas, don't leave me, please."

"I never left you."

"Then why do I feel lonely?"

"You silly dreamer. Look, I am right here." Panchali turned and saw Prahlad staring at her.

"What was that, didi? You let the kite fly away. Slacken on it and it will escape your grip."

"Such is life, Prahlad."

"Didi, why are you crying?"

"It must be the sun spray in my eyes." She disappeared down the stairs.

* * * * *

A scooter grunted insistently outside the house, begging Anand to part the curtains. He saw his daughter getting off the back seat. Dropping the pen he came to the window for a better view of the stage. Roshan was switching off the ignition and Panchali swung herself down. Anand observed she was holding his shoulder to perform the stunt. They talked for a brief minute and Anand replaced the curtain thoughtfully. This Roshan chap was getting too close to his daughter. All this play acting was a lot of pretence to get this pretty butterfly trapped in his eager ... what were those finger like projections called in flowers? He had no time to think, for Panchali was back un-strapping her sandals and singing, yes, singing a love song too.

"*Mere ranga me ranga ne vale,*" It was from the recent super hit film, Maine Pyar Kiya, I am in love.

"Panchali, are you coming from college?"

She allowed the phrase to finish, then said, "No," and continued singing.

"I am talking to you, stop singing."

"Oh sorry baba, I thought you had finished."

"Come child, we need to talk." He went to his room and

waited for her to enter, then closed the door to the whistles of the pressure cooker and his wife's sharp ears.

"So where are you coming from?"

"What can I say, it was such an adventure!"

"Adventure? with Roshan?"

"Yes. We drove out to the outskirts."

"For a picnic in the fields?"

"No baba, we had more serious things to do."

"Serious things with Roshan?"

"You don't think I changed drivers half way through, do you?"

"All right, I can picture you and Roshan on that scooter. Did you stop anywhere?"

"Yes, that's where the adventure began."

"Go on, my dear, I am listening." Panchali noticed he was cracking his knuckles noisily.

"We stopped by a temple, a real forlorn looking one, with a bleak saffron flag pasted to a trident mast."

"I have seen forlorn temples myself, so skip the detail."

"There was a lemon on the tip of the spear, smeared with sindoor. Why do they do that?"

"Will explain later. Continue your story."

"So we got down and from inside came sounds, it was already taken."

"Sounds? Someone praying? Crying?"

"No baba, don't be old fashioned. There was a young girl and a lad, who saw us approach and shut up."

"Did you tell them anything? Desecrating a temple like that!"

"They were just talking; that is no offence surely? We remounted the scooter, still on our search."

"Searching for what?"

"I was just coming to it. Then we found the place. It was a broken-down house."

"Were you looking for such a ruin? Does Roshan have some archaeological interest or what?"

"No, I doubt if he can spell the word. So we parked the scooter, and went in. Let me get some water, I am parched."

Anand had started pacing the room. She had done it. In the clear light of day, with a joker, Roshan. And now what? She was back chirping that love song.

"Where was I?"

"In that ruin, with that loafer, Roshan."

Panchali swallowed the remark, then went on nonchalantly, "Oh yes. It was not just a lightning-struck or burnt-down place, but a mausoleum. Some stones lay on the floor with the Urdu calligraphy on it. The windows were like mouths with ill-fitted teeth. From the dome above a tree had grown, and some of its roots hung loose from the ceiling like nooses."

"I am interested to know what you did."

"That's what I was saying. We were seeing all that."

"All right, go on."

"Then Roshan asked me the question." She paused as if replaying the question in her head in mute mode.

Her father urged her, "What question?"

"What other question can one ask in such a place?"

"You tell me. I would not know. I never went to a haunted house with a girl."

"He asked me if I was scared of ghosts." Anand wiped his sweating forehead.

"Are you? I don't think so."

"That's what I said, very confidently. Then a bat flew out of the dome, and the nooses, or roots you may call them, started swinging. I don't know why I did it, but I screamed in terror and hid my face."

"Hid your face in your hands?"

"No, I was on Roshan's chest. Don't know how I managed to jump there."

"And he just stood there, chivalrous as hell?"

"No, he too screamed and fell back. I don't think he was expecting fifty kilograms thrust on him all at once."

"Wasn't it dusty on the ground?"

"Oh yes, Roshan was covered with dirt, or more likely bone dust."

"And you?"

"I was on him, remember? May have at most dragged some cobwebs on the way down. Baba, you look so pale. Can I get you some water?"

"Yes, water please. No, no, make it sherbet and add some extra sugar."

In the kitchen Panchali returned to the tune she was singing. Her mother's ears were burning in curiosity. "What's happening in there between you and baba?"

"Nothing, he just wants to know if I did it with Roshan."

Her mother drew in a breath. "And did you?"

Panchali exhaled in exasperation. "Don't be silly, ma," and she disappeared with the glass of sherbet. Binapani wondered, if that meant "of course", or "not at all".

Her father was lying down on the bed now and the fan was running at full speed. He jumped back upright when she came in.

"How long were you on the ground?"

"What do you think, I would look at my watch in that position?"

"Just give me an approximate number, how many minutes?"

"Minutes? Are you joking? It was just ten seconds or thereabouts."

Anand let his breath escape noisily. "Ahh, this sherbet is so refreshing."

"Then we had a good laugh and I helped to dust the poor fellow."

"Don't 'poor fellow' him too much. Adventure was over I hope?"

"Yes. This place is adequate and with a little sweeping it will work perfectly."

"Work for what, child?"

"For our rehearsals, baba. What else do you think we were looking for?"

"Why can't you practise here?"

"At home? And have the neighbours scream at us? We need to practise talking loudly, really loudly, so that our voices reach far without a mike. No, it has to be in a place far from the crowd we could madden."

Anand scratched his chin. He had not shaved yet.

"Why don't you practise in the school then, after hours?"

"Is it not locked at that time?" All government premises were thus kept safe from harm's way.

"I have a key and you could use the stage at your heart's content."

"Oh, thank you, baba."

Anand fiddled with his keychain. "Make a duplicate of the main gate."

"Baba, why don't you give me both the keys? They are so tightly bound. Which of them is the right one?"

Anand almost agreed, then changed his mind. The other one was his office key. He had an ominous flash-forward of Roshan and Panchali snugly practising in his office. Oh, girls were such a responsibility! Panchali held the key in her palm and tripped at the shoe rack in a hurry to get out with it before her father changed his mind. Binapani caught her. "Hey Panchali, I did not know Roshan could drive a scooter."

Her disappearing heels answered, "He can't. He can start and stop it though."

It was such a labour to get the principled guardians of government resources to share their privileges. And for what purpose? For educating the masses, so well aligned to their own goals.

* * * * *

"Baba, how can you stand this?" Asked Panchali leaning over and whispering in Anand's ear.

"That is why I am sitting," he moaned. That year the family was attending the Durga pooja in their neighbourhood. Cosmopolitan Bombay had residents of all states, and each had set up their special replicas of homeland. People sat on chairs watching Durga in the act of planting a spear in Mahishasura's neck. On the dais a priest uttered Sanskrit chants rendering all the pronunciation in Bengali, since he read from a palm leaf book, written in Bengali.

"He has just massacred Brahma's invocation to the Goddess. She will hardly have been roused to wake Vishnu." The Brahmin was brought from Bengal to give an authentic touch to the ceremony. He held his sacred thread in his thumb and performed the chants, as prescribed. He knew when the hibiscus was to be offered and when the marigold. He rang the bell and sprinkled water at the right time, but the power of the mantra was lost as the words came out of his mouth all deformed.

Binapani tried to defend the meticulous old man, "Bengali does not have 'sa' or 'ya'. What can he do? He is being faithful to the text."

Anand disagreed. "The problem is in using Bengali script to write Sanskrit text. A priest should read from the original."

Panchali was sitting with a copy of the Devi Mahatmyam in Devanagari script that she was following.

Yuyutsu agreed, "The chanter of the Mahalaya, Birendra Krishna Bhadra, has a good pronunciation. A priest can be trained to do it right."

On the next day of the worship, Mother Durga would be created from the combined power of all the Gods. And it would have to be dramatic, full of emotion, energetic enough to call upon Her. Panchali woke up with a little plan in her head. She wore her mother's garad, the traditional Bengali sari reserved for worship, of white silk with a broad red border. She wore the aaltaa, a red dye drawn around the edges of the feet. Thus was painted Durga, so all could see the beautiful foot that crushed the life out of the Mahishasura. The demon could change his appearance at will and played the trick several times during the battle. Lion, mad elephant, enormous buffalo – the mahisha – that made the earth quake with its hooves and churn the clouds with its horns. A famous classical Sanskrit poet had written a whole epic in praise of the Mother's foot.

Before people assembled and the priest made his appearance, Panchali sat on the prayer mat and offered some flowers at the Mother's feet. Then she started reading from the Devi Mahatmyam in her impeccable Sanskrit, paying no attention to the gathering crowd. The incense was lit and Durga was being invoked. Then she noticed a commotion that grew louder and then abated. She turned back once after a chapter and saw the hall had only three people, her parents and brother. They nodded an encouragement and she continued. After the reading was over, Panchali was surprised to hear conch shells blowing. People crowded before the statue, their hands cupped for the flower offering. The organizer indicated with his eyes that she was supposed to pick the basket of flowers. In each palm she placed the offering and they were thrown up in the air in the direction of the Goddess. The pushpaanjali was over and they cupped their palm, left supporting the right hand. Panchali scooped out a little spoon of Ganga water for each person and they drank it.

She was praised for her good work as priestess. The background story was simple. The Brahmin had turned up and began cursing them for allowing a woman, and not even a Brahmin, to utter the sacred chants. So they laughed at him, "We are worshipping a warrior Goddess and won't allow a non-Brahmin woman to conduct the offering? What kind of hypocrisy is it?"

He argued, "It is written, women and lower castes are not allowed to utter the sacred chants."

"Written where? Show us."

He was not sure, but his fourteen generations knew it, he swore. He was mostly concerned about his fees and when they assured him of it, he slunk away.

* * * * *

"Baba, Roshan has come to see you." Panchali held the door open for Roshan to pass through.

"Oh Roshan, come in, sit, so how are the rehearsals going on?" asked Anand wondering why Roshan would want to visit him, if not to announce something apocalyptic.

"The one in the haunted house?" grinned Roshan.

"I thought you were practising on the school stage!"

"Relax, sir, I was teasing you."

"I never know when you two start and stop acting. Don't make it a habit of life. You must take some things seriously."

"Yes, sir, that is why I have come to have a discussion with you." Anand looked for his handkerchief. "Panchali told me you think I am a loafer."

Anand was flabbergasted. Was she his daughter, or some stranger? Why could she not keep a secret within the family?

Roshan was serious, "I wanted to know why. Yes, in a way you are right, we Sindhis are loafers, wanderers, nomads. Because we don't have a land of our own any more. Because we have been exiled from our ancient country and nobody will stand for us, not even a professor like you."

Anand felt sick within. "Roshan, what are you saying, why are you taking my casual remark so seriously?"

"Because I am Sindhi, and Sindh is now in Pakistan. We, Hindu Sindhis, are scattered all over India, and our brothers, the Muslim Sindhis, are on the other side of the fence. You know sir, we Sindhis were a cohesive group. We have a common guardian deity for our people, Jhulelal, and we have worshipped together for centuries at shrines of Sufi saints. In fact when the Partition was finalized and we realized Sindh was not divided, we rejoiced, both Hindus and Muslims, together. Punjab's and Bengal's fate was not ours. We could still sail on the Sindhu River and launch our ships on the Arabian Sea. But then we heard rumours about Hindus and Muslims killing each other. We were scared and suddenly our neighbours were Muslims first, Sindhis second. We flocked to Karachi and stood in a huddle, like the gladiators, armour-less, surrounded by hungry lions. Then the ships started leaving for India with us. Those who could not travel to Karachi crossed the border on trucks, trains, camel, foot, or cart. Then here we dispersed. I suppose in a way we are still roving the country in search of a place called home. And we may never find it in India. Yes, sir, you have a right to call me a loafer. You are lucky, you live in Maharashtra, the great land of the Marathas, your mother state."

Roshan's eyes were watery. Anand looked at Panchali with an eloquent plea for help. She opened her notebook and scribbled a line, and handed him the chit. Roshan sighed and waited. Anand hoped she would share some medicine to neutralize Roshan's pathos. The line was from the lyrics of an old Hindi film song, *"Jo gham diye jaate ho, us gham ki davaa kar naa.* O you who wound, forget not to create its remedy." The girl was spinning out of her orbit. But she was following his lead, and he was pleased, even as he sat on his own tribunal.

"Roshan, Sindhis are welcome in India. Of the few names of regions mentioned in our national anthem, Sindh is one". Anand sang the line, "Punjab, Sindh, Gujarat, Maratha, Dravida, Utkala, Vanga."

"As far as I remember, the anthem was written in 1913 when Sindh was indeed very much part of India. But I believe, now, some of you don't utter the word 'Sindh' when you sing the anthem."

"No, not at all. Nobody does it. Circumstance has made Sindh part of Pakistan, but that does not mean the Sindhi people are not part of our country."

"How many Indians are there who do not have a State of their own? We Sindhis alone, and that's what makes us a minority, insecure, at the mercy of others. Shouldn't the government provide special privileges for minorities?"

At last Panchali came to her father's rescue. "That is such an artificial sentiment. Minority indeed! One could say you are Hindu and therefore one of the majority. Anyone can parcel himself into a minority group. My father is Marathi and mother Bengali, how many of my kind are there? I feel like a minority. Help, help, I need concessions from the government, for example, free train passes from Bombay to Calcutta. Don't overact, Roshan."

Anand felt surefooted now, "You know the Sindhi language has more Sanskrit words than most other Indian languages, because it is one of the oldest. What script do you use to write it?"

"I use Devanagari, same as Sanskrit, Hindi and Marathi."

"And Nepali. In Pakistan Sindhis use the Arabic script."

"In India too. My mother knows it, as she went to a Sindhi-medium school."

"You see, this makes the language adaptable to both countries at once. Roshan, I would be proud to be Sindhi. You are the most adaptable of people. You have made Hindustan your home, this is your homeland whether it is called Bombay or Delhi, this is the country that was named after the river that flowed in your province. You represent India more than the rest of us."

"All right, baba, you don't overdo it now. Roshan, are you happy?"

"Yes, sir. All clear. So I am not a loafer, agreed?"

"Roshan, if I find you were acting and making me sweat for a dirty prank of yours I will be very angry."

"I assure you, sir; it is not as dirty as the Partition prank."

Panchali defused the situation. "Roshan, just give up. You look comical when you are trying to be solemn. Shall we tell him at last what we came for?"

Roshan cleared his throat which did not portend well for Anand. These two monkeys were up to no good.

"Sir, in this rapidly changing world,"

Panchali supplied the details, "The Iraq-Iran war has ended, Soviet troops have withdrawn from Afghanistan, the meltdown of the Communist Bloc has seen drastic changes in Eastern Europe, and martial law has ended for our neighbours."

"The Pakistani General, Zia-ul Haq, died in a plane crash in

August 1988, and the next elections brought Benazir Bhutto to the forefront, daughter of the former prime minister, Zulfikar Ali Bhutto. The army chief, Ershad, in Bangladesh ended martial law. Begum Khaleda Zia, widow of the former General, Ziaur Rahman, won the elections."

Anand was itching, "Yes, we know all that, the thirty-year Cold War has ended, the Berlin wall was demolished, a student uprising in China brought the cannons out in the Tiananmen Square."

"But one revolt quashed is no cause to lament. It had a ripple effect throughout the world. In Chile the dictatorship of General Pinochet was replaced by a democratic government. He was convicted of corruption and human rights violations."

"And South Africa is celebrating. Nelson Mandela has been released from prison and apartheid is dying a long awaited death."

"It is the age of the awakening of the common man." Roshan concluded theatrically.

"The question, baba, is, where does India fit in this global drama?"

Roshan answered her, "India is grappling with her biggest problem, and cannot participate. And do you know sir, what that is?"

"Corruption?" Prime Minister Rajiv Gandhi's term ended miserably under corruption charges against him regarding kickbacks in a Swedish weapons deal, the Bofors scandal. The Sri Lankan peace-keeping stunt-turned-battle against Tamilians also did not help his image. Consequently he lost the elections to the Janata Dal in late 1989.

"Baba, there is something more pressing than corruption."

"Sir, we think the first issue India ought to look into is her uncontrolled population growth."

"And so, we decided to create some awareness. It will be a street show in the most affected areas – villages and city slums."

Anand's head was swimming. In public, her daughter and Roshan, not the loafer, but a dignified citizen of Mother India, would teach family planning? How?

"Children, I think it is a bold idea. Perhaps a little too bold."

"Surely sir, you agree something has to be done. The population bomb is ticking."

"Baba, don't worry, we will not do anything explicit. We will not promote pills and other consumer contraceptives."

"Good, those are beyond the reach of the poor."

"We will not even force people to get neutered."

"We will show them the opportunity they and their children lose when they are numerous in the family."

Roshan continued, as if the two had even rehearsed these lines, "But at the end we will have to talk about sex."

Anand hoped they were not going to get too close or touch each other in front of strangers.

"Baba, we have prepared wonderful visuals they will remember. Here they are." She got out some enlarged pictures of couples in romantic poses, all carved in stone.

Anand flipped through the photo plates. "These are sculptures from ancient temples. That one is from Khajuraho, this from Konark. Bina, look what these children are doing – mixing oil and water – oh, what a soup! I just hope your extreme youth will save you from the more sensitive guardians of our culture."

"Oh, don't call ma, she is such a prude."

Binapani overheard the last hasty comment. "What makes you say that, Panchali?"

"You told us we were flown in by a stork and dropped at your doorstep."

"That was when you were five."

"All right, sorry. We need your permission to go on the tour."

"What tour? Where will you stay? How will you reach these places? Somebody has to announce your skit in advance." Binapani was more concerned about the practical details than the moral implications of the topic.

"We have contacted the Ramakrishna Mission and the Bharat Sevashram. They have volunteers in villages who will take care of logistics. We will go by bus and stay in their guest houses. Our skit will be part of their routine literacy programmes."

"Ma, can you contact Mrs Nair? Isn't she a member of Chinmaya Mission? They have several units too. Here, give her this poster and explain that this summer we are ready to go wherever they can arrange. We hope they can raise the funds for our travel and lodging."

Binapani looked at the poster and handed it to Anand without comment. It was a Shivalinga, the black stone symbol used to represent Lord Shiva.

Anand slapped the poster on the table, face down. "Now I must protest. This is blasphemy. You cannot use this to represent copulation."

"We could not find anything more appropriate. And remember, many of these people cannot read, so we had to find a visual." Panchali had found some text explaining that the Shivalinga is an erect genital half way into a vagina. It also said, Shiva is the proto male in the Hindu pantheon. Unmarried women in India pray that they get husbands like Shiva. After Sati, his consort, died, he waited for her to be reborn and married her again. He is the most faithful of husbands. His symbol is thus suggestive of his masculine prowess.

"Roshan and Panchali, you are too young to understand how certain minds can pervert truth. You have heard my warning and I shall rest my case here." Anand was silent. He did not want to be the wet blanket on his daughter's first public venture.

Panchali tried to placate him, "Baba, we actually asked people and found they associate the Shivalinga with the God, and they don't think of its derivation. It is like the love sign. Do we think of the anatomical heart's shape when we look at it? The temple pictures will be the real material to help us convey the message. Or would you prefer us to do something more explicit?"

Her parents both agreed that images were the better way to go. Roshan winked at Panchali. Now they had to tackle his parents.

* * * * *

The play was a success as the two acted confidently and unabashedly. They alternated being doctor and patient, so the audience developed a respect for them and believed in the simple methods they suggested. After the play, women flocked around Panchali and asked her clinical questions. Roshan looked hassled, "I wish I had paid attention to biology."

Panchali was puffed up being addressed as nurse, "Send them to me."

"They won't talk to you. They are all men!"

"Ah, of course. Why don't I teach you something this evening, Motu?" Motu was the sweet name she had reserved for Roshan, meaning "fatso". He knew she was feeling especially content.

"You know, Motu, something tells me people do not know the law, even among the educated circles in the cities."

"Right, no court will pardon one who commits an offence simply because he did not know the law of the land."

"I am not talking about laws in general, but about *the* law."

"The abortion law?"

"Yes, as you know I am proud of it, that it has existed in India for a long time, whereas in so many countries it is mired in controversies. But has it helped in controlling population?"

"I have not seen any statistics, but I suppose not."

"None of the women knew about it, or so it seemed, since one cannot get a direct answer about such matters. The whole topic is taboo."

"Our school in the biggest metro did not teach us, no TV or radio programme hinted about it, and of course our parents lent us no hand. What can we say about villagers?"

"Actually the law addresses the social stigma associated with unwanted pregnancy. When a woman gets an abortion, the paperwork is sealed in an envelope marked 'secret' and is kept in a safe place. Five years later the records are destroyed. I don't understand why this important law is not disseminated."

"Abortion is not considered a good option because it has emotional effects on the woman."

"That lasts a few months at the most, but an unwanted child is a burden for many years. And it is not fair on that innocent child. Besides I am emphasizing that abortion is the last resort. If their menfolk cannot be persuaded to get vasectomy done, there is a simple operation the women can do which will not affect their health, for example the IUD, Intra Uterine Device."

"Panchali, I think we should do this play in cities too."

In a political party office overhung with saffron banners, a reporter walked in with photos in hand.

"Boss, look at these two college kids doing a skit in villages. The poster has a Shivalinga, with the words 'Family Planning Awareness' written under it, which is lost on the illiterate folks, but they are using photographs of our temples."

The boss answered gruffly, "Are they ridiculing Hindu architecture?"

"Maybe, you are the better judge. They say these erotic postures comprise only a tenth of the temple sculptures, and moreover they are not carved in prominent places."

"Is that true, only a tenth?"

"People did not seem to be pleased. So they explained these sculptures were on the outside and had a symbolism."

"And what is that?"

"That these acts and their thoughts should be left outside. Once inside the house of God, the person's mind had to be clean. But sir, using the Shivalinga as a sex symbol, is that allowed?"

"Who are these kids? Khan, Ali, Hussain?"

"No, Deshmukh and Chainani."

The boss yawned, "Why are you boring me? In fact let all know how liberal our religion is. That it does not shy away from using symbolism even if it is open to misinterpretation. We can say, 'Look how our Hindu culture helps people from the grassroots'. Who are sponsoring them?"

"Hindu organizations like Ramakrishna Mission and Chinmaya Mission."

"Why are we left out? Shankar, Shankar, where is that rascal? Hey, go with this man and talk to those kids."

After one of the shows Roshan and Panchali were collecting their display plates when they heard footsteps approaching. The man wore a garland of rudraaksha, the maroon marble-sized seeds that resembled red eyes, and thus were called rudraaksha. It indicated he had chosen a spiritual path over that of a householder's.

"Jai bholenath" he greeted them loudly, "Victory to Shiva."

"Oh my God" whispered Panchali. Her father's apprehension slid into her mind.

Roshan joined his palms above his head, "Jai bholenath!"

"You two, come with me." He needed no permission.

Roshan indicated with his hands to Panchali, "Let us follow." She shook her head. Roshan came close, "Better to comply. We will run if it gets knotty."

They entered a house that resembled a den. "Welcome to our cave." announced their guide, "Gurudev wants to talk to you."

The master was seated on a tiger skin, his muscular chest decorated with a single rudraaksha garland. Hair from his head fell in dust coloured strands around his neck, like snakes. He was a living image of Shiva.

"Children, I was told you are using the Shivalinga in the wrong way. Are you making the naïve error of looking at it as a sex symbol? It is an occult Tantrik yantra, not to be played with, but to meditate upon. It is kept in sanctums of houses and temples, flowers and incense are offered, sandalwood paste decorates it, people drink the water that is used to bathe the linga. Do not interrupt, son." Roshan had opened his mouth, but snapped it shut. "The union of a man and woman is merely a paradigm used to depict union between the Lord and his creation. It is a dynamic posture, evocative of a continuous outpouring of the divine seed to fertilize the manifestation. One has to be a deserving vessel to accept his creative energy."

Panchali got in a word. "But baba, it is open to

misunderstanding. One could think our religion invites people to have sex, as if the divine sanctions it by doing it himself."

"Why else does India have such a population problem?" joked Roshan. He liked the baba who was fatherly, not at all like the strict elder-brother guide.

"You," the baba pointed to Panchali, "Are Bengali, and you should have seen Kali standing on Shiva's chest."

"Yes, that is a common calendar theme. Kali was dancing when she stepped on her husband, Shiva, lying on the earth. She hung out her tongue in shame."

"That is a children's folklore. But what does the symbol represent? Kali and Shiva are Nature and Soul, prakriti and purusha. When Kali danced on Shiva, he was the shava, a dead body. But when he was aroused, he became the player and she his toy. That image on your poster depicts this truth, Soul dominating Nature. These are two branches of Tantrism. For the Shaktas, Nature stands above the Soul, the Shaivas worship the Divine over his Force. Those who place the Lord and his beloved at equal footing are the Vaishnavas. Radha and Krishna stand together for them. Then there are other philosophies – those who believe in a transcendental Brahman, those who think the creation is an illusion, and so on. People align themselves according to their bent of nature, because thus they can walk fastest on the road."

"Sorry baba, we will change the poster."

"Why, did I scold you? Did I say it was wrong what you did? I was just letting you know."

"No, we see our ignorance."

"There is no such thing as non-ignorance. We are all a shade of it. Our religion does not force. Merely indicates. It allows everything. You choose your path, Shaktism, Shaivism, Vaishnavism, dualism, non-dualism, illusionism, Christianity, Judaism, Islam, what difference does it make? Only the web is different; the spider is the same. Even if the web is sundered, it will recreate it. For it does it with its own saliva."

*****

Roshan and Panchali had made plans to travel to the villages for a second round of their family planning campaign during Sundays. But a big pimple developed on the face of the country, which soon became a boil. Prime Minister V.P. Singh had started his series of mistakes. He brought out a report drafted by Mr Mandal, which reserved a lot more seats for the backward castes in professional colleges. It was a way to apologize further for the centuries of segregation, or was it a way to ensure future votes from these classes? Reservation was not new to Independent India, but the Mandal Commission's recommendations increased it to an enormous percentage. A college admission meant a good career, which meant a good livelihood. A bad education was unemployment, destitution, poverty. Students stopped trains by sitting on the tracks, strikes paralysed the education machinery. When the government pushed forward adamantly, some kids performed incredible feats. They threw kerosene on their bodies, and torched themselves. Ghastly images of burning youth flashed on the front pages of newspapers, and V. P. Singh lost support in the parliament. He had lasted less than two years. New elections were declared for mid 1991.

It was the decade of the common man, the substratum of a populace for which the edifice of government actually stands for, and stands upon. That unit was angry, hurt, cornered, and made its voice heard. The world was opening up through globalization and people knew what was happening in other parts of the world. It was no more possible to suppress truth, however ugly. And it was no more possible to silence global forums where people shared their opinions.

* * * * *

The year-end programmes were over and the junior batches threw a farewell party for the outgoing students. Panchali sat in her corner feeling very sad. She would not see Shreyas any more. Yes, he lived with her every day of her life, unknown to the world, but still, to see the outward form gave her immense pleasure. Just to be in his aura was like taking a monsoon shower after the summer heat. Seema and her boyfriend were chatting in one corner head to head. Abhijit and Sharmishtha were holding hands, perhaps pledging the world to each other. The lights were dimmed and someone put on the "enigma" song. It said as much – switch off the light, relax, close your eyes – and such mea culpa confessions. Panchali leaned against the wall. Sights of love around her were becoming painful and she had to close her eyes to feel Shreyas' proximity. Then she heard his voice in her outer ears.

"Panchali, sleepy?"

The many wounds of the past years ruptured all at once. She looked at the ground but the tears were gathering fast, so she looked at the ceiling to drink them back. She would not allow herself to be wounded by him again. She would have to protect herself. Shreyas sat down beside her to chat.

"I wanted to tell you I am joining an institute to study ecology."

"Congratulations." She heard her own grating voice.

"In Dehra Dun, flanked by the frothy rivers – Yamuna and Ganga – leaning against the Himalayas ... where forests are green and the brown earth is bursting with life!"

"Is that also where the special seeds were planted during the Green Revolution, those that increase the yield dramatically?"

"Those were planted all over our country. There is an environmental activist from Dehra Dun, Vandana Shiva is her name, who condemns the Green Revolution as a theft against the indigenous methods of agriculture. I believe it too. Selling those seeds to the developing nations is an organized crime. The plants kill the nitrogen-fixing bacteria in the soil along with weeds. But these so called weeds are cattle-feed and greens that we eat in India. Then these foreign companies use film stars to advertise and don't tell the farmers they need lots of water in addition to fertilizers and pesticides. But let's not get into the humanitarian violations. If I start talking about patents I won't stop till you walk away."

Shreyas looked at the quiet girl beside him, "So what are your plans, after you finish next year?"

"Why are you asking me all this, Shreyas?" she spoke to herself, "You don't care for me; so leave me alone. You have no idea what you mean to me. I am a cloud precariously balanced in dew point. A single word from you could let loose a storm within me." Then she sighed. It was not his fault he did not love her. She dared to look him in the eyes. He was as handsome as ever and she fell in love with him afresh.

"Shall we keep in touch?" he asked casually.

Was he playing cat and mouse with her? She smiled, but did not answer. He understood, and did not press her. Then he said goodbye and was gone. She looked at him for the last time, and thought "Shreyas, today you are free. And I am bound forever to a ghost of my past." Such was Radha's tryst with destiny. Or maybe because her love was unrequited she never ceased loving. The "enigma" had died and a melody from an old Hindi film came to life.

Chalte, chalte mere yeh geet yaad rakhna,
On this journey of life remember my song ...
If, on the path, our ways should part
And should you feel lonely
Call upon me still, my love
And I shall return.
Never say farewell, never say farewell.
Khabhi alvidaa naa kehenaa,
Khabhi alvidaa naa kehenaa.

Chapter Twenty-three

Tulsi

Panchali and her brothers strolled in the shopping mall, both the boys swaggering beside her, each a head taller and sporting a thin moustache. She was buying them clothes for Holi and was strongly opposed to Prahlad's choice of an army uniform.

"That is against my philosophy of non-aggression and I will not allow you to pick one of those ugly camouflage shirts. Do they sell such nonsense in Delhi or did you splash green and brown randomly on white fabric?" she looked at Prahlad's clothes distastefully.

"Suraj joined the Indian Air Force, and man, you should see how smart he has become. He stands apart in a crowd now. You can sense a new confidence in his very gait. And the way he talks one knows his mind is flying at MiG-21 speed."

Prahlad flexed his biceps and thrust them in Yuyutsu's face.

"Stop it. I am not even competing with you." Yuyutsu could not help but admire those muscles. Panchali looked her younger brother up and down, not like a sister, but as a girl. He was getting to be a wee bit smarter than his age no doubt, she had to admit.

"The actor, Salman Khan, has lots of muscles. You can keep your biceps and yet not join the armed forces."

"But didi, you miss the point. I want to serve the nation."

"Kid, you have no idea what war means. It is an unnecessary sacrifice. None of the wars these days are unavoidable. Just some jawans get killed initially, they are decorated and everybody moves on, except for the affected families. Why would you choose such a dangerous career?"

"Didi, you are too much of a woman. Too soft."

She agreed. If ever her lover decided to join the armed forces, she would stand in his way with her life.

They passed by the film hero, Rajnikant, and all three of them stepped back in surprise. It was a life-size manikin, but so real. Then Panchali smiled, for indeed it was a real person, and one she recognized from an old mischief. Yuyutsu cried out before her, "Swami, is that you?"

"Yes, my dears, do I look like Rajni or not?"

Panchali massaged her eyes, "Are we that luminous, Swami?"

"Oh sorry, I forgot to remove my Ray Bans." He could have said dark glasses or goggles, but then he would not be a Rajni.

"Panchali, don't think this is my job, to pose as Rajni and stun customers." At least Swami knew the effect he had on people. "I was standing here to talk to you and then thought I could as well do some marketing stunt meanwhile." No, he did not guess the effect he had on innocent shoppers. Swami had left their school after class twelve for his hometown, Madras.

"You were waiting to talk to me, is that what I heard you say?"

"Yes, if the young men could excuse us, for a few minutes."

"Swami, why don't you meet me after we finish shopping? I don't want to keep these boys waiting."

Prahlad squared his shoulder, indicating he was not one to leave his sister with this strange man, even if Yuyutsu seemed convinced he was harmless.

"Oh my, who is this bodyguard with you, Panchali?"

"This is Prahlad, my brother from Delhi."

"I would rather not have to duel with him." Swami hesitated, then said, "OK, if you don't mind I can tell you right here, while your brothers do the shopping. I am leaving Bombay in a few hours and came to talk to you particularly, Panchali."

As they walked, Swami told Panchali about Tamil sentiments regarding the civil war in Sri Lanka. He condemned Rajiv Gandhi's peacekeeping manoeuvre vehemently.

"But Swami, he was scared the LTTE issue will spill into India. We don't want another state demanding autonomy. Besides, the methods used by the LTTE ..." she shuddered, "Terrorism taken to another height."

"Panchali, don't call them terrorists, please, at least to humour me. They are freedom fighters."

He became moody and stopped talking. "Swami, I am sorry. I have really no opinion on that political issue. You see, I tend to shun any kind of violence."

"Listen, I want you to do a play on the LTTE cause."

"That is all too political for my taste."

"Hear me out please. Just send one message to the political parties fighting the general elections – that they should not interfere in Sri Lanka's internal affairs."

"But didn't the Sri Lankan government request India's help? Like it was during the Bangladesh War?"

"India could choose not to intervene. I tell you, the LTTE issue is not going to be solved overnight, and it is best for Rajiv Gandhi to know, or whoever else comes to power, that no more peacekeepers are needed. The LTTE is, as you know, an organization that is ruthless. Children and women are recruited at a tender age to play with their lives. They are trained to sacrifice. They don't have the easy-going outlook of a half-hearted attempt. They will succeed."

"Swami, I am sorry. This is all the reason I should not take up the cause."

"Panchali, there is enough money in this that you will not have to worry for a year. Don't look at me that way; I know you work for art's sake, not money. It is good money, collected by expatriate Tamilians – Indians and Sri Lankans – from Canada, UK, USA, and we want to put it to good use."

"We? Swami, I did not know the Sri Lankan War was an Indian Tamilian cause."

"Not all Tamilians believe in Eelam, the ancient Tamilian home in Sri Lanka. But I do. And I want your help. Is that a yes then, for old times' sake, for Aamir's sake?"

"Now if you drag Aamir in this, how can I refuse?" Panchali

had an idea. "But there is one condition – the message will be hidden. It will be set in the medieval period – the story of alliances between small kingdoms."

"That will work. We will get a reporter to interpret it the right way and send the message to Delhi. Let's go back to my friend's shop. I have a cheque ready for you as an advance."

"Swami, are you in a hurry? I am working on a script right now."

"Yes, you have to agree to take this up. Within a month we want to see results."

"I am having my doubts now. I am a social awareness worker, not a political propagandist. I think I can do without this contract."

"Panchali, please, it is best for the Indian government. They will thank you some day."

"You are as mad as ever," she sang.

He handed her a cheque. "I will keep a watch on you, sweetie." He teased her, "I have to rush to Madras now."

"Didi, I don't like all this business you are getting into," commented Yuyutsu. Panchali ignored him.

"Prahlad, did you get your shirt? Oh no, not another army uniform!"

"No, it is of the Navy! That is why we call it navy blue."

* * * * *

The red, pink, green and yellow powders were piled on the plate along with a lamp. The three children waited excitedly for the last hymn to finish. Anand walked the plate and his hymn outside the apartment, followed by the human flies. He kept chanting till he had reached outside the building into the cement walk. There he finally surrendered to the madness of Holi. There are a lot of Kangra miniature paintings where Krishna plays Holi with the people of Brindavan. In a pastoral setting merry faces shine below powdery clouds of yellow, red, green, blue, orange. Some revellers can be seen holding spray cans emitting the red gulal water. Holi is a festival of friendship, of fun, of forgetting past wounds, of rejuvenation. Binapani hid behind Anand, who declared he would protect her from the kids. But when she felt safe, he got a handful of abir, the red powder, swivelled around, and smeared her face with it. Then Savita came galloping with some vicious pink powder and threw it in the air. The two boys had attacked Panchali who was fighting a losing battle with her uncle, Atul, as ally. Some passersby joined in the fun and got themselves coloured. Then the milk booth boy took a break and contributed his bit to the chaos. The newspaper deliverer cycled through the crowd emerging yellow on the other side. The vegetable vendor rang his bell from a mile away to be safe. The cement pavement resembled a child's wilful water-colour wash. A stray white dog had come to join the fun and very soon was red, like the plastic dog with a perfumed erasure. Someone hopped into the garden and turned on the hose. Families from all around came to whitewash each other with water. A rivulet of colour drained off the pavement. The three children ran up to the terrace to dry themselves in the wind.

Prahlad said, "I will teach you a Holi song. Listen. *Jeevan hai paayaa jis liye*", the other two followed him as he repeated each line,

"*Jeevan hai paayaa jis liye*
I have been granted life for a cause
And that I will accomplish."

*Khelenge Holi aag se
Tufaan hum ban jaayenge,*
I will play Holi with fire
I will become the hurricane
For you, O mother, I will live
And for you will I die."

"Prahlad, this is too powerful a song for this simple festival."

"But this is the real Holi that pumps life in you. And you spray it out on others. Does it not inspire you to love your Motherland, ever more? Let us play the real Holi, with fire. We are her leonine children. She is the mother Durga driving us."

Savita brought a tray-full of laddus. She had changed from the bedraggled discoloured sari. "I just heard you sing Prahlad's favourite song." Three hands darted forward, "Wait, let me feed you the first laddu." But it was too late as three contrite sorry's escaped stuffed mouths. Before she could scold them, Savita had to swallow her words down with laddu crumbs. Some delicacies make diabetes seem too small a price to pay.

The LTTE skit was poised to go live and true to his word Swami and his friends arranged the venues and sold the tickets. Panchali noticed how deep was the sympathy for their island brethren. It was May 21, 1991, when the phone rang in Panchali's house.

"Panchali?" It was Swami's voice, but it sounded out of character, not the confident accent, but a tense whisper.

"Did you hear the news? Switch on the TV now."

"What happened?"

"See for yourself. I will call you in a few minutes."

She switched on the TV. In the next two minutes she called her whole team one by one and cancelled the shows, all of them. Nobody questioned or protested; they seemed to be waiting for just such a direction.

"Swami, I saw everything. It was simply ..." Panchali was out of words.

"Now you know. Listen, I am going underground. You will not find any of the volunteers either who helped you in Bombay. Can you do me a favour? Destroy all evidence of our plan."

"I will do that. Don't worry."

"Also your phone bills. You never met me, we never talked."

"Swami ..."

"Yes, what is it? Tell me quickly. I must call others before I vanish."

"Will you call me when all this is over? I will be worried."

"If I can, I will."

Panchali tore the script to tiny shreds. Bills and bank deposit receipts were added to the pile. The horrific image of Rajiv Gandhi's remains in tattered bits of shoe and flesh haunted her mind. When he was campaigning in Tamil Nadu, mingling with the crowd, a bomb suddenly burst in his face, mincing him and at least fourteen others. Curfew was imposed in Tamil Nadu. The country was shocked at the audacity of a foreign organization to massacre an Indian leader, in India. It was a suicide bomber, a woman LTTE cadre, who had garlanded the former prime minister and had bent down to touch his feet detonating a bomb she wore in her belt. Seeing the last pictures from the camera of a dead photographer, her accomplices were traced down by the police. The mastermind shot himself, and the others bit into cyanide capsules before they could be captured, three months after the incident, in a hideout in Bangalore. The Indian army would definitely not be sent to aid Sri Lanka any more. Some people had become impatient to drive the lesson home. Panchali's covert message would not be needed.

* * * * *

"Why are you here, miss?" asked an angry man. "There are entire compartments reserved for women."

Tulsi mumbled "This is my first day in the local train at this hour. I did not know it will be this crowded."

"You can still make it to the ladies' compartment." She was scared the train would leave before she could reach her rightful place.

Some more voices addressed her, "It is for your own good. People will fill up till they are hanging out, how will you get out?"

"Quiet please," persuaded a voice. "She said she made a mistake. No need to beat a dead donkey, eh?" That convinced the grumblers to leave her alone.

Tulsi looked up gratefully at the owner of the voice. He was a boy much younger than the men but he looked like one who could plaster a dozen of them with one fist. He was tall and broad and when the train started moving, the breeze caught his hair, long enough to reach his shoulders. When Indra, the Lord of Gods, came down on earth on his white horse, he would have looked like this. No wonder the apsaras of heaven considered it punishment to be exiled from his presence. Indra was an ancient God, a hero in the Vedas, who delivered man from his travails. Buddhism had taken several Gods from the Hindu pantheon; among them was Indra. He was known by another of his names, Shakra, the luminous one. Tulsi was woken from her reverie. This Indra had started talking to her, since he observed she could not keep her eyes off him; they returned like two mares proud of their stallion.

"Now that you are snugly seated at the window, miss, it is best you sit there till the terminus."

"Churchgate?" She asked in alarm.

"Yes, then you can take the next train back. And please choose the ladies' compartment. See how the bodies are getting thickly packed. They will thin out after Santa Cruz, just a little bit. What happened?" Tulsi had started sniffing and hid her face. Tariq crouched down to face her. His voice was a gentle whisper, "What happened? Did I say something to make you cry?"

"It is my first day at college. I need to do the registration; otherwise they will give my seat away."

"Oh no, they won't do any such thing."

She kept crying.

"OK listen, I will help you get down at the right place. Where is your college?"

"Andheri."

"All right, we will start walking towards the door from Goregaon."

She nodded and tried to compose herself.

Tariq walked ahead and cleared the way. There was just a fraction of a second before the wave of human bodies collapsed at his back after he parted it. Tulsi managed to squeeze herself in that spot. At Andheri he jumped down and held back the wave ready to pour in. She would have been sucked back if he had been a little smaller in stature, but Afghan warlord blood ran in his veins, he was an eagle among sparrows. He jumped back in and the train started. Tulsi looked at his hand waving her goodbye and she screamed back, "Shukriya, shukriya, thank you, thank you!"

"And Panchali", Tulsi regretted, "I did not even ask him his name. He was so handsome I can't get him out of my mind."

"And skin," added Panchali pointing at her gooseflesh.

"Tell me, what is the chance that a person will meet another in this city of ten million people?"

"None, unless you get into the general compartment again."

"Oh no no!" shuddered Tulsi, then she said, "But if I meet him it would be worth a second experience of that nightmare."

Panchali's mother loved to fiddle with the radio. She had even tried some disastrous recipes on her family, suggested by friendly voices. The comments were usually "Very tasty, but don't try again." Today she found a better channel and Panchali's ears thrilled to the lilting melodies of old Hindi songs. Then light bulbs lit in her mind. She met her friend at the rehearsal that afternoon.

"Tulsi, I know how you could meet your dream boy."

"How, tell me quick!"

"What will you give me?"

"A kiss."

"Go to hell. I don't want a kiss from you, nor from Mister Long Hair. I was just teasing you. There is a radio programme of Hindi songs hosted by some lady called Supriya Dighe. You can call her number and she will play the song of your choice. I heard someone dedicating a song to his girlfriend because it was her birthday. Why don't you ..."

"Yuppy!" She hugged Panchali and gave her a kiss on the cheek. "You are an angel. Now pray for me, please, that he listens to the programme."

"I promise, but really you should accept the chances are slim here too."

Panchali tuned the radio to the new programme and waited. The first caller was not Tulsi, nor the second, then the third caller was her crazy little lovelorn friend. After the greetings she said, "I want to dedicate it to a handsome young knight I once met in the local train. He helped me get down at my station in Andheri and left me wishing I knew his name, so that I could dedicate this song to him. The rest of my words will be in the song. If he is hearing this, I am Tulsi Savarkar from Kandivili, Lokhandwala complex." The song was an old wine ever the better for its age. Binapani shouted from the next room. "Panchali, raise the volume. You know, Uttam Kumar danced in that song with Vyjayanthimala." Uttam Kumar was the Bengali film legend who did a handful of Hindi films. Panchali tweaked Tulsi's cheek in her mind, in appreciation of her ruse. The song was a little too bold for the short encounter on a train. But then how can one find subdued love songs from Bollywood? If he were as Tulsi described him, he would not mind the overstatement.

"*Ek chhotisi mulaaqaat...*
A small encounter became love,
And love became a garland round the neck,
yaa yaa yippie yippie...*"

* * * * *

For the next few days Tulsi jumped whenever the phone rang. Her father was roped in her game, but had insisted on screening the callers. He rejected all of them. They were drunkards, eve-teasers, old wheezing men, he said. "Bad idea" he concluded, making sure she would not invite such publicity any more. What was the chance he was listening to that radio programme on that specific day? Tulsi lost hope.

Then one day she heard her father bang on the bathroom door. She silenced the shower,

"Call for you, Tulsi."

"Who is it?"

"He will not tell me."

"Wow daddy, what makes you allow him to do it?"

"His voice. It is very gentlemanly."

"Oh my God, I will be there in an instant." She manhandled herself with the towel and almost tore her dress in a hurry to get into it. Then with dripping hair she pounced on the phone.

"Hello, this is Tulsi."

The voice on the other end did not talk, but it sang. The song was from a Hindi film, where the hero comes to meet his prospective bride, and on the way he imagines all sorts of possibilities.

"*Aaj unse peheli mulaaqaat hogi...*
Today I will meet her for the first time
And we will talk face to face about many things.
Then what shall pass who can say, who can guess...*"

Her "small" mulaaqaat was answered with his "first" mulaaqaat. She recognized the voice that had soothed her in the train and looked like vanilla ice cream topped with a pair of blushing cherries.

"So when will this mulaaqaat happen?" she asked, breathless.

Now he was grave. "Hey Tulsi, my name is Tariq Aziz. You better ask your father if such an encounter can happen."

"It depends on you and me. Not my father. Besides he already likes you. He is a psychiatrist and judges people by their voice. Not religion."

"In that case I say it will happen in five minutes."

"Really, Tariq, where are you?" she looked outside the window, stretching the phone cord to its limit.

"Somewhere in this concrete jungle of flats. The good watchman at the gate helped me with your phone number. Now give me directions to reach your place."

Tulsi could not risk losing him once again. "Wait at the poolside, there is just one pool and I will be there in two minutes." One of Tariq's co-passengers had heard Tulsi's dedication, and had also witnessed the escort scene. When he next found Tariq in the train he conveyed Tulsi's message.

* * * * *

"Prahlad, this is didi from Bombay."

"Thank you! Thank you!" Panchali heard her brother's enthusiastic voice on the phone.

"What are you thanking me for? I have not congratulated you. In fact I am very angry with you."

"Didi, do you know how many people appear for the exam and how few are lucky to get through?"

"They are the unlucky ones, and I will not allow you to be one of them."

Savita took the phone extension from her son and went to the kitchen, so that he would not hear. "Panchali, you know from childhood he has been dreaming about the army. Now finally he got through. I hope he will tire of it soon and change his mind. The more you reason with him now the worse it will be."

Prahlad snatched the phone back, "Didi, this is not a game I am trying to play one round and see how it feels. Every Republic Day I marched and saluted the Indian flag. Was it just for a passing fancy? I exercised and studied hard for this exam, but finally when I pass it my family discourages me. This is so unfair."

"Prahlad, we care for you. You know what war is. Leaders cook a fight and youngsters are used as firewood."

"Didi, we have to choose our battle and fight for it. This is mine, no matter what others think about it."

Panchali wondered, do I have a battle? Have I chosen yet? Am I a blade of steel carving my own path, like Prahlad, or a bubble flowing with the stream?

"Didi, are you there?"

"Yes. I am here. Trying to choose my battle." Her younger brother had found it. She was still a kite drifting in the wind.

"Prahlad, fly like the arrow you were meant to be. I wish you all the best."

"Didi, that is such a relief. Thank you."

"No matter what we do, the vocation we choose, or we think

we choose, we are driven by Him who has strung us in the garland like jewels. That is what Krishna had told Arjuna in the battlefield of ancient Bharat, *mayi sarvam idam protam sutre maniganaa iva.* He knows what He is doing. And what greater assurance is there?"

Yuyutsu took the phone. "Hey Prahlad, congratulations!"

"And you too, Ullu. Baba is thrilled you will follow his footsteps."

"Yes, he is my inspiration, and my battle, I suppose, is civil engineering." He laughed, as the word "battle" hardly suited the context. "Ma says, she came from Jai Hind to Hey Ram, and I am going from Hey Ram to Jai Hind."

"Are you going to Calcutta?"

"Close by. The college is Bengal Engineering College, on the other bank of the Ganga. I dug up some information about it. The college started in 1856 as Civil Engineering College to train workers of the Public Works Department. In 1880 it shifted to the lush campus of the Bishop's College in a region of Howrah, called Shibpur. It added science and other engineering subjects to its curriculum and after Independence, architecture and Town and Regional Planning. So Shibpur is my next stop."

* * * * *

The drama called "Harmony" opened with five students strolling together during an excursion. They came upon a Hindu temple in ruins. There were granite statues standing on podiums, some in niches and some embossed in pillars. The five dispersed and did their own exploration. One of the boys stood out. He had long hair and was built like a pathan, an Afghan, tall and fair, sharp-featured like a model. Aditi called out to the boy next to her,

"Hey Roshan, look at this idol, it may have been Goddess Durga seated on her lion. But her nose is chopped off."

Panchali called to Tulsi, "What a sorry state for ancient art! This God has no fingers and no nose either."

Roshan announced, "This one is worse. He does not have a head, and his toes are gone. Some barbarian was here."

"No", said Aditi, "Not a barbarian, but the conquerors from the Near East. Tariq, say something, you are Muslim. Is that a right guess?"

"Yes, Islam does not believe in idol worship. I think that is why these statues have their noses slashed, to literally symbolize the shame, 'naak kaat diya'. It was an ancient punishment to cut a person's nose and disfigure him so that he roamed the world displaying his notoriety."

"Somebody else's religion is of course notorious, and one's own harmonious." Tulsi looked around at the three others who were Hindus.

"Tariq, are you saying it was not intolerance, but just aesthetic disgust?" the four stood against Tariq.

"No, I agree it was intolerance, since all non-Islamic people were heretics, considered lesser human beings."

Panchali was willing to help Tariq, "At least our idols were disfigured. But the whole Buddhist library at Nalanda was burnt. So many spiritual texts are gone for ever. The monks were killed too as they did not hide daggers in their belt, as the Sikhs taught themselves later."

"Yes, which monk would have thought he had to learn karate along with his sutras?"

"And Hindus were plundered because they were not aggressive. They allowed each one to follow his own propensity."

"Yes, Hindus don't proselytize."

Panchali now joined Tariq's side wholeheartedly, "Tulsi, Roshan, Aditi, you say Hindus are tolerant toward outsiders, but within their own ranks they have created enough stratification to disgust even insiders. I say the Turks, Persians, Afghans and Arabs were repelled by the Hindu caste system and protested with their swords."

"So Panchali, you are saying what they did was right."

"I am pointing out that the Hindus should not be such hypocrites as to blame outsiders when they themselves have done much damage to their religion."

"So should the Hindu blame his fate and stick to his non-violent ways? Should they not retaliate?" asked Aditi.

Roshan took the lead. "Yes they should, and we will too. Even if it is a few centuries late, we will avenge the deformation to our deities. Close up, I have an idea." The five of them put their heads together. Tariq was also included in the conspiracy.

The next scene was at a deserted mosque at night. Around the arched entrance were drawn the fluid lines seen in most mosques. Tulsi climbed up a ladder with a paint brush and bucket of paint to reach the top of the arch. From below her friends threw up instructions.

"That curve you see there on the right, add a dot to it; that will make a naked woman."

Tulsi's hand shook, "This brush is too heavy for me. Roshan, why don't you come up?" Roshan was up there and he leaned in all directions, "I can't find any curve that looks like a human organ. This one is a reed, and that a bird in flight. This one is a cup that is lying on its side. And there is a conch shell."

"Yes that one, dot it, desecrate it."

Roshan complained, "It already has a dot below it."

Aditi said, "Then add a curve to match the dot."

Roshan was climbing down. "Panchali, I can't see well so close up, choose a pattern from down there and you make the dots."

Panchali went up and came down and Aditi did it too, shifting the ladder to another spot, but none of them could make a single mark. They sat down dejected.

Tariq asked, "What happened to your plan?"

Panchali said, "If the patterns were not so beautiful, I might have added my poor taste to them. But this I just don't have the heart to destroy."

Roshan agreed, "Me too, it seems perfect as it is and so skilfully inlaid. The brush would make an ugly blotch."

Tulsi sighed, "This revenge business does not resonate with me."

Tariq spoke in a measured tone, *"Allah ho akbar, bismillah ar rahman, ar rahim.* God is great. I proclaim it in the name of God, the all-compassionate, the all-merciful..."

The rest of them came around and stood alongside Tariq. They followed his gaze up at the arched entrance.

Roshan asked hesitatingly, "Tariq, are you chanting this from memory?"

Tariq shook his head. "No, I am reading."

"Is that what is written there?" cried the other three.

Aditi moaned, "Oh, I thought they were just decorations; stylized plants, tendrils, vines and creepers."

Panchali shook Tariq, "Tariq, why, why did you not tell us before what it was? Were you waiting for us to make fools of ourselves?"

"When the Muslims came to India, did they ask what these statues meant? Did they try to understand how much it would hurt the native people?"

Panchali sat down on a stone. "When the early conquerors came to India, they were thieves who looted the land to enrich their own country. The Persian, Nadir Shah, stole the peacock throne carved in gold. Muhammad of Ghazni made seventeen raids into India and every time destroyed the Somnath Temple in Gujarat, carrying away caravan-loads of jewels. But when the Turks, Afghans and Mughals came, they made India their home. They did not loot from their own land; instead they beautified it with the Red Fort, the Grand Trunk Road, the Taj Mahal. And as part of keeping their home clean, they did away with idols."

"But is that justified, Panchali?"

"As much as it is for Hindu temples to blare chants from four mikes at five in the morning and burst firecrackers in crowded streets."

Roshan argued, "But Panchali, five times a day the minarets dust out their prayers on the city below."

Tariq came between them and put his hand round each one. "For eight centuries Hindus and Muslims have lived side by side. By now we are an old couple and we can pardon each other's snores. After the Id festival I go to my neighbours who are Hindus and give them the feast biriyani."

"You are right, Tariq," said Tulsi, "We too share our sweets with our Muslim neighbours after Dussehra."

"All this hatred is conjured up by vote bankers, also known as politicians."

Panchali turned to the audience, "I ask each of you, raise your hand if, in your life, a person of the other religion has harmed you."

No hand went up.

"What we see are people of all religions working together in the fields, in mines, in offices, everywhere. And yet when someone shows these artefacts of history we allow our blood to boil, and we start hating those who were family a few days back."

Tulsi came forward, "I feel my nose is cut, that I have lived with the Tariqs in this shameful love-hate relationship. Is it true we enjoy hating?"

"How can that be? We cry out for love, sit through two hours of filmy melodrama just to live it by proxy, we steal it at enormous cost, we buy it for a night, we risk everything for one season of festivity. No, given a chance we would rather love than hate."

"And we do have that choice. Make it now. Boycott division. That was an old trick played on us by the colonists. How is it that our own so-called leaders are making us drink that rancid potion in a new bottle?"

"A question for you all." The lights in the audience lit up. "Would you rather wake up at four in the morning and queue up for water? Or would you like running water in the tap? It is a stupid question. But it seems we, as a people, are making the wrong choice."

"We don't have good roads, affordable hospitals, clean water to drink, proper schools, and yet we seem to have time for religious vengeance, to break a temple or mosque."

"I invite any of you who feel the need to act thus, or have met such people, to raise your hand."

Everybody looked around and none raised their hands.

"So where do these people come from? Villages? Do they know what they are supposed to do?"

Tariq and Roshan mimicked the villager and the leader.

"What is it this time, sahib? Do we have to vote for the hand or the lotus?"

"No, today's gig is breaking a dome."

Panchali engaged the audience again. "I will offer this evening's proceedings to the one who will sincerely say he can break a religious structure."

Many hands flew up.

The five on stage came forward. "Thank you all for participating. You have yourselves proved how politics manipulates people. With money. If educated citizens like you are swayed by it, what of those for whom ten rupees means a huge sum?"

"We request you to send this message to the government, that you are intelligent human beings who demand civic amenities. Let the monies be rightly allocated. Let the poor man be paid to pave a road, not to break it."

"Vengeance does not improve the common man's lot. Revenge begets more revenge ad nauseam. Meanwhile a country, or two, or three, suffers. Let us forget the past ills and join hands in harmony. We have a long way to go and a lot of work to do."

Panchali thought the drama ended with a high note, the audience would go home, introspect and apply themselves to nation-building. But the critics were diligent too. Hindu papers criticized her for calling the Muslim, family, and wiping the board clean while so many raw wounds festered. And the Muslims were angry because she suggested the verses from the Quran could be desecrated in a mosque. At a theatre Hindu party workers guarded the ticket counter so that none of the tickets were sold. At another, Muslims did not even let the troupe enter the greenroom. Luckily for Tariq, they were not physically hurt. He negotiated every bit of the way in his gentle style. And when it came to managing the Hindu crowd, the four of them protected Tariq. Finally Panchali decided she would enact the play in the villages, the real victims of political exploitation.

But her timing could not have been worse. A Hindu political party, the Bharatiya Janata Party, had just then decided to fly its saffron flag from hilltops. A chariot similar to the ones that are used to parade a deity around the city, called a ratha, was used ostentatiously, to attract attention. From the south to the north of India it journeyed, overhanging with floral decorations, rallying followers along the way, and making the police prick up their ears wherever it passed.

Roshan was as sporting as ever, "Whoever thought the Hindu is laid back is getting a taste of his virility."

Panchali was furious, "Tolerance, one of the strongest principles of Hinduism – as Krishna professed in the Gita, 'No matter however the devotee worships, in whichever form, I accept his oblation' – is tossed out."

Tulsi cupped her ear to hear Panchali. They were on a bus headed towards a village to show "Harmony".

"Do you know what an oxymoron means?" Panchali asked again.

"Two contradictory ideas thrown together."

"Such as?"

"Snow in Bombay."

"Good one."

"Now your turn."

"Fundamentalism and Hinduism. It is an unholy union."

"And yet Panchali, people keep filling up the seats and they clap at the end."

"Luckily, the fanatics have not appealed to everybody's reason, especially those who apply common sense. A little foot in the doorway is preventing it from being slammed shut. Some day the gates will fly open."

Chapter Twenty-four

Yuyutsu

Didi

    I cracked the ragging secret code. All you need is a single trait worthy of pity. If you are "Mister Perfect" the seniors will fell you like a tree. But if you have a "poor me" attitude, you will have fooled them. Now don't read ahead. Imagine what in me should have evoked pity. Did you guess it? My name, of course! At first I thought only the lab assistants could not pronounce it, but then I found many of my college mates got their tongues tied too. I had resigned to being Jujutsu, but they pitied me so much they have renamed me. I am Bruce Lee now, the Jujutsu champ. Oh, there is an important etiquette I have to tell you about. You must address your seniors as elder brother and elder sister. Even those who are a single batch senior are Arindam-da, Susmita-di, Abhijit-da, Mala-di.

    Within a week I figured if you don't eat fish, you don't eat. And if you don't speak Bengali, you don't speak. Yes, I have begun to eat fish. The people here consider fish vegetarian. They even use the word "cultivation" for fisheries. After the mad race of Bombay, Calcutta seems like a vacation; of course not in college (don't think I am not studying). There is a holiday for Buddha's birthday, for Ramzan and Id, Durga pooja, Kali pooja, Holi, Gandhiji's birthday, Netaji's birthday, Christmas, Independence Day, Republic Day, and students' union strike day, and transportation workers' strike day, bankers' strike day, factory lockout day. People march in a human train kilometres long, chanting slogans and waving banners. Traffic is paralysed. All are asked to stay at home. If anyone tries to open his shop, he will be forced to close it; first with words, then with the sticks. Once I was returning from didima's house and got caught in one of these human snakes. The whole Howrah Bridge was jampacked with buses and cars stuck for hours. I ditched the bus and walked across the Ganga, squeezing past these unionists. The Communist government and the same Chief Minister, Jyoti Basu, has been ruling West Bengal for the last fifteen years. Phenomenal! I am told busloads of poor and ill-informed folk are brought to the ballot boxes and tutored to vote for the sickle-and-hammer on the patch of red. They return home after the day-long picnic and a precious ten rupee note in their hands.

* * * * *

"How about this inkpot?" The stationery vendor pushed the glass jar in front of Yuyutsu's face.

"Stop it, Manik-da, I have already told you I don't like green ink."

"That's what everyone says. And I have these in stock for ten years. They will dry out now. Do you think I will write them down in my will for you students?"

"Why did you get them in the first place?"

"It was a wrong delivery and since it would cost more to send them back I just kept them. Who knew you kids are so choosy."

"No offence to the colour green. It is to protect our colour blind lecturers. They use red usually, but if they see us using red too how will they correct? I say, the only recourse you have is to gift them to us."

"If I give you for free, in the next ten minutes there will be a queue of students and after I have finished my green stock they will force me to gift the blue and black, and who knows the students' union will be on my back to dispense with justice towards all."

"Achha Manik-da, why don't you catch some Muslim customers to buy the green?"

"Why so?"

"It's an impression I have. Green is the Muslim colour. Yes, I know why. The Bangladeshi and Pakistani flags, are they not mostly green?"

"So?"

"They surely use it to copy out passages from the Quran, or use it for drawings. Maybe they dye cloth in green to make their flags. Try selling your pots in Metiaburz and you will know what I mean."

"Bruce Lee, people in Calcutta are Indians. Why should they fly the Pakistani or Bangladeshi flag?"

"Is that a challenge? If I find one of these flags in Metiaburz can I get the inkpot for free?"

"If you find a Bangladeshi flag anywhere in Calcutta I will give it for free. I have a very cunning mind and can find out if you cheated. You will give me the exact location and I will get it verified."

"Deal. Boss, keep the inkpot packed."

The next Sunday Yuyutsu crossed the Ganga on a ferry. The Howrah Bridge looked like an ostentatious ring in the river's finger. The ride was too short to dive in a daydream. He jumped on the bank and started scanning the tops of buildings. The skyline was a nest of television antennas, telegraph wires and clothes hanging from parapets to be dried. No green signal was to be found. Yuyutsu walked through the narrow streets, then stopped at the paan shop.

"Bhai sahab, have you seen any green flag around here?"

"This is Calcutta saar, only red flags fly here."

"Is this not the Bangladeshi area?"

"Yes, can't you understand from my accent that I came from the other side of the border myself?"

"Then should not someone fly a Bangladeshi flag?"

"My family came here ages before Bangladesh was formed. Even the newcomers don't fly that flag. Arre arre, watch out!"

Yuyutsu had bounced back on the road and had not seen a cyclist coming his way. The handle felt like a bullock's horn in his ribs. The cyclist never stopped or looked back, but scolded him, "Didn't you hear the bell?" It was a girl. Yuyutsu could only think of a song as answer to her insolence,

"*Jaane waalo zaraa murke dekho hame ...*

You folk who pass by, turn awhile and look at me,
I too am human, just like any one of you."

The melody was from the film Dosti and it was the turning point in a blind man's life. His song touched people's hearts and they filled his begging bowl.

The cyclist slowed down, but did not stop.

"Don't be offended by her, saar. That girl I know well. She has just learnt to cycle and can't stop unless she finds a mound of sand. She rides past two blocks from her house near the construction site, then walks the cycle back."

A boy approached Yuyutsu. "Did it hurt a lot?"

"Arre, no. I was just embarrassing her."

"You have a wonderful voice. Sing some more."

Yuyutsu started the song again and sang most of it.

"Hey listen, my name is Hamid. My brother is getting married soon, and next week we have the song majlis, where the two parties will have a competition of songs. But I have no songster friend. We cannot lose to the girl's side. You understand, don't you, question of honour. Will you sing with us, please?"

"Sure, I am always ready for a party."

"I will send a taxi for you."

"It is easier to cross the river and walk up here."

The next week Yuyutsu was welcomed with open arms in a huge house. Hamid's family was one of the wealthiest of Metiaburz and thus the honour factor. Yuyutsu was whisked indoors and given a sherwani to wear, embroidered every millimetre. The art of making decorative fabric and tailoring them was an ancestral trade among Muslims. The colloquial word for tailor was not the Sanskrit word, but darzi, an Urdu word. Yuyutsu looked into the mirror and was shocked to find a prince in there. Even his sandals were hand-stitched, gold thread patterns on black velvet. Since their religion did not permit drawing human figures, they excelled in pattern designs. Yuyutsu was given a fat pillow to lean against and a glass of rose sherbet. Youth of his age surrounded him, and declared they could suggest songs if he ran out of stock. He looked at his adversaries. They were a row of maidens in purple, pink, maroon, and red. They dazzled his mind, but did not tie his tongue, fortunately, since the men who encircled him were either tone deaf, or had sore throats from eating too much kulfi. It was an antaakshari bout, where each side had to sing a song that started with the last syllable of the previous song. At least his companions kept a close watch on the songs that were already sung. Twice they caught the girls repeating a song and teased them red. After every phrase Yuyutsu sang, they showered him with "Wah wah" appreciations. The women were nightingales, compared to the crows around him. But they were running out of stock and Yuyutsu wondered if living in the heart of Bollywood did have some advantage. When the sound "Ja" came along, he sang the "*Jaane waalo*" song he had sung on the road after the cycle accident.

Finally Yuyutsu's one-man-show won the singing bout and there was much applause, from both parties. He wiped the sweat out of his forehead. The sherwani could be hot. Someone came with a plate-full of steaming chicken biriyani. Was he going to eat meat too now? But the smell was too alluring and very soon he wondered why he had wasted so many years of his life not eating this delicacy. He finished with sweets, packed with dry fruits, dripping ghee. "Man, these people know how to cook!" It was getting dark and finally he disengaged himself from his new fans. But at the door someone threw an invisible noose round his neck. She was the purple one he had conquered.

"So, Yuyutsu, where did you learn singing?"

"In the school of life. Now let me see where my career began. Yes, serenading. I think I was seven."

"Chasing girls that early in life?" she mocked.

"Oh no, not for myself. I was hired as playback singer. For my own sister!"

"Well, here is an advice. Don't sing too many songs on the road for girls. You will be arrested for eve-teasing."

"I don't usually sing on the road. But how did you know I

did it recently? Were you the rude one who rammed a cycle handle in me and sped off?"

She bit her lips in embarrassment. "Sorry, I am new to cycling. Actually I don't even see the people on the road. I have to keep my eyes focused ahead. But when you sang the *jaane waalo* today, I recognized the voice."

And so Yuyutsu visited Metiaburz again, and yet again. He did not see the Howrah Bridge pass by, nor the fishermen whistling to the fish, nor the crimson dusk over the smoggy sky. He just thought of the one on the other end of his journey, Selma.

"Selma, I already have a Christian name, Bruce Lee. Now I want a Muslim one. How does Salim sound? Prince Salim, son of the emperor Akbar?"

"No, it will not work. Salim is too close to my name, as if you were my brother."

"So? Do you mind?"

She gave him a punch in the ribs. "You naughty thing! Of course, I mind."

"Oof, what have my ribs done to you? From that first encounter you have been punishing them."

* * * * *

At the same time an engineering student in Karachi in Pakistan, threw up a handful of shooting stars in the night sky. He would begin his career as a pop singer strumming his guitar in the college corridors while his friends drummed on the canteen table Ali Haidar's song "*Purani Jeans aur Guitar*" captured the hostel life of thousands of students across the three countries, immortalizing their fond memories in a catchy tune. Those days when they wore old jeans and played the guitar, were thrown out of class and complained about the system, stayed out late and scaled the compound walls, smoked cigarettes and brushed teeth to hide the smell, wrote love letters and borrowed money to give her gifts, were scolded by papa and supported by mummy. Those days when one dreamt of achieving something really big, *woh dil me shochnaa karke kuchh dikhaa dein* and planned it afresh every day, *woh karnaa planning roz nayi yaar*.

* * * * *

Yuyutsu sat watching the news with Selma's family. People had climbed the three domes of a mosque, the Babri Masjid, waving saffron flags. The camera swung around the crowd. Some khaki colours could be seen, policemen, standing at the outskirts of the melee, watching the drama. Men started striking the old domes with hammers and stones. The bricks of the five-hundred-year-old edifice crumbled sending up a cloud of dust. There was an uproar of battle cries. Numerous ochre-clad men, in the robe of Hindu ascetics, had assembled and were enthusiastic contributors to the demolition. People wanted to participate in breaking a mosque that Babar, the first Mughal emperor, had built in 1527, supposedly over a Hindu temple. The venue was Ayodhya, in Uttar Pradesh, the capital of Lord Rama of the epic age. Some Hindus claimed this very site had once been the spot on which Rama was born. In 1949 Rama's idol was sneaked into the mosque, and ever since the place has fomented communal disharmony.

Selma's father shook his head in concern. Breaking a place of worship, however unused, in that mob-like fashion, was wrong. Then suddenly alert, he snatched Yuyutsu by the arm, "Go, go, now. I fear Metiaburz is not safe for a Hindu." Yuyutsu looked at Selma's wide eyes. Was she shocked that her father was throwing him out, or was she shocked at what the Hindus had done to her religion? He got up, a minute too late. On the road a few paces from Selma's door he collided with a man running in blind haste. Yuyutsu held his elbow and steadied him.

"Thank you," gasped the man and pulled Yuyutsu along with him. "Come, let's crack some skulls as they cracked our dome."

Yuyutsu stared at him, shocked at the animosity. The man turned around, "You hesitate, shala, you must then be one of them. Scoundrel, how dare you destroy our place of worship!" Yuyutsu covered his head from the stick pounding down on him, "I did not! How could I? We are not in Ayodhya!" Then the stick struck his skull and blood oozed out on his eyes. More feet were heard and punches beat upon him from all sides. He could hear Selma's voice crying out "No ... no ...", then it became muffled as if a hand was put over her mouth. Her door slammed shut and the last thing Yuyutsu remembered was the stench of the gutter and an excruciating pain in his stomach.

* * * * *

Yuyutsu opened his eyes and saw angels with white wings hovering above him. They had women's faces ringed with haloes. The next time he saw the vision he knew it was paradise and told himself all was good and fell asleep. Surely, him being Bruce Lee, had landed him in a Christian heaven. The third time something was amiss in paradise. The woman angel's face was distorted in fear. She was whispering although the veins in her neck suggested she was screaming. He was intrigued and stayed one more second awake to listen to her words. It said, "Bruce Lee, can you hear me?" The shock of hearing his college nickname in heaven gave him a jolt. The woman clapped her hands over his eyes, and exclaimed in delight, "He blinks!" Yuyutsu tried to talk but something was wrong with his mouth. He could just rotate his eyes and catch a glimpse of a complex array of bottles and tubes. All the endings of the contraptions seemed to disappear somewhere inside his body. Slowly the last event came back to him, like a dream remembered vaguely in the morning. He was in a hospital and his eyes were intact, that's all he knew.

Sister Lucy was given the charge of reviving Yuyutsu if she could. When he opened his eyes and looked around she knew the worst was over. She had won the battle. Among her friends she could hardly stop describing the state in which he was brought in, and what she did to tease life back in his body. She said it as if she was delivering a baby from a very complicated case. When Yuyutsu had found his voice and thanked her, she took his hand and placed it on his chest, "Thank Him, child." Yuyutsu realized he had a Cross hanging round his neck, with the small replica of Jesus suffering in the last moments of his life. "The Lord has resurrected you."

* * * * *

The first feeling Malini remembered was hunger. She was three years old, crying in the street. A woman in white sari with thin blue border held out a biscuit in her hand and Malini grabbed it.

She followed the lady who visited huts and handed these savouries. Finally she was lost but happy to be with someone who cared and fed her. Malini was brought to the children's orphanage and baptized as Lucy. She grew up in the shadow of the Cross and Mother Teresa, the angel sent to the impoverished land of India by the Lord Christ.

Christians arrived in Kerala on the western coast of India, perhaps within a hundred years of Christ's death, starting Syrian Christian churches. The next wave of Christians came with the Portuguese colonists in the sixteenth century, and these were followed shortly by the Dutch, the British and the French. Using India as a foothold, Christianity travelled to other Asian countries. The last wave of evangelical missionaries that poured in during the British Raj set up educational institutions and hospitals all over the country.

Mother Teresa was eighteen in 1928 when she left her native country, Albania, and travelled as a missionary to India. While she taught at the Loreto convent in the metropolis of Calcutta, she was struck by the abject poverty around her. An inner call drew her towards these slum dwellers, these shadowy beings hugging the peripheries of society, these unwanted, sick, destitute souls, the poorest among the poor. She went begging from door to door to collect money to set up her "Missionaries of Charity". She had to face uncertainty and the temptation to return to the safety of the convent, but every time she saw an innocent face like Malini's light up with her simple gesture, she returned to the street and walked on ahead. Funds started rolling in and Mother Teresa set up institutions around Calcutta – orphanages, hospices for the dying, soup kitchens. Then all over India and around the world such institutions of charity sprang to life. Some of her wards grew up to work in these hospitals and looked after the children whose parents had no means to search for them when they strayed in a crowd. Sister Lucy paid her own way to a professional nurse's training programme by working in a tailor's shop at night. On Christmas day she went back to Nirmal Hriday, the "pure heart" orphanage she was brought up in, her hands full of sweets and pens and notebooks and comics for the children. One day these little ones would be mothers and fathers, doctors and nurses, scientists and artists and honourable citizens of the world. And they would know how to help another human being, how to love unconditionally, how to be grateful.

* * * * *

"What day is it?" asked Yuyutsu.

"Oh, you look fresh today! January 6." replied Sister Lucy massaging his hands. He was drifting in and out of consciousness, and she hardly left his room. Everybody complained she was showering too much love on that unknown boy. But she ignored them. She gave him a second chance to live, and therefore he was her son.

Yuyutsu tried to think, what had he done for Christmas that year? And New Year? Why could he not remember? Then he asked fearfully, "When did I come here?"

"On December 6 of course, that horrible day."

He was mortified. Who had informed his family? Or did they not know? Where was everyone? Were they safe? Did anyone else get beaten up like him? He asked "Did you inform my family?"

"Bruce Lee, you have not told us about your family. All we could catch from your delirium were the words, ma, baba, didi, and a Muslim girl, Selma. It is not safe these days to be confused with a Hindu or Muslim. That is why I have hung a Cross pendent on you. They thought you were Hindu and almost killed you! Of course when they found you were Christian, they brought you here."

Yuyutsu looked down at his leg and hand in cast. His body had more stitches than the stitches in his shirt, his head was bandaged and without morphine in his blood he would die of pain.

"Can I call Shibpur Engineering College and tell them I am here?"

"I have already done that. One of the boys who brought you here left a message to call as soon as you woke up. He has called quite a few times already. And I think I saw some people looking at you from outside the ICU."

"Who is this boy?"

"Says he is your friend. The name is Sam D'Souza."

Yuyutsu looked everywhere in his memory but could not find any Sam he knew. Out of exhaustion, he fell back unconscious.

The next day he woke up outside the Intensive Care Unit, to the sound of approaching determined footsteps. A woman shrouded in a black burqa was walking towards him. He smiled in wonder, could it be Selma? She clutched the bedstand and her hands trembled with emotion. It was the same hand that carved out the watermelon seeds before giving him the fruit, the same that held the book when he recited a poem from memory, that wiped his head when he returned drenched from the rain, tied his shoe laces when he broke his arm. He reached for the hand tenderly, "Didi." The next moment Panchali threw her veil away and brother and sister embraced. The wound in his lip reopened and blood fell on his chest. None paid attention to Sister Lucy complaining about the torn labial stitches and her surprise about the visitor's religion.

Panchali declared she would take Yuyutsu back home.

"But you cannot do it; he is practically on life support."

"Sister, you are sister to many, but I am sister to just this one boy. I will find a way to look after him. Please bundle all the bottles and tubes."

"Do you live far?"

"Bombay."

Sister Lucy almost fainted. Her best piece of work was being stolen. But she had to yield.

Once in the plane Panchali removed her veil. Yuyutsu was recovering fast and she did not need to give him as many injections any more. She furnished him with the events of the missing month from his life.

"After the mosque demolition, all the Muslim pockets of India rang with cries of revenge. Baba and ma were first concerned about me, because my latest drama touched upon religious sentiments. As soon as I reached home they felt less tense and called you that day, on 6 December. But the phone lines were not connecting. For three days the lines were down, then they got through, but you know how the hostel boys are, they go off to call, and never return. We left messages that you should call. But you did not. We did not want to scare didima, as she is not keeping well, and with Raja mama gone on his tours, she was alone too. We actually lied to her and told her all was fine. One week had passed and reports of deaths were trickling in, especially from Calcutta. We had begun to worry. Bombay too had her fair share of riots. Ullu, you never told us about your Muslim connection."

"I was scared you will all oppose it."

"You were right not to tell us, but for another reason. We would be doubly worried for you. We sent a telegram to the College warden. And he replied you were missing from that day. It was then that a lightning struck home. My friends started looking at me as if my brazenness had cost me the first victim."

"They blamed you for my disappearance?"

"If you really had, it would mean my martyrdom too."

"Are you saying they would have killed you?"

"No, but I would shut my mouth, which is tantamount to killing me."

Yuyutsu patted her hand. "Hit me, I deserve it. I have caused you much trouble."

"Wait till you hear the rest. So I disappeared too, just like you."

"Not like me, I was in a hospital, half dead."

"All right, not like you. But to the world I had vanished before the press could start speculating and blaming me for the mosque demolition, and the fuel crisis and the drought."

"Surely you are exaggerating!"

"Yes, just flattering myself. Even art has no place right now. It is about survival. Ishmael was banished from his father's house, and he survived the privations of the desert. His descendants, who made a dwelling of that wasteland, were united by

Mohammad under one religion. And the Hindu civilization has not been destroyed despite repeated defeats, political and ideological, from without and within. Yet again these colossal forces have met."

"When the survivors meet it is like the finals in World Cup Cricket – India versus Pakistan."

Panchali felt hurt, "Ullu, I was being dead serious."

"So am I, didi. And so are the cricket fans. It's not a game out there – where losing is an option. People sit on the edge of their seats, crack knuckles, leap up for an out or a six and dispute the umpire's calls passionately. Many of us wonder what a solid team we would make if we were the same country."

"Yes, then so many things would be different."

Yuyutsu touched her arm gently to wake her from her reverie. "Didi, you were saying something. How did you vanish?"

"Ah yes, I hid myself behind the burqa. It is a most convenient disguise, in winter though. If you had done your stunt in summer I would not have come to get you."

"Stunt indeed! I suppose that is why I am called Bruce Lee."

"The next time I will try a wig. Breathing through a veil can get on your nerves."

"Next time? I thought you were not coming for me?" they both had a good laugh. "Now you should sleep, Ullu."

"How can I sleep at the climax of the story? Didi, please tell me the rest. How did you find me?"

"So I jumped on the next train to Calcutta. It was half empty as people were scared to travel after the curfew was lifted. But Metiaburz was still under army surveillance."

"Why do you mention Metiaburz?" Yuyutsu was surprised since the hospital was elsewhere.

"That is an important clue to finding the treasure. I will come to it."

"Treasure?"

"You, Ullu. The Ticket Checker was a Hindu, and was scared

to even ask me for a ticket. I had to show it to him myself. I went to Shibpur, to your college and asked around for you. Then I went to the authorities and told them to put up a notice about me, your relative. If anyone knew about your whereabouts they should contact me. I stayed in the guest house close to your college. Nobody came for two days and I started sweating in fear – imagine in winter!"

"Didi, hurry up. But finally someone did come surely. Was it Sam D'Souza?"

"What's the hurry, now that we are safe? We can as well relish the story. Then came your saviour – don't look at the Cross – it was a person of flesh and blood. He is Muslim; so he wanted to be at home on 6 December in case there were riots. And of course in Calcutta the safest place for a Muslim is Metiaburz, whereas it is the worst for a Hindu. What were you doing there sitting in the lion's den? Don't you read the newspapers?"

"I read about the ratha yatras, those decorated chariots that pulled crowds wherever they went, and invited people to reclaim a temple from a mosque. Frankly, they sounded like a lot of filmy cameos, full of gas. Who would guess a sane government could allow such a thing?"

"He was returning home just when the Babri Masjid was being broken, and he saw a mob beating a boy. He went right in the crowd, recognized you and managed to scream out that you were in his college and that your name was Bruce Lee. The punches and kicks stopped. You were not Hindu any more, but Christian. He and two others got an autorickshaw and brought you to the hospital, the only place safe from communal riots. And that too you were lucky, because within hours a curfew was imposed on Metiaburz. It ran out of control and the army was called in. There were sand bags posted at street corners. Tear gas bullets were fired, some soda bottles were used as bombs by the mob. People were butchered across the country. Hindus as first, then came the retaliation and Muslims were killed. So far reports say two thousand have died countrywide. He said he had phoned the hospital several times. He wanted to know about your family so that he could inform us. But neither could he step out of his house because of the tense situation in Metiaburz, nor could you be woken to supply him the information. The college phone lines were busy every minute, for days, and there was nobody to look up student details. Finally he managed to get through to someone who could find your local contact."

"My local contact is didima! Oh no, she must have worried herself sick."

"She is no worse; she was a policeman's wife. In a sense that was a blessing. She informed baba and ma immediately, which was a day after I started off. I was the only one who did not know."

The young man met Panchali at her hotel and told her everything. Ullu was alive. It could have been much worse. She was very grateful to him.

"Thank you, thank you, for saving my brother's life. I owe you a big one."

"Actually you owe me another."

"Oh my God ..." She was thinking of Raja mama holed up in Hyderabad with the football team he was coaching. Hyderabad was under the Nizams, the Muslim rulers, for centuries and was a city chequered with pockets of Hindus and Muslims. "Whom else have you saved?" she asked fearfully.

"You"

"Me?"

"Panchali, so you did not recognize me?"

She stared at him.

He smiled, "I am Ra the Egyptian Sun God."

"You mean you are the Rahim I met in Gaur, when we were teenagers?" Then the two talked like friends reunited after years, and filled each other in about their lives and hobbies and career aspirations. Rahim said he liked the play she had done, "Harmony".

She was aware of him being from the other religion, "You didn't mind my insulting the Muslims?"

"Insult? Not me. But I thought the Hindus would feel insulted."

"They did too. I managed to alienate both the communities."

Panchali's face became sad. "Rahim, can I tell you something? Something that is disturbing me?"

"Yes, tell me. Tell me all you would not even tell your best friend."

She was instinctively led to trust him, "I feel an anguish within, as if I have been raped, torn asunder. I had a faith that the common man does not harbour hatred towards a person of another religion. A wicked minority manipulates an innocent majority. Then I saw the frenzy atop the Babri Masjid. Who were those people?"

"A mindless mob."

"Those who see the need to avenge centuries of temple destruction, torture, forceful conversion, disrespect of their womenfolk, robbing of citizenship rights ..."

Rahim was hurt. "Panchali, at least you should not use the word 'need'. This is a politics of hate, and we know better than to give credence to it."

"Rahim, when it comes to human sentiments, everything gets muddled up. Maybe there is some genuine grievance that needs to be addressed."

"In other words, you are questioning if a person can shake off the history of his people." She was pensive. Rahim goaded her on, "Didn't you say revenge begets more revenge? Where's the solution here? Sant Kabir, who is revered as the apostle of Hindu-Muslim unity, denounced orthodoxy within all religions."

They got on a rickshaw and headed towards the hospital. She was still morose, as if it wasn't enough that her brother was alive. As if her many other dead brothers were crying out to be alive.

At last she spoke, "Rahim, this was long overdue, I have to admit."

"What? The demolition?" He whispered, careful not to be overheard by the rickshawalla.

"Hindu fundamentalism. But if a people cannot forget, they can still try to forgive. For the good of all. And I don't mean just the Hindus, Muslims too can."

Rahim laughed aloud, "Aha, the romantic is back."

Panchali also became jovial, "As Bernard Shaw says – people see things and ask, 'Why?' But I dream things and ask, 'Why not?'"

"And remember the other dreamer, Rabindranath Tagore?
Where the mind is without fear and the head is held high;
Where knowledge is free;
Where the world has not been broken up into fragments by narrow domestic walls;
Where words come out from the depth of truth;
Where tireless striving stretches its arms towards perfection;
Where the clear stream of reason has not lost its way into the dreary desert sand of dead habit;
Where the mind is led forward by Thee into ever-widening thought and action –
Into that heaven of freedom, my Father, let my country awake."

* * * * *

"Ullu, do you know Rahim?"

"Actually I cannot place him."

"He said so too. You do not know him; he is in the last year of college. I would recommend him as a friend. He could be your second Muslim connection." She laughed teasingly. "He is the kind of audience I would love to write my plays for." Panchali caressed Yuyutsu's sweating forehead. "Sleep now."

"Didi, is everything fine in Bangladesh?"

"Is she from there?"

He nodded. Panchali shook her head to indicate it was a sad story. "Temples, perhaps the very few that withstood the Partition and the Bangladesh War, were demolished. Again a stream of Hindu refugees came knocking at the Indian door. Same in Pakistan."

"I did not know there were Hindus in Pakistan."

"Maybe now there are none. Or some, you can count on

your fingers. After all, it was their home, and it is not so easy to abandon property within hours. One always hopes for better days. Besides, neighbourhoods take care of each other. We have seen this happen several times. Remember how the Sikhs were saved by their neighbours?"

"Yes, Selma's neighbourhood would take care of her, but not any Hindu." Yuyutsu said sarcastically.

"People are not vile. I believe it firmly. But when they form a mob a strange dynamic takes hold of them."

"Did Selma ever call the hospital?"

"She sought out Rahim as soon as the curfew ended. The poor girl did not even know if you were alive. He advised her not to contact you. Helping a Hindu could land a Muslim in trouble. It was best Sam D'Souza called you."

"Rahim is a smart one, isn't he? I was so angry with Selma I had decided not to meet her again."

"Oh, in that case she should blame you for the mosque demolition."

"You seem to take her side, as if you would not mind my being her friend."

Panchali swivelled around to face him, "Don't you love her any more?"

Yuyutsu turned his face to hide his emotion. Panchali stroked his hair.

"Love is a gift from God. Only a lucky few get it. Who am I to deny or grant it?"

Her brother squeezed her hand in gratitude.

A sad loneliness landed like a black raven in Panchali's heart. Yuyutsu slept happy as a child by his mother. She leaned her head on the glass pane of the airplane and looked out at the setting sun. She did not see her own reflection, but Shreyas, looking at her from among the clouds. He rested his forehead against hers and together they flew into the pink sky, her dearest companion, in joy and sorrow, always present, yet ever absent.

Chapter Twenty-five

Vasant

On Sunday mornings at ten, Sulaiman used to garage his taxi after denying passengers their ride. At nine-thirty some frantic person would hail him,

"Boss, I have to get home fast, the Mahabharata will start in a few minutes."

"Me too," said Sulaiman, "If you live in Metiaburz I can drop you, otherwise sorry."

The Mahabharata was not the code name for some disastrous attack that would wipe out anyone found out of doors, but was a television serial of the epic Mahabharata. All roads were on self-imposed curfew except those in front of shops that sold television sets. People watched the serial standing inside and the crowd spilled on the road. Two years back the epic Ramayana was screened on Sundays. Monkeys were seen peeping from windows at Lord Rama's army of monkeys. Sometimes they got so excited telegraph wires were in danger of snapping with their jungle acrobatics. The actor who played Rama got into some embarrassing situations. Simple-minded folk touched his feet in obeisance. In 1993, after the Mahabharata ended, the serial of Krishna's life was being telecast on Sundays, prime time. Mumtaz sat before the television in an attitude where only the incense was missing. Rahim tuned his amateur radio set and scribbled down Morse code messages he was receiving. He grew tense and called out, "Can you reduce the volume, abba? I am picking something interesting." His father closed the door after him leaving Mumtaz at her prayer seat.

"What is it?" The atmosphere after the Babri Masjid demolition was electrified. In several cities Hindu-Muslim violence broke out weeks after 6 December, as if someone was enjoying the division among people, and was making sure the Congress government would be condemned for mismanaging the situation.

Rahim placed his finger to his mouth, "Shhh!" After some more long and short beeps, the transmission completed. Rahim read what he had jotted down. "I picked this up from Bombay. Someone says he overheard a conversation about planting bombs in strategic locations. He was sure some major terrorist attack would hit the city shortly. I think the police department also caught the signals. One of the ham operators said adequate precaution would be taken immediately."

"I wonder how long it will take for us to forget the mosque. Weeks, months, years maybe. Is it asking too much from political parties to have some foresight?"

"But this is very much part of their plan. Parties play at ballot box politics. This Hindu party can get a straight eighty percent of the votes if they endear themselves to the Hindus."

Mumtaz had joined them in the commercial break, "Hindus don't like violence. I am sure the Bharatiya Janata Party has managed to alienate itself from the masses."

"No, that is not what I overhear from my passengers. Some of them seem to harbour a lot of hatred for Muslims and they are happy to find a political voice. The Congress party is doomed."

"Not so soon, abba. There is one person in the Congress government who is saving the day, Finance Minister Manmohan Singh. He is trying to globalize the Indian economy, inviting multinational companies to set up their offices in India, relaxing licence rules for entrepreneurs. India should soon be in the world's economic map."

"The opposition party has a tough task ahead. It needs a big item to wean away voters from the Congress. And so communalism is chosen." Sulaiman threw up his hands in frustration.

Despite tip-offs and police precautions, on March 12, 1993, in the early afternoon, a car parked in the basement of the Bombay Stock Exchange exploded, damaging much of the building and killing many people. Within hours thirteen bomb blasts rocked Bombay detonated from cars and scooters. Shopping malls, upscale hotels, cinema halls, a double-decker bus, the Air India building and a Hindu party office suffered from the explosions. In all 2450 people were killed and 700 injured. The Muslim underworld dons claimed it was in retaliation of the attacks on Muslims and destruction of their property after the Babri Masjid incident.

*****

Panchali waited to be called for the audition. The Dharma Theatre Company was looking for fresh female talent. She had seen the director-cum-hero, Vasant, act in many plays, was impressed by his performance, and was at that moment praying for a break in her career. The other co-worshippers were of all feathers – sophisticated storks in high heels, rustic peahens with rough features, tall as a crane, small as sparrows, chirpy bulbuls, proud eagles, jealous hawks, desperate vultures. The atmosphere was especially tense as nobody knew what role Vasant was looking to fill. Beauty was not the only criterion for stage acting; there were many other factors that came before a pretty face and perfect figure.

Panchali was called in. She repeated dialogues from the plays she had done. Vasant observed her from all angles; she was asked to imagine the audience in front. Then he raised her chin with his index finger and slowly traced it down her throat. She had stopped talking and waited for the finger to end its journey. But it ran on down the entire neck and continued. She looked at Vasant staring unblinking at her, in a challenging fashion. The finger had reached the limit of her tolerance. Panchali gripped his hand and snatched it away from her body. "I am not here to sell myself for this role." Vasant asked thoughtfully, "Are you sure? This is going to be your first taste of fame. From here on the audience will love you. I can make it happen for you."

"Not if my honour is at stake, because I will not allow it." She was angry and her eyebrows arched like two cobras ready to strike. What else did these men think they could get away with? Nobody has so much power over another. Vasant had started orbiting her, his gaze fixed on her flushed face and blazing eyes. He heard her rant but uttered not a word. Then abruptly he walked away, "Relax Panchali, you will get the role."

"What?" She was incredulous.

"I was looking for a lady to be Razia Sultan. You know her, don't you? The first female ruler of India in the thirteenth century, of the Delhi Sultanate epoch. If she did not have anger in her she would be wiped out. I wanted to see if you could get sufficiently enraged and how you expressed it, proudly or crudely."

"Sir, I am so sorry I misunderstood you."

"You were supposed to. Otherwise I would have failed you, like I did so many before."

"Nothing is worth the loss of your dignity. Razia honoured hers. From now on imagine you are a princess, daughter of a Sultan, heir to the throne of Delhi, with enormous power, but living with venomous snakes around." Vasant handed her the script and explained details of the role. She was hardly hearing him. In her ears sang a tune of jubilation. A dream had come true. She would act in the Dharma Theatre Company, and in the lead role of the Queen Razia.

There was a celebration at home for her appointment. After the revelry she declared her intention of dropping out from the master's degree programme.

Her mother was upset, "How is that possible? Your father and I are both M.A. You are the new generation and will be stuck at B.A.?"

Anand blew away Binapani's concern, "Why does she need an M.A degree when she has a career as an actress ahead of her? She can teach herself whatever she is missing with the faculties she has gleaned from formal education. Go, Panchali, follow your star."

"Oh baba!" She embraced him, "You are my hero."

Her mother was grumbling "And this is coming from the head of the department. What an example you are setting for the students, Anand."

"Bina, I will encourage talent over pedagogy and make no exception for any child. How many lucky ones are there who have the opportunity to hone their talent? Rarer still are those who can make a career of it. Lectures, exams, degrees are pitchers to hold water for the one who has thirst for knowledge. She can always get her fill from wayside ponds and God's gift of rain."

"And tears!" added Binapani, still angry.

* * * * *

Prahlad woke up with a start. The emergency siren was blowing. He scrambled to his feet and splashed water on his face. In the corridor he found the other cadres were buttoning their shirts, tightening their belts and running at the same time. It was dark outside. A thrill mixed with fear and anticipation rushed down his body, making the hair in his arms stand upright. Piush caught up with Prahlad, as breathless as him, "What do you think it is? War?" "Nah, I doubt if they would send us in a real attack. We are still learning."

The hall was packed with a hum of expectation, and red eyes shocked to wakefulness. The Colonel rapped on the table, "Is there anyone from the Latur district of Maharashtra here?"

It was the Maratha Regiment he was facing and many hands went up.

"You have been granted leave to be with your family. For the rest of you we have a big task ahead." The boys looked at each other in impatience.

"This morning about an hour back an earthquake struck Latur. From the reports rolling in, this has to be a massive rescue operation. We are going to fly in as close as we can get, then we will travel on trucks and jeeps. But the roads miles around are destroyed, so be prepared to trek and jog for long distance. Also there will be aftershocks. All you have learnt so far will come to your aid, plus much more will be demanded."

The Latur boys had started congregating, frowning in concern.

"Any questions so far, gentlemen?"

"How long will we be on duty there?"

"Well, we have seen severe quakes along the Himalayas, and elsewhere too, but in the recorded history of India such a devastating earthquake has never happened. It is too early to gauge the extent of damage, but we have been assured it is unprecedented. Pack your canteens for many days. I warn you, you may not get any rest henceforth. Every minute is precious for a person trapped in an airless hole, or with a concrete slab on his leg. Also the hardest lesson you will learn is to make the right choice. Those who cannot be saved, even if they are alive, should be left behind. The doctors will be overworked, you must remember, so do not burden them unnecessarily. Work as a team, do not waste energy, be safe yourselves and God speed."

He called out names of officers and showed them the map of Latur. Prahlad's leader handed out the roles and the boys ran to assemble the ladders, torches, ropes, axes, stretchers. They could see the planes landing in the indigo pallor of the fateful morning. Some people in Latur went to sleep on the night of September 29, 1993 and never woke up. It was a shallow quake measuring 6.4 on the Richter Scale, the kind that can cause the most damage. Mud and thatched huts were crushed like matchboxes, concrete buildings crumbled, roads split open. Food packets were airdropped, doctors, nurses and relief workers battled for weeks, but like destruction in a war zone, Latur, for miles on end, was left with deep gashes, hillocks of debris and the cries of helpless, destitute human beings. About 8000 people died and 30,000 were injured in the disaster. And the loss of livelihood and savings is beyond the domain of statistics. Some people migrated out of the devastated region to rebuild their lives elsewhere from the bottom up.

* * * * *

Panchali arranged her suitcase and chatted on about her upcoming trip. Binapani watched her silently. Finally the excited girl caught her breath. "Ma, are you still angry about the college thing?"

"No."

"Then why are you morose?"

"Traditionally when a girl leaves home, her parents cry

because who knows when her husband's family will bring her back to visit her old place?"

"Oof ma ... I am not getting married! I'll be back."

"And yet it feels the same." Binapani sighed, "You are embarking on a new journey. But before you leave, I have to tell you something important."

Panchali abandoned her packing and came to sit beside her mother. Binapani walked to her cupboard and brought out a small book.

"What is this?" asked the mother.

"A book," replied her daughter.

"It is also a spiritual map you will use on your inner journey. This cosmic poem encompasses a universe of human emotions, demoniac agonies, divine possibilities, worlds visible and invisible. It speaks of hope and discovery, love and tragedy, truth and beauty, and much more. It is a living experience, a power in action."

Panchali received the book on her palms. Then slowly she turned to the first page. "Savitri, a legend and a symbol, by Sri Aurobindo. Thank you, ma," she whispered.

Binapani weighed every word she uttered, "'This world is the heroic spirit's battlefield.'" The vision of a young man passed before her eyes. He touched his heart with his fist and said, "The revolutionary dies, but the revolution lives on."

Binapani held Panchali by her shoulders, "Go, my child, fight and win."

*****

Razia Sultan was a big hit around the country. The script was very powerful, in beautiful Urdu, and the performance was gripping. The troupe travelled to Delhi and Panchali got front seat tickets for her uncle and aunt. Then they went to Calcutta and there too she had a family reunion. Vasant himself acted as Yakut, Razia's stableman and her lover. Panchali adored the scene where she rode on the elephant out to the battlefield. She danced to the beats of the battle tambourine and learnt a little bit of sword fighting that Chitrangada knew so well by then. Panchali showed her love so deeply on the stage for Yakut that Vasant one day joked, "Panchali, I hope you have someone you love." He knew how impressionable young girls could be and one of the dangers of the performing arts profession was falling in love with the co-star. Then next month a new role comes up with a new hero and the woman's heart is muddled up. Sometimes before she can recover from one love, another is thrust on her. Or she imagines the on-stage pretence of love to be real, and when the hero walks away, she feels shattered. So Vasant wanted to make sure right in the beginning his heroine was not falling in that old trap.

"Yes, I love someone," she answered.

"Ah, that explains your realistic acting. And who is that if I may?"

"My hero, of course." She was getting into an actress' skin. Vasant smiled, "Keep your secret, little girl. I won't pry it open."

Razia Sultan was interested in her father's courtly activities from childhood. She wore a man's tunic and did not veil her face as was the custom among women. They were the first Turkish dynasty in India. She reigned from 1236 for just four years, but her achievements were significant. Her rule was marked with religious tolerance. She set up educational institutions that included teachings from the Hindu books of science and literature. She was a shrewd diplomat and played one noble against another to safeguard her position. But they could not tolerate a woman commander for too long. They conspired and attacked her. She and Yakut were killed, and her brother ascended the throne.

* * * * *

"Prahlad, how can you wear just a banyan in winter?"

"Aai, once you have spent time in the Siachen Glacier, you can chew ice and not rattle your teeth."

"Ah Kashmir, my dream vacation. Is it beautiful? Will you take me there some time?"

"Not yet, aai, sorry. They are trying to find the bodies of

those four hostages for a month now. I can vouch they were all killed."

"Shh, don't speak inauspicious words."

"Prahlad, your mother thinks all hostage crises end like in the Roja film."

"Yes, I saw that. It showed the trials of a honeymooning couple when the husband gets kidnapped. The militants demanded in ransom are not released from prison, the husband is tortured, but ultimately he escapes after many hoaxes of his death."

"We heard of that film from our Tamil friends. Then when the Hindi version was released, what a rush there was to get tickets! I think Maniratnam is a very sensitive director. Did you notice how he plays with light? Makes it magical."

"Finally through Roja in 1992, we saw the new face of Kashmir, once a paradise on earth."

"Savita, I promise, I will take you to Kashmir as soon as the problems are solved. Did you not hear what Rani's family went through when they were there?"

"Baba, what happened to them?"

"They were stuck in a hotel without food and hot water for four days. Curfew! Then on the fifth they were escorted out by the army, fearing for their life at any moment. Rani had never seen a gun before, and these men were sitting inches from her, holding machine guns. She trembled the whole way down to Jammu."

"Serves them right. Do you know how much tention these tourists cause us? It is hard enough to safeguard civilian lives."

"How about the army personnel? How safe are they?" Savita's forehead was furrowed with a frown.

Prahlad threw his arms round his mother's neck and sang
*"Saare jahaan se achha hindostan hamaaraa
Hum bulbule hai iski ye gulistan hamaaraa*
We are the birds in the garden we call Hindustan. Aai, how

will Kashmir become a gulistan, bed of flowers, if the gardeners don't work hard for her?"

Savita noted in her mind, her question was not answered. Atul hoped he had a normal kind of a son, with aspiration to build a house, like Yuyutsu, or teach in a school, or design a car, sit in a shop, a bank, a post office, work the fields, do anything other than this. He said not a word; just popped a blood pressure tablet into his mouth.

From 1989 militancy in Kashmir escalated to a state of constant armed conflict. Pakistani infiltrators were often found wielding sophisticated weapons. One of the strategic high altitude bases was the Siachen Glacier, 70 kilometres long in the Karakoram Range. It looked down upon Pakistan Occupied Kashmir and China. It was just 33 kilometres from Mount K2, the second highest peak in the world. It was the world's highest battle ground at 6000 metres above sea level. All along the ranges the Line of Control ran like a zipper, ready to split open. In winter the peaks were abandoned by Indian and Pakistani battalions because of the harsh climate. In October 1994 four Western tourists were kidnapped in Delhi by Kashmiri militants who demanded the release of ten members of their group. On November 1 in an encounter with the police, these militants were killed and the hostages freed. But the second foreign hostage crisis in July 1995 ended sadly. Out of the six tourists who were kidnapped in Kashmir, one escaped, a second was found beheaded. Intense search yielded no result, nor would the government hand over the twenty-one militants demanded in exchange. In December 1995 the militants announced they had no more hostages. These four people were never found – dead or alive.

* * * * *

Vasant noticed his plays were becoming heroine-centric. What was the matter with him, did he not want to be the lion of the jungle? Why was he satisfied to lick his paws and allow his partner to capture the hunt? Sometimes he wondered if non-professionalism had crept into his life, and he was beginning to love her. Or maybe it was luxurious to be loved, as Panchali did in her acting. He deliberately chose outstanding roles where the heroine was exactly Panchali's age. Jhansi Ki Rani, the queen of Jhansi, who had participated in the Sepoy Mutiny of 1857; Devi Choudhurani, a story by Bankim Chandra, about a woman who defied the colonists; the Rajput princess Jodhabai who married emperor Akbar; Noor Jahan, wife and political advisor of Jahangir, Akbar's son; Mirabai, the Rajput widowed queen who roamed India singing hymns of Krishna; Satyavati, matriarch of the Kuru family in the Mahabharata; Padmini who committed Jauhar when her husband lost the battle. Vasant played the romantic hero's role, to counterbalance the powerful character Panchali portrayed.

One day after a successful show, the troupe went to celebrate in a plush restaurant. The revellers exited one by one, and Vasant was left with a drunken Panchali. She was bubbly and acted out her many romantic roles. Waiters buzzed around them, catching snatches of the melodrama. Others came to congratulate and some who had seen the poster made up their minds to see the play.

"Shall we go on a boat ride?" asked Vasant.

"Yes, let's do that, like Satyavati did." She giggled at her naughty joke.

They walked through gullies packed with shining brassware and mounds of colourful spices. The noise of the market, a few bullocks and cows caught in the rush, ash smeared sannyasis, temple bells and mosque azans all mingled in this one fascinating city, Benares. Near the ghats of the Ganga the crowd had thinned out and a pleasant breeze played with the waves and Panchali's dupatta. She recited a poem bowing to the breeze as her paramour in a Shakespearean mood.

"In such a night as this,
When the sweet wind did gently kiss the trees,
And they did make no noise, in such a night,
Troilus methinks mounted the Troyan walls,
And sigh'd his soul toward the Grecian tents,
Where Cressid lay that night."

Vasant wanted to hold her in his arms so badly his ribs hurt. Something had to be done with his inner turmoil.

He found a cosy boat lined with cushions and tipped off the boatman to take his bidi break on the shore, in such a night as this. He rowed the boat till the city was a line of burning embers. Panchali was playing with the water,

"In such a night
Did young Lorenzo swear he lov'd her well,
Stealing her soul with many vows of faith,
And ne'er a true one."

Vasant set the oars down and came to sit beside her.

"In such a night
Did pretty Jessica, like a little shrew,
Slander her love, and he forgave it her."

Panchali leaned her drowsy head on Vasant's shoulder.

"What is it, O mighty sage? Why have you wrapped us in this white mist?" Vasant had hardly looked at anything other than Panchali so far. He was scared she would fall overboard. But now he was surprised at the charming sight that engulfed them. The fog was rising from the river and had indeed created a screen around the boat. Which way was the shore? Or did it matter? Panchali pretended to be Satyavati, daughter of a fisherman, who ferried people across the river. Once the Sage Parashar was crossing on her craft when he was struck by her beauty and wanted to possess her. So he created a cloud around the boat. Thus was Vyasa conceived, the sage who composed the epic Mahabharata, recounting the story of his own family. Later, King Shantanu, the greatgrandfather of the Pandava and Kaurava brothers, fell in love with Satyavati and they got married.

"Panchali, will you stop reaching down for the water, or do I have to do it for you?" Vasant retrieved her wet hand and held it in his. "We are not on stage now, this is real life."

"What is that?" She feigned to be scared, "Who is Panchali? Am I not Razia, or Padmini?" He wrapped her in his embrace, "No, you are Panchali. Now tell me, do you still love someone else?"

"As Razia I loved Yakut, as Padmini, Ratan Singh."

"And as Panchali, whom do you love?"

Her mind began its descent into reality through the thick clouds of intoxication.

"It was me you loved, through all these roles, you just saw me, Vasant, is that not true? Say it, say it, my love." He was kissing her now and her lips parted in a delicious smile. It wasn't just the superficial caresses on stage, but her body he had touched which met this unknown delight with eagerness. "Can love be thus too?" She surrendered into his arms. Vasant did not know what he had denied himself for art's sake. Human beings have hearts that rule over the mind, and so be it, for the heart is often purer than the mind. Why is it reined in like a wild horse, broken and tamed and tethered? Vasant looked at the rapturous face of the girl he loved, and as he looked her lips moved,

"Ah, Shreyas."

Vasant felt the sting of an electric wire. "Who is Shreyas?"

Panchali's plane crash landed on the earth. With a shock she realized she had uttered his name.

"So it was Shreyas all the time! Even I, Vasant, was just role acting for Shreyas?"

She had gone mute. "Panchali have you been so blind that you did not see me falling in love with you? Why didn't you stop me? Why did I give you the lead roles? Why did I pick the scripts that would fit your character? Why did I launch you into this theatre world, make your name a catchword, why did I place myself as your lover, in every drama we did together?" He was shaking her now, "Why? I eclipsed the hero's role to promote you. Are you saying all that sacrifice was in vain?"

Panchali whispered, as white as the fog around them, "Have you not warned me yourself from the beginning? That our friendship would be strictly professional?"

Vasant wanted to break something. He dug his oars into the river and the water accepted his rage submissively. The lights of the river bank grew larger. The only sound was the violent strokes slicing the water. Panchali spoke at length, so softly he had to stop rowing to hear her,

"If that is any consolation, Shreyas does not love me."

Vasant threw down the oars. "Then you are a mad woman to continue loving him. You are famous now, Panchali, anyone will come for your hand. You are talented and pretty and rich. I love you. Panchali, look at me; surely you could try to love me. There are no rules any more between us. I imposed that discipline on you, and now I am shattering it to pieces." He returned to her side and held her weeping face against his chest.

"Oh Vasant, it hurts so deep I cannot breathe sometimes."

"Yes, it hurts not to be loved. You just gave me a glimpse of it." He was crying too. "We are a helpless lot, we human beings."

Panchali spoke through her sobs, "I pray that I forget him, but I cannot. Even if I have no happy memories with him, I just imagine them. He is constantly with me in the deepest recesses of my heart. Vasant, I cannot deceive you, I am his bond slave, although he has no clue about it. Please, please don't cry. Let's forget about today and resume our lives as before."

"Resume what? Do you know what my life has become, for your sake? Panchali, I gave you sola anna mohabbat, and you return with do anna ka ehsaan." He had given her all the love he could muster and she returned it with a pittance of kindness.

Panchali wiped her tears, "At least that is more than what Shreyas gave me. Not for a day did he love."

"And yet you spin dreams around him! You have a deranged mind." He was getting wild again.

"Vasant, before you tear me apart with your words, take me to the shore and I will disappear from your life. I have honoured you and am much indebted, so do not tarnish that impression I have. You have been a mentor, a friend, and I will respect you for ever."

They had reached the banks and the boatman came running to catch the ropes Vasant flung overboard. He looked from one to the other and held his tongue. Vasant helped Panchali down, "Whatever has happened between us today, can I trust you to keep it a secret?"

Panchali was relieved to hear his composed voice, "Yes I promise, nobody will know it. Will you also keep a secret for me?"

She could not see his face shadowed by the faint light of dawn. But she knew he was a broken man, because she did not know how to be grateful to one who had sacrificed so much for her.

"Shreyas is your secret."

"Yes."

Vasant nodded, "I will keep it." She really loved this Shreyas, a lucky man, but hardly richer by his good fortune. To herself Panchali made another promise. She would never drink again to lose her head to such an extent that the deepest layer of her being could float to the surface and find an outlet through her mouth. They climbed the steps together in silence. The phantom of Shreyas walked in between. In the last stair Panchali turned to look at the river, and Vasant disappeared in the narrow lanes. The sun's heat was raising the curtain of the mist. Thin catamarans could be seen silhouetted against the orange wash of the sky. Fishermen cast their nets that fell soundless like cobwebs. Bells of the Vishwanath Temple started pealing and the Durga Temple answered back. Soon an orchestra of tinkling bells filled the air. A knot in her heart shook loose of its foundations and escaped the cage of her body towards the mark in the sky's forehead. A hymn of many voices rose up in the sky. She felt free of her past. It was an hour of new beginnings. One cycle had given way to another. And she would reconstruct everything brick by brick. She was herself again, Panchali, the princess who leaped out of the fire to clean up the debris of an era.

The sacred Ganga flowed before her, the Ganga who was called down from heaven, whose forceful descent was checked in Shiva's matted locks, who flowed over the ashes of the cursed princes and brought them back to life, purified of their past deeds. Like a mother, she soothed Panchali with her eternal song. "Look at that banana leaf that floats upon me. This morning it was on a tree, in the afternoon in a wedding banquet and now is its journey's last act. Those sheaves of hay bound together with string were limbs of a Goddess worshipped by thousands of people. One day after their little scene on earth all shall pass on. These moments of pain shall pass, the joys shall pass. The arms around your neck you imagine to be love shall pass, the pain of rejection shall pass. I shall absolve everything, I shall pardon everything, I am oblivion, I will wash your sins, I will wash your sorrow, I will wash your body away and you will keep the essence. What did Nachiketa tell the Lord who was bribing him with worldly wealth? Not with the ephemeral can the eternal be found, *Na adhruvai praapyate tad hi dhuvam*. Give up Shreyas, give up Vasant, give up your little person; grasp your true Self and you shall find All in it. Every stream empties in the sea – the one called Shreyas, the one called Vasant, the one called Panchali."

She walked down the steps that trembled under the surface of the water. Her feet found the clay riverbed. She was touching the body of her Mother, the Ganga, on whose lap lay the slain in eternal peace. The cold water felt her heart wounded by Shreyas, it smothered the lips Vasant had kissed, it caressed her hair as it rolled over her. Panchali raised her head from the holy dip and looked the sun in the eye. A man waist deep in water was chanting his morning prayer, "*Tatra ka moha ka shoka ekatwam anupashyata* – one who sees Oneness everywhere, how shall he be deluded, whence shall he have grief?"

Part Six

Chapter Twenty-six

Rustum

"Roshan?"

"Yes, Roshan here."

"It's me, Panchali."

"Oh hello, Panchali. What makes you think of me?"

"I am back. What are you doing these days, Motu?"

Roshan smirked silently at the endearment.

"Working with a theatre company, same as you, I suppose, only not as well known as yours."

"I have quit."

"Why? I thought you were all over Vasant."

"I want to get back to our old haunts – education, social awareness, population control, communal harmony, work with villagers, children ... what do you say? Motu, are you there?" There was a long pause. Roshan was fighting some emotion.

"No, I am not there for you."

"Are you serious? I was looking forward to our working together again. I have been thinking of a play on ahimsa, non-aggression. It is the story of ... "

"Stop, Panchali. You cannot use me whenever you like, and then just walk away when someone else turns up! Did you ever look back when Vasant picked you up? Did you think of me? I was just the jester in your life, a shadowy extra. When the king walked in, you danced away with him. I like the Hindi word for 'Joker' in the game of cards – ghulam, slave."

"I am sorry, I did not know you had expected anything."

"You blind girl! Did you even think how I felt when you deserted me?"

"Motu, what are you talking about? We were friends, right, just casual friends?"

"Yes, just that."

"Motu? Roshan?" The line went dead. She slammed the phone, and hissed in rage,

"That boy has ruined me and I don't know how long he will keep ruining me."

Her father had stopped to hear the strained conversation. He came and patted her head, buried in her hands.

"Who? Has Roshan ruined you?"

Her throat was choked with sobs. She shook her head in answer, "No, not him."

"Panchali, I can't stand you sitting there depressed all day. Maybe you should join the university, it will keep you occupied. Poor girl, you are lonely. Go visit your uncle and aunt and take your mind off the past."

"Baba, I have a drama to perform. And if no one is ready to help me, I will do it alone."

Binapani encouraged her, "That's the spirit, child. Like Rabindranath says,

*"Jodi tor daak shune keu naa aashe,
tobe eklaa cholo re.*

If no one responds to your call,
Walk on ahead alone.

It was Gandhiji's best song, I heard. And you said you wanted to do a play on ahimsa, isn't it coincidental?"

Anand rode on the swelling wave, "We will make it a family production, your solo debut, Panchali."

"And I will contact my Chinmaya Mission, Ramakrishna Mission friends to send you out again to villages."

"That will not be necessary, Bina. The city theatres all know Panchali, and lots of drama lovers will support her."

"But I will go to villages too, to entertain the poor who cannot afford a theatre ticket in a city, but who will come on an evening to the temple dais to colour their life by one little stroke. Then they can go home richer by the thoughts of compassion."

"Let me guess, you have chosen an episode from Mahavir Jain's life."

"You are close, baba. This is from Mahavir's younger contemporary – Buddha. It will be a start, and then I can employ full-time actors with accompanying musicians. All I need is one break away from the Dharma Company banner. But this venture is not a mono acting. I need a man opposite me. It is the story of Amrapali and Ajatashatru."

"If not Roshan, how about the other boy who used to act in your troupe?"

"I never thought of Tariq! I wonder what he is up to these days."

And so it would be Tariq, and no kinglier a person could be found for the monarch, Ajatashatru. Tariq had joined a software firm, but was willing to shift his career if the opportunity came knocking at his door. Anand said he would be glad to review her script, and offer the school premises for their practice.

Atul and Savita begged Panchali to stay in Delhi since they felt Prahlad's absence dearly. But their niece was too busy with her new play.

"Why ahimsa, Panchali? When we are attacked how can we not retaliate?" asked Atul.

"Uncle, don't think of ahimsa as a political doctrine or a military policy. It is a dharma, a process of self-purification, a way to rid ourselves of selfishness."

Savita answered, "OK, I have thought of one way we can apply unselfishness to our daily life. When you are sitting in the bus and you squeeze up on the seat to let another person sit."

"Or offer your place and stand up. Lots of people give up their seats to the aged and to women."

"Atul, I have another," said Binapani, "When you do not break a queue and respect 'first come first served'. Often a queue becomes a crowd and then the strongest ones shoulder their way ahead."

Anand saw a way to practise ahimsa. "When you speak

sweetly with everyone. It is especially useful when one is on the better side of a counter, like in a post office, or railway station, or bank. As the Upanishads say, *jihva me madhumattamaa*, let my tongue drip honey."

Panchali read aloud what she was jotting down, "Be gentle, be kind, be forgiving."

"And ask for forgiveness."

"Yes, of course."

"Here's another. When someone is waiting for you, you attend to him immediately. Some people enhance their importance by being hard to reach." Atul had worked with town planners.

"Yes, dishonesty is violence on others and unto one's own nature."

"The same degree of awareness is required for not coming late. It means you respect other people's time. Panchali, add to your list – be sympathetic."

"How about withholding information, like it is done to sell some questionable products?"

"Sounds like violence to me. Would you sell that to your own family?"

"I think we stumbled upon a clue. When unsure whether an action is aggressive, ask yourself if you would do it to someone you care for."

"And of course we cannot forget the contributions of Jainism," said Savita, "Even if some of us may find its practices too austere – sweeping the street to avoid stepping on insects, wearing a cloth over the nose, a vegetarianism that prohibits anything under the ground – we must follow its principles of ecological balance. Using water, soil, electricity, metals, trees, stones, food – in short all the gifts of nature – wastefully, is an aggression."

"And polluting is outright cruelty towards this great living Being – the Earth."

"You know, ahimsa is not just an inner strength. It has a powerful outward expression too. Think of the difference it makes when we are encouraged to attempt something hard or praised for our efforts. One who upholds ahimsa is not mean or jealous."

"Yes, benevolence is a gushing river that can break many dams. One kind word has a tremendous potential to transform a person's whole life."

Atul concluded "Now we see the utmost importance, and I can even add, the pressing need, of ahimsa as a social doctrine."

* * * * *

Anand had started making marginal notes, then threw away the sheets.

"Panchali, this won't work. Start again."

She rummaged in the dustbin for her discarded effort, "What do you mean?"

"Why have you used so many Urdu words?"

"Because it is the most romantic language I know."

"But think of the period, this is a historical event. Five hundred years before the Common Era there was no Urdu in India. Buddha preached in Pali, the language of the common man, and that is one of the most prominent contributions of the Master – his breaking away from Sanskrit, language of the educated class, and adopting the simplified spoken tongue."

"Pali is not spoken any more. How do you expect me to write, or the audience to understand?"

"I am not asking you to write in Pali. Choose your vocabulary to match it as much as possible. Which means no Turkic, Persian, Arabic words. Think in Bengali, it is derived from Pali. You will see that will disqualify some of the metaphors you have used."

"Which ones?"

"Farishta for example is a male angel with wings. There is no such being in Hinduism or Buddhism. Gods can fly by levitation, or are borne by their vahanas – the peacock, the eagle, the horse, the swan, the owl, and so on. Here's another. Don't use wine to describe the intoxication of love, but amrit, nectar, for exalted passion. Wine has a negative connotation, for reasons of its immoderate use."

"Oh baba, I was looking forward to ordering my genie around and flying on magic carpets," joked Panchali, "But you have snatched the Arabian Nights from me and given the Enlightenment of day."

The practice sessions had begun on Anand's school stage. Tariq and Panchali had a devoted ally, Tulsi, who played many roles off-stage – critic, prompter, props setter, light's woman and provider of dinner. Once Tulsi got irritated with Tariq,

"Are you some sort of wooden puppet? Ajatashatru is expressing his love for Amrapali. Show some emotion." Panchali observed Tariq looking up at the sky in resignation. It was a poignant scene, but Tariq was being a difficult lover. He could not reply to Tulsi in words, using the coarse tongue of human language. But his sentiments spoke lucidly. That night Panchali tossed about in bed thinking about Vasant and Roshan. Poor Motu, he had loved her when they were doing those fake romantic scenes. It must be quite burdensome to Tariq to love the wrong Amrapali. The next day, Panchali asked Tulsi to act out the scene as Amrapali. Ajatashatru held her hand and they looked at the moon together. Tariq's face was rapturous. No better pair of actors could fit the roles. Panchali despaired at her own blindness. She had been too eager to steal the limelight to notice the drama in the shadows. From now on, she would direct, be the witness, enjoy from afar, and allow those more fortunate, to love and be loved.

* * * * *

King Ajatashatru, "the one who has no enemy", did have an enemy in reality. He had enlarged his kingdom of Magadha, most of which was later known as Bihar, but failed to conquer the beautiful city of Vaishali. A brave tribe called the Lichhavi lived there and had weapons Ajatashatru's artillery could not match. So the king came up with a plan. During a battle, he took the clothes of a killed Lichhavi soldier and wore them. The disguise was so fitting that immediately one of his own soldiers knocked him off his senses. After the combat he was dragged back to Vaishali, and since nobody could recognize him, they sent him to be cared for by a ganika. Now ganika is synonymous with the word courtesan, but not so in those days. These were highly respected ladies of society with unmatched intelligence and many cultivated skills. They were sought after for their wide range of talents, including political counselling, soirees of poetry and dance, effervescent conversation. One such beauty, Amrapali, "Mango Blossom", nursed Ajatashatru back to life. When he regained consciousness he had forgotten his ruse and imagined himself to be king of Magadha, not a Lichhavi soldier. He ordered the attendants around the house, and Amrapali complied imagining him to have lost his mind with the blow on his head. Then Ajatashatru regained full control of himself, and slipped back into his role acting. Gradually, living with Amrapali, he enticed her to share the secrets of Lichhavi warfare. She disclosed everything and showed him the barracks and the weapons in them, for she was in love with this handsome man, no matter who he was. And Ajatashatru too fell deeply in love with Amrapali, and would have never returned to his earlier life as king, if he did not have the disquiet of royal blood coursing through his veins. Often he almost told her he was the mighty king, but refrained because every time he uttered the name of Ajatashatru, he realized Amrapali and indeed every citizen of Vaishali, hated him.

When he had learnt enough, one night Ajatashatru left the bedside of his beloved Amrapali, and walked out of the city gates. The king had returned and the people of Magadha were ready for battle. He shared his knowledge with his generals and they laid a death trap for the Lichhavis. In the battle that ensued, Vaishali was sacked, its people massacred, fire licked at the stately houses, and a rumour flew around that an insider had sold the most precious of Lichhavi secrets. It reached the ears of Amrapali and she came out to glimpse this rapacious monarch. One look at him made her shudder. There he was, her paramour, on the horse leading his army against her homeland. Not only was she betrayed in love, but he had beguiled her into betraying her own people. She alone was responsible for the defeat and the carnage. Shattered within, Amrapali, wandered out of her house in search of death. She walked to a forest and there she hoped a wild creature would take pity on her and end the anguish that tore at her breast. But it was not to be. Instead of a wild beastly roar, she heard a soothing hymn of many human voices fill the air with its sweetness, "*Buddham sharanam gachhaami*, I follow the path of the Enlightened One." She came upon a glade where sat a luminous being encircled by disciples drinking his words. She stumbled on his feet and wept bitterly. It was the Enlightened One himself, the Buddha, who lifted her from the ground, and filled her broken jar with the nectar of his words. She listened till her heart was calm and her faith in life restored.

Meanwhile Ajatashatru, the victor, rushed to Amrapali's house to reclaim her as his queen, to fall at her feet and beg for forgiveness, to do anything she wished of him. But the house was deserted, ransacked. He feared she too was pillaged like the rest of the city. He ordered his soldiers to find her and waited in terror, a king, yet slave of his desire. They found her among the mendicants wrapped in saffron. Ajatashatru came running to her and called her by the many names of love. But she did not betray a single emotion. "Amrapali, it is I, the wounded soldier. You gave me life, now you are my life, return to me, O my only one." He knelt down and placed his crown at her feet. "Amrapali, I am your slave, do what you wish with me. I have sinned against you, and I shall accept all punishment. But do not spurn me. What use is this lavish life if not shared with you?"

But Amrapali stood firm on her course, holding the begging bowl before the man who was ready to sacrifice everything for her. The mighty Ajatashatru's achievements, his kingdom, his wealth, the honour he gave her, were all too petty to fill the bowl. A person can be tortured, bribed, coerced for anything, but cannot be forced to fall in love. That is the difference between rain from heaven and the water teased out of the earth in a well. Even a king does not have infinite power. Ajatashatru had no right to turn his beloved away from the path of the spirit. He let her pass out of his life and followed her to the one who was more powerful than himself. He laid his crown at Buddha's feet and embraced ahimsa.

* * * * *

Tariq knocked on the door of the ladies' greenroom. "Panchali, someone is here to see you."

Her visitor, a young man from the audience, had a message "Ahimsa is wonderful and always relevant, but unless we identify with Ajatashatru, we will look upon it as someone else's problem."

Panchali considered his point.

"Madam, if you don't mind my suggesting, you could work on exposing the himsa, the cruelty that exists in our society."

"Why do I feel you have a real story to share?"

"Yes, if I may? The girl was the best student in the class, and her foolish father thought an academic degree would make up for lack of dowry. The groom's family pretended it would, but now they torture her. They abuse her and taunt her for being more educated than her husband, and yet at his mercy. She is treated worse than a servant, beaten and locked in the house."

"And of course she cannot complain to the police."

"Neither to her father. He does not have money to support her. So she does not tell him about her misery. If there is way to shame these people, to spit on their faces in public, make them realize their meanness ... I am hoping that would bring some sense in their thick skull."

"You know this girl well?"

"Yes, I ... I am her brother."

"You loved her?"

"No, no, I admired her. I am from a low caste. Marriage was not even a dream, but I cannot bear to see her so unhappy. I fear she will be provoked to kill her husband. And then the police will be all over the place."

"I will do as you say. If there is a way she can tell her own story it will be best."

"Impossible. Her family will not allow the defaming and they will torture her even more. But if you want women to tell their own stories, you could ask those trapped in the red light district."

"You know any?"

"Yes. She was widowed and do I need to tell you how she was treated after that?"

"No."

"She ran away and joined one of those establishments. Now she is trying to save money to rent a place and find a proper job."

"Was prostitution a better option?"

"Oh, yes!"

* * * * *

The Madam glanced at Panchali and from her expert reading of character changed her smile to show respect. Panchali explained she ran a theatre company and wanted to make a play. She talked to the women painted garishly for other people's nightly romp. The pathos that drove them to this profession transcended religion, caste, beauty, intelligence. The girls had these in common – poverty, misfortune, dependence, weakness and above all they were treated cruelly. One was abandoned by a husband who had chosen to marry a younger girl, another dealt with a sadist, some escaped murder attempts. There were rape victims whom nobody wanted to marry; orphans peddled in childhood; abandoned widows. Panchali took notes of the devious ways of destiny that brought these ladies knocking on this gate. She paid for their time and trained them. Since the women had to recount their own stories they acted spontaneously. Some cried on stage.

There was a hermitage called Tapasya where Panchali tended to a garden. Anyone who was sad could come and cry and none would question them about their sorrow. Some women met in silence at Tapasya, wept and left feeling a little restored. Then gradually they talked about their pain, and decided to support each other. They asked Panchali to help and she converted Tapasya into a school where the sixty-four skills were taught, as outlined in the Kama Shastra. These women became the talk of the town and cultured people welcomed them to their celebrations as entertainers. They travelled from town to city, creating their own Tapasyas, the gardens where flowers bloom on plants that were once twigs. When the curtains fell and rose again, Panchali disclosed the shocking truth that the story tellers were recounting their own life history.

"Tapasya means seeking the true Self is us. Every person needs a little bit of space and time for inner growth. There are many amongst us who have had no opportunity for either. Part of tonight's proceedings will be reserved to create the garden house of Tapasya. But this will not suffice and we would be grateful for your continued support."

Tapasya travelled around the country planting a smile on a sad face. The young girls were optimistic; they would contribute to build Tapasya, even if it were a hut in a village. Some wives told their stories, bravely risking the anger of their family. Some had the courage to walk out of their marriage, a practice regarded as taboo in Indian society. A magazine started criticizing Panchali for creating a feminist movement. "Divorce? That too initiated by a wife, the Lakshmi of the house? At this rate of westernization, young mothers would soon smoke and wear skimpy clothes."

The father-in-law wrinkled his nose, "Chhi chhi, my son's wife has a counter opinion, and threatens to walk away! I had never wanted him to marry a girl with a job. Now he is going to suffer!"

Then the reporter laughed, asking himself, "What was Tapasya after all – a fancy, not a reality. The women would go back to their brothels, and the proud ones at home would cover their heads in shame. As for Panchali, she would remain a spinster all her life. For who would love a woman with prostitutes as friends, who would tolerate her arrogance?" He was feeling very confident, "If there is any man who can defy my claim, I promise to shut up."

Panchali tossed the magazine aside. Vasant and Roshan should be happy they don't work with her any more. And Shreyas? Was he reading this and feeling pity for her, or was he shocked that she was a kidnapper of decency? It did not matter what the real Shreyas felt. The one beside her, the Shreyas of her imagination, gave her the thumbs up. He had walked holding her hand when she knocked at the rickety doors of ill repute. He had soothed her when she cried unable to bear the burden of knowledge. He knew her pain was as light as snow compared to the boulders that crushed these women. Panchali closed her eyes in peace. Shreyas stood by her, and nobody else's opinion counted in her scheme of things.

Contrary to Panchali's scheme, somebody else's opinion did count. A letter to the editor praised Tapasya and the author said he would be happy to be with Panchali all his life. His letter read like an art critic's and carried much weight, enough to flatten the flippant observer's mouth. Panchali looked at the address and the name. Slowly a vision rose before her eyes. During one of the shows from her days with Vasant, the troupe had stopped at Pune for a month. She was a devadasi, a lady offered to the temple to look after the deity. She captivated the landlord of the village and changed his corrupt ways, to the benefit of all. The devadasi performed a dance during the evening prayers, and later alone on a moonlit night. Apart from the zamindar on stage eavesdropping on her, there was another off-stage admirer. Once an actor was missing and Panchali called him to fill up the place. Rustum was very shy and declared he had never acted. But Panchali waved his excuses away. They became friends and he volunteered to be the ticket checker for the shows.

Panchali was grateful that after so many years Rustum should remember her and have the courage to stand by her. He concluded by underlining the importance of women's education. "In a nuclear reactor the fast subatomic particles are absorbed by a substance called moderator. Without it, a reactor would explode like an atomic bomb. Women are the moderators of society. They have the strength to absorb the pain and anger and insult and frustration men cannot deal with alone. That is how they control the explosions. That is how they heal emotional wounds. They embody the principle of harmony, of sympathy, of sacrifice. The collective will gets a higher precedence than their personal ego. They have compassion that weeps for the downtrodden, and kindness to stretch out a helping hand. A society that denies opportunity to women is doing itself much harm. Therefore women's education is essential for world peace."

She took the train to Pune and hunted down Rustum's house. Her steps slowed as she rounded the last corner. Children were singing a song that made her nostalgic, reminding her of the carefree days of youth.

"*Aao baccho tumhe dikhaaye,*
Jhaanki Hindustan ki ...

Come my little ones, let me show you
Glimpses of our country, Hindustan.

Is mitti se tilak karo
Ye dharti hai balidaan ki.

Wear this soil as a mark of honour on your forehead,
For this earth is soaked with the martyrs' blood.

Vande mataram,

Victory to the motherland, victory ..."

What a joy it was to meet a friend from the past, such a dear one as a song! She had reached her destination and right in front of the rows of children stood Rustum. The name of the school was painted on the façade, "Jagriti Vidya Mandir", – Awakening, the Temple of Knowledge. Ah, of course Jagriti! That was the film with the famous song they were singing. It was a 1954 super hit about an idealistic schoolmaster who instills patriotism among his students. In 1957 its twin film was made in Pakistan, called Bedari, which also means "awakening" in Urdu. The children filed out and Rustum came to greet his guest.

"Panchali, I am so happy you have come. It took me so many years to entice you here. Now you are my captive. That house over there is ours." They had entered the principal's office. Panchali looked around,

"What am I doing in the principal's office?"

"You are giving him company. He forgot to put flowers in the vase, so you have come yourself to fill the gap."

"Rustum, you are the principal! To think that we used you as a ticket checker!"

"It was my pleasure to work in your team. Besides I was just a student then."

"You give me courage to believe in Tapasya. Rustum, the second part of the letter to the editor was..." Panchali was about to say, "It was not necessary", but Rustum anticipated the hesitation,

"Yes, I do. Any day, when you want a shoulder to rest upon, I will be here for you."

"But I hardly know you."

"Oh Panchali, not all relations depend on number of interactions."

Rustum and his brothers were running their late father's several businesses and institutions. They were Parsis, Zoroastrians from Persia, living together in their joint family property and were always glad to welcome guests. Among themselves they spoke in jovial Gujarati, which Rustum tried to translate hastily, but Panchali stopped him. "Once you know Sanskrit, you understand all north Indian languages." She guessed the Persian words from her knowledge of Urdu. Rustum's mother fattened her on the world's softest chapattis dipped in ghee. She teased her son, "Rustum, we need a Sohrab in this house." Then she explained to Panchali, "It is a Persian legend of two valiant warriors, the seasoned Rustum and the young Sohrab. A long duel between the two ends with Sohrab mortally wounded. It is then that Rustum learns from the boy that he himself is the father, but neither knew it. It is too late and Sohrab dies in his father's arms."

Panchali conducted drama workshops in the school and enjoyed her new life so much she had almost forgotten about Tapasya. Rustum's sisters-in-law sat on the long swing with Panchali, shelling peas and telling her stories.

"We came from Persia a long time back. No one knows for sure when. The coast of Gujarat lies on the maritime Silk Route, which attracted merchants from the Middle East."

Dinaz continued the thread, "Commerce was one reason, but a huge group came when Arabs were Islamizing our country, which is now Iran, and were imposing the jiziah tax on us."

Gulbadan, the youngest jumped in, "Oh, let me tell this story. A boatload of Zoroastrians came to the shores of Sanjan in Gujarat and asked for permission to drop anchor. The king had very little room to accommodate so many new people. So he sent a message – a cup of milk full to the brim. The messenger returned within a day with the same cup, and offered it to the king. Upon drinking the milk, he realized it had been sweetened. The newcomers were saying, 'Sire, we will not be a burden to your land, but will enrich it'".

Parviz was passing by, and had stopped to listen to his wife's tale. "This is our popular legend. But one fact was, the king had wished us to adopt the Indian custom of clothing and language. Thus we brought our fire from the Zoroastrian religion, our prayer books and burial habits, but women gave up trousers for the sari. Within a few generations we spoke our own dialect of Gujarati and blended perfectly with the local culture."

Nazneen let the bowl of peas rest on her lap. "At first, most of us worked in the fields and just about made ends meet. When the British turned Surat in Gujarat into an industrial town, we joined the factories and were praised for our diligence. One of us came to Bombay and started a successful brokerage firm. He helped many more migrate to Bombay and within decades banks, shipping companies, textile mills, heavy industries were owned by us."

"We have a strong concept of helping the needy, and soon we became one of the richest Indian communities with large charitable organizations, hospitals and schools."

Panchali nodded, "The small Jain community is also like that – prominently wealthy and equally generous."

Gulbadan strung her arm around her new friend, "Culturally Zoroastrians and Hindus have no jarring note as both believe in the policy of 'Live and let live' and allow each other ample freedom."

Panchali asked, "And have the Parsis sweetened India as they had promised?"

Feroza answered, "Though a minuscule part of the vast

population, we have made our mark as doctors, in the armed forces, as educationists, as industrialists. Some have even reached rare summits."

Everybody around Panchali got excited and started fluffing up their feathers.

"The Tata family manufactures locomotives, trucks, cars; it started the airlines service, software consulting, a hydroelectric power station, the TIFR scientific research centre, the TISCO iron and steel company."

"The Bombay Stock Exchange was started by the cotton trader, Dinshaw Petit."

"Dr. Homi Jehangir Bhabha is the father of the nuclear energy programme."

"The Godrej family is famous for home appliances."

"Sorabji Pochkhanwalla started the Central Bank of India."

"Zubin Mehta is a world renowned orchestra conductor."

"Nani Palkhiwalla is a leading constitutional lawyer."

Rustum came and sat beside Panchali in the prayer room. She was scrutinizing a hand-woven rug hanging from the altar. Rustum explained, "This winged angel you see is the creator, Ahura Mazda. And on the altar is the fire we worship. It is called Aatash Bahram, Fire of Victory."

"Aatash? We use it in Marathi and Bengali. Aatash bazi means fire crackers. And what are these words embroidered here?"

"They are the three principles of Zoroastrianism – good thoughts, good speech, good deeds."

Panchali repeated the words slowly, tracing her finger over the words.

"Not that way." Rustum held her hand and pointed to the words "Start from the right side. Good thoughts, good speech, good deeds." He tightened his grip, "Hey Panchali, will you stay here? Forever ... ?"

"It is so tempting. I love your family. And you too. But I have to get back to my Tapasya."

"Bring your Upanishads and the Bhagavad Gita and let them rest beside the Avesta. You can pursue Tapasya, your spiritual practice, right here."

"And the other Tapasya? For which you have given me a new lease of life?"

Rustum was thoughtful, "Yes, I know, I cannot cage a bird, however pretty the cage."

"Rustum, can I return whenever I like?"

"Oh, that would be a treat for us!"

"Next time maybe I could learn some Persian to read the Avesta."

"You can read it now." He handed her the book.

Panchali's eyes widened, "It is written in Sanskrit! How is that possible?"

"It was translated by our priests way back in the twelfth century. You forget we have been in India for a thousand years. We are more Indian than Persian."

* * * * *

"Panchali! Where are you? Why do you keep your cellphone switched off? What if there was an emergency?"

"Ma, let's say I was in a forest hermitage, in a retreat from society. What is it?"

"How about letting us know? Oh forget it! Listen, there is some lawyer who is trying to get in touch with you desperately. He won't tell me anything, the old frog. I hope you are not in trouble."

"I don't want to speculate. I am back now and he can get in touch with me."

The city was so dusty and dry and fast and heartless, she wanted to catch the next train back to Pune. Maybe she was missing Rustum's manly shoulder to lean upon. The lawyer came to Panchali instead of calling her over to his office. Surely he had something very special to discuss.

"My client is impressed with your Tapasya project. He wants to sponsor it."

She was still thinking of the Jagriti school and planning more projects for the children.

"How much does he want to contribute?" She asked paying him a fraction of her attention.

"The whole of it. He says it will be a house with a large garden."

She snapped awake. Was it possible she heard him right?

"Who is this person?"

"Madam, I cannot disclose it until you sign the contract. Here." He turned the page around for her to read.

"Bunch of legalese! I have no patience for these long-winded sentences. Give me a gist of what it says. Surely he wants something in return? The plan was to make Tapasya self-sufficient. It is not a business enterprise."

"He knows it is not a regular investment." The lawyer inserted a paan in his mouth and took his time to chew it. "But he does want something in return, you are right. He wants you."

"He wants me to do what? Why did you stop?"

"Madam, you did not understand. He wants you."

Panchali flew into a rage.

"What kind of insolence is this? Do you think I am a person of easy virtue? I was fortunate enough not to have to sell myself like those poor women."

"Madam, madam, control yourself. I will tell him you do not agree."

"Sorry, Munshiji. I understand you work for any kind of client, but given your reputation, should you not exercise some discretion? Tell him I felt deeply insulted. Namaste." She got up abruptly. Munshiji polished his reading glasses before putting them in the case, "If you would like to reconsider, you can always call me."

"Get out! Obviously it does not hurt your self-respect to come with such a proposal, but it does mine to keep you around here another second."

Her mother called, "Panchali, so what was the lawyer business about?"

"Nothing important. He is researching someone I knew a long time back. I am going to have some more Tapasya shows".

"Good, the women have been pestering me to bring you back."

She would have to multiply the shows and present Tapasya in many cities for the garden house dream to come true, to create a shelter for broken souls, to build a place they could call Home.

Chapter Twenty-seven

Prahlad

Binapani heard the phone ring; Anand picked it up.

"Hello, is that you, Atul?"

She dropped the rolling pin, switched off the gas and came running out of the kitchen. Had the war ended? Was Prahlad back?

But Anand was quiet, and his hand trembled. "Can I speak with Savita?"

"Anand, I don't think she can talk now, we have just got the news ourselves."

"Atul, we will be there by the first available train."

Anand sat on the chair with his face hidden in his hands.

Binapani held him in an embrace and they both wept. It was better he cried now because Savita would need a strong shoulder to lean on.

Anand at length composed himself, "Bina, can you arrange for us to go to Delhi, now?"

"Yes, I will arrange everything. I will inform your college."

"And can you tell Yuyutsu ... can you inform our children?"

The word "children" stuck in his throat. His sister's only child was dead.

In 1990, more than 250,000 Kashmiri Pundits, of the Hindu priestly caste, left their homes for refugee camps in Jammu and elsewhere, harassed by the insurgents and their armed sympathizers infiltrating from Pakistan Occupied Kashmir. Only a few thousand chose to stay back even after witnessing the killings of their brethren. In March 1997 Pakistani infiltrators lined them up and gunned down seven Pundits in one go. The community was outraged, Muslims included, who paid their last respects alongside Hindus and Sikhs in the burning ghats. Again in January 1998, twenty-three Pundits were massacred, and this time women and children too. Analysts said, outrage against the innocent was just another way to lure India to battle and internationalize the Kashmir issue, which was supposed to be solved bilaterally under the Simla Agreement.

From 1996 to 1998 the various coalition governments in India played musical chairs with the prime minister's seat. In 1996, despite the unstable leadership, India decided not to sign the Comprehensive Test Ban Treaty, the CTBT, which was to prohibit nuclear tests, though she had endorsed its forerunner in Nehru's time when it was the Partial Test Ban Treaty. Her reason was, the other international nuclear treaty, the NPT, Non Proliferation Treaty, which pushed for disarmament, was not being taken seriously by the countries that had nuclear weapons. If it would be laissez faire in the nuclear race, India was in it. In May 1998, when it came to Atal Bihari Vajpayee's turn to be the prime minister, a series of five nuclear tests were conducted in Pokhran, in the desert of Rajasthan. Same place, same auspicious day, Buddha Poornima, twenty-four years after the first test. Before the Indian public could finish applauding Vajpayee's audacity, they were stopped by Pakistan's nuclear tests. The world watched this new nuclear theatre with apprehension, crying at the top of its voice, "Nukes are a deterrent, not war weapons! Caution! Do not use."

To defuse the tension, Vajpayee took a decisive step not taken by any premier since the formation of Pakistan. In February 1999, he went to Lahore in Pakistan, to accomplish a much-awaited, long-desired, gesture of friendship. He travelled on the maiden journey of a trans-border bus service from Delhi to Lahore, along with Indian celebrities – actors, sportsmen, artists, journalists, etc. Vajpayee and his Pakistani counterpart, Nawaz Sharif, made plans to increase mutual cooperation, share responsibility for nuclear weapons, safeguard human rights, and pledge non-interference in each other's internal affairs.

Ironically, at the same time, troops were being mobilized in the Himalayan heights along Leh-Kargil by Pakistan's Army Chief,

General Pervez Musharraf. There the temperatures dipped to -48 degrees centigrade, making every step a struggle for survival. When the Indian army returned to patrol the peaks in May, following their annual schedule, a shepherd told them about the occupation of some strategic peaks in the Kargil district. India launched Operation Vijay, "operation victory", deploying 30,000 troops in the sector. At first there were many casualties as soldiers were shot from the occupied peaks while trying to negotiate the only roadway connecting the border posts. The heights thereupon had to be scaled at night when the extreme cold could freeze one to death. The Air Force pitched in to help despite the limited visibility, and was successful is bombing some of the enemy strongholds. Thousands of land mines had been planted in the snow by the infiltrators within the Indian territory.

* * * * *

It was mid-June. In Delhi, soldiers marched bearing three coffins wrapped in the Indian tricolour. They were followed by unfortunate parents, a young widow, some little children, and the family of Prahlad. Other ceremonies for the martyred soldiers followed ... guns were lowered in salutation ... wreaths were placed on the caskets. Savita, held by Atul and Anand on either side, kept repeating through her sobs, "I don't want the Param Vir Chakra, I want my son back. Keep your titles and honours, give me back my little boy."

Panchali placed a golden rakhi beside the flowers. Prahlad had pledged to save his sisters and had braved all for it. The band played the anthem at a slow pace,

"*Jana gana mana adhinaayaka jaya he*
Victory to the guardian Lord of Bharat
Master of her people's destiny ..."

Yuyutsu looked at the camouflage cap Prahlad had gifted him a long time back. With a lump in his throat he placed it beside his sister's rakhi. Atul lit his son's pyre, and head bowed returned to his spot beside Savita. Panchali was blinded by her tears.

"Didi, open your eyes!" she heard Prahlad say, "Look and marvel at this beautiful creation. It too exists on earth!" She opened her eyes and there in front of her was not the Taj Mahal, but tall flames. Her brother, who played Holi with fire, had chosen his battle, had fought and died for it. The soldiers saluted their officers, and Panchali in her heart bowed low to the short but intense life. Somewhere on the other side of the border, a band played another anthem, and other set of widows and fathers and mothers and sisters cried for their loved ones.

Binapani was reminded of a song the poet Nazrul Islam wrote when his son passed away.

Shunno e buke paakhi mor aae phire aae,
In this lonely heart of mine, my little bird, return, O return.
"Jana gana mangala daayaka jaya he
O well-wisher of the people,
O destiny of Bharat,
Victory to you, a thousand times over, victory to you."

Anand prayed for the soul that had come on a short sojourn on earth as Prahlad, his nephew. A hymn from the Bhagavad Gita escaped his trembling lips,

"Ajo nitya shaashwatoyam puraano
Na hanyate hanyamaane shareere
Unborn, eternal, perennial, ancient
The soul perishes not in the perishable body."

*****

From mid-June onwards the war turned in India's favour as peaks were reclaimed one by one. Pakistan was criticized internationally and by her allies, USA and China, as the aggressor nation. In July, India regained most of the military posts and Nawaz Sharif called off the war. In the fifty days of war, 527 Indian soldiers died and more than a thousand were injured. Pakistan suffered comparable losses. Vajpayee became a hero and won the general elections for a five-year term. Almost immediately after, in October 1999, a devastating cyclone hit Orissa, killing more than ten thousand people, rendering 1.67 million homeless, uprooting and snapping 90 million trees, killing 2.5 million domestic animals, flooding 6600 square miles of crops, stealing the livelihood of 5 million farmers. Those who had donated for the Kargil War found themselves now donating for the cyclone relief. Many in the affected districts died of starvation and disease.

The defence budget was increased and a physical fence was being erected along the Line of Control in Kashmir. Already the largest weapons buyer among emerging countries, India started importing military hardware worth billions of rupees, from the Western nations. The chief suppliers were Russia, Israel, France and Britain. Pakistan suffered great economic hardships due to the war, Nawaz Sharif was ousted in a bloodless coup led by General Pervez Musharraf and martial law once again returned to the country.

* * * * *

Panchali stormed into Tariq's house.

"I need your help urgently. Sing me the Pakistani national anthem."

"Panchali, I am so sorry about your brother ..."

"Tariq, sing me the song, now." Tariq looked at her and knew she was in earnest. He picked up his electric guitar, plugged it in and made it peal in delight. Panchali jumped around. "Wow, you have an electric guitar. Excellent!" She was trembling in excitement.

"Why don't you sit and let me recall the tune." He hummed a little; then cleared his throat to sing,

"Paak sarzamin shaad baad
Kishware haseen shaad baad
Tu nishaane azme aalishaan
Arze Pakistan
Markaze yaqeen shaad baad.
Blessed be the sacred Land
Happy be the bounteous realm
Symbol of high resolve
Land of Pakistan
Blessed be thou citadel of faith."

Tariq stopped playing, "Seems like I have forgotten the words."

"Try to remember the tune at least."

"Relax Panchali! What's the hurry? I was too young and after we came to India I never heard the song again. What's the matter with you? Do you know how you look? Mad. Yes, raving mad."

Panchali went to the bathroom and looked at herself in the mirror. Who was this person? A loser? A crazy woman? Her younger brother had died fighting his battle, and she had not even begun hers. Tariq had brought her a glass of water.

"I think you are exhausted from the Delhi trip, I mean emotionally."

"The Pakistani national anthem. I need it, Tariq. Try to remember."

"I can ask my sisters. They were old enough to remember. I think Darya had sung it on radio too when we were in Peshawar."

"Where is she?" Panchali had got up to meet Darya.

"No, you will rest. I put you in house arrest right now." He dialled Tulsi's number.

"Yes, call her here. I have a plan for a new play, and we will have to launch it before people forget about the war. Call your sister too. She can teach us something."

The play was about the hardships faced by the common man because of the Partition. It was woven in with songs from all three countries where poets wrote about the fundamental unity in the culture of the subcontinent. In the second half, the three united to become one nation, and life changed drastically in all three regions. At the end all voices together sang the Indian national anthem. The audience had stood up to show respect, but sat down afterwards. The first chords of the "Paak sarzamin" played on a solo electric guitar, a poignant strain rending hearts. Nobody got up ... the violins and the keyboard joined in and played the same phrase. Panchali instructed the musicians to repeat till everybody in the audience stood up. People looked around at each other ... noticing the same few notes were being played again and again. After the tenth time, Tariq could stand it no more. He leaned towards Panchali, exasperated. "What are you doing? Is it their fault they don't know we are going to sing the anthem? If not for me, you would not recognize it yourself." Panchali bit her lips in sudden realization and took the microphone, "We are now going to sing the Pakistani national anthem followed by the Bangladeshi one." The audience rose en masse. Tariq heaved a sigh of relief, as did the rest of the participants on stage. Tulsi felt embarrassed at Panchali's public display of stubbornness, "Our team will desert you if you repeat that. I think you should take a long break and grieve for your brother."

"Where is the time? People are dying in Kashmir every day, my brothers, from both sides of the border. We need to stop spending for killing and getting killed ... can't we divert those funds for humanitarian causes?"

"You think it can be done by screaming from podiums, '*mazhab nahin sikhaataa aapas me baira rakhnaa*, religion does not teach us to hate each other'? Or singing the anthems?"

"I don't know what to do, Tulsi, Tariq. Help me. Guide me. I just know it is my battle and I need to fight for it. I cannot find the right weapons. Ahimsa is the only one I have. I can plant the seed, and hope some day it will sprout."

* * * * *

While the jubilant world was all prepared to welcome a new millennium, a drama of a very different nature unfolded in the subcontinent. On December 24 an Indian Airlines flight was bringing tourists from Kathmandu in Nepal to Delhi when it was hijacked by five armed Islamic militants based in Pakistan. The plane was diverted to Amritsar for refuelling but the hijackers suspected they would be overpowered on the airstrip and decided to ascend in the last minute, just missing the fuel tanker by a few feet. Fuel was so low the pilot wanted to make an emergency landing in Lahore, but the Pakistani government did not want to get linked with the hijackers and shut down the air traffic controls. All the lights along the airstrips were switched off, forcing the pilot, Devi Sharan, to try to land by sight. He almost landed on a well-lit highway instead of the runway, then pulled up just in time. Realizing this would mean a plane crash, Lahore airport allowed the landing. Once on the ground the pilot requested women and children to be let off, but again the Pakistani authorities rejected the request. The plane was refuelled and on direction from the hijackers was flown to Dubai, where 27 passengers were released, including the passenger who had been stabbed, and later succumbed to his injuries. The rest of the hostages were flown to Kandahar, in Afghanistan, where the plane, along with passengers, was stranded for days. The fact that the Taliban government was not recognized by India complicated matters. Fighter aircraft surrounded the hijacked plane, as if to make sure no attempt could be made by the Indian Special Forces to storm it. Indian negotiators managed to bargain the demand from the release of thirty-five imprisoned militants and payment of two hundred million US dollars in cash, to the release of three militants. The five hijackers and the three released militants were given a safe passage by the Taliban. On the eve of the new millennium, the remaining 166 hostages were flown back to India.

* * * * *

"Didi, didi, please save me" Panchali lifted a girl from the road clutching at her feet. "My father wants to sell me to the night club."

"Why?"

"My elder sister got married and had two daughters. Her husband blames her for not bearing a son, and now he has remarried."

"What does he do? Where does he live?" Panchali's voice was angry.

"No didi, please do not tell him anything. He said he will kill my sister. He does not do anything. When he needs money he forces my father for it, in return for keeping my sister alive. She is blue with bruises. But she has two daughters, so she fights on."

"I suppose your father needs money so badly he wants to sell you?"

"Yes, he cannot marry me off anyway. Please give me a little spot in Tapasya. I will wash the dishes, mop the floor, do whatever you say, but don't force me to return home. The brokers are waiting."

There was no Tapasya, it was an idea, an appeal, a prayer.

"Come with me, I have place in my house for you". That is where Tapasya would begin. "Some day we will rescue your sister too and her daughters."

Panchali took her leave from the three women who had found shelter in her house. Word was going around about Tapasya, and more hapless souls came begging to be accepted. But this was hardly the Tapasya of her dreams. How many could she keep and for how long? She went to Benares and encouraged prostitutes to share the story of their lives on stage. She worked with tribal women in Orissa and mothers in Rajasthan who had to abort their female foetuses. She contrasted the women of cities, the entrepreneurs and independent girls, with village wives beaten by their husbands, slum dwellers, cheated, overworked, ailing. She requested for grants from Non Governmental Organization sponsors, but they were interested in rape victims, those who were violated forcibly, not those who "chose" to sell their bodies voluntarily. That such self-degradation could not be voluntary was evident in every story, yet people did not have funds for Tapasya.

* * * * *

Yuyutsu left Kolkata and joined a construction project in Delhi so he could be with his uncle and aunt. Anglicized names were being replaced by Indian ones. Calcutta was Kolkata, Bombay became Mumbai, Madras was Chennai. Yuyustu's presence was especially necessary in 2001 because of a sad incident that enraged Atul to suffer a minor stroke. The defence budget was always enormous, and when a sting operation by a media company, called Tehelka, exposed the ugly corruption in the ministry, families who had lost loved ones in the many wars, were shattered. The Indian Armed Forces inspired the youth, their discipline was exemplary, they were rescuers of last resort, honourable and dutiful towards their nation, brave and self-sacrificing. Children like Prahlad grew up dreaming of the Ideal because of them. Yuyutsu tried to explain, "Uncle, corruption is within the ministry of defence, which is mucked up in red tape and politics. It is not the Armed Forces."

Tehelka created a bogus weapons company and sold fictitious binoculars by paying kickbacks to the tune of one crore rupees. During the conversations, that were being secretly video recorded, the officials boasted of other kickbacks they had received.

The low intensity war in Kashmir continued unabated, massacre of Hindu and Sikh villagers, burning of tourist buses, attack on the assembly house in Srinagar, capital of Jammu and Kashmir. Militants were trained in Pakistan Administered Kashmir and in the bases vacated by the Afghan Mujahideen. Their only aim was to annex Kashmir for Pakistan, contrary to the Kashmiris' dream of an independent country. To add to the woes of the ruling Hindu party, constant reminders of the Babri Masjid demolition dogged their tenure. In Gujarat fifty-eight Hindu pilgrims returning from Ayodhya were burnt in a train at Godhra. In retaliation, through March and April of 2002, Muslims were massacred, and then Hindus suffered the same fate. Instead of acknowledging the Tehelka report, the government drained the company resources in lengthy court cases. In 2003 when the company was all but bankrupt, private well-wishers kept it afloat. In the next elections the Congress party bounced back, led by Rajiv Gandhi's widow, Sonia Gandhi. The renowned finance minister, Manmohan Singh, was sworn in as prime minister in May 2004. Heads started rolling as the new government proceeded to act on the Tehelka report. The press was honoured; an essential limb of democracy.

* * * * *

"Throw these jihadis out of here!" a tipsy man banged on the table with his glass tumbler. Rahim held up his hand, Liaqat pulled himself off the guitar, Mir silenced his drums.

"Jihadis? Us?" asked Rahim in a cold voice.

"Of course! Who has destroyed Kashmir? Muslims! Who bombed our temple in the sacred city of Benares? Who attacked pilgrims going to Amarnath?"

"What has terrorism got to do with Islam?"

"Everything. Isn't it written in the Quran that you will go to heaven if you kill infidels?"

Rahim looked around at the gaping crowd in the club, "Have you read it yourself? In Arabic? A transliteration? A translation? An interpretation? An explanation? An inference? An extrapolation? A wishful thought? A hunch? A propaganda? You equate the word 'jihad' with murder, but do you know what it means?"

"Holy War!" cried Rahim's opponent.

"Very good." Rahim's voice cut through the silence like a razor blade. "Can you tell me the first word of the Bhagavad Gita?"

Someone immediately started singing out the verse "*Dharmakshetre kurukshetre samavetaa* ..."

"Stop, stop, stop. Dharmakshetra – doesn't that translate into 'Holy War'?"

"How dare you!" The drunkard was already up on the chair, had placed his foot on the table and was fiddling with his shoe laces. Liaqat approached Rahim and whispered, "Steam off, friend. We are a minority here."

Rahim turned to Liaqat, still holding the mike to his mouth. "What minority? What is the difference between Islam and Hinduism, or any other religion for that matter? We all believe life to be a pursuit of the Divine. And is the Divine so limited that only one narrow path should lead to Him?" Rahim composed himself and faced the audience. "The word 'jihad' means to struggle – a struggle against enemies within, a struggle against evildoers, a struggle to uphold dharma."

"Oh, really?" mocked the man holding a shoe in his hand. "What about the blasts in Mumbai in 2002 by Muslims to mark the tenth anniversary of the Babri Masjid event? Explain why in July 2006, seven bombs burst in the local trains of Mumbai. Do you know how crowded these trains are? Within minutes, 209 people were dead and more than 700 were injured."

Someone sighed in a loud voice. "I wonder how long we will be reminded of that shameful act."

The drunken addressed him now, "Which shameful act? Babar's demolition of the Rama temple?"

"Peace, peace." Boomed another voice. "Let the Supreme Court decide the fate of that disputed complex. Till then let's agree to call it 'Babri Masjid – Ram Janmabhoomi', Babar's mosque – birth site of Rama."

He was countered immediately, "Well, if it was just a nomenclature it would not be so painful. We don't want to create a new Jerusalem here. Do you know a wall cordons off the area and a unit of the Central Reserve Police Force guards it round the clock, always on alert? In 2005, they overpowered five terrorists who attacked the makeshift Rama temple. And this case just drags on."

The belligerent man turned back towards Rahim, "Jihad is a war against non-Muslims. What else is taught in a madrasa, may I ask you?"

"That view is just an interpretation of certain groups, and originally a madrasa was an Islamic school for religious studies ..."

"Yes, yes come to the point, young man. Hasn't it lately been disseminating radical ideologies?"

The club manager walked in with hands folded and faced the accuser. "My good man, you cannot possibly blame all Muslims of being terrorists! Let me remind you of the killing of Muslim villagers by Muslim separatists in Kashmir. These villagers had opted to cooperate with the Indian Army, and in return were given weapons to defend themselves. They hated the militants so strongly that they did not even bury those who died in the encounters. They said these militants were acting against the teachings of Islam."

"That is very true!" answered a voice from the back of the room.

The tipsy man curled his lips in disgust and turned around, "You Muslim?"

The man replied amiably, "I Indian." People smiled and many laughed aloud. A person walked over to Rahim and indicated he wanted the mike. He faced the audience.

"I am a journalist and my name is Harish. May I speak?"

Those who had stood up in excitement sat down to listen.

Harish started, "The Indian Army had launched operation Sarp Vinash, 'destruction of the snakes', in January 2003. Extensive bunkers, well stocked with provisions, were found in the mountain heights of Jammu and Kashmir and several militants were killed. Four thousand engineers worked round the clock to construct the 600 kilometre long fence along the Line of Control. Ground sensors – pressure activated and infrared sensors – were fitted along the high altitude fence. One night in June 2004, when in a border hamlet Muslim villagers were asleep, militants swarmed it to take revenge and started shooting randomly at them. Twelve people were killed. But within fifteen minutes the armed villagers retaliated and chased them off."

Applause broke out. Someone tapped the drunken man on his shoulder, "Take it easy, boss."

The manager grabbed Rahim's mike, "Now, I am no scholar, and have not touched the Quran, but the militants were accused of being un-Islamic by the simple-minded villagers of their own faith. So I say, let us not imagine division where there is none and let us not comment on somebody else's religion. And for heaven's sake let us keep religion out of politics. Rahim, sing!"

Rahim did not sing yet "One of the battles we need to fight together, people of all religions, is the idea that links Islam with terrorism. Does anyone know what the word 'Islam' means?" Rahim waited for a few seconds, then answered, "It means to bow down in submission."

* * * * *

Atul had a sudden heart attack and within days left this earthly abode, and his wife, all alone in the world. Savita had cried for so many years she had no more tears left when Panchali came to be with her. She was her daughter almost, the person who could read her sorrow without the need for words. One who had not found love was now closest to the one who had lost all love. They visited the Taj Mahal, hoping its beauty could heal the destitution in their heart. Savita and Panchali walked linking their arms, aunt and niece missing dear ones around them.

"Aai, I am here!" Prahlad waved from the bush, "Don't tell baba."

"Savita," called Atul from behind, "Have you seen Prahlad?"

Savita turned back but there was no Atul. She looked ahead, and Prahlad was gone. "Panchali, why are we here?" she cried out.

"To find Him who plays hide and seek with his devotees." Panchali looked at the magnificent Taj Mahal, she who will remain while men come and go. Where was He, the charmer of hearts, Mohan, whom she sought all her life, maybe for many lives? Would He wait till she bled, her feet pierced by thorns, would then her pilgrimage end? Was He really heartless, made of wood, of earth, of stone? But hadn't he told Arjuna that the Lord is hidden in every heart? He is the doer, they his instruments.

Ishwara sarva bhootaanaam hriddeshe Arjuna tishthati
Bhraamayan sarva bhootaani yantra aaroodhani maayayaa.

Then why was there still so much pain? Where was the shoulder she could rest her head on and go to sleep, and never worry about waking up? Where was his human reflection for Panchali? Did Krishna not love her enough? Or did he love her too much? The human lover wasn't there, he had never been there. Yet she desired him, wanted to hide him safely in her heart, wanted them to be happy, together, her and Shreyas.

Savita and Panchali sat on the ledge of a minaret looking down at the Yamuna, in a sort of peace, the calm that comes from being accustomed to long suffering. Two white birds, one widowed, one never married. "Aai, shall I sing a song I composed?" Savita embraced her "You called me aai, mother?"

"Yes, ma is in Mumbai, and aai is right here." She touched her heart. "Now if you make me cry, how will I sing?

I walked alone in the eucalyptus grove
Surrounded by the mystic scent,
And all I asked was to hear the leaves
Trampled by someone at my side.
I sat on the beach and watched my steps
One by one coming from afar.
And I longed for another pair of feet
To write its lyrics across the sand.
Did I hold the moon in my hands,
Or treasure a star in my ring?
Did I want to fly like a bird,
Or cascade down a mountain path?
But for the world it was easier to forget
The little figure in a lonely shrine,
And seal its multitudinous ears
To the muted prayer and the silent sigh."

The border between Amritsar and Lahore had changed. Savita and Panchali sat in the gallery with hundreds of others looking at the soldiers marching below. Two iron grill gates, a few feet apart, were latched, one painted in the saffron, white and green of the Indian flag, the other with the Pakistani crescent, moon and star on green background. The gates were then opened for a few minutes; two soldiers from the opposing sides met in the midpoint, shook hands and unfurled the two national flags. Pakistani tourists could be heard on the other side of the tall wall. In Amritsar, Panchali and Savita touched the bullet holes in the wall of Jallianwala Bagh, a garden where once a crowd had assembled to celebrate the harvest festival. It was the year 1919 when the people of India rallied for freedom from every nook and cranny of the country. The government looked with suspicion at any large gathering. That Baisakhi day in April, British soldiers stood at the narrow entrance of the garden and without any provocation, fired at the unarmed crowd of 20,000 people. Within minutes a thousand had died, many jumped in the well to escape the bullets, some perished in the stampede and many more succumbed at night, unable to reach the hospital. The event added fuel to the already burning fire of freedom struggle. At the Golden Temple, the dams the aunt and niece had carefully erected, fell apart and memories came flooding in.

> "I watched the sunset melt in the sea
> And the light through the fingers of the tree,
> And all I asked were a pair of eyes
> To share this beauty with me.
> Did I ask for the desert to fill with trees
> Or the mountains to lay down flat?
> All I did was to cup my hands
> For a drop of heaven's clemency.
> But for the world it was easier to deny
> Than lift my face to plant a smile
> And wipe away these pools of tears
> By the single gesture of a hand."

Punjab was back in the fold, grazing like a sheep. The shepherd, K.P.S. Gill, the police officer in charge of crushing the Punjab insurgency, had eliminated all troublesome elements, even the suspects. All had seen a film by the director, Gulzar, called Maachis, "matchsticks". It had shown the pain Punjabis went through in the 80s when insurgents and the police had both turned militant and terror ruled the state.

"It is so difficult to govern a country," sighed Panchali, "Khalistan was bad, but so were the killings by the police. Life is indeed a journey on the razor's edge, *kshurasya dhaaraa*."

They got on a rickshaw, and Savita nudged Panchali. The driver was pedalling with one foot; then waiting for the wheel to come round. His trousers flapped in the air where the other leg should have been.

Savita whispered, "Amazing how often we are reminded of our good fortune."

She clutched Panchali with both hands, "We have our limbs intact. What a blessing!"

A struggling man in the street, his leg blown away by a landmine, was God's messenger to light a lamp in Savita's dark house. Evenings were jolly again in Punjab. People were not afraid to come out singly or with their wives. The merry spirit was back, although some were maimed from the conflict, they had survived it, and India would too.

*****

One Sunday morning Panchali opened her door to a mother and her six-year-old daughter. The woman wore a soiled old sari, but her eyes shone with intelligence. It was obvious she had seen better days. Her husband had died in a factory accident. When she was alone at home, a man tried to break in. She screamed watching him chisel at the netting in the window, but none of the neighbours came to help. She screamed till she vomited blood. Her vocal cords were torn and took months to heal. Then she appealed for protection from the factory owner, for whose negligence her husband had died. He made her the family tutor and raped her at will. Not he alone, but any man in the huge house had unrestricted access to her. For a morsel of food he provided.

"Panchali, they are planning to abuse my daughter now. Will you keep her with you? Please?"

"And you?"

"Whatever I earn I will send you."

"No, I meant what about the way they treat you?"

"When one wants something very badly, one can sacrifice anything for it. I want to give my daughter a better chance than I got."

Panchali felt her own beating heart. Did she want Tapasya so badly that she could sacrifice for it, sacrifice something precious?

The lady went on, "Look, I know Tapasya is a dream. If there was such a place I would gladly fall at your feet and beg for acceptance. But we are those who lie awake at night and dream, we sleep during the day and dream, our minds and hearts are made of dream stuff. It is only our bodies that remind us to keep fighting."

"Tapasya is real." Panchali tried to steady her voice.

"Then show me the building you call Tapasya. How many women can it protect? Even if Tapasya is as big as the state of Maharashtra it cannot house all the women who are suffering in silence in our country."

"Tapasya is a state of being. It is not just a structure of brick and cement. It is compassion in people's hearts. Tapasya is in every home. Or will be. One day when a little grain of it materializes on earth, I will welcome you with open arms, and you will be the first teacher there."

*****

Panchali toyed a long time with the business card before calling the number on it.

"Munshiji?"

"Yes, speaking"

"This is Panchali. Do you remember me?"

"In fact I do. I am losing my hair but not brain yet."

"Remember years ago you had a client who wanted to donate for a project I was doing?"

The voice sounded interested. "Yes I do. Now let me see, you called it Tapasya, right? He was no mediocre client, and I would have made a fat commission from it."

"So Munshiji, is that offer still open?"

"After so many years? I really doubt it. But there is no harm in asking, haan, what do you say?"

The lawyer started laughing and ended up in a long cough. A fleeting verse passed through Panchali's mind, from Shankaracharya's poem, Bhaja Govindam. In his brief thirty-two years of life he had travelled the entire length and breadth of the country and had set up four mathas, monasteries. The hundreds of poems he had composed had caused a spiritual revival, in his era, around the start of the ninth century CE. Bhaja Govindam was a gentle rebuke to those attached to material life. "As the drop of water is fickle on a lotus leaf, such is life, short and uncertain." Panchali sang one of the stanzas to herself, "The body has rotted, the head is bald, teeth have fallen, he is walking with a stick, and yet he does not abandon desire, *tadapi na munchati aashaa pindam*. Therefore, before it is too late remember the Lord, you fool! *Bhaja govindam, bhaja govindam, bhaja govindam moodha mate.*"

Munshiji came hobbling on his stick, as Shankaracharya had foreseen, a file under his armpit.

"You are a lucky one! So what has made you change your mind?"

"My first white hair, I suppose." She brushed aside his nosy question.

"Ah yes, one is not growing any younger with time."

"But before I see the contract, I would like to add two conditions."

"Oof!" the lawyer was irritated now. "I cannot return again and again. Do you know I have arthritis?"

"Then maybe I should come to your office next time?"

"Can I just make a call right now?" He would risk no more delay to collect his precious fees. "What are your conditions?"

"Until Tapasya is built, I and your client do not meet, and his identity remains hidden from me."

"Now now, you ask for the moon, lady."

"Yes, something like that."

"Let me hear the second condition, and I hope it is reasonable."

"If I can pay off the expenses, then my contract with him is dissolved."

"Now this makes sense to me."

"Let me step out of here and you can call him."

Munshiji called her back in a few minutes, "I have no idea what he sees in you. I have never seen your plays and admit cannot appreciate art. What is all this about Tapasya?"

"Surely you don't want me to bore you with performing arts? So what did he say?"

"He agreed. He just asked where you would want Tapasya to be."

"You mean I get to choose the place?"

"Madam, you did not want to know who he is. But I assure you, some people are richer than you can imagine."

Panchali was smiling through her tears, "Then let it be in Brindavan, away from the city, on the banks of the Yamuna."

"That city of widows? You know that's what it is called. For some reason abandoned widows crowd there. I know why. There are so many temples from where they can get free food."

"You would not understand, Munshiji," thought Panchali, "What Brindavan means. One has to walk over deserts to know the true taste of water."

Chapter Twenty-eight

Chandidas

Pilgrims were walking in a crowd up the steep zigzag mountain pathway accompanied by loud devotional songs. Muleteers without passengers were bargaining with some breathless pedestrians. Four men carrying a doli, a basket with a person precariously hanging on to it, passed by, calling out from behind, "Side, side, please." It hardly seemed ten at night. But gradually in every bend they saw the city of Katra getting smaller, its lights grouping together and one by one switching off. When a mule frisked by kicking the dust, people pasted themselves against the mountain wall and let it pass. A landslide had killed many pilgrims a few months back. The rubble was still piled on the side, which constricted the road and often forced people to make a single file. The lassi and puri shops were getting sparse. It was a relief since each of these also sold the full worship regalia; a coconut, two betel nuts and its leaves, marigold and hibiscus flowers, some kumkum, a packet of red powder to dot the forehead, a lump of camphor. Competing vendors clamoured from all directions, "Sister, aunty, brother, uncle, won't you worship the Goddess up there? Come, come here." The songs blaring from loudspeakers repeated, Jai Mata Di, victory to the Mother. The higher they climbed, the air got cooler, the night quieter, and the crowd thinner. Panchali passed the same few people, who rested on the roadside parapet, then when she rested they passed her. They had formed a bond, and after a while they encouraged each other. The switchbacks were endless and at one point the landslide debris choked the passage to create a dangerous staircase. Panchali saw a hand reaching down and she quickly grabbed it. The mules clambered up slipping and getting back a foothold. Since they had four legs they could afford to have one of them dangle in the air for a while. The last of the shops passed by. Panchali stopped to drink water and fill her bottle. The sky was resplendent. There stretched the Milky Way galaxy, the Akash Ganga, the celestial Ganga.

Panchali had lost her companions and would have to find the next batch of pilgrims. She passed a woman, her belly full of her child, walking up step by step, panting and holding her back. "When had she started?" wondered Panchali. "Surely not at nine at night, like most able-bodied pilgrims." Katra was in the administrative region of Jammu, tucked well inside the Indian half of Kashmir. A divine child, Trikuta, born in south India, meditated on Lord Rama. She met him on his way to rescue Sita. Rama renamed her Vaishno Devi, spouse of Lord Vishnu, and sent her to a cave hermitage in the Manik Mountains, in what is now Jammu. He gave a tiger for her protection, an army of monkeys and bow and arrows. Every day thousands of pilgrims walked for fourteen kilometres to pay homage to the Goddess Vaishno Devi. Many would have come with a request for a boon; some as fantastic as stardom, or sudden wealth. The pregnant woman might have wished for an exceptional son. Or maybe she did not have children for a long time and had promised the Mother to return when she did conceive. But even more pathetic was the next sight. Panchali saw a man walking up performing a strenuous feat. He lay prostrate on the road, in the posture used to bow down before an idol, stretched fully, shaashtaang. With a chalk he marked the road where his fingers touched. Then he got up and planted his heels at the mark. Again he knelt and stretched himself. And thus he progressed, in a caterpillar's gait. His eyes were red and he was reeling with fatigue. He might lose his balance and fall off the precipice. Panchali remembered the little "Welcome" milestone at the start of the journey. It gave a statistic of the number of people who died in landslides, by exhaustion, by slipping off the sheer edge. Pilgrims uttered an extra prayer to remove obstacles from their present journey. What was he asking the Goddess, to suffer such punishment? Was he asking her to cure a terminal disease, or he had an invalid child he wanted restored? Was the Goddess that powerful? Could she reverse the dictates of fate that his soul might have himself chosen?

Panchali heard a man's voice behind her and felt glad she

had company. She hoped it would be a family with women. But her ears picked just one pair of steps and knew he was alone.

"What have you come here for?" asked the voice.

She did not answer, nor look back.

He continued, "All these pilgrims have a desire they want to see fulfilled. 'Give, give, give' is their loud cry."

She walked faster hoping to catch up with some others in every bend. It was disquieting to walk with a man all alone in the dark so close to the borderline between life and death.

"Women don't come here alone. Women don't do anything alone in India. It is not safe. Night is unsafe, this road is unsafe. If you are risking all this you surely want something dearly. Tell me."

"If you don't leave me I will scream."

"But lady, why did you come here alone?"

"If I tell you, will you leave me?"

"I am walking the same path as you. I cannot leave from here just because you are scared of me. I mean you no harm."

"Then prove it by walking ahead faster." She was unable to go any quicker herself.

He was not in any hurry to put her at ease. "Since you are on this arduous pilgrimage, you should also ask something from the Mother, however unreasonable. You know, miracles do happen."

"If you don't leave me alone, I will jump."

He scoffed at her. "You cannot."

"Are you challenging me?"

"No. I know you cannot because Shreyas won't allow you."

Panchali's foot as though hit a stone. She stumbled. "Careful, the road is narrow." She could feel his breath on her back.

"What do you know about Shreyas?"

"Whatever your mind suggests. Let me read; someone very close has died. You are mourning him. Maybe that's what his name is, Shreyas!"

"No!" Panchali turned around to face her pursuer. She wanted to fly the distance that separated her from Shreyas that very second and cover him with her wings. No harm would come to him as long as she was alive. He existed and that was enough for her to continue living, just as the Taj Mahal existed. They balanced off all that was ugly and mean and dark and sad. The man's face was creased with age. He wore a dhoti and a home-spun lose shirt. He had a metal pot in hand to carry water, a kamandalu. She smiled in relief. He was a spiritual man, maybe a sadhu, no mischief monger.

"Babaji, I lost my cousin brother; then his father passed away, all within the last few years."

"And Shreyas? One, two, three, four, five, six, so many times scribbled over and over again in your mind, like the names of Gods devotees write on paper to drop in temple offering boxes." Panchali walked beside him, but did not answer.

"Is that why you are alone?"

She nodded.

"Ask the Goddess and she may grant him to you."

"No, I don't want Shreyas. But I do want something else. Can you guarantee she will give what I ask?"

"Guarantee is not a word Gods care about. Their scheme is different from ours. But depending on your tapas, you could barter one for the other."

"How does that work, babaji?"

"Do you know the story of Vishwamitra?"

"Sage Vishwamitra who composed the Gayatri mantra?"

"Yes, him. This story tells of a time before he became a brahmarshi, the highest rank among rishis, to use popular language. He was a king who gave up his kingdom and started doing tapasya, spiritual practices. At that time Sage Vashishtha was the greatest of them all, a brahmarshi, one who knows the Brahman intimately. Vishwamitra was badgering Vashishtha to grant him the brahmarshi accolade, but Vashishtha insisted on calling him rajarshi, a king-sage. Then comes the twist in the tale. Trishanku, an ambitious king, wanted to ascend heaven in his mortal body and had approached Vashishtha to help him. The sage did not want to grant an unnatural boon. So Trishanku went to Vishwamitra who was arrogant and wanted to outshine the one he considered his rival. He made Trishanku rise, but Indra, lord of heaven, pushed him down. Vishwamitra used his power to stop him midway in his fall and created a heaven for Trishanku in the middle regions. All his tapas was used up, he had to return to rigorous austerities. Again he demanded the brahmarshi title, and was refused. So he attacked with his whole army and killed Vashistha's many sons out of rage. Then he started hurling his lethal weapons at the Elder. Vashistha resisted the attack with just his short wooden stick, the brahma danda. Only then did Vishwamitra realize his folly. These are his famous words,

Fie on the strength of the warrior,
True strength is spiritual power.
A single stick endowed with it
Has destroyed all my weapons.

Dhik balam kshatriya balam
Brahma teja balam balam
Ekena hi brahma dandena
Sarvaastraani cha hataani me.

This is the power I was talking about – tapas – to create a heaven, to conquer an army."

"But then when did Vishwamitra compose the Gayatri mantra?"

"Ah yes, the story goes on. Vishwamitra was still very angry with Vashistha for holding back the title. So he stormed into his hermitage. But when he was outside the hut, he heard his name being mentioned. Vashistha's wife, Arundhati, was complaining to her husband that Vishwamitra had killed their sons, why was not her husband, the most powerful rishi of all, punishing this cruel man?

"Because I love him," said Vashistha. "How can I wish ill of him?"

"Hearing this Vishwamitra had his last transformation. Can you guess what that is?"

"Repentance?"

"Yes, which comes from humility, an essential virtue, superior to knowledge and power. He fell at Vashistha's feet and the elder said, "Arise brahmarshi." That was the moment when Vishwamitra became a brahmarshi. Later he composed the Gayatri mantra. Now do you understand – ask that for which you can match your tapas."

"What if I ask for the unification of India, Pakistan and Bangladesh?"

The ascetic looked at her sharply in the dark. Was it possible she was also a member of the fraternity? No, she wasn't. She was a seeker of unity in her own way. Maybe his and her ways could meet. But did she want it that badly? He wanted to find out.

"And what are you capable of sacrificing for it? Do you have such a lot of tapas? Ask something simple for yourself. Not that which will affect millions of lives."

"I have no dearer wish than this, in my heart."

"Start then with sacrificing Shreyas."

"I cannot. Remember when Yudhishthira lost the gambling game he bartered himself first, then his wife. But he was disqualified because he did not own his wife at that point. I don't own Shreyas."

"But you could sacrifice your love for him."

"Would you ask me to sacrifice my love for Lord Krishna?"

"No, but Shreyas is not Krishna."

"For me, babaji, he is the human representative of Krishna."

"No, he is not. Don't fool yourself. You desire him, and since you know you can never get him, you say he is Krishna. Don't belittle Krishna to be human. Shreyas may never love you, but Krishna always loved you, and will always love you."

Panchali was thoughtful, "Will it suffice if I give up my love for Shreyas?"

"No. Have you done any nishkaama karma, a deed done as an offering to the divine without expectation of reward?"

She started tentatively, "When I loved Shreyas I did not expect anything back from him."

"Again, don't fool yourself, child. If you loved without expectation, why is your heart crying all the time? There is only delight in that kind of selfless work. What better feeling than to be an instrument of the divine? Does the flute decide what the musician should play?"

"Then is there no way I can ask for peace between the three countries?"

There was a devastating famine in the year 1770 in Bengal, which wiped out a third of the population. The wandering spiritual seekers, Muslim fakirs and Hindu sannyasis, organized themselves in groups and lived in forests. They looted from the British tax collectors to distribute wealth among the hungry multitude. These were the men Bankim Chandra lionized in his novel, Anandamath. They were the ones who sang Vande Mataram and worshipped their country as the Mother Goddess. The fakir-sannyasi rebellion was suppressed with much difficulty, but could not be put out completely. The legacy of the revolutionaries continued down the ages, through the turmoil of the World Wars, the madness of the Partition, and the conflicts ever since. And none felt it stronger than those in Kashmir. The man Panchali called babaji was one such sannyasi for whom India's independence was a sacred duty. His motherland had to be freed before she could assume her rightful place in the world. For, the sannyasis believed, she had much to do for humanity. And her bondage was her fractured psyche in a divided body.

"I am a worshipper of Shiva. You may have heard about Kashmir Shaivism. Our practice is the control of energies. Do you know the word for 'control' in Sanskrit?"

"Tantra."

"Yes, we are Shaivite tantriks. You know, these Himalayas are home to thousands of sages who can change world events with a single thought?"

Panchali was suddenly animated. "Show me such a man. Surely one of these luminaries would want India and Pakistan to stop this bloodbath?"

The sannyasi directed his piercing regard and searched her inner being. What he saw pleased him. Panchali had the marks of a suitable sacrifice. But she would have to come on her own.

"I am willing to pay. Will anyone help me?" Panchali's questioning was urgent.

He laughed. "Money? They can get whatever they like sitting on spot – knowledge of the remotest part of the world, things precious and rare, people's obedience, control of destinies. Offer something else."

Panchali rummaged her mind but could find no answer. The sage continued,

"What did your brother give to the cause?"

"His life."

"Can't you do the same? Were you not going to jump some time back anyway?"

"Give up my life too? Isn't it enough that so many soldiers are dying?"

"This will be a different death, a ritual sacrifice." His tantrik friend from Bengal, another freedom fighter, believed such a deed could appease certain forces. And these forces were powerful enough to reverse the Partition and heal the nation.

He assured her, "I know a man, a worshipper of Kali, who has the power to make it happen."

Panchali was not assured. "But when Arjuna says he would prefer to die rather than kill his kinsmen, Krishna chides him for being faint-hearted. He asks Arjuna to be his instrument. *Nimitta maatram bhava Savyasaachin.*"

"Not all instruments are destined to live on, child. Imagine, one death can save millions of lives. Sage Dadhichi sacrificed his life so that Indra could make a mace of his bones and kill the demon Vritra."

Panchali heard Prahlad's voice whisper in her ears, "Didi, this is my battle and I need to fight for it."

At the summit they queued up to visit the cave temple of Vaishno Devi. People were chanting Jai Mata Di and touching their earlobes with their fingers. Mules standing in a line chomped from sacks hanging from their neck. Men, women and children were scattered on the ground, sitting, sleeping, eating, talking. On the way down Panchali saw trees hosting monkey circuses. The tamer creatures sat by the roadside – mothers picked lice out of children's bodies, sisters played at catching each other's tails, fathers hollowed their mouths at men challenging them to step closer, sons extended their cute little black palms for groundnuts. The walk down was much smoother with daylight breaking through the clouds. Panchali repeated the Gayatri mantra – the chant that is whispered in the ears of boys when they start on a spiritual quest, the chant that is repeated by men at the two twilights – beseeching the supreme sun to illumine their mind. The mantra vibrated within, filling her with peace and joy and provided a cadence to her walk.

Her companion left her at the entrance of Katra.

"If you really wish for unification, consider sacrificing your life. It may work. I have read what is written in your inner being, and the fire I see is pure. Meet me in Murshidabad during the fakir mela, this year or any year, when and if you are ready."

* * * * *

The contractor for Tapasya called Panchali, "He, you know who I am talking about, says you wanted a Krishna temple in the complex. Shall we make it on the riverbank?" The contractor had accompanied her to Brindavan and worked through the details of the arrangement. He also kept her apprised of the sum spent, as specified in the contract. She saw the numbers rise and knew there was no way she could pay herself out of this debt. He wanted to use marble for the mansion, but she said she would be happy with a floor strong enough to stand a hundred dancing feet and a roof that did not leak. No fancy materials or designs were needed. She wanted to keep costs down. But for the temple she agreed to marble, the purest stone the earth could produce out of her meditation, her own tapas. Panchali would touch it, close her eyes, and imagine she was sitting in the Taj Mahal. She would hear the same Yamuna cascading by, and feel the river's breath on her cheek. Kadam trees would be planted around the temple and the women would play Holi like the gopis of yore. On Diwali each girl would float an earthen lamp down the river. Those flickering points of fire would travel far, bearing the message of hope.

* * * * *

The year 2007 saw major changes in the subcontinent. Prabhakaran, leader of the LTTE, was killed in a special operation. Tamilians in Sri Lanka would be integrated with the Sinhalese, and peace would be established in the island after the thirty-year civil war. In Pakistan from 1999 General Musharraf had ruled and now, in 2007, the democratic forces were clamouring to return. Benazir Bhutto ended her exile and came back to lead her party in the elections, but a bomb in her car ended that wish. Her party won and her husband, Asif Ali Zardari, rose to power.

In Bangladesh, Mohammad Yunus of the Grameen Bank was awarded the Nobel Prize for peace in 2006. His schemes had provided livelihood for lakhs of poor people who would have otherwise been recruited in the terrorism industry. Mother Teresa was awarded the same peace prize in 1979 for her charitable work in India. The Indian economist, Amartya Sen in 1998 had received the Nobel for his contribution to welfare economics, that which affected developing nations. Financially, India was growing by leaps and bounds. The information technology boom swept many in the middle class to the upper echelons of prosperity. Wireless networks won over the mosquito-net of overhead wires. The milkman, the istriwalla, the newspaper boy and the rickshawalla, all had cellphones. Televisions replaced radios, cables replaced antennas, computers replaced typewriters, e-mails replaced letters.

And yet there was terrorism. Several bombs ransacked Uttar

Pradesh. The Samjhauta Express, the train that ran from the Indian capital to Lahore in Pakistan, was a symbol of "accord", as the word Samjhauta meant. It was started in 1976 after the Simla Agreement between the two countries. A bomb burst in that train while passing through Haryana, India, killing sixty-eight people, mostly Pakistani passengers and some Indian guards. Clearly, some factions were opposed to friendship between the two countries. The Delhi-Lahore bus which had started operating from 1999, did not stop even during the Kargil War. But in 2001 when the Parliament House in Delhi was attacked by Pakistani militants, the service was halted for a few months. On the positive side another connection, that used to be the oldest, over the Thar Desert, was revived after forty-one years, in 2006. The Thar Express connecting Jodhpur in Rajasthan to Karachi in Sindh had stopped operating when its tracks were bombed in the 1965 war with Pakistan. A bus connecting Srinagar to Muzaffarabad, cities on opposite sides of the Line of Control in Kashmir, started operating from 2005. There were talks about starting several other bus services in the same region.

* * * * *

Panchali could wait no more. She journeyed to Murshidabad and found the fakir mela, the fair that was the confluence of three spiritual paths – the fakirs who were Sufis, tantriks, a sect of Hindu yogis and bauls, renegades of all classification. She stood in the middle of a colourful crowd wondering how babaji would find her. The three shades of ascetics commingled and regaled in each other's discoveries. She recognized the bauls playing the ektara, the single stringed guitar. Some wore orange clothing that shone in the sun, and others were wrapped in patchwork. She came close to their merry throng singing verses couched in double meaning. Baul songs pine for the mystic being within. They called him the moner maanush, the man of the heart.

> Where will I find him, the man of my heart?
> Forlorn I seek him all over the land
> For that precious moon

My heart is ever in swoon
Would I not rejoice if I found him again?
My eyes would regale night and day.
The fire of my love is burning me out,
Yet in his absence my being cries aloud
See it for yourself, tearing my heart apart.
It is not easy to find him, friend
Whosoever has perceived him
Alas, has covered himself in ashes
In this world of outward things.
I do not know where he resides
The heavens too wonder where he hides.
Friend, if you see that mystic man
Hasten to ease this painful knot
And tell me where he can be caught.

Panchali observed the fakirs in their long white robes. They anointed one another with couplets of profound beauty inlaid in a tapestry of qawwali songs. A chorus of Wah wah flew up in the air like gentle applause. And the tantriks were there too, rudraaksha garland dangling over a red robe, ash smeared forehead, seated on tiger or deer skin. Some of them had imposing physiques – straight back, oily skin, bare torso, jet black locks, hand resting on a wooden stick shaped to hold a formidable wrist.

"That is a brahma danda, the one Vashishtha used to destroy all Vishwamitra's weapons." Panchali turned around.

"Babaji, how did you find me?" She felt glad to meet the man she spontaneously called "father".

He waved the question aside. "Come, I will take you to my Shakta friend, Chandidas." Under a banyan tree surrounded by fakirs and bauls were seated some tantriks. They wore a red kumkum mark on their forehead and had matching red eyes, enough to scare Panchali.

He bowed to an imposing figure, "Pranam Chandidas. This is Panchali."

"Babaji, where are you going?" Panchali's voice shook in panic.

"Don't worry, child. His outward appearance is like a pumpkin but inside too he is as soft as one."

Chandidas placed a jute mat on the ground and indicated with his hand, "Sit." Is this what a Shakta tantrik looks like? The Shaivas were less frightening. Babaji was like the soft spoken fakirs.

"My friend says you desire something."

She looked around not to be overheard "Unification of India, Pakistan and Bangladesh." Suddenly a political wish seemed out of place in this celebration of the spirit.

"And are you ready to sacrifice that which you hold most precious?"

She nodded.

"Do you know what sacrifice means?"

"Whatever Krishna says in the Gita. Yad karoshi ..., whatever you do, offer that to me."

"Do you offer everything to him?"

"I pray before writing a script or going up on stage for acting. I mean I invite him to act through me, but I know that is not offering everything."

"Do you know what human sacrifice means?"

"I did not even know it was still practised."

"What you know is a single shell on a vast ocean bed. As long as you are dependent on linear knowledge you will know only what a journalist reports. It started with the practice of offering one's blood to the mother Goddess. You know she was created to drink blood, the blood of a demon called Raktabeeja. Blood is her food, but it is not that red thing which flows in the body of creatures. It is a symbol of the praanamaya kosha, the life plane. To gain power or knowledge in the higher planes people sacrificed in the material and life plane. Shakta tantriks who adore the Mother do not think worship using blood is a barbaric act. Offering life is superior to offering material oblations. Over the centuries it got watered down to spilling the blood of animals."

"Yes, I have seen goats in the Kalighat Temple waiting to be slaughtered."

"Then the animal lovers stopped that practice and in most places it is a pumpkin. The sacrificial vermillion powder is applied on it and it is quartered in one stroke, like in a guillotine." Panchali's breath ran out of her. She saw a giant blade crashing above her neck.

"Are you afraid to die?"

"I am afraid of the path it will take."

"This is better than dying of disease. It will happen in a fraction of a second."

"Is it necessary?" She suddenly wanted to be far away from her own resolve. Wouldn't she be a better instrument if she were alive? Then she saw Prahlad's face before her eyes. Her one death had the power to save so many lives. She had to believe in it. She would force herself to believe in it.

The tantrik smiled, "Look at you clutching at life! Don't you believe in reincarnation?"

"Yes, but will it really bring unification, at least amongst the people? I mean I will not be there to know the results, and I want some assurance that it will work."

"You are afraid to sacrifice. People do it all the time. Look at mothers taking their children from football practice to singing class, fathers working in factories to feed their family, boys and girls studying to earn a living, to marry, and sacrifice for their children. Such is the cycle of life, full of sacrifice. People have accepted, not knowing what it is. Because the intermissions are filled with festivals they think it is a leela, a divine game. But no, it is sacrifice of their entire life. The whole creation is a giant yajna, a sacrifice, of the Lord. Only those who can step on the shore can see the river flow. Only they can choose a cause to sacrifice for. And you, who have no husband or child, are that lucky person."

"I understand," came a subdued reply. Panchali was not convinced of her lucky state.

"But let me tell you, it will not happen without effort. You have to do your tapasya."

"On myself, to increase the spiritual potencies in this body?" She saw a long path vanishing into a mist.

"What I mean is you have to work towards making Love amongst people a concrete reality. Your sacrifice will be the concluding act. You have to convince people about its possibility. All their positive thought energies are needed for this work. I will entreat the Mother on your behalf. The rest is Her will."

"Then I have a lot of work to do."

"Get started right now. And find me when you are ready. I need to prepare the offering – that is you."

"Find you where?"

"In Tarapeeth at the temple I worship, or in any of the three fairs, the baul mela at Kenduli, the fakir mela in Murshidabad or at the tantrik mela in Kamakhya."

"And where will the sacrifice happen?"

"It will happen in a burning ghat in the middle of the night."

"In Tarapeeth?"

"It can be anywhere. Give me a date and place and I will be there."

"Then as my last wish, can it be in Agra?"

"Yes, it can be."

She could then spend the last minute of her life in the eternal edifice of hope, the Taj Mahal.

"Wait." He said. Panchali sat down again. "Do you know the mahamrityunjaya mantra, the hymn that will remove the fear of death? Repeat it to gain courage."

"Yes.

Trayambakam yajaamahe
Sugandhim pushti vardhanam

Urvaarukam iva bandhanaan
Mrityor mukshiya maa amritaat.

We worship the three eyed one, Lord Shiva,
Who is fragrant and nourishes all beings.
As the gourd is severed from its bondage to the creeper,
May he liberate us from death and lead to immortality."

The tantrik's voice became soft, as if he was talking to his own daughter, "Panchali, have you seen a fat pumpkin dangling from a thatched roof? It is attached to its tendril but tenderly. A little wind can drop it. Let your attachment to death be as slender as that. Then will you taste immortality. Bondage is an illusion, maya, a disease that hurts. Drop it. Your friend and lover is within you and walks by your side. Illusion is looking for him outside. Rishi Yajnavalkya, the 'one who wears sacrifice as bark', was a man of great knowledge taught by the Sun God himself. Students came flocking to his gurukula; he was wealthy too in worldly ways. But one day he decided to drop them all, like a tree drops its bark in winter. That is the sign of a jeevanmukta, the free in life, the true enjoyer. All this sweetness you crave after, a man's love, people's respect, wealth, security, are nothing but sugar, artificially manufactured. Once you taste the honey of the divine, these will fall away. Be the jeevanmukta and conquer death. The one who denied you love has done you a great favour. One less snare to snap."

Panchali recalled a line from Sri Aurobindo's writings describing the state of union with the Beloved. "All that is left of the personal soul is a hymn of peace and freedom and bliss vibrating somewhere in the Eternal."

Chapter Twenty-nine

Rahim

One shrill vibrating note woke Panchali from her reverie. A grinning baulini, her hair tied in a bun above her head, brought her ektara close to Panchali's face, "*Moner maanush dharaa dilaa naa*, so did the man in your heart slip away?" She pressed Panchali's cheeks as she would to a little girl, "I know why you are sad. He had promised to return and did not."

"Oonhu," Panchali denied it.

"Then maybe he did not send a letter?"

"Oonhu," she shook her head from side to side.

The lady pulled Panchali up by the hand and the two of them skipped to the clearing. A man followed them beating a dugdugi, a drum that hung as a side bag from his shoulder.

"Then tell me, shoi, little friend, what is weighing on your heart?"

"Ah," sighed Panchali lacing her arm round the baulini's neck, "It is a long story and life is too short to tell it."

"Did he not fill your pot with his essence?" asked the baul.

Other bauls had come scampering like children. They danced in rhythm at the dugdugi's pace, surrounding Panchali and posing her tricky questions.

"Did he steal in like a thief when you were asleep?"

"Oonhu."

"Did he tear your veil like a despot?"

"Oonhu."

"Did he part the curtain gently like a lover?"

"Arre, then why would she be so sad?" a baulini shoved the silly baul with her elbow.

"O ho, I know what happened."

"What? Please honour us with the revelation." Panchali pretended to be curious.

"He went away with someone else."

"No, not even that. Let me tell you the secret. He never came."

"Then shala he never loved. Forget such a heartless one."

"Tcha tcha," clicked Panchali's tongue, "He is in Mathura, a busy king. Why should a slave of his bother him?"

The bauls and baulinis rested their hands on their waist ready for a fight.

"What kind of king does not pay tribute to love?"

"I say he is a thief. He stole your heart and never paid for it."

"Eyi baandi, hey slave girl," a baul leaped in front of Panchali's face, "Forget the cruel lover. Come with me, and I will fill you with nectar."

The baulinis burst into raucous laughter.

"Why do you laugh?" asked Panchali.

"Because he had promised us the same treat."

The baul came to embrace Panchali. "I tried. They were all broken jars. But come my sweet one ..." Panchali darted off like a doe and hid behind one of her new-found sisters.

"Is our prince floating on a cloud of ganja?"

"He is ever in love, shoi, and is there anything called sober love?"

"Then love me!" A fakir tripped in on uncertain feet, "My beard is white but my love ever green."

"Why, father," retorted Panchali, "Have you lost your staff that you need to loan my shoulder?" All the ektaras echoed the same question.

"This one is conquered by wine, that one by ganja. Now sister, which of these vices would you rather choose?" asked a baul.

"Ah, you make me long more for my absent lover."

"A lover who cannot love!" They all tittered like birds.

Then a wonderful voice leaped on the stage, "Here am I that rascal lover who can indeed love."

They all encircled the newcomer. Panchali stopped her dance, "Rahim, you?"

"Yes my dear, you pine for me and yet cannot recognize me?"

"If you disguise yourself as a kitten, how can I spot the tiger?"

"Look you all, how she mocks me while I suffer for her. Panchali, I have been waiting for you from the day I aimed the arrow at your heart."

"How so? I saw no arrow flying hither."

"Witness feminine cruelty, brothers. Here I stand, Partha, for five thousand years, and she, Panchali, pretends to love another."

The prancing bauls and whirling fakirs clucked their tongues, "Is that so? Panchali ignoring Partha! Then it is a great injustice unto him. Come let us fling her in his arms." In one sweeping gesture Panchali was lifted off her feet. "One, two, three!" She flew off in the air wondering how she allowed these little chimps to play their game. She landed in Rahim's strong arms, yet again.

"You better bear your own burden; we have other hearts to mend." The colourful crowd scampered away.

They were alone and Rahim put her down on the ground. He then kissed her in the mouth, a long sweet kiss. When the intoxication receded she pushed him away. "Rahim, what are you doing?" She was angry with herself most of all.

"I could not help it. The golden light of the dusk has embraced you as a flame lights up its earthen lamp. This is the hour when prospective brides are shown to their new family. The crimson sky touches up a face with its pink make-up palette. The girl looks as if she is visiting the earth for a brief lifetime and would return to Indra's court as the apsara she really is."

"And what was all that about Partha?"

"I am Partha. And Rahim too. It is an interesting story. I will tell you if you stop frowning."

"Tell me, Rahim-Partha, what you are doing here."

"Can I ask you the same question?"

"You first."

"I come here every year to this fair for the past many years. I have a fakir friend, who is my murshid. He is too old to travel alone and so we come together."

"What is a murshid?"

"Madam, you are standing in Murshidabad and asking what a murshid is? Oh sweetheart, I was teasing you. Murshid means 'teacher' in the Sufi lineage. Now you tell me."

"Oh well, I got to know a tantrik who invited me here. This event is so rich in songs, poetry and spiritual discourses; I thought maybe I could use some of these in a play."

"Panchali, do you like it here?"

"It is wild and intense, as if an undiscovered person in you rushes out and you have no control over it."

"It is deep too. There is much to learn. I always go back full of spiritual wine."

"Rahim, I want to hear your story."

"Not today. It is not a sunset story. Shall we meet at the banks of the Ganga tomorrow before sunrise?"

Panchali nodded. Again it would be the enchanting Ganga and a handsome young man by her.

* * * * *

Rahim pointed at the eastern horizon where the clouds had just begun to blush. "That river is Padma and this one flowing southwards is Hooghly, the same Ganga, sacred river of Paradise. I will tell you a story of many rivers, of confluences of religions, of broken lives adding up to a whole family. The Padma flows into Bangladesh where she is joined by Jamuna and Meghna. Together the three journey towards their bed of eternal rest, the sea. Between Meghna and Padma is a town called Sonargaon, where once lived a young couple, Madhumati and Balaram.

The story was sad and hopeful, a lyric of struggle and victory, a ballad of love and sacrifice. Panchali laid her head on his shoulder and he strung his arm around her. The dome of the mosque was silhouetted by the rising sun, and it shimmered on the river's face. Rahim recited from Omar Khayyam's Rubaiyat he loved so much.

> Awake! For Morning in the Bowl of Night
> Has flung the Stone that puts the Stars to Flight:
> And Lo! The Hunter of the East has caught
> The Sultan's Turret in a Noose of Light.
> Dreaming when Dawn's Left Hand was in the Sky
> I heard a Voice within the Tavern cry,
> "Awake, my Little ones, and fill the Cup
> "Before Life's Liquor in its Cup be dry."

"Panchali, do you think it is just a coincidence that we should meet again and again in such wild ways? I have been waiting for you for a long time, over the span of lifetimes perhaps. Those little stars that hold the keys of our destiny have created a Partha and Panchali so that in some life they can be together, happily united. What do you say, my dove? This time their conspiracy will not have failed."

Drops of tears ran down her cheeks and wet his shoulder.

"What is it moonbeam, unburden your charm on me."

She nestled in his chest and cried for a long time. "It is all over, Partha. Some deed has been signed and I am enslaved."

"Is there some Yudhishthira, some elder brother I am not aware of?"

"No, but there is a Duryodhana I have sold myself to."

She told him about the sponsor for Tapasya, but did not mention the other contract with Chandidas.

"At least you have one way out. By paying off your debt."

She looked at the sky. "It is beyond my means."

"Let me see if I can rescue you, once again." He was hatching a plan.

They went to a shop that sold magazines since Panchali

wanted to know what Rahim did. He had said, "There is an article in Science Today you can read. Why would I waste our time together talking about quantum mechanics?" The shopkeeper disappeared under a desk and got out a whole pile of Science Today magazines. They sneezed and waited for the dust to stop dancing. Splitting the pile in two they started their hunt. Suddenly her heart stopped beating. He was there on the front page, Shreyas, looking as dashing as ever, not a day older, as if screaming to his teammate, "Hey, pass the ball." She took two magazines home and rushed to read about Shreyas. He had set up a seed bank in a rural area at the foothills of the Himalayas, close to Dehra Dun. He said the Green Revolution was a failure in the long run as fertilizers and pesticides poisoned the soil. Genetically modified seeds had to be replaced with natural seeds and the earth nursed back to life. Farmers were fooled into buying these High Yield Seeds because they produced more food, faster. But the seeds were expensive, depleted the soil, and worst of all they were unusable after one season. Some ghastly term called "terminator seed" shocked Panchali. Even if the seeds could be collected, the farmers were not allowed to, because a foreign company had a patent on them. In Shreyas' farm indigenous seeds were gathered, saplings were grown and distributed. There was an analysis of the farmers' suicides, the numbers of which were staggering. The more Panchali read the greater grew her conviction that Shreyas was doing a valuable service to the agriculture community. He encouraged farmers to end their slavery to foreign producers of genetically modified seeds. Workshops at his place taught natural methods of agriculture, which were the traditional ones, but now had to be re-inculcated. Panchali's heart swelled with pride; yes this was the boy she had admired from ages back. She imagined a street play using the Ramayana parable. Rama would be a farmer, Sita his land, whom he would have to rescue from Ravana's clutches. At the end they could burn an effigy of the demon, this seed company.

* * * * *

Rahim returned home and asked his mother about the Chakraborty house. The last they saw of it was a charred ruin.

"I want to see what has happened to it."

"After all, it is his," pointed Sulaiman, "But why after so many years?"

He told them about his beloved, Panchali, and her Tapasya. So the three got Bangladeshi visas stamped on their Indian passports and flew to Dhaka.

"Mumtaz Begum, we left the country with Mujibur Rahman as the leader of the oppressed Bengali people, and we return in his daughter's tenure, in a free land of the Bengalis."

"Yes, mia sahib, I am doubly proud because she is a democratically elected woman leader." Sheikh Hasina Wajed was the prime minister of Bangladesh from the beginning of 2009, in her second term in office.

They took a train to Sonargaon and Sulaiman and Mumtaz walked along the streets as bemused as Rahim. They could not recognize any feature. Housing colonies, schools, markets, honking cars, heaving rickshaws, watertanks. No ponds, or huts, or birds, or fields. It was a city, not a village any more. But surely the sacred banyan tree would not be felled. They asked the hotel manager, "Accha bhai, have you heard of any ancient banyan tree around here?"

"Yes, the one opposite the haunted house? People go there to pray. Don't go at night. You can hear ghostly screams."

"Which haunted house?" Mumtaz whispered the question.

"The Chakraborty house."

A shiver ran through the three of them. They hastened to the banyan tree, each one shut in his own world. Sulaiman held the iron gate and patted the creepers. This was where he had met his wife, and soon Rahim was born. Mumtaz pushed the clanging gate, but a chain padlocked from inside resisted her attempt. She shook it impatiently. "It stands, the house stands. It is not taken, Rahim, my child, it is yours."

A man appeared from inside, his dark oily skin shining in the sunlight. "Go away," he indicated, "This is a haunted house."

Sulaiman cried out, "Badal!"

The man swivelled around.

Mumtaz said, "Badal, I am your boudi. Will you not let us in?"

The gardener had peppered hair. He scratched his stubble and looked at Rahim.

"This is Partha, remember? Rahim."

Badal thought for some more time, then waved them away. "Other impostors have tried this before. Go away."

"Mumtaz, after coming so far is this the welcome we get?"

"Think of something, ammi, can you remember some feature of the house that only you would know?"

She shook her head. "We had the Durga Pooja here, the whole neighbourhood came, everybody knows this house as well as me. And then there was the Gopal temple in the garden where we played Holi."

Sulaiman suddenly grabbed the iron gate and screamed, "Badal, do you still have Gopal under the earth?"

Badal this time came right back walking fast. He approached the three of them and looked carefully at their faces.

Sulaiman spoke again, now full of hope, "Remember that day we dug the hole under the mango tree and put Gopal in a box, wrapped with your father's silk dhoti?"

Badal had stretched his hands through the bars and held Sulaiman's. His eyes were moist, "I knew he would answer my prayer some day. Boudi, Partha!" he held them each through the bars and his voice choked.

His story was simple. As long as the Chakraborty family did not return he would protect the house and Gopal's temple. Immediately after the 1971 war ended he dug up the wooden statue and re-established it on the niche. The temple emanated fresh incense fragrance. Mumtaz sat at the feet of Gopal and went off down memory lane. Father and son left her alone, to inspect the remains of the house. Badal stopped at a spot and held them back.

"There, I found her one morning, dead."

"Who?"

"I don't even know. She had come shortly after the war that December. She mentioned your name and I knew you had sent her to stay here. Poor girl was pregnant too. She said nothing more, not a word. I fed her and made her a bed here. But one day she took a handful of sleeping pills and that was the end of her story."

"The hotel manager told us about ghosts. Does her spirit scream?"

Badal laughed, "Those screams were what I practised on passers-by. They knew she had committed suicide and henceforth to keep people out I made up all sorts of yarns. Some contractors were eyeing this place like hawks and would come around ever so often. It is then that I started issuing forth bloodcurdling shrieks. Do you want to hear?"

The real birth certificate of Partha Chakraborty was fished out and handed to the town council. Partha's house was put up for sale, minus Gopal's temple and Badal's garden. But there was a problem. Nobody wanted to buy a haunted house.

"Badal kaku, you did your duty a little too well. Now what shall we do?"

He had an answer. "Call an ojha. He will chant incantations and chase the ghost out of here."

"Excellent plan, but why did it not strike others to bring an ojha?"

"Oh yes, they did. But every spirit-chaser said he needed to know the girl's name and religion. The Muslim ojhas were scared of the many Hindu Gods pursuing them, and Hindu ojhas said a Muslim ghost would sit on their back for the rest of their life. But surely you know her name?"

Gopal had indeed taken charge of the house. What else made Aleya so secretive that she did not disclose her name to anyone in the city?

Mumtaz thanked the Lord in her heart, "We know her name. Call the ojha". The ceremony attracted much attention, and Partha suddenly had lots of kakus, telling him stories about the most important family of Sonargaon of a century ago. The Chakraborty's were generous when they were landlords and upright when they were pauperized. The property value rose daily, as bidders shouldered each other. Gopal's temple would be handed over to the city council after Badal passed away. Finally the family sold the property to a hospital.

* * * * *

"Panchali, you are free!"

"Partha, did you go to Bangladesh?"

"Yes, and I have brought you a gift. Our house was sold."

"What are you saying? I cannot take the money. It is yours, from your ancestry."

"Panchali, listen, I have not missed a home, a father or a country. But I have dearly missed a companion, Partha's Panchali. Take it as if it came from Gopal."

Panchali felt a dagger pierce her heart. He was helping her write off the contract she had signed with ink, but what about the other one she had written with blood? Partha insisted she take the money and use it as collateral to pay off her debt. She accepted the packets of Bangladeshi taka and silently said it to his yearning eyes, "Partha, if I could I would return to you."

"Wait, what is eating you, Panchali?"

"The Partition. I am working to stitch the torn dress and cover the Motherland's shame."

"Can I help?" She looked at the bundle of notes wrapped in brown paper, stamped Sonargaon, Bangladesh. Sonargaon, Sonargaon ... she had heard the name before. A sudden flash illumined everything. Her mind raced ahead.

"Yes, Partha, yes, yes. You can help. Go back to Sonargaon and start walking on the Grand Trunk Road towards India. Remember, in 1540, Sher Shah Suri, an Afghan warrior, had defeated the Turks and started the Suri dynasty ruling out of Delhi? One of his contributions, above all, stands today. He built a highway that ran from Peshawar at the Afghan border to

Sonargaon of Bengal, spanning his entire territory. Like a river, it became an artery for a flourishing civilization. Traders, pilgrims and soldiers stopped at the cities that sprang on its banks."

Panchali was so excited she hardly paused to breathe, "Starting from Peshawar it crosses the bridge over the river Jhelum in the Punjab province of Pakistan and reaches India at Amritsar. Thence it runs down to Delhi, passes the tanneries of Kanpur in Uttar Pradesh, and lands in Sasaram in Bihar, Sher Shah Suri's hometown. It touches the coalfields of Dhanbad and crosses over to Bengal past the Durgapur steel and power plants. From Kolkata it swings upwards to the old capital, Murshidabad, and stops at Sonargaon."

"And so, Panchali, you plan to use this road as a geographical handshake?"

"Yes, people will walk from both ends and meet in the midpoint, Agra, city of the Taj Mahal."

"And will you walk with me?" His eyes were bright and face jubilant.

She shook her head, "But I will be there in Agra waiting for the end."

"Panchali, when you give me the signal I will start marching from Sonargaon. But promise, when I meet you in Agra, you will come with me."

Panchali thought to herself, "I will, when the three countries become one nation." But she said aloud, "I have a sister in Pakistan and one is Bangladesh I have to meet first."

"Do I know them?"

"Yes, they are Sindhu and Meghna."

"And you are Ganga?"

"Didn't you tell me ours is a story of confluences?"

Partha kissed her forehead, "This time you won't slip away. Now go gather your raindrops, little storm."

"Partha, remember me from a fairy tale
A dear old friend who'll never fail."

"I shall think of you when the day will advance
In a maddening whirling dervish's dance."
"Remember me as a song that rings
In the magic of your guitar strings."
"I shall see you smile in the crimson light
Of a blazing fire in the solemn night."
"Remember me caught in a photograph
Cheating old time and having the last laugh."
"And when the rains will set us afloat
Moored at your shore you will find my boat."

Panchali brushed her last tear away and whispered to the retreating figure,

"But above all remember me
As one who died for unity."

Partha waved from afar,

"I will not have hoped in vain
For you'll surely be mine again."

* * * * *

Dehra Dun was famous for three "ch*s*" – chai, chawal and chandan – tea, basmati rice and sandalwood. The soil was fertile at the foothills of the Himalayas and the climate pleasantly cool. The bus passed through the teak and sandalwood forests and deposited Panchali before a dirt path. In front of her rose the Shivalik hills, with the tea bushes on its body, like a host of woolly sheep seen through green goggles. "It is a few kilometres off the main road, isolated from all habitation, a self-sustaining community of farmers and scientists," had said the article in the Science Today. A cyclist passed by and said, "Behenji, sister, a little further on." After an hour of walk another cyclist also pointed ahead, "A little more." She wished these simple gestures of extending the hand could be quantified as one kilometre, or ten, or simply, camp here for the night under the stars or turn back and hire a car. For a long time Panchali was the only person from horizon to horizon. It was very hard to believe she was not lost. Did wolves prowl here at night? What if some lewd men found her, a lone woman? Panchali quickened her pace. If only she had thought of renting a cycle. She could not ask his help, or rather would not ask, because he had rejected her before. Her feet were sweating and she realized a blister had formed. Her mind spun on its own,

> In this tug of war played by life
> You and I have been flung apart,
> But if I dial SOS
> Will you, my dear, pick up the phone?
> When the sailboats have reached the shore
> And the rosy dusk tiptoes past us,
> If I write a note in the sky
> Will you read it and smile awhile?
> I cross deserts to reach your home
> Lose my way and stumble and fall,
> Then if I faint on the last step
> Will you carry me, dear, indoors?
> And in some distant eve
> When you see the incense burn,
> Will you watch me in the smoke
> Curling my way up above?

Then thirst hit her. She forgot all pain and limped on ahead. It was late afternoon when dazed and cracked-lipped she saw human activity up ahead. It was a farm, no, a greenhouse, with a barn, and granary ... whatever it was, it would be her night's refuge, even if it were an army barrack or a prison. She was exhausted and too dry to produce tears to drink. "Foolish girl!" she kept telling herself. She met a man driving his cows back from the pasture.

"Do you know Shreyas?"

He shook his head, "Have not heard that name."

"What is this place?"

"A farm."

"Who runs it?"

"Doctor sahab."

"What? Is this some animal care centre?"

"No, not that kind of doctor, but the other kind."

She walked on and met women binding sheaves and loading them on a bullock cart.

"Shreyas? Water?"

No to both.

Panchali stumbled past the entrance and called a boy pumping water at a bore well, "Take me to your doctor sahab. I need to rest for the night". He looked at her stomach and decided she was so tired because she was pregnant. He gave her water from a mug. She sat at the foot of the well, panting. Suddenly the blisters cried out and she saw her sandals were patched red. She limped towards a greenhouse following the boy.

"Doctor sahab, someone wants to see you." Panchali looked in and her eyes were dazzled by the light. Through the haze of her fainting sense she saw Shreyas turn towards her, and then she felt herself sinking back to the dark womb of the mother earth.

"Doctor sahab," called the lady he had appointed as nurse, "She is waking up." Shreyas scurried down the school corridors for a happy moment. It was always special to meet someone from those bright islands of childhood. But, Panchali was a pale shadow of the girl he knew. Her feet were bandaged and her face was sun burnt.

"Panchali, what have you done to yourself?"

"I walked from the highway."

"Why didn't you tell me you were coming? Our van picks up people. There is not even a village in between and the forest becomes quite alive at night. Have you eaten? Why have you come alone?"

She thought to herself sadly, "Alone? I should ask you, Shreyas, why am I alone?"

But to him she said smiling, "How are you, Shreyas?"

"When you can walk, I will show you around. What a journey of rediscovery it has been! You know the simple festival our grandmothers used to perform before the planting season?" He was as excited as a student.

"I can't recall any pastoral ritual, except the sankranti, where the first harvested rice is cooked with the first batch of jaggery."

"But there was a ceremony before the sowing. They took the various kinds of rice grains and planted them in a pot. The shoots came out within days. We thought it was a game. But actually it was a scientific experiment. The best grains were planted that harvest. Those that grew slowly or defectively were kept for another cycle. Nature tells us which seed she will prefer for that season. So many secrets are hidden in this handful of soil – the climate, soil pH, concentration of insects, potential pollinators, migration of birds, health of germs, soil salinity, natural fertilizers, earthworm population, the promise of monsoon."

"Oh my God, it is a whole book in a palm."

Shreyas was scrutinizing her, "I wonder why they said a pregnant woman was here to see me."

She burst out laughing, "Then it is time I should tell you about my child. Shreyas, will you do something if I ask you to? Will you teach your techniques to the people of Pakistan? Get a seed bank started and train them to make it self-sustaining?"

"Panchali, are you serious? Whoever goes to Pakistan?"

"I know someone who was born in Peshawar and he will accompany you. He has loads of family there who know all the ins and outs of the system. Shreyas, don't think so much. Just do it. For the sake of our motherland. They are our own brothers; we should share our knowledge with them."

"It sounds right, but this place has grown with government grants and loans."

"Oh Shreyas, how silly of me, that's what my child is. I brought you money bundled in my belly. Here, take it."

"Taka? From Bangladesh? How can I take it just like that? Is it yours?"

"Shreyas, say yes, please. Tariq will go with you, and he will arrange everything."

* * * * *

Panchali rested and observed Shreyas, busy as a bee in his happy hive. He did not need anybody to distract him and certainly not human love. One who has found nectar does not tarry in a toddy shop. There were water cisterns created for rainwater catchments, biogas plants that provided cooking fuel, windmills to irrigate the land and solar panels for electricity. A vegetable garden supplemented the crops of pulses and rice. But above all, the farm was a seed bank that sold grains to farmers at a cost lower than the genetically modified variety. Every summer students came to work with Shreyas in his greenhouse. Panchali saw the line of saplings and inspected the labels.

"Shreyas, these first five are all rice."

"This whole section is just rice, each a different kind. And here we are experimenting with a strain that requires less moisture. It is very important not to be dependent on monsoons, or the release of water from dams."

She nodded, water disputes were an old evil.

"What is that device, Shreyas?"

"It's hardly a device. See, how simple it is. A little pressure from above opens up this valve and a funnel is exposed. The water passes through a sand filter and is collected in this earthen jar. Cup your hands and drink some of it. Isn't it heavenly? The surplus drains in that well."

"I see, rain water is trapped, and dust, insects and birds are kept out."

"It is clamped to the ground by a giant corkscrew. Even a storm or a kicking bull will not topple it."

"Ingenious! Do you have a patent on it?"

Shreyas turned towards her, a little hurt, then saw her face, ready to burst into laughter. He smiled mischievously, "Now Panchali, I will really start my lecture on patents."

Panchali read the name of the farm at the entrance –

Madhuvan. Of course, she smiled, Madhuvan was the right name, the garden in Brindavan where Krishna danced with the gopis, where he played with the cowherd boys – the glade of sweetness, where Shreyas lived. She opened the window of her heart and sent a gentle breath to help the butterfly drift away. Tenderly she released the hand she had held for the last twenty years. All was for the best. Alvida, Shreyas, farewell. He was her king, but not her God. At last when the dusk had turned to night, she knew Krishna transcended his million guises. At last she was alone with Him, her Friend, her Guide, her Beloved.

Chapter Thirty

Panchali

Binapani and Anand came to drop Panchali off at the railway station. She was headed towards Brindavan with an exuberant circle of women. They filled two compartments, leaned out of the doorway, waved through the window bars, teased one another, laughed, sang, clapped.

"Look at those free birds chirping merrily!"

"Ma, baba", Panchali held them both in an embrace. "Thank you for everything."

"Panchali, ma", Binapani patted her daughter's back, "Baba and I think you should engross yourself with Tapasya and not meddle with Pakistan."

"Why?"

"You know how Pakistan is perceived internationally. Ever since the attack on the New York twin towers, it is believed the perpetrators get safe refuge there."

Anand explained graphically. "Imagine a rat has died in the middle of the road. Your pet dog is curious and runs to it. Then you run after your dog, and just then a bus comes and runs over all of you. Is Pakistan really worth all that running?"

"You are asking me to leash my desire for unification. But the rat is the political leadership, not the common man. It is the best time to act, since the gap between the people and the government is widest. People have suffered from an inflated defence budget, from a corrupt state machinery, from floods and droughts and poverty and neglect – in short they have always had the worst deal. Now is the time to help each other. We will re-establish the link amongst people, who have nothing to do with gunpowder or kickbacks, who want to live peacefully and enjoy life. I am not planning a rally or strike. It is a peaceful march called dosti, friendship."

"But Panchali, things have improved. In 2010 after popular unrest, stone-pelting and curfews in Kashmir, the Indian government had promised to engage all parties in dialogue, including separatists. Schools were reopened, students arrested during demonstrations were released, and a permanent group was formed to address grievances."

"And on another front, in September 2010, the Supreme Court had come to a decision about the Babri Masjid-Ram Janmabhoomi debacle. The premises were to be split between the Hindu and Muslim factions. There is also more trade between India and Pakistan. Don't you think there is reason to hope?" asked Binapani.

"Are you saying there is no more terrorism? No more hatred? No more cruelty? This internecine war is harming us all. We are on the path of self-destruction. Surely everybody sees it?"

"You mean mutual destruction."

"No, I mean self-destruction. We are one people."

"Bina, she is right. I fear if it is not checked our civilization will disintegrate. And this time we will only have ourselves to blame."

Binapani agreed, "I remember a cartoon, from a nursery rhyme, or perhaps it was a fable, where two snakes are fighting, and each starts chewing the other's tail. The ring becomes smaller and tighter, until it disappears altogether."

Panchali nodded. "Besides, ma, baba, I am just an instrument of a superior power. Call it the Divine or the Time Spirit or the *Bhaarata bhaagya vidhaataa*, Destiny of Bharat."

Anand and Binapani hugged her, "Panchali, let your deepest wish be granted." She bowed down, touched their feet and turned away hastily.

"Girls, our new journey begins now."

On the way, Surmayee approached her, "Didi, will you teach me English?"

"Yes, surely, and many more subjects."

"Start with English."

"Do you want to read novels?"

"No, that book you are reading. You can't see yourself, but you are smiling like an apsara, an angel. I too want to read it."

"The Savitri, of course you will read. Listen to this. Just hear the music of the words. I will explain later."

The other girls in the compartment came around. Surmayee disappeared returning with the rest. "Didi, tell us the story before you read."

"Ashwapati was a king of ancient India. He was a sage too, one who had reached great spiritual heights. He invoked the Divine Mother and implored her to descend on earth. She granted him his wish and was born as his daughter, Savitri. Her very presence made the earth beautiful, people felt spontaneously happy, ascetics saw magnificent visions. Her friends clustered round her as bees round a hive. When she came of age, her parents sent her out to seek a husband. She roamed the country and after many months found him whom her soul recognized as her mate. He was Satyavan, once a prince, but his father lost his kingdom and became blind. When Savitri returned to the palace, she met Narad, the Divine messenger, who was visiting her father's court. With his prophetic vision he saw Satyavan was fated to die within a year."

"And sure enough he would have told it to Savitri?"

"Yes, as soon as he dropped the hint, Savitri's mother beseeched her to continue her search. But Savitri and Satyavan had come down together on earth to move the human quest by a further step. It was not by chance that Satyavan was thus fated to die. Savitri married Satyavan and started living in the hut with her new family, breathing not a word about the prophecy. When the fated day arrived she accompanied Satyavan to the forest where he chopped wood. Suddenly a terrible pain assailed him and stole his life away. She saw the dreadful God of Death come to take his soul. Savitri followed him to his abode challenging him at every step."

"What kind of challenge was it?"

"Oh, they had lengthy debates. He sneered at life on earth; she upheld it as a priceless opportunity."

"And did she win?"

"Ah, for that you will have to wait till the end. He granted her boons to reward her perseverance and also to turn her away. She asked Satyavan's father be cured of blindness and his kingdom returned. When he gave her another boon, she asked for children. Death granted her all. Then she pointed out that her husband needed to be revived for it. He scoffed at her, saying she could always find another man to marry. But Savitri is the Divine Force, and her very purpose of embodiment was to conquer Death. After a long occult battle, Death was conquered. He vanished, returning her husband back to life."

"I love happy endings."

"But it is not yet the end. The Supreme Lord appeared before Savitri and gave her the boon of moksha, freedom from the cycle of birth and death, release from the web of good and evil. But she is our mother and did not accept her own salvation alone; she wanted us all to be free and happy. This is what she said,

> Imperfect is the joy not shared by all.
> O to spread forth, O to encircle and seize
> More hearts till love in us has filled thy world!
> O life, the life beneath the wheeling stars!
> For victory in the tournament with death,
> For bending of the fierce and difficult bow,
> For flashing of the splendid sword of God!"

* * * * *

Tariq opened the door smiling broadly, "Panchali! Here you are at last. We thought you would spin around the country forever. So I hope you have come to give us the green signal?"

A little boy ran past Tulsi as she came in, looking as charming as on her wedding day. Panchali drew in a breath, "If you two are planning to get any prettier the Pakistani film industry will never let you return to India."

From behind the sofa a tiger-masked creature jumped on

Panchali, "Halum!"

Tulsi whispered, "Better be afraid, otherwise he will cry." Panchali looked at the boy and was lost in the galleries of time. She was waving aside Jalal's claws and saying, "Who is afraid of a fake tiger?" Panchali grabbed the boy, pushed his mask back and saw a baby Krishna face in a pout. "Oho, I am so scared, help me!" She hid behind Tariq and the boy came laughing after her.

"I need to go now, see you both in Agra."

"But when do we start?"

"Ten days from now. Partha will start at the same time from Sonargaon."

"Where are you going?"

"To Amritsar."

Tulsi and Tariq looked at each other. They knew Panchali by now. She would have made up her mind a second ago, as if she had finished her toothpaste and was stepping into the nearest shop.

"Bye bye, aunty," waved their son, Anant Azad – Forever Free.

Tariq called after her, "Listen Panchali, my sister, Dunya, is immigrating to Pakistan."

"Oh don't use that word, we are the same nation."

"Right. She will settle in Peshawar back on the lap of our doting aunts and join Lollywood – you know, that's what the Lahore-based Pakistani film industry is called. She will take with her one of the biggest success stories of India – the entertainment industry."

Tulsi added, "And the reason is quite obvious – it does not discriminate by religion."

"But listen, Panchali, here is the good news. Dunya says the ban on Bollywood films was lifted from 2008."

"That is indeed good news!" shouted Panchali from the staircase as her farewell message to her dear friends.

"My cousins will start the dosti march with us. And Darya is going to tour with her troupe of singers. She has stumbled upon some old Urdu melodies, pre-independence, patriotic, like *saare jahaan se acchaa*."

Panchali had returned to the door, "How is Shreyas doing?"

"He is itching to come back, but the people have all but imprisoned him. They are coming in hordes to learn. Right now he has found a man, Ahmad Shah, whom he is training to be Doctor sahab."

"Good, he needs to go to Bangladesh after that. Will you tell him when you meet him? Ask him to contact my brother, Yuyutsu. His wife has relatives in Bangladesh."

"Why don't you tell him yourself?" he shouted, but she had flown down the stairs.

* * * * *

The same electrician brushed past Savita a third time and stopped in front, "Madam, I told you he is busy. Call his office and get yourself an appointment."

"It's all right. I can wait."

"Hey Chhotu," the man called a boy hurrying past with tea cups on a tray. "Come here." He handed Savita a cup. "Really madam, if I could, I would call him out, but we are in the middle of a shoot." He ran off sweating. It was seven in the evening. Savita had sat five hours on the plastic chair. People were streaming out and among them was the person she was waiting for. Shaan's eyes grazed hers, then returned and fixed themselves incredulously. She got up and tried a nervous smile.

"Savita!" he cried, "What a surprise!" He came close and time froze between them, "I wanted to sit by you and watch your hair turn white, one by one."

"Shaan, Shaan ..." her voice broke and she hid her face.

He took her inside his office and closed the door.

"What happened, Savita? Was life unkind to you?"

She calmed down a little "I had the best possible son and a wonderful husband."

"Had?"

"Yes. Kargil War. My son was an officer in the army. Then a few years back Atul died of overstrain. He could not forget Prahlad and used to work like a madman."

"Ah, Savita," Shaan sat down feeling a knife edge in his heart.

"We women survive, isn't that nature's mandate? We don't die, we just suffer. But let's forget that. Tell me about yourself."

"Oh, I have grown this camera business into a full-fledged production house. Look at that." He pointed to a glass case.

"Isn't that the camera you had when we met?"

"Yes, she is the one who immortalized you."

"Shaan, what about your family?"

"Oh that! Where was the time? I had to marry off my sisters, then this studio, shooting three films all at once."

"Were you not lonely?"

Shaan became absentminded. He traced his finger on a framed photo sitting on his desk, "Lonely? I think I was too busy ..." Savita made a sudden move, reached out for the photo he was caressing and turned it around. She was staring at herself from ages back, dreaming a young girl's dreams. "Arre Savita, why are you crying?" Shaan came to her side and wiped the tears from her cheeks.

"Shaan, I have still not been to Kashmir."

He embraced her and she heard him say in a choked voice, "We will settle in Kashmir if you so want, on a houseboat, on the Dal Lake. Nobody will have to go to Switzerland any more, Kashmir will be again the paradise it used to be."

"Shaan, you made me forget the reason I was here. I had come to ask you a favour."

"Granted, jane-e-man, my sweetheart."

"Ahh, listen first. I have a niece, Panchali, who has fallen in love with Pakistan and Bangladesh. She has a plan to unite the people of the three countries, heart to heart, brother to lost brother. And for that she wants some television time, just once in a while, to send the message."

"It will be like the national integration programme we had years back, remember, *mile sur tumhaaraa hamaaraa*, 'across the land let our songs unite'? At noon for a few minutes every day we will have the 'unity' show."

"Shaan, how can I thank you? Panchali will be so grateful."

"You have already thanked me regally, mere sapno ki raani, O queen of my dreams."

"Do you think Pakistan and Bangladesh will show it too? There will be a march on the Grand Trunk Road from either side, meeting in Agra. That is her contribution. But she hopes people will find their own ways to participate and the show could bring their ideas in focus."

"I can then film you, Savita."

"Why me?"

"You are participating by asking this of me. While you talk, I will jump in beside you on the houseboat with the mountains of Kashmir as backdrop. And we will scream, 'Let us rebuild Kashmir together. Every barrack should be replaced with a house, every police station with a school'."

* * * * *

The first episode began on the border of Amritsar and Lahore, the twin cities of Punjab. Panchali said an idea was like causing a ripple in the consciousness space. Here was one,

"Unification of Pakistan, India and Bangladesh. We know our past hasn't always been of filial love, but that does not mean our future cannot be. We have made mistakes together and suffered for them. And that is why we stand here today, a little wounded, but not so weakened, to create a new tomorrow. What is sixty years in a history of five thousand? Let us blow it away like a bad dream. Let us share our future joys and bury the past sorrows. Let us build bridges and tear down fences. Let us find ways to collaborate and celebrate our family reunion. We have passed the last crossroads and are now headed on a straight path." She invited people to join the dosti march.

Shaan added, "Anybody with an idea of unification send your video or let us know and we will announce your contribution."

The border security forces spoke, "We will play cards with each other. When the government is tired of paying us for having fun, they will find us other assignments."

"What do you say, Amar?" asked a Pakistani soldier.

"I say it is a deal, Armaan," replied his Indian counterpart.

A few days later Vasant was on screen, offering his service as director to shoot the progress of the Grand Trunk Road dosti march. He had a little poem to share,

"From Padma to Sindhu
From the Hindu Kush to the Arakan
The rivers and mountains
Are but facets of the one.
So let us join our hands
Across the three lands
To sing a melody
Of peace and harmony."

In the next telecast Yuyutsu showed a blueprint for an office complex he would build in Srinagar, capital of Kashmir. "We need to rebuild the state; we want people to settle there and work happily, uninterrupted by fear." The following day a construction worker spoke about how he was taught to use a Kalashnikov in exchange of money. He treated it as a job and killed when asked, suffering the bites of his conscience. Then he found this construction company's poster and life has ever since been wonderful.

One day Rustum called Shaan for the shoot in Pune. He gave the background of the 1954 film, Jagriti. It was about a school principal who taught his students in an unorthodox way and inspired them to live honestly. Rustum himself as principal tried to follow that role model and had adopted a song from the film as the school's invocation prayer. Then the clipping showed the students in the school courtyard singing the familiar tune. But as they listened to the words they heard, "Pakistan Zindabad, long live Pakistan". Where was "Vande Mataram, victory to the Motherland"?

After the song Rustum was back. "Did you like the song?

You will have to excuse me for my little joke. The song is from a film called Bedari, the Pakistani version of Jagriti. Both films created a lot of national sentiment. Our students in India want to send their brothers and sisters in Pakistan this message of fraternity."

A few days later a clipping arrived at Shaan's office. It was the song from Jagriti sung by students in Pakistan. Some of the kids appeared on screen and said they wanted to have Rustum's students as penfriends.

Panchali was overseeing the mandala painting on the floor of the Tapasya dance hall when noon struck. A girl grabbed her hand and rushed her to the television. "Didi, someone is addressing you."

"Hello Panchali", said a man in French cut beard.

Panchali slapped her mouth to stop a loud laughter, "Get those dark glasses off, for heaven's sake!"

Swami, as though he heard her, said, "Oh, sorry folks." He freed his eyes from their shackles. "This is Swami from ..." An elephant came ambling to Swami and placed its curved trunk on his head as blessings. A little bell jingled from its neck. "Do I have to tell you now where I am? In front of a temple of course, in south India. The other day I said to myself, just because we are far from Pakistan and Bangladesh shall we not participate? So we decided to do it at the community level. We are going to visit Muslims and we welcome them to our homes. We want to learn about each other's religion and share our jokes and mythologies and fairy tales and recipes and songs and... Then we got a huge letter from the church people. They said all are God's sheep and wanted to be included." He checked his watch, "I got to leave now, Hussein and George are waiting at home. All right folks, we in the Deccan plateau will follow your dosti march on TV. So long, khuda hafiz, namaste." Swami made five quick wrist twists with his glasses and placed them on his nose.

At midday everybody enjoyed seeing Roshan and his grandmother doing a skit together.

Roshan said, "Dadima and all of us are going to Sindh, to our hometown, Karachi. I say dadima, do you have one of these?"

He waved a blue note pad in front of her. The old lady wrinkled her nose to adjust the glasses, "Why do I need a ration card?"

"Dadima, this is a passport. It says IN-DI-A. And look inside, there is a visa. It says PA-KIS-TAN. Do you have one of these?"

"When I was young and wanted to go home I knocked at the door and my father let me in. Did he ask me to identify myself? I don't know about ration cards and voting identity cards. I just know I am going home. If you young folks don't want to come, don't come."

"OK dadima, then we will also leave our ration cards behind and come with you." Roshan winked at the audience and then gave some details of a ship his family had booked. "It would have been faster to take the Thar Express to Karachi, but that train is jam packed now. Then dadima said she wanted to retrace her steps. We are leaving for Karachi in two weeks from Mumbai. Any Sindhi is welcome. There is no guarantee the ship will return. But this much is guaranteed; we will reach Karachi and will be welcomed home."

Binapani accompanied Yuyutsu's wife, Selma, and daughter, Tiasha, to Kolkata. Selma and Tiasha would fly to Chittagong in Bangladesh. That was Selma's ancestral home, which she had not seen herself. After Sher Shah Suri's time, the Grand Trunk Road was extended to the port of Chittagong. And that is where Selma would start her dosti march, along with her cousins and their friends and family. They had planned to reach Sonargaon on time to catch up with Partha's group. Tiasha was excited and asked her mother, "When was the last time you walked like that, and camped in roadside inns?"

Selma passed on the question to her mother-in-law. Binapani handed Tiasha a small paper camera. "You will take pictures of the march and show your father and grandfather. None of us alive have done such a thing before." Once there were caravanserais all along the Grand Trunk Road, and trees on either side provided shade. But with the passage of time some sections became frayed. Selma had brought lots of different seeds with her to plant on the way.

Anand accompanied Yuyutsu to Kashmir and found ancient Sanskrit documents in the private collection of Pundits. Kashmir had a rich history of spiritual masters from early days of civilization. The first thesaurus, Amarakosha, was composed in verses by a scholar from Kashmir, Amara Singha. Anand collected Shaivite texts and pored over them and one day appeared at midday, laying out elaborate plans to set up research facilities in Kashmir to study these ancient works of wisdom. There would be gurukulas, residential schools, nestled among the hills where students would learn spirituality and the practice of Yoga. He called Kashmir 'the forgotten culture in a hidden valley'.

*****

Binapani entered her house in Kolkata and was amazed to find the grass well trimmed, roses on the walkway, rajanigandhaas spreading their fragrance. Fifty years of her life melted away. She was standing in her knee length white socks and frilly frock. Raja rushed out, taking two steps at a time, lifted her off her feet and pirouetted with her, "Bina-didi, I have a surprise for you!" He was as athletic as ever though his hair was whitening, not so common a sight, a youthful grey-head. The house was sparkling new. The last time she was here her mother had passed away. Everything was in disarray but she was too sad to care. A pair of soft hands shut her eyes from behind. "Who is it?" Binapani asked caressing the hands. It was a woman's surely.

"Raja," She asked pretending to be stern, "What have you been up to?"

The hands slipped off and Binapani saw Aparna's bright face before her. "Aparna!" The two hugged. Then Aparna started her story.

So after your mother left I got a frantic phone call from your silly brother here,

"Eyi Aparna, why is the pressure cooker not whistling?"

So I ask, "Maharaj, did you switch on the gas?"

He was really offended by that. Aparna imitated Raja's voice, "What do you think, I have no common sense?"

I ask, "How much water have you added?"

Then our man, who, mind you, has a lot of common sense, asks, "Water where?"

I tell him to drop the phone that instant, run to the kitchen and switch off the gas.

Binapani clapped and laughed, much to Raja's annoyance.

"Aparna, this sounds like Ramer Shumati, the story by Sharat Chandra. Ram was upset and left home. Then he was trying to cook rice without water and all the grains got stuck to the vessel. He went hungry, poor boy. Remember how we cried at his plight?"

Raja mimicked them, "Oho, how we cried. And in my case only mockery?"

"Raja, there is a tiny difference. Ram was fifteen, and you fifty-five."

"Anyway", continued Aparna, "I came to check on the house, maybe I would find it half burnt."

"Look Bina-didi, she is exaggerating. Everything was tip top."

"Yes, so tip top I had to run from the grill gate to the door. Who knew how many snakes were living in that garden! Then inside the house the kitchen was so unused the cobwebs were waist deep – from the ceiling down. And the tool shed floor was an inch thick with droppings."

"I had kept a family of bats as pets," Raja was quick to add.

"So Aparna, come to the sweet end, my dear friend," Binapani pinched her cheek.

"Well, one thing led to the other, and I never left your brother. Oh Bina," Aparna flung her arms around her friend's neck, "I did not know how lonely I was."

"And I never learnt to cook," grinned Raja.

The boys of the football team were going to Murshidabad with Raja where they would meet up Partha and walk down to Kolkata. Aparna's girls would start from Kolkata and go up to Bardhaman.

"Some of my boys want to escort the girls," said Raja assuming a matter-of-fact tone.

Aparna mimed the words to Binapani avoiding Raja, "Not some. All."

"I suppose because their coach wants to escort the teacher?" teased back her friend.

Binapani said she would walk with her cousin, Ishani, and Ishani's husband, from Kolkata to Dhanbad, the first city beyond the Bengal border.

"What about Ishani's daughter, Chitrangada?" asked Aparna.

"She has been faithful to her ancient past. Remember the Chitrangada of the Mahabharata, princess of Manipur? She has settled in the Seven Sister States of the Northeast."

Raja continued, "Our Chitrangada is a warrior in her own right. She has been working with the tribal people there, looking after their education, health, crops, protecting their rights. Maybe you missed her part at noon. Her contribution is the integration of the Bangladeshis who cross over. You know they have a very different culture than the tribal people, and most of the tension arises from the fact that they don't trust each other since they don't have a common language. Chitrangada has made herself the interpreter and mediator. She teaches Bengali to the tribal and the tribal languages to the Bengalis. She appeals to the central government for funds on their behalf, oversees contracts, advises, translates, teaches martial arts, dispenses with justice too. In short, she is as good as a sarpanch of many villages."

"Aparna, isn't that nice? A woman head of state, working at the grassroots?"

"And this is not a political post that she has to worry about elections. She has earned the trust of both parties and they go to her with their disputes." Raja was very proud of his nieces.

"Eyi Aparna," Binapani tickled her friend, "Don't you feel young again?"

"Bina, I can hear the *uttishthata jaagrata*, 'arise, awake', ringing in my ears."

"Naxal style? Are you following the rise of Naxalite activity in India starting from 2009? They call strikes, create skirmishes, engage the police in encounters, sometimes derail trains, cause quite a headache to the government, in short."

"Oh no, not that way any more. I believe in peaceful methods. Call it age or wisdom."

* * * * *

The women were so excited for the opening of Tapasya they hardly slept. They worked alongside the painters and carpenters. At night Panchali heard their merry chatter. She looked at the calendar. Tariq and Partha would start their dosti march tomorrow. She anticipated a month for them to meet at Agra. A last journey to Tarapeeth and her march too would end.

Mumtaz came on the noon show and said she had made two rakhis for her two brothers, men who had protected her as would a brother. One was a West Pakistani soldier who saved her life when she was a Hindu, during the Bangladesh War. The other brother's name was Mohan, whom she had met in Jaduguda, when she was a mine worker. He was a nuclear scientist. She related the two poignant incidents of her life. Mohan's reply to Mumtaz was telecast at noon shortly after hers. He remembered every detail of that day and was eager to meet her. A clipping came to Shaan from Pakistan. "Mumtaz, I am Jahangir Khan, your lost brother. I live in Baluchistan and was wondering how I could participate in this dosti celebration, when I heard you. Now that I have a Bangladeshi sister waiting for me in India, I will join the march at Lahore and meet you and my brother, Mohan."

Sukhvir announced he would to go back to his childhood haunt in Rawalpindi and join Tariq from there. His cousins jumped at the proposal and said the whole family would unite in their ancestral town. Muslims of Rawalpindi responded with open arms, "Return home and see if we have loved the land as much you did before us."

One midday, people had a good laugh. The visa officer in the Pakistani embassy in Delhi called the visa officer in the Indian embassy in Islamabad.

"Arre bhai, these days I don't even get time to drink tea. Everybody wants to go to Pakistan."

"Same here, but brother, I think our job is in jeopardy. At this rate very soon visas will not be necessary any more. We are doing away with the Partition!"

As a follow-up to that conversation, the next day's clipping showed a line of placid camels in the desert of Rajasthan. The camel driver asked, "Why are you all rushing to get visas? Are we out of business? Look at these sturdy beasts. And I tell you we have been in this trade much before there was a need for visas. Only one question puzzles me. They accuse me of crossing the border. Help me, friend, locate this elusive line." The camera spanned the horizon end to end. "Where do you see a line here? I just see a circle of sand."

The midday television clippings were posted on internet sites and people started showering their good wishes through comments. Social networking websites and emails connected people around the globe. They gathered in groups to celebrate their common identity. The Diaspora found new friends among their old neighbours. Many travelled long distances to join the dosti march. Shaan and Vasant came together one day. "Thank you all for contributing generously for this programme. We have created a dosti fund for the surplus. We hear Rustum wants to open other Jagriti schools and Anand has applied for gurukula loans."

Shreyas talked about his endeavours to heal the earth and took his audience on a tour of his farm in Pakistan.

"Do you see this giant L-shaped bracket? Now when a wave hits it from the front it bounces back from the other wall and there is destructive interference. Create a line of these, like a fortress, and you cut the water's speed manyfold. In the next level we have these dykes and sluices to direct the water where we want it. For storage or irrigation. You may have guessed where this portable and inexpensive device will be most beneficial – in flood zones, like the Padma Delta. And that is where I am headed next – to the low-lying fertile land of

Bangladesh." Panchali knelt before his image, holding her heart, overflowing with gratitude.

When the dosti march began, Shaan and Vasant were the busiest of men. They shuttled between the two sides of the Grand Trunk Road, filming, editing, enjoying themselves to the hilt, making the two minutes at noon a sacred moment. There was much singing on the way, cleaning the road, planting trees, storytelling, sharing of food and blankets. Houses became inns to provide shelter to the marchers. The gates at the borders were kept open for the crowd to pass through. The Army band played till the last man crossed over. Partha had reached Asansol when Tariq reached Amritsar. At Benares, temple bells chimed to welcome Partha's team, and chants from the mosque trailed the marchers with a goodwill message. Tariq's group was treated to mattar paneer and chapatti in Jalandhar by the hospitable Punjabi inn-keepers. Throughout Punjab there was a festival of homecoming as Pakistanis circled back on their family history. The confluence of the black Yamuna and the brown Ganga in Allahabad saw the confluence of people from Bangladesh and India. Tariq reached Karnal in the state of Haryana, and headed towards Delhi.

Panchali sat beside the Shakta priest, Chandidas, her forehead smeared with vermillion powder, herself a blood red flower offered to Kali. The Goddess stood astride the fallen demon, her sword tipped with blood, her tongue hanging out. But her eyes were large, full of motherly love. She was killing the demons that tore us apart – anger, jealousy, hatred, greed, selfishness. Panchali took her leave from Chandidas and returned to Brindavan, for the finishing touches before the opening ceremony. Their next assignation would be at the Taj Mahal, a week hence, at the twilight hour, confluence of day and night. The same day Tariq's group from Peshawar would greet Partha's from Sonargaon. And on the very same day the first Tapasya building would fling her doors open to a world of new possibilities.

Partha was at Kanpur and he thought of Panchali. A few more days and they would be together. The nights were like speedbreakers. At the bonfire he sang a bhaatiaali song she loved so much. Anant Azad seated on his father's shoulders towered over all the heads.

"Papa, papa, look at that amazing sight!"

Tariq turned towards the Jama Masjid. "That was my dream when I was your age, and it is your reality. She is called ..."

"Unity." It was uttered by the old lady Tulsi was escorting. She and many of her age had travelled by bus from Lahore to Delhi, for one purpose – to camp at the Purana Qila, the Old Fort.

"My parents debated over going to Pakistan, in 1947. If we were further from Delhi, we would have remained at home, or perhaps gone to Lucknow or Kanpur. We were told the Hindu majority would maltreat us and we were scared. So we camped here in the fort under the open sky, till the train took us to Pakistan, so many of us that the burning roof of the metal cage was also packed with people. I did not understand why my family was abandoning the country they had fought to liberate. Pakistan was conceived in fear and her birth pangs were traumatic." She paused to look around the happy crowd.

"But your generation does not need to regret, Tulsi, and your son's can as well forget the grave mistake my father's generation made."

When Mohan joined the march a ripple spread forth in the human sea, "Mohan is here." An answering wave brought the news, "We see Jahangir." The chain of messengers rapidly grew short and very soon Mohan was embracing Jahangir. The crowd rejoiced as everybody knew their story and looked forward to meeting their sister as much as they did. Mumtaz saw her brothers waving to her on the screen of a cellphone. Hundreds of women inspired by their reunion busied themselves making a few extra rakhis. Sulaiman got himself a rickshaw and dressed her up like the faithful craft of his journey to India. Partha ferried his parents on it, aiming towards the legendary Taj Mahal and his new future.

Savita started her march from Delhi at the monument of the Immortal Soldier, the India Gate. "Prahlad beta, my dear son, today your battle has been won." She stopped at Raj Ghat, on the banks of the Yamuna, to kneel before the memorial of departed leaders. She touched the black marble Samadhi platform made for Gandhi, with "Hey Ram" inscribed on it: "Bapuji, it has happened through love after all .... Many times we tried to hate, but we are flowers of the same garland, one that the caprice of ages could not rip apart."

* * * * *

Panchali sat on the ledge of her favourite minaret at the Taj Mahal. Before her eyes stretched the ancient land shaped by the thought of sages and the sword of kings, the sacrifice of heroes and the labour of love. The bard of time traced a silver line on the Yamuna and recounted the story of a people, from the glory that was to the glory that will be. The monument of love would henceforth be an emblem of friendship. Her fountains would flow with the nectar of joy and her white body would be illumined with the many firecrackers at night. When the two groups would meet, there would be tying of rakhis. The people of Agra were prepared to receive them, to spread their mats, to bring sherbet and food. Houses had rangoli designs on their thresholds, Christmas tree lights lined terrace parapets. Schools and offices declared a holiday. When Panchali had left Tapasya the day before, the women were also ready. Hundreds of lamps lit the pathway to welcome the townsfolk and the generous donor. The temple made of pure moonlight had clay-carved statuettes of Krishna and Radha. He played the flute and she rested her head on his shoulder. The floor would be decorated with flowers of many hues. Every girl had a new dress to wear. In the dance hall a show had been planned to entertain the guests. Singers would accompany the dancers and some would play the pakhawaj, the side drums, all members of Tapasya, each a flame saved from the storm. Panchali saw these happy scenes with her soul's eyes as if they had happened many times before. Henna beautified the palms, betel leaf juice reddened the lips, sandalwood paste smeared every limb with its fragrance. Anklets rang, bracelets sang, eyes sparkled with tears of bliss. Krishna was coming to steal every heart.

And Anant Azad would sleep in his mother's lap and look at the stars of a new nation. One that used to be three countries. Tiasha would see the photographs of merry men who had carried her piggy-back on the dosti march. She would wonder, was there really a time when our nation was split like that, in three bits?

A single musical note swelled like an anthem of delight. Panchali looked at the river below and saw what her heart had dreamt a thousand times. The first boat was set afloat and from the other bank the auspicious sound of a hundred conch shells thrilled the air. Panchali closed her eyes and felt a vastness within her. It was as if all the people she had known were together at the same time, their lives mingling in an ageless river that lived in her. A marvellous power, one she could not question, made her arise. She stood tall and spread her arms to embrace life, life in her manifold beauty, life with her infinite possibilities, life that triumphs in the face of death.

"Panchali, it is time to go."

Her lips parted in a gentle smile. She looked at the formidable figure of the tantrik standing at her feet, and said, "Yes, it is time. Time to go from delusion to strength, from ignorance to revelation, from defeat to eternal victory. Time to go to the Satyam, the Ritam, the Brihat, the True, the Right, the Vast. Do you hear those millions of voices down there chanting,

Asato maa sat gamaya
Tamaso maa jyotir gamaya
Mrityur maa amritam gamaya."

Chandidas heard the mantra echo in his heart.

"From falsehood lead me to truth
From darkness lead me to light
From death lead me to immortality."

He saw the boats cross the twilight of an age. He saw the luminous throng climb up the bank. Above him stood the figure on her pedestal, the ancient one who had arisen from a fire, her battle now won, her sacrifice complete. He bowed to the Mother. Her children had called and she had descended in their hearts.

She had kept her promise. Finally the nation was united. Finally she was free.

The sun was setting in the horizon. A strip of red line marked the forehead of the river as if she was the bride of the sky. The tender night embraced the earth, and the Supreme Lord granted Savitri her wish –

"Thy peace, O Lord, a boon within to keep
Amid the roar and ruin of wild Time
For the magnificent soul of man on earth.
Thy calm, O Lord, that bears thy hands of joy."

Glossary

apsara	—	female angel adept in dancing (Sanskrit)
arre	—	an interjection to draw the attention of the listener (Hindi, colloquial)
chapatti	—	flatbread (Hindi)
churidar	—	tightly fitting trousers worn by men and women (Hindi)
dal	—	lentil soup (Hindi)
do anna	—	one-eighth of the full amount, a pittance (Hindi, colloquial)
ehsaan	—	favour (Urdu)
istriwalla	—	man who irons clothes as a profession (Hindi, colloquial)
kurta	—	a loose-fitting knee-length gown worn by men and women (Hindi)
lassi	—	sweet buttermilk (Hindi)
mandap	—	a pavilion for public rituals (Hindi)
masala	—	spice (Hindi)
mattar	—	pea (Hindi)
mohabbat	—	love (Urdu)
neem	—	a plant with medicinal and insecticidal properties (Hindi)
paneer	—	cottage cheese (Hindi)
poorna swaraj	—	complete self-government (Sanskrit)
sherwani	—	a man's formal knee-length coat buttoned to the neck (Urdu)
sola anna	—	hundred percent, full amount (Hindi, colloquial)
upasana	—	meditation or worship (Sanskrit)
veena	—	a stringed musical instrument (Sanskrit)
vihara	—	a monastery (Sanskrit)